Romantic Suspense

Danger. Passion. Drama.

Cold Case Tracker
Maggie K. Black

Her Duty Bound Defender
Sharee Stover

MILLS & BOON

COLD CASE TRACKER
© 2024 by Mags Storey
Philippine Copyright 2024
Australian Copyright 2024
New Zealand Copyright 2024

First Published 2024
First Australian Paperback Edition 2024
ISBN 978 1 038 90770 7

Sharee Stover is acknowledged as the author of this work
HER DUTY BOUND DEFENDER
© 2024 by Harlequin Enterprises ULC
Philippine Copyright 2024
Australian Copyright 2024
New Zealand Copyright 2024

First Published 2024
First Australian Paperback Edition 2024
ISBN 978 1 038 90770 7

MIX
Paper | Supporting
responsible forestry
FSC® C001695

Published by
Harlequin Mills & Boon
An imprint of Harlequin Enterprises (Australia) Pty Limited
(ABN 47 001 180 918), a subsidiary of HarperCollins
Publishers Australia Pty Limited
(ABN 36 009 913 517)
Level 19, 201 Elizabeth Street
SYDNEY NSW 2000 AUSTRALIA

Cover art used by arrangement with Harlequin Books S.A.. All rights reserved.

Printed and bound in Australia by McPherson's Printing Group

Cold Case Tracker

Maggie K. Black

MILLS & BOON

Maggie K. Black is an award-winning journalist and romantic suspense author with an insatiable love of traveling the world. She has lived in the American South, Europe and the Middle East. She now makes her home in Canada with her history-teacher husband, their two beautiful girls and a small but mighty dog. Maggie enjoys connecting with her readers at maggiekblack.com.

The Spirit of the Lord is upon me, because he hath anointed me to preach the gospel to the poor; he hath sent me to heal the brokenhearted, to preach deliverance to the captives, and recovering of sight to the blind, to set at liberty them that are bruised.
—*Luke* 4:18

DEDICATION

With thanks to Emily
my editor for ten years
for all the incredible books we did together

Chapter One

There was a man standing on the sidewalk across from the Clearwater Bookstore, staring at Amy Scout through the storefront window. She froze as her hands instinctively cradled the unborn child in her belly. This was the third time today she'd spotted the stranger with his imposing black and tan German shepherd outside the store, which was unsettling considering how deserted the tiny town in Northern Ontario was during the offseason. But if he was going to eyeball her then she was going to take down every single detail she could about him in return.

Amy grabbed her sketchbook and a charcoal pencil, letting her fingers find his face on the page. His beard was dark, and his jawline was handsome in an intimidating way. He had curly hair and a build that was muscular and strong. There was an intensity to his gaze, although in the gloomy light of the late afternoon she couldn't quite make out the color of his eyes.

As if sensing her gaze, the man turned and said something to his dog. Then the pair continued down the sidewalk, leaving Amy with just the charcoal picture of his face. She studied it a moment. There was something oddly familiar about him.

Had she seen him somewhere before? Was he there to hurt her? Did he have anything to do with Gemma's disappearance?

She had a whole lot of questions but absolutely no answers. Amy closed her eyes and prayed.

Lord, please keep me safe. Help me keep my baby safe too and bring Gemma home soon.

She had to believe her missing friend was still alive, despite that law enforcement had told her Gemma had probably drowned and her body might never be found. Two weeks ago, Gemma's empty car had been found submerged in a dangerous river, at the bottom of a steep waterfall near the town of South River, about an hour from Clearwater. Amy had no idea where Gemma had been going when she'd left the cottage that day or what she'd even been doing in that area.

It was like her best friend had been hiding something from her. Gemma had started going into the store early in the morning and returning there late at night after dinner, but she would never give Amy a straight answer when she asked why. There'd been some big secret, something that was bothering Gemma. Whatever it was, Gemma had refused to talk about it. She kept Amy in the dark and then she disappeared.

Amy closed the blinds firmly, locked the front door and switched the hand-painted sign in the window from Open to Closed. Her unborn daughter kicked within her and a smile crossed Amy's lips. The doctor told her this fluttering would become stronger and more frequent in the next six weeks before the child was born. To Amy the poking and prodding always felt personal, as if her child was trying to communicate with her. She liked it, and it made her feel less alone.

"Hello, Skye," Amy said. She couldn't remember exactly when in her pregnancy she'd named her daughter that, but it seemed to fit. The sky was immense and beautiful. It was peaceful at times, yet life-changing and powerful too.

"I'm just closing up shop now," Amy went on. She walked over to the front counter, opened the cash register and began to count the money. "Gemma still isn't here. But I want to make sure that everything is in tip-top shape when she gets back."

They'd been best friends since they met in seventh grade. Amy couldn't remember a time—day or night—when Gemma hadn't been willing to drop everything to be there when she needed her. Vice versa too. Amy wasn't about to let Gemma down now.

"This place is a ghost town right now," Amy added. "Most of the stores are shut and the cottages are empty. But from the May long weekend to Labor Day, it's going to be packed around here. The lake will be crowded with boats, and there will be tourists and vacationers everywhere. Not to mention busloads of campers."

She moved from the cash register to restocking the bottled drinks and snacks in the minifridge, then started straightening the books on the shelves. The store itself was a former barn that Gemma had painted a bright turquoise. Oddly it always seemed smaller on the inside than it looked from the outside. In the main room they displayed newly released and best-selling books, along with DVDs and VHS tapes for rent since there was no cable television up here and the internet signal was weak.

A smaller room off to the side had floor-to-ceiling bookshelves filled with mostly used books, including an entire back wall dedicated to crime, cold cases and unsolved mysteries. It was also home to the store's resident conure parrot, Reepi Cheeps. The little bird was only a few months old. His name was a twist on a character from one of Gemma's favorite childhood books. The green and gray conure more than lived up to his name with constant cheeping and chirping, as he bounced around the high shelves. Reepi lived in the store during the warmer months and was allowed to roam free when it was quiet.

"See, I'm not alone," Amy told Skye, as she continued to tidy. It comforted her to talk to her daughter. "I've got a birdie and a baby on the way. Plus, we had a pretty good day, all things considered. We had twelve sets of customers, which isn't bad for a Tuesday in April. One of them even bought a couple of my postcards—the ones I drew of Reepi. I think I might paint him on the side of the building when the weather gets warmer. We can make him our unofficial mascot."

She just had to think positive, keep moving and not let herself consider that Gemma might not come home. It had been Gemma's idea to start selling Amy's sketches in the bookstore. When some of the customers balked at the sticker price, Gemma then started selling postcard prints of Amy's artwork alongside the originals. There was no way Gemma was about to let anyone haggle over the price of her best friend's art.

Gemma had always been protective. Maybe even overprotective. When Amy called her in a flood of tears to tell her that Paul—the man Amy had just eloped with—had turned out to be a liar and a conman who'd robbed her blind, Gemma had immediately driven through the night to pick Amy up and bring her back to the cottage.

That was long before Amy even realized she was pregnant with Paul's child.

She paused with her hand on a misplaced DVD as a sudden chill ran down her spine at the memory of the man who'd ruined her life...

It was my fault for being impulsive. I always jump into things without thinking.

And then I ended up prey to an evil man…

Skye kicked again, jolting Amy back out of the dark rabbit hole of self-recriminations and regret she had almost tumbled into. It was a hard kick this time too, and Amy silently thanked God for the distraction. At her last doctor's visit, Amy was told her blood pressure was worryingly high and she needed to lower her stress level. All the more reason to focus on happy thoughts now, despite how much her memories might want to wander.

"You know, Gemma and I met up here when we were kids?" she told Skye. "She's a year older than me. But we did everything together. I don't know if you'll ever have any brothers or sisters. I never did, but I always had Gemma. And she had a younger brother named Ajay."

She was sure she'd told Skye all this before. Amy tended to repeat the same stories. It was hard to keep thinking of lighthearted things to talk about. Not that Gemma's problems with her brother were a happy thought, but it sure was a lot better than thinking about Paul.

"Ajay was my age and he loved adventure books. But Gemma never let him hang out with us, because he was really loud and silly. He would climb on the roof of their cottage and jump out of windows. Once he set off all these fireworks. And then on my fourteenth birthday, he drove my grandma's car into the lake, while my cake was still inside. The police came and the whole party was ruined."

Even though she'd been really upset at the time, it was the kind of memory she laughed about now. But for some reason, Gemma never had. There was a deep-running tension between the sister and brother that Gemma never wanted to talk about. And Amy never wanted to push her to open up about it. She hadn't even known how to contact Ajay when Gemma vanished.

Amy walked into the smaller room where Reepi was bouncing around between the bookshelves, like Amy's own scattered mind. The green-cheeked conure was incredibly good at playing hide-and-seek. She opened the cage door with one hand and stretched out the other to make a landing platform for the bird.

"Come on, Reepi!" she called. "Playtime's over."

There was a flutter of green and gray feathers as the bird glided out from somewhere high above Amy's head and landed on her palm. Dutifully, he began to hop down her arm toward the open cage door.

Suddenly the lights went out, plunging the bookstore into darkness.

Amy's heartbeat quickened, but she took a deep breath and tried to calm it, as her eyes adjusted to the dark. She listened for any sign of trouble. Only silence filled her ears. Okay, so the store had probably blown a fuse or she'd forgotten to pay a utility bill. Gemma had taken her laptop with her when she disappeared, and Amy still hadn't figured out where she kept her bills and files.

She felt Reepi bounce off her arm and then heard the gentle creak of the bird landing on his perch. Amy pulled out her cell phone and used the screen's glow to double-check that Reepi was safely in his cage, then she closed the door and latched it. She put her phone back in her pocket, slid her jacket on and turned to head out the door at the back of the store.

A tall masked man blocked her way. Amy screamed. His cold eyes narrowed through the holes of his ski mask.

She turned and ran toward the front door. Her fingers fumbled for the lock. There was a small canister of bear spray in a pocket inside her jacket, but she wouldn't deploy it until she was outside, in case inhaling the toxic spray hurt Skye.

Strong hands grabbed her from behind. She struggled and kicked back hard against her attacker. He yanked a thick cloth bag over her head, blinding her vision.

"Now you're going to stop fighting," a coarse and heavily accented voice filled her ear, "and you're going to help me find what I'm looking for."

Sergeant Jackson Locke of the RCMP's Ontario K-9 Unit opened the back door of his double-cab pickup truck and watched as his partner, Hudson, leapt inside. The German shepherd promptly lay down on top of Jackson's coat.

"Now what am I going to do if the temperature drops?" Jackson asked. Hudson rested his head on his paws and looked up with big brown eyes. "Just be thankful I've decided that today is not my day. I'm too rattled to interview Amy. We should just pack it in and go find a motel before it gets dark."

For almost three hours, they'd paced laps around the tiny town of Clearwater, as he tried to gear himself up for talking to Amy Scout about his sister's disappearance. Jackson and

Hudson had been in the Yukon on an under-cover assignment and imbedded in an orga-nized crime ring when his boss, Inspector Ethan Finnick, had slipped him the news that Gemma had gone missing and was presumed dead.

It wasn't until Jackson had closed his Yukon case and gotten back to Ontario last night that he realized just how weak and dicey the evi-dence was for his sister's disappearance. Nobody had a clue what she'd been doing in the area where her car was found, totaled and empty and submerged in a river. And no one had heard from her since. But the local cops who inves-tigated had no idea how strong, stubborn and downright difficult his older sister could be.

In many ways, he and his sister were polar opposites. But for all their disagreements, he respected the fact that Gemma wasn't the kind of person to give up without a fight.

While the RCMP's Ontario K-9 Unit didn't have official jurisdiction over the investigation into Gemma's disappearance, Finnick had of-fered Jackson forty-eight hours off work to come up to Clearwater and see what he could find.

What Jackson hadn't been expecting to find was Amy Scout.

Unbidden, Amy's hazel eyes and long honey brown hair filled his mind. For reasons he couldn't begin to guess, it seemed the girl Jackson had a huge crush on—for his entire childhood and well into his teens—was now all grown up, living alone in his family's cottage, heavily pregnant and even more beautiful than he remembered. Unfortunately, his foolish heart had started beating just as fast at one glimpse of her face as it always had. He felt like a teenager again. Back when he'd known Amy, he'd gone by Ajay—short for "Arthur Jackson." It was a nickname he'd despised but his mother had insisted on because his father was an Arthur too. He'd changed his name to Jackson when he was eighteen.

He was a new man, but he suspected Amy probably hated his guts just as much as she always had.

He hadn't spoken to her since he'd ruined her fourteenth birthday party by hopping into her grandmother's car and crashing it into the lake. He'd been a troubled teen, lashing out after his parents' divorce. At the time, he'd been upset Amy hadn't invited him to her party. And maybe he wanted someone to pay attention to how much he was hurting. He'd tried apologizing to Amy after, but that hadn't gone well.

Jackson ran both hands over his head as if trying to get his brain in gear. He'd parked a little ways from the bookstore in a narrow alley, in the hopes that walking a couple of blocks to the bookstore would help settle his nerves.

It hadn't.

Hudson's shaggy eyebrows rose, as if he knew there had to be a good reason they'd spent five hours driving all the way up from Toronto and it wasn't to just wander around for a bit and leave.

"You're right—I'd better get this over with." He had to go talk to her, whether she still hated him or not. For Gemma.

He wasn't sure if Amy liked dogs—Gemma didn't. Gemma also didn't like cops. Just in case, he was sticking to plain clothes and leaving Hudson behind, at least for now. He rolled the window down, shut the door and then prayed as he jogged down the alley.

Lord, help me be wise. Help me find the right words to say. And help me find my sister.

The back of the bookstore came into view. The door was ajar. At first silence fell. Then he heard a faint and muffled cry. He ran faster. The door flew back on its hinges and he saw them.

A tall man in a dark ski mask had his arm around Amy. He was forcing her backward into the alley. A white cloth bag had been pulled down over Amy's head as a blindfold. She was thrashing against him and fighting for her life. His heart leapt in his chest.

"Stop! Police!" Jackson shouted. "Let her go! Now!"

He ran faster, not even certain they'd heard him over the sound of the scuffle. Jackson reached for his badge, then realized he'd left it with his gun back in the truck. The masked man dropped Amy and ran. She sank to her knees. Her hand reached inside her jacket as if searching for something.

"Amy!" Jackson shouted. He dropped to the ground beside her and grabbed her by the shoulders, trying to steady her enough to pull the bag off her head. But a fresh scream tore from her lips and she struggled against him. "Hey, it's okay, I'm not going to hurt you—"

But the words had barely left his lips when her right hand darted up in front of his eyes. She was holding a small black canister of bear spray. The ring was wrapped around her finger. The nozzle was pointed directly at his face.

"Stop!" He let her go. "Put that away, it's me, Jackson—"

Amy yanked the pin and fired.

Chapter Two

He had to hand it to her. Amy hadn't even hesitated and her aim was perfect. Two qualities Jackson would've really admired, if it wasn't for the thick stream of noxious chemicals now hitting him right in the face. Immediately his eyes began to burn and stream with tears, blurring his vision. Despite himself, Jackson practically yelped in pain. Amy scrambled back, dropped the canister and began to claw at the hood still covering her face.

"Stop!" he called, only to burst into a heavy coughing fit as the bear spray seared his lungs. "I'm not going to hurt you! I'm a cop!"

She hesitated. "Who are you?"

"Jackson!" He'd told her that. "I work with the RCMP's Ontario K-9 Unit now."

"You're a cop? Why didn't you tell me you're a cop!"

"I did!" he insisted. His voice rose and he

nearly choked from the pain. "I'm guessing you didn't hear me. It was kind of chaotic. Now let me walk you away from the blast zone. I'm going to take your hood off but first we're going to move upwind a bit." It felt like fire was filling his lungs with every breath. "Trust me, you don't want to breathe in this stuff. Looks like the blindfold was tied in a knot and you won't be able to reach it."

She paused another moment. Then she turned her head away from the bear spray that still lingered in the air. She let him take her arm and walk her a few feet away from the detonation.

"Who was that guy?" Amy asked.

"I don't know," he admitted.

"He was completely silent," she said. "I didn't even hear him until he was on top of me. Does he have anything to do with what happened to my friend Gemma?" she asked.

"Again, I have no idea," he said. "But I'm here to find out what happened to her."

Amy's head rose defiantly. "I don't believe she's really dead."

"Well, neither do I."

He started coughing again. His lungs and eyes were still stinging, and he could barely see. The first thing he needed to do was rinse his eyes out with water. That would give him temporary but much-needed relief. He'd then have to wash his skin with soap and water, change his clothes too, and see if he could give his eyes an extra rinse with saline solution. It was a whole complicated procedure not made any easier by the inability to properly see and breathe. But he couldn't just leave her there. He wrestled with the knot until it came free. With his help, she pulled the hood off her head. Then she turned around.

Her hazel eyes met his and widened.

"Wow, I got you good," she said. "I'm so sorry about your face. That looks really painful."

Just how bad did he look right now?

"Thanks for your help," she said. "Your name is Jackson, right? I'm Amy. I'll go grab you some water. I've got some in the store."

Wait, didn't she recognize him? It was true they hadn't seen each other in over a decade. He'd lost his youthful chubbiness, bulked up, gotten a new dent in the bridge of his nose thanks to a bad break and grown a beard since then. Not to mention the bear spray was probably doing a number on his features. Then it hit him. In the chaos of the moment, he'd called

himself Jackson instead of Ajay. Furious barking filled the air. He turned to see Hudson gal-
loping down the alley toward them. The dog's
teeth were bared. Hudson snarled. He must've
heard Jackson cry out, managed to wriggle his
way through the open truck window and was
now charging to Jackson's rescue. Or maybe
he'd just smelled the spray and knew it meant
trouble.

Amy gasped.

"Hudson, stop!" Jackson ordered. He held
up his hand. "Sit. I'm okay. Amy is a friend."

The dog sat promptly. Hudson's head cocked
to the side and he whimpered softly.

"Sorry, bud," he added. "I'm sure this stuff
smells even worse to you than it does to me."
Then he turned to Amy. Her face was pale.
"This is my K-9 partner, Hudson."

"Hi, Hudson," Amy said, hesitantly.

The dog thumped his tail in response as if
trying to reassure Amy that he hadn't meant to
scare her. She turned back to Jackson. "Hang
on a second. I'm going to get you some water
for your face."

Amy dashed through the open door and was
back seconds later with a bottle.

"Thank you." He took it gratefully and

splashed it over his eyes. "I should get changed too and wash my skin. Can you help me find somewhere to do that? Then we should sit down and talk about what just happened."

Which was kind of hard to do while it felt like his pores were on fire. The closest motel was over an hour away—the longer he went without changing and washing, the worse it would be for him. He wasn't about to let himself into the family cottage without asking Amy first, even if he did co-own it with his sister. He splashed his eyes again and when he glanced back, Amy was fiddling with her cell phone. Hang on, was she taking his picture?

"Give me a second," she said. "You said your name is Jackson, right? And you're a cop? Here to investigate Gemma Locke's disappearance?"

"That's right."

Amy really did have no idea who he was. But maybe that was a good thing. The police who'd interviewed Amy before had thought she might be hiding something about Gemma's disappearance. In a normal family, the fact he was the missing person's brother would be an advantage, but Amy knew better than anyone that he and Gemma had never been close. The Amy he'd known back when they were teenagers would never have told Gemma's little brother any of her best friend's secrets. Maybe if she didn't know who he was, he'd have an easier time getting her to open up. He could find out the truth...and maybe he'd be less anxious.

"And do you have a last name, Officer Jackson?" Amy asked.

"It's Sergeant Jackson, actually. And my last name is... Finnick."

Before he could think it through, his boss's last name slipped over his tongue.

"Which division?" she pressed.

"The RCMP's Ontario K-9 Unit."

"Do you have a badge?"

"In my truck," he said. "Hudson's got a badge too."

She paused for a moment as if considering his answer. Then she stuck out her hand. He shook it.

"Nice to meet you, Sergeant Jackson Finnick," Amy said. "Sorry again for your face. Now, if you'll excuse me for a minute, I'm just gonna pop back into my store and close everything up for the night. Back in a second."

"I'll come help you," he said.

"No, thanks," Amy said. "You stay out here with Hudson and keep rinsing your eyes."

She walked back into the bookstore.

Jackson looked at Hudson. The dog cocked his head.

"Well, partner, do you think I just made the biggest mistake of my career?"

Amy closed the door almost all the way, leaving it open a crack. Then she calmed her breathing and looked around. The bookstore was eerily quiet now except for the sound of Reepi bouncing happily in his cage. The power was still out but solving that problem would have to wait until tomorrow.

She closed her eyes and prayed.

Thank You, Lord, that I made it out alive. Please keep me safe now and give me the wisdom I need.

She ran her hands over her belly, feeling for the comforting form of Skye. She held her breath and waited until she felt the flutter of her baby move inside her. Amy exhaled.

Thank You, God.

Skye was okay.

Now, what to do about the intimidatingly handsome Sergeant Jackson and his fierce partner? The cottage was only a few minutes' drive away. He could get cleaned up there and they could talk. She even had a bottle of saline solution for washing out his eyes. But, he was still a total stranger and she didn't know how much she trusted him. Amy glanced down at her sketch pad on the counter. The picture she'd drawn of the man she now knew as Jackson Finnick stared up at her.

Was he really who he said he was? Sure, he'd just told her that there was a badge in his truck, but it could be a fake or even his attempt to lure her to his vehicle. She sighed. Maybe what had happened with Paul had ruined her ability to trust anyone.

She pulled out her cell phone, dialed 911 and told the operator that it was imperative she speak to an officer in the RCMP's Ontario K-9 Unit immediately. There was a click. She waited. And after a long moment, a voice came on the line.

"Constable Caleb Perry, RCMP." The voice was confident and professional. "How can I help you?"

She blinked. "I didn't realize the RCMP had constables."

"Beats calling us entry-level grunts," Caleb said.

"My name is Amy Scout," she said. "I'm calling from Clearwater, Ontario. I have a man here with a large dog who claims to be a K-9 officer with your unit. I wanted to verify his identity."

And get someone to send help right away if he was lying.

"Absolutely," Caleb said. "Though, I can tell you we do have someone in Clearwater at the moment. Is his name Sergeant Locke?"

As in Gemma Locke?

"No." Amy frowned. "Finnick. Sergeant Jackson Finnick. His partner is a German shepherd named Hudson. But Locke is the last name of the person he's here to investigate so maybe there's a mix-up there?"

There was a pause.

"Maybe," Caleb said. His tone was indecipherable.

"I took a picture of them if it helps," she added.

"Yeah, please do send it through," Caleb said. Now he sounded surprised. Or maybe even impressed. "I'll give you my personal cell number you can text it to."

She typed in the number as he rattled it off, then she sent him the picture she'd furtively taken of Jackson and Hudson.

"Yup, that's Jackson Finnick and Hudson all

right," he said, after a long moment. "I grabbed some food with Jackson yesterday actually and he told me about the case. They're in Clearwater right now to look into the disappearance of Miss Gemma Locke."

"Yeah," Amy said. So that all checked out. "Gemma was a friend of mine. I'm staying in her cottage and manning her bookstore for her until she gets back."

"So, you don't believe she's dead either," Caleb said, almost as if to himself.

"No, I don't."

"Well, neither does Jackson," Caleb said. "So, you're in good company. Jackson is one of the very best officers I've ever known and Hudson is second to none. If you need more character references, I'm happy to pass the phone around the unit. Everyone will say the same."

"No, that's all right," she said. She was beginning to feel a little foolish. "Thanks so much for your help, officer."

"No problem," Caleb said. "I'll text you the unit's direct line. Feel free to call either the unit or myself if you need anything."

"I will," she said. "Thank you."

"No problem."

They ended the call. Okay, seemed like

there were still some people in the world she could trust.

She found Jackson and Hudson where she'd left them.

"Come on," she said, "grab your bag and I'll take you to the cottage where I'm staying. I've got saline solution and a special soap that's good for getting bear spray off your skin. You can get cleaned up and we can talk about Gemma." She gently grasped his arm. "I'll steer."

"Sounds good," Jackson said.

They made their way to his truck, where he grabbed his jacket and a large bag from the vehicle.

He glanced in the rearview mirror as he did so, clocking his reflection.

"Yup," he said. "I'm a beauty all right."

His eyes were still red and swollen, and his whole face was puffy. Guilt pricked her heart. She couldn't imagine how much pain he was in and yet he hadn't even complained.

As opposed to Paul, who'd lose his temper whenever anyone so much as got his drink order wrong. She would know. When they'd met she'd been a waitress.

"My car's up here," she said brightly. It was a twenty-year-old Volvo with more dings and scrapes than she could count. But it was reliable and it was hers.

Hudson stretched out in the back, Jackson got in the passenger seat, and she started to drive through the woods and down the narrow roads that would lead her back to the cottage.

"So, you have a place up here?" Jackson asked.

"I'm staying at Gemma's, actually," she said. "Making sure everything is taken care of while she's gone."

"I know that you spoke to the local police for their investigation," Jackson said. "But they didn't mention you were living here."

"I hadn't really decided what I was going to do by then."

She still wasn't exactly sure what she was going to do. Skye was due in less than two months and Amy still didn't know what kind of life she could even provide for her.

"How long have you been living at Gemma's?" Jackson asked.

His questions were casual and his tone was light, but she could tell he was interviewing her. She wondered why he'd started by talking about her living situation instead of the attack.

Maybe it was his way of easing into the conversation and trying to make her comfortable.

"A few months," she said. "I had some financial problems and she invited me to come live with her."

That was the easiest way to explain it, without going into the wreck Paul had left her life in.

"Where were you before that?" he asked.

"Niagara Falls," she said. "For a little over a year."

"And before that?"

"Traveling the world. I never really settled down anywhere."

Although now that she was about to be a mother, that life was behind her, with nothing left to replace it.

Thick trees pressed in on all sides. Before Paul, her life had been spent leaping from one adventure to the next. She'd just gotten back from backpacking around Europe when she'd taken the waitressing gig in Niagara Falls for a few months to save up for her next adventure. Paul would come in alone and ask for a table in her section. He'd told her he was a real estate developer from Southern California who was visiting on business. She hadn't even found him attractive at first. He was short, balding, and seemed older than the thirty he claimed to be. But she'd thought he was interesting. He'd worn her down slowly over time. There'd been large tips, then dates and gifts, until the next thing she knew she was in a long-distance relationship receiving dozens of calls and texts from him every day.

She frowned at the memory. He'd been so persistent that she never imagined he didn't actually care.

Then he'd surprised her with the most incredible gift of all—blueprints of the tiny seafront art gallery he bought for her. She could fill it with her own sketches and use it to support other up-and-coming talent too. She could hire staff to run it when she traveled. All she had to do was say yes. They'd elope that afternoon and she could start the emigration process immediately. He'd even bought her a ring and booked a wedding chapel in the hopes she'd agree. And impulsively, she decided to jump into the promise of a new adventure.

Only none of it turned out to be real.

He hadn't even lived in California, and she

didn't even know his real name. Everything about him was fake.

"Everything okay?" Jackson asked. "You look upset."

A look of genuine concern moved behind his puffy red eyes. Like he actually cared about how she was doing beyond just investigating the case.

"I'm fine," she said. "Just lost in thought."

"Are you okay if we go over the details of what happened back at the bookstore?" he asked. She nodded. "What do you remember about the guy who attacked you?"

"He was tall, masked and, like I said, he was silent." She sighed. "I didn't even hear him until he snuck up on me."

"And you don't have any idea who he was?" Jackson asked. "Could he be an acquaintance or someone you were once in a relationship with?"

"No," she said. "I'm pretty sure I've never met him before."

"Did he say anything to you?"

"Yeah, and he had an accent too."

"What kind of accent?" Jackson asked.

"Australian, I think. Really thick, like he was putting it on."

Jackson nodded. "What did he say?"

"I don't remember the exact words," Amy

admitted. "But he told me not to fight and that I was going to help him find something."

"Find what?" Jackson asked.

"I don't know." She shrugged. "But the police never found Gemma's laptop. It wasn't here or in her car, and I'm pretty sure she took it with her."

Jackson's cell phone began to ring. He squinted at the screen. "My eyes are so watery I can't even read it."

She glanced over. "It's Caleb Perry."

He slid his phone back into his pocket. "He's a colleague."

"I know," Amy admitted. "A low-level grunt."

Jackson's eyes widened slightly, then he winced as if it had hurt him to do so. "He's a constable... How did you know that?"

"While I was in the store, I called 911," she went on. "I asked them to patch me into the RCMP's Ontario K-9 Unit. Maybe I shouldn't have gone through 911, but if you had turned out to be a liar, I would've needed emergency help, now wouldn't I?"

"Yeah," Jackson said. He sounded a bit thrown.

"Caleb answered, and I asked him to verify your identity. I even texted him a picture I'd managed to snap of you and Hudson."

"Wow," Jackson replied. "That's really impressive." There was an odd tone in his voice she couldn't quite place, like he was picking his words very carefully. "What did Caleb say?"

"He verified that you are who you say you are and that you're here looking into what happened to Gemma," she said.

"Did he say anything else?" Jackson asked. He sounded like he was holding his breath.

"Only that you and Hudson are really great."

He exhaled slightly, and Amy wondered what he'd been afraid Caleb might've told her. She turned off the small, rural road onto an even narrower dirt track. The cottage came into view, and beyond it, through the trees, she could see glimpses of the lake. It was a long and meandering body of water that curved through the forest in such a way that no matter where a boat sat on the lake, it was impossible to see all of it at once. Half a dozen islands dotted its surface, most not much larger than a few rocks and trees.

The cottage was two stories. But the second story was a loft, only a third of the size of the bottom floor. It contained two small bedrooms and a landing that jutted out over the living room, which could be reached by a spiral staircase. Most of the cottage consisted of a large living room and kitchen, with a wood-burning stove and floor-to-ceiling windows. She pulled to a stop.

"Welcome to Gemma's cottage," Amy said. "It used to belong to her grandparents, but she bought it from them when she was in college."

Jackson stiffened slightly.

"Actually," he said, "the way I heard it, Gemma and her brother jointly bought it from their grandparents."

"Huh, I didn't know that," Amy said. It looked like Jackson really had done his homework. "I've never seen him up here."

"I take it he's busy with work," Jackson said. There was that odd tone in his voice again.

She pulled to a stop by the back door.

"Do you know if anyone questioned him about what happened to Gemma?" she asked. "Because wherever she was going that day, it was important to her and she didn't want to talk about it. Maybe he had a financial motive, if she was living in a cottage they jointly owned, or he was in some kind of trouble."

As much as she hated to think it.

"Oh, police have talked to him," Jackson

said. "But do you suspect him? Do you think there's something wrong with the guy?"

"No," Amy said. "Not really. But Ajay was into some really stupid petty stuff when he was younger. Pranks, trespassing, that kind of thing. Maybe he went downhill and got involved in even worse stuff since then."

Jackson didn't answer. They got out of the car and started for the cottage.

"Would you mind if we let Hudson chill outside on the front porch?" Amy asked. "Gemma isn't a fan of dogs in the house, and he's a pretty big guy."

Not to mention, he'd seemed downright terrifying when he'd been charging toward her back at the store, despite how sweet his shaggy face was now as he looked up at her.

"I'm happy to put out a bowl of water and a blanket for him," she added. "But I don't know if I left out things he might eat or things he could knock over. I wasn't expecting—"

"It's okay," Jackson said, cutting her off. "It's fine. The weather's clear and it's a nice temperature out for a dog with a coat like his. He won't mind."

"Thank you," she said, feeling truly grateful at how quickly Jackson had agreed.

They walked around the side of the cottage to the front porch that looked out over the lake. Thick trees ringed them on all sides, hiding their neighboring cottages, all of which were empty this time of year. They left Hudson on the front porch then walked through the sliding glass door into the main room. Amy found Jackson the soap, saline and a towel then pointed him toward the washroom.

She busied herself with tidying up. Enough chicken stew for six people bubbled gently in a Crock-Pot on the kitchen counter. She turned off the heat to let it cool enough to eat. Amy had left her charcoal pencils, sketch pads and pictures scattered around the room. She arranged them into a single neat pile on the dining room table.

Her stomach rumbled. Skye was hungry and didn't want to wait. She walked back into the kitchen and pulled out a box of crackers, a jar of peanut butter and a knife. Amy spread a dab of peanut butter on the first cracker, popped it straight into her mouth without pausing to put it on a plate, and then did the same with the second. She was about a dozen crackers in when she realized Jackson was standing in the bathroom doorway in a fresh, clean blue shirt, watching her. She blushed, realizing he'd just caught her snacking.

"How are you feeling?" she asked. "You're looking better."

Some of the redness and swelling had subsided. She noticed for the first time that his eyes were green, reminding her of Gemma.

Her missing friend had green eyes too. Not pseudo-green, like Amy's hazel ones, but the kind of bright green that silently caught a person's attention from across the room.

"I feel better," he said. "Do you have enough crackers for two?"

"I actually have chicken stew if you're hungry," she said. "There's plenty if you want to stay for dinner. It's a lot better than crackers, I just couldn't wait until it cooled. Pregnancy hunger isn't like any other form of pangs I've ever experienced. There's something that feels really urgent about it. Do you have any kids?"

"No," Jackson said. He walked over to the couch. "Never married, no family and no kids. It's just me and Hudson. I'm not really cut out for the parent life." He chuckled sadly as he sat, and something in his tone made her suspect there was a story there. "Is this kid your first?"

"Yup." She put the peanut butter and crackers away. Then she got out bowls for stew.

"Do you need a hand with that?" he called.

"No," she said. "I'm good."

"How far along are you in the pregnancy?" he asked.

"Almost thirty-four weeks," she said.

"Do you know if you're having a boy or a girl yet?"

"A girl." She smiled. "I call her Skye."

"I like it," he said. "And you moved in with Gemma after you were pregnant?"

"Yeah." Now his steady string of questions was beginning to feel more like an interrogation. She guessed Jackson wasn't one for meaningless small talk. Steam rose off the stew as she lifted the lid. She stirred it slowly, letting the warm aroma fill the room. "But I moved in before I knew I was pregnant. My so-called husband left me before either of us knew I had a baby on the way. We were only married a couple of weeks actually."

"Wow, I'm sorry," Jackson said.

"Don't be. I'm better off without him."

The morning she'd gotten home from buying groceries to find Paul gone, all she knew for certain was that his cell phone had been disconnected, the eight thousand dollars she'd had in savings had been drained from her bank account and he'd taken every expensive gift he'd ever bought her. It was only due to Gemma's internet sleuthing afterward that she'd found out Paul had at least three different names he used, several children by multiple women, a wife in Michigan and another in Wyoming.

What he didn't have was an art studio.

Getting the marriage annulled had been a snap. Getting any form of justice had been another matter entirely. Turned out Canadian law enforcement wasn't about to dedicate a lot of resources to scouring the United States for a man whose real name and location she didn't even know over the theft of a few thousand dollars.

Amy scooped large ladles full of chicken, potatoes and vegetables into bowls. Then she walked over and handed one to Jackson. He stayed on the couch, while she sat in the rocking chair, and they talked about Gemma. Amy went over everything she knew about the days before Gemma's disappearance and where she could have been going, which wasn't much.

"It goes without saying that I searched every inch of both the bookstore and this place for clues in the days after Gemma left," Amy said.

"Of course, the police searched too. So, whatever the intruder was looking for, I don't think he's going to find it." She stirred her stew slowly and watched as steam rose from her bowl. "At this point I'm wondering if I should start checking every book in the place for hidden messages. But there are thousands of them."

"The police who interviewed you indicated they thought you weren't being fully honest with them," Jackson said.

"Really?" She felt her eyebrows rise. Was this why Jackson was grilling her? "Well, I told them everything I know. I can't tell them what I don't know."

"How was the bookstore doing?" Jackson asked.

"Good," Amy said. "I think."

"Was anything upsetting Gemma?" Jackson asked. "Was there anything out of the ordinary going on?"

"I don't know." Amy frowned and pushed the stew around in her bowl. "She was working incredibly long hours. Gemma used to talk about going back to school or making a career change. But since I moved in, she's been really focused on being at the store. Sometimes she'd be there until after midnight and then right back there in the morning. But I have no idea why."

She'd wondered if Gemma had been continuing to look into Paul, even though Amy had asked her to drop it.

"Gemma was always a very private person," Amy said. "She was the kind who'd avoid conflict at all costs."

She blew out a breath.

"My doctor has been worried about my blood pressure and told me to keep my stress levels low," she added. "Knowing Gemma, she'd have thought twice before telling me anything that might've upset me."

Jackson nodded. "Where did she tell you she was going the day she disappeared?"

"She didn't," Amy said. "She just told me she needed to run an errand and asked me to manage the bookstore while she was gone. That was the last I heard from her." She set her bowl on the coffee table. She'd suddenly lost her appetite. "I just keep wishing I'd asked her what was going on."

Jackson put his bowl down beside hers. His fingers brushed her hand and then squeezed reassuringly for a moment before letting go.

There was something about the simple gesture that sent tears rushing to her eyes.

"None of this is your fault," Jackson said. "You hear me? You can't blame yourself for any of this. Now, I'm going to take Hudson to the closest dog-friendly motel for the night, then come back here in the morning and see what we can find. It'll be okay. I promise."

His phone began to ring again. This time she couldn't see the name when he checked the screen. But whoever was calling, Jackson's face paled slightly.

"I'm going to take this outside," he said. "Give me a second."

He walked out the front door with the still-ringing phone in his hand and closed the door behind him. He signaled Hudson, and the two of them walked around the side of the building and still the phone rang. Seemed he was waiting until he was completely out of earshot before answering it.

The sun was beginning to set over the lake in shades of pink and purple fading down to a deep royal blue. This place was so beautiful and peaceful. For years it had been her favorite place on the planet. It was hard to think of anything bad happening here.

Something moved in the trees to her right. She turned quickly. But all she could see was an indistinct blur disappearing into the night. Had someone been there? Was her imagination playing tricks on her or was someone watching the cabin?

Chapter Three

Jackson stared at his ringing cell phone as if it were a hand grenade about to explode.

Inspector Ethan Finnick, head of the RC-MP's Ontario K-9 Unit and Jackson's boss, was calling. No doubt to ask what Jackson had been thinking using Finnick's own last name for an impromptu cover identity. Jackson had never imagined that Amy would immediately try to verify that he was who he said he was. Clearly he'd underestimated her, in more ways than one. He'd been beyond relieved when Caleb had covered for him. Caleb was a good friend and an outstanding officer who'd only recently transferred into the K-9 unit and still hadn't been assigned a partner.

He didn't expect Finnick to be equally as understanding.

"Jackson!" Amy called.

He declined the phone call, stuck the phone

in his pocket and turned to see her running around the side of the cottage.

"Is everything okay?" he asked.

"I don't know," she said and gasped a breath. "I think I saw someone in the bushes, but I can't be sure."

Jackson signaled Hudson, and together they ran back around the side of the building. He scanned the darkness but couldn't see anything.

"Where did you see him?" Jackson asked.

"There." Amy pointed to a gap in the trees a few feet from the water.

"Get inside the cottage," Jackson said. "Keep the door locked and your phone in your hand. I'll be back in a moment."

He waited until Amy was safely inside, then together he and Hudson ran in the direction she'd pointed. They burst through the trees. There was no one there and yet multiple sets of footprints marred the ground in indistinct and overlapping shapes, some more faded than others. Someone had definitely been there in the past and not just once, but he couldn't tell how long ago.

Had they been watching Amy, Gemma or both of them?

He instructed Hudson to search. While the

dog seemed to pick up a scent, he lost it again a few feet later at the water's edge. Frustration burned the back of Jackson's throat and he channeled it into prayer.

Lord, help me figure out what's going on and catch whoever's behind this. Help me keep Amy safe and find my sister. He took a deep breath and let it out slowly. *And whatever I face, through all of this help me be kind, wise and the type of person I want to be.*

He and Hudson went back to the cottage, where he found Amy waiting for them just inside the door.

"I'm kind of hoping you're going to tell me there was nobody there and I was imagining everything," Amy said.

"Sadly, I think someone has been watching the cottage," Jackson said. "I just don't know how recently."

Worry flooded Amy's eyes. He watched as her arms wrapped around her belly as if trying to cradle her unborn child and keep her safe.

"Change of plans," Jackson said. "I'm going to stay in Clearwater tonight, so I'm close by if you need me. It doesn't feel right leaving you here alone until we find out more about what's going on. I'll sleep in my truck."

"There's a camper parked around the far side of the cottage," she said. "You're welcome to stay there. It's probably twenty years old, but it'll keep you both dry."

He almost smirked. Yes, he knew the old camper very well. He'd practically lived in it all summer long when he was a kid and wouldn't be surprised if he found dog-eared copies of his old adventure books hidden behind the cushions. He fed Hudson dinner and they walked him together. Then they returned to the cottage, where Amy and Jackson shared another bowl of stew and some homemade cookies. All the while, his phone kept buzzing in his pocket like an angry mosquito, until he eventually muted the ringer.

Jackson knew he'd have to call Finnick back eventually. But for now he was putting it off. There was something just so easy and comfortable about talking with Amy that made it hard to walk away from her. She had the most incredible laugh—it wasn't just pretty but generous too, and it made his own lips turn up in a smile. He couldn't remember ever having seen her art when they were younger, but now every corner of the cottage seemed alive with vibrant lines, shapes and colors. Besides, the longer they

talked, the greater the possibility she might remember something important about Gemma.
He didn't just enjoy her company; she was a
vital part of finding his sister.

Or so he kept telling himself.

The sun set completely, leaving nothing but
an inky black sky with an almost-full moon
hanging high above them. Amy drove Jackson
and Hudson back to the place where he'd left
his pickup truck so he could retrieve it. Then
they came back to the cottage and wished each
other a good night. Jackson hauled his gear, a
sleeping bag and a blanket for Hudson through
the trees to the old camper.

He was a little surprised that Gemma had
never suggested removing it, and wondered if
she'd kept it up as some kind of olive branch
because she knew how much it meant to him.
It was cleaner than expected, with no leaks and
few cobwebs. The ceiling was lower than he remembered. But the smell of canvas surrounding
him was just the same as always. He unfurled
his sleeping bag on one of the bunks, hopped
up and sat there leaning back against the wall.
Hudson leapt up beside him and lay his large,
furry head on his knees. Jackson stroked the
soft fur between his partner's ears.

"Thank you for being so patient with Amy today," he said. "I hope you didn't mind chilling outside. You're a really good dog and I'm sure she'll see that too."

Finally, he turned to his phone and called Finnick. His boss answered on the second ring.

"Finnick here."

"Hi, it's Jackson," he said. "I'm so sorry for not calling you back sooner and I know we have to talk. But I was with Amy. Somebody tried to kidnap her."

Finnick inhaled sharply. "This would be Amy Scout? Your sister's roommate?"

"Yeah," Jackson said, "and best friend since childhood."

"Is she all right?" Finnick asked.

"A little shaken," Jackson said, "but fine. She's one of the strongest women I've ever met. She bear sprayed me when I rushed to the rescue, thinking I might be working with the guy who attacked her. Got me right in the eyes."

Finnick snorted. Seemed he was Team Amy on that one. So was he. Jackson quickly ran his boss through the kidnapping incident at the bookstore and the evidence that someone might have been watching the cottage for days, or even weeks. Finnick was an incredible officer, and Jackson was thankful that no matter how confounded he might be by what Jackson had done in borrowing his name, Finnick's top priority was still making sure the civilian was safe. Jackson had never met an officer who was more dedicated to making sure victims and their families got the justice and closure they deserved. More times than Jackson could count, as he was packing up for the day, he'd glance into Finnick's office and see his boss still sitting at his desk, with his K-9 partner Nippy curled up at his feet, poring over cold cases with such intense focus it was like Finnick took the fact each one was still unsolved personally.

"Amy's very pregnant," Jackson said. "Late third trimester. As much as I appreciate everything she's done to help keep Gemma's store running in her absence, I don't feel safe leaving her up here alone."

"Neither do I." Finnick blew out a breath. "All right, this is where jurisdictions get tricky. Because I can't just easily step in as a head of the RC-MP's Ontario K-9 Unit and wrangle a case out of the hands of the local police who are heading the investigation into Gemma's disappearance—"

"Even if they've bungled it and let it die?" Jackson interjected.

"Even if they've made a dog's breakfast of it," Finnick said. "But I can definitely open an investigation into the attack on Amy and ask local police for their files to help in our investigation."

A wry determination moved through his boss's voice. It was reassuring. Jackson closed his eyes for a moment and thanked God that Finnick had given him a couple of days off work to look into his sister's disappearance on his own and that he sounded willing to throw resources behind helping Amy.

"Now, the only description we have of her attacker is that he's tall, moved silently and has an Australian accent?" Finnick confirmed.

"Correct," Jackson said. He opened his eyes. "Amy thinks the accent might be fake. Like I mentioned, I suspect someone has been watching the cottage for a while. I don't know why she was attacked today or what that has to do with what happened to Gemma. All I can think is that the investigation into my sister's disappearance had been fairly dormant until I got back yesterday and started pulling on every thread I could find. I might've attracted someone's attention."

"I'd agree with that," Finnick said. "They'd

practically closed the case until you started kicking up a fuss."

"Maybe I rattled whoever's behind this," Jackson said, "and they decided they had to act fast."

"It's a definite possibility," Finnick said. "Any new leads on what happened to your sister?"

"Not yet," Jackson said. "By the sound of things, Gemma was spending very long hours at the bookstore in the weeks before she disappeared, but we still have no idea what she was doing in South River. It's in between here and Huntsville, so maybe that's where she was really headed. Amy thinks she was hiding something, but she doesn't know what."

"And you're convinced that local police are wrong and she's still alive?" Finnick asked.

"I am," Jackson said. He had to be. He couldn't afford to think anything else or the grief would overwhelm him. "Gemma is the most tenacious and relentless person I know. She's a lot more introverted than me. We butted heads constantly as kids, because I was really outgoing and she was conflict avoidant. But if anyone could survive a hit job, it's her."

Despite their differences, she'd always looked out for him in her own way. Like how she'd

never been a fan of cops after Jackson had encountered a couple of truly terrible ones. This
was when he'd ended up in a special program
for kids with behavioral problems, after the
whole car incident. It was ironic. Gemma was
so protective she couldn't get over the fact he'd
forgiven the cops who'd mistreated him and
even joined their ranks.

"Well, I hope you're right," Finnick said.
"Now, to face the elephant in the room. What
I don't understand is why, faced with all this,
you then decided to lie to Amy Scout about
your identity? Or how you thought it would
help anything in regards to this investigation?"

The fact that Jackson had been anticipating
the question didn't stop it from stinging. He'd
worked on almost a dozen undercover opera-
tions in his career, both large and small, and
never once had he been accused of lying, especially not by a superior officer.

"The officer who'd interviewed Amy initially about Gemma's disappearance wondered
if Amy was hiding something," Jackson said. "I
have an unfortunate history with this witness,
and I didn't want that to get in the way of finding out what she knew. So, when I realized she
didn't recognize me, rather than dredging up

the past and risking the investigation, I made the split-second call to turn this into an undercover operation."

"But that's not what we do." Finnick's tone was so sharp it could've cut straight through the flimsy canvas walls surrounding him. "You know better than most that we spend days preparing for undercover work. I will not have my officers running around whipping up new identities willy-nilly on the fly. Did you even put an ounce of thought into your cover story?"

"No," Jackson admitted.

"Great, so you're winging it," Finnick said, and Jackson could practically hear him rolling his eyes.

"I know. I need to take a breath and figure out my cover before it comes back to bite me," Jackson said. Then again, if he managed to keep Amy at arm's length he wouldn't have to. There was no need to let things get personal between them, any more than they already had.

"Ha," Finnick said. "It's going to bite you either way at this point. What you need to do is apologize and tell her the truth as soon as possible. What exactly is your history with Amy Scout?"

He paused. "It's personal."

"Not if it has the potential to impact both an attempted kidnapping and a missing person's case," Finnick said. "And I have the authority to pull you back into the office and dispatch another officer to apologize to her for what you've done."

"Okay, truth is, I was a real idiot back when she knew me," Jackson said, quickly. "I was obnoxious. I had a lot of energy and a lot of pain over my parents' divorce, and rather than channeling that in a healthy way I pulled a lot of stupid pranks, which eventually landed me in a program for kids with problems, and that saved my life and got me on the right track. But before that, when I was fourteen, I took a joyride in her grandmother's car because I was upset Amy hadn't invited me to her birthday party. I crashed right down the hill, practically through the party, hit a couple of tables and ended up in the lake. Thankfully, nobody was hurt."

Finnick didn't say anything. The silence on the other end of the phone was almost deafening.

"A year later, I wrote her a letter," Jackson went on, "as part of my therapy process. I was supposed to make amends to people I hurt. I apologized for what I'd done, and what I'd been like back then. I also admitted I had a crush on her and had acted really immaturely when she didn't invite me to her party."

"And did she respond?" Finnick asked.

"She sent my letter back with big block letters printed across it saying she never wanted to see me again," Jackson said. "She said she hated me. And she had every reason to."

"Such teenage dramatics," Finnick said, under his breath. "Both of you."

"The issue is that I'm genuinely embarrassed and ashamed about the person I used to be," Jackson added. Even now, when Amy asked him if he had a family, he couldn't help but think that he'd mess up any kids he had so badly they'd end up behaving even worse than he had. "My sister and I were never close, while Gemma and Amy have always been joined at the hip. I was afraid if Amy remembered me, she'd shut up tighter than a clam and refuse to speak to me." He clasped the back of his neck. "She even suggested that I could be the one who'd done something terrible to Gemma. She practically implied I murdered her for her share of the cottage."

"And you thought if she knew that you were Gemma's brother, you wouldn't get the information you needed to figure out what happened to your sister," Finnick said.

"Pretty much," Jackson said, "especially considering she was already terrified from having almost been kidnapped and had just bear sprayed me. But I take it you think I made the wrong call."

"Probably," Finnick replied. "But I also think that at this point we're stuck with the situation you've made for yourself, at least until tomorrow. But, as you know, due to a problem with our usual dog breeder, I have a couple of incredible new constables in our unit who don't yet have dogs to continue their training with. So, I'm going to get constables Caleb Perry and Blake Murphy to help you on this. You've already roped Caleb in, and Blake has a wonderful knack for dealing with challenging cases. Expect them to make contact with you in the morning and to meet up with you in Clearwater by early afternoon."

Which also meant they'd be able to take over the case and help deal with the fallout if Amy wanted nothing more to do with him once he told her the truth.

"Understood," Jackson said.

"I have to admit, I'm surprised you've pulled

it off so long," Finnick said. "I would've imagined the cottage was full of family pictures of you."

"We're not that kind of family," Jackson said, feeling a twinge of regret. "My parents' divorce was really toxic. And I guess neither Gemma nor I had any great desire to remember our childhood."

Or repeat it with families of their own. At least, he didn't.

"Out of curiosity, why do you think Amy hasn't recognized you yet?" Finnick asked.

"I didn't spend a lot of time up close with Amy when we were kids," Jackson said. "I was a chubby kid then. I've gotten more lean and added more muscle. I've broken my nose since I saw her last. Plus, I've grown a beard."

But the fact Finnick had used the word *yet* hung in the back of his mind like a flashing warning sign.

"One more thing," Finnick said. A warmer tone moved through his voice, which suddenly reminded Jackson that the seasoned officer was almost old enough to be his father. "We all made mistakes when we were younger that we've spent the rest of our lives kicking ourselves for. The wise ones among us learn to face up to those mistakes and learn from them. You're a good officer, Jackson. Don't let the mistakes you made over a decade ago jeopardize this case or your career."

Jackson looked up at the plastic roof above his head. That was easier said than done.

Night came early for Amy like a heavy blanket, dragging her down into unconsciousness before she'd even had time to ask herself what she thought about the handsome man and protective dog who were keeping guard nearby in the camper.

But it seemed her initially peaceful sleep was too good to last. Her body was jolted awake shortly after one o'clock in the morning by the feeling of Skye kicking inside her. The small baby's kicks were urgent and relentless, as if her unborn child sensed that something was wrong and was trying to get her attention. And for the first time since the terrifying incident back at the bookstore, Amy could feel the full extent of her fear seeping into her veins. Her shoulders began to shake as if the temperature had dropped. She took in a long calming breath. Then Amy pressed her hand against her belly, feeling Skye's tiny foot against her palm.

"Hey, it's okay," she said. "I'm awake. What do you need? Are you hungry? Or do you just randomly feel like doing jazz aerobics right now?"

She closed her eyes to pray and felt her lungs tighten in her chest. It seemed the fear wasn't about to leave her so easily.

Lord, I need Your help. I don't feel safe staying here alone at the cottage. But I don't really have anywhere else to go. All I want is to keep Skye safe, but I don't know how, let alone who's after me or why. Am I being foolish by holding onto the hope that Gemma's still alive out there somewhere and everything's going to be okay?

She opened her eyes and looked out the window at the dark woods, searching for the shape of the camper. There'd been something comforting, almost peaceful, about sitting with Jackson in the living room talking earlier. He hadn't once snapped at her or made her feel bad about hitting him with the bear spray. And he seemed to really listen when she talked and paid attention to what she was saying. It was different from what she was used to. But it was nice. It made her feel relaxed and safe, in a way nobody ever had before. Being with Paul had felt like riding a roller coaster. And as much as she loved Gemma, lately her friend had a tension to her, as if she'd been battling some unknown enemy just outside Amy's view.

Being with Jackson felt like stepping outside into the sunshine on a warm day.

"I'm not sure how to tell you this," Amy said out loud to Skye, "but before I saw your tiny little shape on a sonogram, I never wanted a permanent home or a family. I was spontaneous, and I liked it that way. Even with Paul, I was lured in by the fact it was a long-distance relationship and he traveled a lot. You're not even here yet and already you feel like the first thing in my life that has ever been permanent."

And what would her life be now? She had no idea. All she knew was that it would be nothing like it'd ever been before.

A crash sounded in the cottage below her, like someone had accidentally knocked her haphazard pile of sketch pads off the table. Had Jackson let himself back into the cottage for a drink of water or something? Was he struggling to find the light switch?

She swung her feet over the edge of the bed, slid her arms through her housecoat and belted it over her long flannel pajamas. Then she crept in her stocking feet to her bedroom door, opened it a crack and peered out. She looked down, past the railing of the landing at the main floor below. The living room lay dark and empty beneath her. Silence had fallen again. The cottage was so quiet that if someone was there, she couldn't even hear them breathing. Then slowly shapes began to form in the dim gray light that filtered in through the windows, and she saw him.

A tall, masked figure was climbing up the spiral stairs toward her.

Amy closed her bedroom door softly and locked it behind her. The man who'd kidnapped her was inside her cottage, coming down the hall toward her. She ran for the window and threw it open.

"Jackson!" She shouted his name into the night. "Help! The intruder is here! He's in the cottage!"

And the intruder, whoever he was, had definitely heard her now. But had Jackson? There was no reply from him, just the rustling of leaves in the darkness. Was he there? Had he heard her? Was he even now creeping quietly through the trees to her rescue?

I don't even know if I can trust him.

Or maybe something had happened to Jackson, like something had happened to Gemma.

She couldn't hear the intruder either. Was he in the next room? Was he just outside her door? If he hadn't knocked over her books, she might never have heard him. She ran her hand over her belly.

"Thank you for waking me up," she whispered to Skye.

But now what?

She heard the soft telltale squeak of Gemma's door opening on its hinges. Maybe the intruder was searching her room. But what was he looking for? Moments later she heard Gemma's door close again and knew the intruder was on his way to her room. The balcony was so narrow and the spiral staircase down to the main floor was so steep that she couldn't risk making a run for it. Not with a criminal out there who might try to force her over the edge or kidnap her again. She looked out the window again. Tree branches rustled beneath her. Was that Jackson and Hudson? Had he heard her calling out to him for help? Were they on their way?

Help me, Lord, I'm trapped! Am I foolish to hold onto the hope that they're coming for me?

She looked out the window, feeling the

mounting fear rise inside her. Then she looked back over her shoulder at the bedroom door. She couldn't stay hidden in here forever. But there was a sloping overhang about three feet beneath her. The room had once belonged to Ajay and when they'd been kids, he used to climb out the window, across the overhang, and leap down onto the water barrels, especially whenever he'd been grounded. She'd only done it once, when he'd been teasing her and Gemma about being too scared to try it.

Well, now she was far more afraid of whoever was on the other side of the door.

A faint rattling sounded from behind her, as if someone was trying to pick the lock.

She slid her body through the window one leg at a time until she was sitting on the window ledge staring out at the night. Was she really going to do this? What other choice did she have?

Her breath tightened in her chest. The doorknob turned behind her. Her bedroom door creaked open. She caught one fleeting glimpse of the same masked assailant stepping in through her bedroom door.

Then she pushed off from the windowsill and let her body drop down onto the slanted roof below. It was steeper than she remembered. She slid toward the edge, prayers spilling from her lips as she desperately grabbed at the shingles, trying to slow her descent. Then her stockinged feet hit the rain gutter, stopping her with a jolt and almost pitching her forward over the edge. Instead, the gutter held firm.

Thank You, Lord.

Something rustled in the trees, but she didn't risk leaning forward to see what it was. Instead, Amy began to shimmy her way along the roof, moving sideways like a crab. But her socks didn't give her much grip. The shingles were loose under her hands.

A light flickered on and off in the forest so quickly that she couldn't tell where it was coming from.

"Amy?" Jackson's whisper was faint in the darkness.

"Jackson?" she whispered back. "I shouted for you."

"I heard. I didn't want to tip anyone off that I was here."

Well, she'd have liked the heads-up he was coming to her rescue.

"Where are you?" he asked.

"Here."

"Where?"

"On the roof."

"You're what?" His voice rose slightly. "Never mind. Hang on and don't move. I'm coming."

She could hear the intruder moving through her room behind her. What if he had a weapon? Or got to her before Jackson did? Should she just wait there for Jackson to rescue her? Or keep climbing down?

Suddenly the decision was out of her hands as she felt the tiles rip loose beneath her fingers. She scrambled in vain for another handhold, but it was too late. The gutter broke free. Amy screamed as suddenly she tumbled forward, off the steep roof and into the darkness below.

Chapter Four

Lord, please protect my child! The desperate prayer filled her heart as—for what felt like an excruciating and terrifying moment—Amy felt herself falling through the air. Then she landed against a sturdy chest. Strong arms tightened gently around her and she realized he must've run for her.

"It's okay," Jackson's voice soothed in her ear. "I'm here. I've got you. What were you even doing up there?"

"The intruder...was in...my room." Her breaths were coming out so sharp and shallow, she could barely speak. "He's looking... He's looking for something."

Quickly, Jackson stepped under the cover of the porch and out of the view of anyone looking out the window. His arms tightened around her. "Are you all right? Did he hurt you?"

"I'm fine. He didn't see me." She tried to pull

in a deeper breath. "It's no big deal. Gemma's brother used to jump off the roof all the time when we were kids."

"You're not him," Jackson said. "Are you sure you're okay?"

No, she wasn't. But her heart was racing in her chest and she had to slow it down, for Skye's sake.

"I need to lie down," she admitted, "and slow my heart rate."

"We need to get you out of here in case he comes looking for you," Jacskon said. "I'll take you to the camper. Hudson will guard you while I go see if I can catch the intruder."

"But Hudson is just a dog."

"Trust me." Jackson's voice was firm and un-relenting. "He's also an RCMP officer and he'll protect you."

He turned and started carrying her swiftly through the trees toward the camper. Hudson ran alongside them.

"I know you and Hudson didn't get off to the best start," he added. "But I promise he'll keep you safe. If anyone comes within a mile of you, he'll bark his head off. His hearing is far better than ours." He blew out a breath. "And if anyone tries to step foot near the camper, it will not go well for them."

When they reached the trailer, he opened the door and gently set her down just inside the doorway. A faint orange light flickered on above a bunk to her right. She crawled onto the bed, lay down and pressed her hands flat against the mattress, willing her racing heart to slow its rapid pace. Skye was kicking so frantically, Amy almost doubled over.

"The light will flicker off when I close the door," Jackson said. "But there's a flashlight with a dimmer in the side pocket. There's a folding knife in there too, not that Hudson will let anyone get within striking distance of you."

He turned to Hudson and directed the German shepherd to jump inside and sit in front of Amy, facing the door.

"Guard Amy," Jackson said, firmly. "Keep her safe."

Hudson woofed softly.

Jackson turned to Amy. "What am I walking into?"

"Same guy as before," she said.

"Did you see him?"

"Yeah," she said. "Really well. He's tall and

masked. He was clearly searching the cabin for something."

"Did he have a weapon?" he asked.

"Not that I saw."

Jackson nodded. "Okay."

Still, Jackson hesitated in the doorway, as if uncertain whether to leave her or not. She didn't want him to go.

Lord, I feel safe with him here. And now he's walking into danger. Please protect him and keep him safe. Keep us both safe.

"You should go," Amy said. "Catch whoever is behind this before he finds whatever he's after and gets away with it."

"Yes, ma'am," Jackson said. She could hear his smile in the darkness.

He turned the lock on the handle and then closed the door. The orange light flickered out. She lay there for a moment listening for the sound of Jackson moving away through the woods.

Hudson glanced toward her and woofed softly as if trying to reassure her. She reached down and ran her hand along his back, feeling the warmth of his soft fur beneath her fingers. Hudson licked her fingers in response. Then he turned his attention back to the door. The dog's ears perked, listening for any sound in the darkness.

She closed her eyes and forced her breathing to slow.

God, I feel as if the world is shifting beneath my feet.

She'd liked living a spontaneous life. It had been fun, like she'd been on a raft exploring one fast-paced river after the next. But now, it was as if her tiny raft had been swept out onto the huge and wild ocean. She was beaten down by torrential rains. And every time she thought for a moment she'd begun to find her footing, another wave would come and knock her down.

I want my best friend Gemma back, Lord. I can't imagine her being dead, and I want so very much for the police to find her alive. I want Jackson to catch whoever is stalking me and for the nightmare I'm living in to stop. Above all, I want a break from the chaos.

I need peace. Please, bring Your strong and lasting peace into my life.

Finally, she felt her breathing begin to slow, and Skye settled within her.

Thank You, God.

She reached inside the camper's side storage flap, for the flashlight Jackson told her was stashed there. Instead, she felt something rectangular. It was soft around the edges. She pulled it out and ran her fingers along it.

It was a book and there was a piece of paper tucked between the pages.

Glad for the distraction, she dipped her hand back into the pocket again and felt around until she finally found the flashlight. Then she pulled a blanket over her head, just like when she and Gemma had been kids trying not to get caught reading after dark.

She flicked the light on. It was one of Ajay's old adventure novels, about two brothers who explored incredible places solving crimes. She pulled out the piece of paper. It was ragged at the side like it had been ripped from a spiral notebook. Words were scrawled across the page in large bold letters, only to be dramatically scratched out as if someone had tried to erase any evidence that they'd ever been written.

Hi Amy,
I like you. Do you like me?

Yo Amy,
I think you're amazing. Do you want to be my girlfriend? Yes or No.

Dear Amy,
Do you like pizza? Want to go get some
in town maybe?

Her heart stopped in her chest. She'd discovered something she wasn't supposed to see.
Ajay had had a crush on her. But she'd had no
idea, and he'd never sent her a letter like this.
But he'd tried to write one…she guessed when
they were about thirteen, judging by the handwriting. Had Gemma known? And if Ajay felt
this way, why had he never told her?

Jackson pressed his body against the living
room wall of his cottage and listened. He could
hear the sound of the clock ticking and his own
breath rising and falling. Trees rustled somewhere beyond the cottage walls. A cold breeze
cut through the air. The door to the front porch
had been left open.

Did that mean the intruder was already gone?
Had he found what he was looking for and escaped while Jackson was taking care of Amy?
Or was he still hiding somewhere in the darkness?

Jackson crept through the main room with
his gun drawn. Every nerve in his body was

on high alert with the knowledge that at any moment he could be ambushed by an unseen enemy. Slowly, his eyes began to adjust to the light filtering in through the large picture windows. Thankfully the open concept cottage didn't provide too many spaces for someone to hide. He missed having his K-9 partner there beside him. If Hudson had been there, he'd know in an instant whether or not they were really alone.

He looked around the main floor. It was hard to even tell for sure that anyone had been in the cottage. But he was certain that drawers and cupboards had been opened and rummaged through. Books had been rearranged on the shelves. Twice now, Amy had told him that the intruder usually moved silently. Seemed like he also knew how to avoid leaving a trace.

Who was this man? What did he want?

Why was he after Amy?

Jackson was grateful he'd gotten to her in time. Suddenly, the memory of holding Amy in his arms as he ran to the camper filled his mind. She'd been shaking and obviously terrified. Yet, at the same time he was amazed by how incredibly brave and courageous she'd been. Climbing out the window, like he used to do when he was a kid, was a pretty gutsy move. It also might've saved her life.

Jackson shuddered to think what could've happened if she hadn't woken up and escaped, and he silently thanked God for protecting her.

He'd always liked Amy. She'd been cute, smart, spontaneous and fun as a teen. But since reconnecting with her, he could see just how strong and caring she was too. The way Amy had taken on running Gemma's store without missing a beat was incredible, especially considering her own circumstances. He needed to find out what had happened to Gemma. Not just because he loved his sister and had to know she was okay. But because he needed to give Amy closure too and try to bring her best friend home.

Jackson finished his sweep of the main floor. Slowly he crossed to the spiral staircase guided by the dim light, the feeling in his gut and the faith that God would watch over him. He planted a foot on the first step. It creaked underneath his weight.

Suddenly, a shadow moved across the balcony above him. Then, before Jackson could even blink, a figured leaped over the railing and hurtled down toward him.

Instinctively, Jackson raised his weapon to fire. But it was too late—the taller man landed on top of him, knocking Jackson to the floor in a full-body blow. Jackson's head cracked against the hardwood. The gun flew from his hands.

The masked attacker's weight pressed down against him. The intruder swung. Jackson blocked the punch with his left hand and leveled a hard blow with his right. He caught the man in his jaw. The intruder grunted and fell back.

He leapt to his feet. So did Jackson.

"RCMP!" Jackson shouted. "You're under arrest for breaking and entering! Hands where I can see them! Now!"

The intruder didn't even hesitate. He leapt over the couch, stepped across the table and ran for the open back door. The man dashed out into the night. Jackson scrambled for his gun, reholstered it and ran after him.

As he got outside, he caught a glimpse of the attacker disappearing through the trees, following the same path Jackson had found before. The criminal was moving so stealthily that Jackson couldn't even hear him. But he knew where the man was going.

Jackson pushed himself faster, praying with every step. Then the trees parted. The dark waters lay ahead. The masked man was standing up in a small speedboat, using an oar to push far enough away from the shore that he could hit the engine without wrecking the propeller on the ground.

Jackson planted his feet in the earth and raised his weapon, silently praying to God that he wouldn't have to take the shot.

"Stop!" Jackson shouted. "I'm—"

"I know who you are, Officer Locke!" the man shouted. His accent was thick and sounded Irish. "And if you fire that gun, you'll never find out what happened to your sister!"

Gemma?

"Where is she?" Jackson shouted. "What happened to her?"

What looked like a long grenade glinted in the man's hand. He yanked the pin.

Suddenly, a blinding light overwhelmed Jackson's eyes and a deafening bang sounded in the air. Smoke filled Jackson's senses. He heard the boat motor roar and when his eyesight cleared, the intruder was gone.

Chapter Five

Amy sat bolt upright as a boom echoed through the air.

Was it gunfire? An explosion?

Please, Lord, let Jackson be okay.

With one hand, Amy cradled Skye in her belly. With the other she reached down for Hudson's comforting bulk. She could feel the rumble of the dog's soft growl reverberating through her fingertips.

Somehow she'd actually managed to doze off in the bunk while praying. She'd felt strangely comfortable and at peace alone in the camper, for reasons she couldn't begin to understand, only then to be jolted awake by what sounded like a hundred bullets being fired at once.

Her ears scanned the darkness. But silence had fallen outside again, leaving her with no clue about what had just happened. Had Jackson managed to stop the intruder? Or had the criminal gotten the better of him?

Then Hudson's ears perked. The dog's tail began to wag happily, banging like a drumbeat against the camper floor.

Moments later she heard a gentle knock.

"Amy?" Jackson whispered. "It's me. Jackson. It's okay. He's gone."

Thank You, Lord.

Amy slipped her feet over the edge of the cot, feeling the warmth of Hudson's fur brush against her legs. Amy's fingers fumbled as she unlocked the door and pushed it open. There stood Jackson, looking tired and breathing heavily. She guessed he'd run back through the woods.

"Sorry to take the extra second getting back to you," he said, "but I stopped for these."

He held up her running shoes.

"You stopped to get my shoes?" she asked.

"Well, yeah." He grinned almost sheepishly. "I thought you'd want them. Right? I mean, unless you want me to keep carrying you around everywhere."

A grateful sob slipped past her lips, as if her brain had finally caught up with her overwhelming sense of relief at seeing him standing there. Suddenly she found herself throwing her arms around him. He wrapped his free arm around her and brushed his hand along her back.

"Hey, hey," Jackson said, softly. "I'm okay. He's gone. You're safe. I'm safe. It's all good."

Just as quickly as she'd grabbed onto him, she let go again. Why had she hugged him like that?

"Are you okay?" Jackson asked.

"Yeah," she said. Amy stepped back, then took her shoes from his hand and dropped them on the floor. She wriggled her feet into them, oddly thankful for the distraction.

"Do you want a hand with that?" Jackson asked.

"No, I've had a lot of practice in recent weeks," Amy said. He waited until she'd successfully gotten her shoes on, then reached for her hand to help her out of the camper. She took his hand, feeling the warmth of his fingers on hers. Amy's arms still seemed to tingle from the spontaneous hug they'd shared just moments ago. She pulled her hand out of his. "Thank you."

Hudson jumped down from the camper. Jackson closed the door and they started walking back to the cottage.

"So, what happened?" she asked. "I heard a really loud bang. It sounded like something exploded."

Jackson broke her gaze.

"Unfortunately, he got away," Jackson said. "He was in the cabin, we tussled, he ran out through the woods and hopped in a boat. And I lost him. He had a flash bang."

She looked up. "What's that?"

They kept walking, with Hudson flanking Jackson on his other side. Jackson still wouldn't meet her eye.

"It's sometimes called either a stun grenade or flash grenade," he said. "You pull the pin, there's a big bang, a really bright flash of light and sometimes a bit of smoke. They're used by the military and law enforcement for crowd control and to disorient hostiles."

"You're making him sound like a magician," she said. "Big flash of light, puff of smoke and ta-da he's gone."

She was trying to lighten the mood, and Jackson almost smiled at that. But he seemed too frustrated with himself to be shaken by the joke.

"All we've got here is a canoe," Amy said. "But the neighboring cottage has left us the keys to their motorboat. The keys are in the kitchen."

"Thanks, but I don't think I'm going to find any trace of him now," Jackson said. There was an odd tone to his voice she'd never heard before. It was bitter and frustrated, maybe even embarrassed. "Whoever this guy is, I think we're dealing with a professional. The question is, a professional what? You were not kidding when you said he moved silently. But his fighting skills were more opportunistic than calculated."

"So, a professional thief?" she asked. "Or a professional hit man?"

"I can't know for sure," he said. "But I'd definitely say he's skilled at breaking and entering."

"Plus, he came prepared." Instinctively, Amy ran her hand over her neck, remembering the cloth bag he'd yanked over her head just a few hours earlier.

Jackson shook his head. "He was running through the woods and I couldn't even hear him. Plus, he was methodical. The cottage barely looked touched."

Still, his eyes were looking everywhere except her face. Uneasiness grew in the pit of her stomach. There was something else bothering him. Something else was troubling his mind, but he wouldn't say it.

She stopped and turned to him.

"What aren't you telling me?" she asked.

Jackson stopped and blew out a long breath.

"I chased him down to the waterfront," he said. He started walking again and so did she. "When I got there, he was pushing a small speedboat out into the water. It's so shallow there that he had to get out a ways before he dropped the motor so that he wouldn't destroy it on the rocks. I identified myself as a police officer. I also pulled my weapon, which was a dicey move, because honestly it would've been a pretty tricky shot from that distance, especially in the darkness."

"And?" Amy pressed.

"And he shouted that if I fired that gun, I'd never find out what happened to Gemma."

Amy's whole body jolted as if her heart had suddenly stopped. She stumbled forward a step and felt Jackson's hand quickly take her arm and hold her up.

"You okay?" he asked.

"I'm fine." Amy shook him off. "You're saying the man who attacked me in the bookstore and who broke into the cottage knows where

Gemma is and what happened to her? Does that mean he kidnapped her? Did he kill her?"

"I don't know," Jackson said, "and we can't jump to conclusions."

Maybe not. But that still didn't explain the odd shift in Jackson's tone. Something had happened between the time he'd dropped her off in the camper and returned. Whatever it was had shaken him.

"He did have a heavy accent like you said," Jackson added. "But it sounded more Irish to me. Either way, I think it's probably fake. Thankfully, I have two colleagues coming up tomorrow to provide extra hands on this case. Constable Caleb Perry, who you talked to on the phone, and also Constable Blake Murphy. Sorry, I confirmed it after you'd gone to bed for the night and forgot to mention it earlier in all the excitement."

They got to the cottage. Jackson stretched his hand over the doorknob. Then he hesitated. "I think I should stay in the living room for the rest of the night. If that's okay with you. I don't want to run the risk of that guy coming back. Hudson can stay on the porch."

"Hudson can camp out in the living room with you," Amy said quickly. She ran her hand over the back of the K-9's neck. "We made peace back in the camper. Hudson and I are good now."

And for some reason, right now, I might actually trust him more than you. At least I know he's not hiding anything from me.

Jackson nodded. "Sounds good."

He opened the door and switched on the light. Finally, she could see the full contours of his face. It was still a little puffy, but his skin had mostly recovered from the bear spray. Dark shadows lined his eyes. He looked tired and worried, like he'd aged a decade since they'd said good-night.

"Hudson and I are just going to do a quick check of the place to make sure all the doors and windows are locked, so we don't have any unwanted visitors," he said. "We'll be back in a second."

He signaled Hudson to his side and turned as if he was about to head to the second floor.

Amy grabbed his arm. He looked back.

"I'm choosing to trust you," she said. "I believe you're a good guy and if you're keeping something from me it has to be for a good reason. But I can tell you're hiding something. There's something else on your mind—something you're not telling me. My ex told me enough lies to last a lifetime and I can't take any more now. So please, tell me what happened, Jackson. Why do you seem so shaken?"

He knew I was Gemma's brother, Jackson thought as he searched Amy's deep and earnest gaze. *Which means, somehow, he knows more about this whole situation than I do. And he knows more about me than you. What does that even mean?*

Jackson wished he could open up and talk to Amy about it. About all of it. But unfortunately, he'd made a rash and foolish decision the day before that had put him in a stupid situation. And now the last thing he wanted to do was upset Amy any more than she already was. What if she kicked him out of the cottage in the middle of the night and the masked intruder came back? What if she got attacked again and hurt—or worse—because of his mistake?

He could forgive himself—mostly—for the rash decision in the moment. But that call was getting harder to defend with every passing hour. It was like he'd drunk something corrosive, mistakenly believing it would be the best medicine, and ever since he felt it eating away his insides.

Amy was still standing in front of him, looking at him expectantly.

"The masked man told me that he knew who I was," Jackson said, dancing as close to the truth as he could. "That really rattled me. Maybe that means he knows I've been looking into the case. Or maybe he somehow saw my badge. I don't know. But I didn't want to worry you. Because, for all I know, he was lying to me and doesn't have any idea where Gemma is."

"But he knows about her," Amy said. "He knows she's missing and you're looking for her."

Jackson nodded.

"But he didn't say anything specific about where she was, what happened to her or even if she's still alive?" Amy pressed.

"No," Jackson said.

Still, she searched his face for a long moment as if trying to decipher a deeper truth hidden behind his eyes. He'd tell her that he was Gemma's brother tomorrow when Caleb and Blake were there for backup. Then it wouldn't matter if she hated him, because at least she'd be safe.

He was the one who'd drunk the poison. He could live with it eating him up inside until then.

Amy waited in the living room while Jackson and Hudson did a thorough check of the cottage. But aside from a few drawers he could tell had been opened and books he could tell had been moved, nothing was amiss.

When he got back to the living room, he found Amy had laid out a mountain of blankets and pillows on one end of the couch for him, and another blanket on the floor in front of the couch for Hudson. The dog promptly walked over to his new bed and curled up into a ball.

Amy was in the kitchen, eating crackers with peanut butter and boiling water.

"I'm making peppermint tea," she said. "If you'd like some. There's some of Gemma's regular tea in the cupboard too. I just haven't been able to handle caffeine since getting pregnant."

"Have you got any instant coffee?" he asked.

She glanced in the cupboard. "Yeah, we've got some of that too." She pulled out an orange container and shook it. "It sounds pretty dry and granular."

"Good by me," he said. "If you can dump about an inch into a mug, and add some hot water and a spoon, I'll take it from there."

A smile crossed her face, and there was something about it that seemed to light up the furthest corners of his exhausted core. "Deal."

He rekindled the fire in the wood-burning stove while Amy put the crackers away and made them hot drinks. A few moments later, they sat in comfortable silence in the living room, in the same chairs they'd been in that evening. Amy and Jackson sipped their respective drinks and glanced at each other over the tops of their mugs. Neither of them seemed to be in any hurry to try to head back to bed and turn in for the night.

"How are your eyes feeling?" she asked.

"Still a bit dry and sore," he said. "But they've mostly recovered."

"Sorry again about that," she said.

"It's really no big deal——"

"Yeah, it is," Amy cut him off. "At least it is to me. I really appreciate the fact you're being so awesome about it."

"But you were totally justified in spraying me in the face like that," Jackson said. "You were startled and defending yourself."

"I don't know how to explain what I mean." She ran a hand through her hair. "But the fact you're right doesn't stop people from yelling at you. I was a waitress and customers yelled at me all the time for things that weren't even a little bit my fault. Not a lot of people are as understanding as you are or as willing to let things just roll off their backs."

Her earnest hazel eyes met his. He held her gaze, and for a long moment neither of them said anything.

"Well, I made a lot of mistakes when I was younger," he said, finally. "And I know what it's like to want to be forgiven. So, I try not to give anyone a hard time when they mess up. Again, not that I think you did anything wrong."

But he couldn't let himself go down that train of thought. She didn't know that he was Gemma's brother or that she'd once rejected his apology.

"You mentioned that some people have a temper," he said, changing the subject to a safer one. "And as much as I hate to ask you this, I need to find out more about Paul. Did your ex have a bad temper?"

"I think so," Amy said. "Not that I ever saw him yell, but he was pretty particular about having things the way he wanted. I never saw him do anything violent, though."

"Is there any way he could be behind what's happened to Gemma?"

"Well, he's not the intruder," Amy said.

"How can you be sure?"

She sighed.. "Look, I know the previous police accused me of not being totally honest, but I have nothing to hide. Just stuff I'm embarrassed by and don't like talking about." Amy rolled her eyes. "To start with, our intruder is about a foot taller than Paul. Also, Paul was a liar and a cheat, but he's not that athletic. Which is ironic, because he always claimed he came from a long line of men who'd served in the military. He loved showing off his grandfather's Second World War medals. They were really impressive ones with wings and crowns and everything."

"Okay," Jackson said. "But what if he hired someone to get revenge on you? Or revenge on Gemma for taking you in? It's not unheard of for a man to leave his wife and then turn around and try to punish her for moving on with her life."

Amy set her mug down on the coffee table with a thump.

"First off, I'll concede that Gemma did spend a lot of time trying to dig into Paul's identity and his various shenanigans after I moved up here," Amy said. "She had this investigative drive, like she'd missed her calling to be a detective or something. She's always been into unsolved mysteries and cold cases. All the dog-eared fiction books in this place are Ajay's and all the true crime ones are hers."

Very true. He'd often thought it was a shame Gemma hadn't gotten into law enforcement. She had an incredibly acute mind. But she'd also always been too independent to even consider it. Not to mention, Gemma felt the police had been too hard on him when he'd been younger—plus they'd botched it when a friend of hers had vanished in college.

"Then we got an email from someone claiming to be Paul's team of powerful lawyers," Amy continued.

"Really?" Jackson leaned forward. "What did it say?"

"It said that Paul wasn't the father of my child," Amy said, "that he wanted nothing to do with me and that he was taking a restraining order out against both me and Gemma."

"Wow." Jackson blew out a hard breath. "What a jerk."

Among other worse terms he resisted the urge to use.

"Yeah," Amy said. "Gemma suspected he'd written the letter himself and pretended to be his own lawyers. Which might be true, but it gave me the closure I needed. I got an annulment, and I asked Gemma to stop looking into Paul because it wasn't good for my stress level. I didn't need to know anything more, and I already felt terrible enough for ever getting involved with him."

Okay, but that didn't mean Gemma had actually stopped digging.

"I'm glad she looked into Paul for a while," Amy went on. "There's a lot of stuff that I only know about because of her."

"Like what?" Jackson pressed.

"He told me his name was Paul Keebles," Amy said. "He told me that he was incredibly wealthy, worked in real estate and lived in California. He said he was never married, no kids, and that his grandfather was a military veteran. Also, he claimed he visited Niagara Falls at least once a month on business."

"What kind of business?" Jackson asked.

"He said he had an important business contact up here," Amy said, "and they were doing some real estate deals. But I never met him and for all I know he had other women he was visiting in Niagara Falls."

She spread her hands as if laying out the information she had.

"Gemma found out that he doesn't work in real estate or live in California," Amy said. "He has two other wives in different states, at least one fiancée and multiple children. He goes by several different names, including Paul Brown, Paul Keane, Paul Kent and Stanley Paul. His only career seems to be catfishing women, stealing small amounts of money and valuables from them, and moving on. Gross low-level stuff."

Jackson could feel heat building at the back of his neck. He took a calming breath.

How can anyone treat people that way?

"Did you try contacting these other women and warning them?" he asked, gently.

"Gemma did, and I think that's partly what sparked that letter from his lawyers."

She ran the back of her hand over her eyes, as if trying to wipe away unseen tears.

"Paul doesn't care about me!" Her voice rose and quivered with what sounded like anger. "He doesn't care about anyone. He discards people. He dumps wives, leaves children and moves on. I wasn't special to him. All I ever was to him was a little blip in a long string of cons."

Jackson winced. There was a pain in his chest that felt so sharp it was like he'd been shot.

"So, I really don't think he'd hire some Australian slash Irish professional thief to go after me now," Amy added. "Because I'm no threat to him and there's nothing I have that he wants. But if you think it'll help in the investigation, I'm happy to tell the whole messy story about me and Paul." She pulled her long honey brown hair back into a ponytail and tied it with an elastic that she'd produced from somewhere he didn't see. "Well, maybe 'happy' is the wrong word. But I'm willing to tell you everything that happened, if you think it'll help."

"At the very least it will help me eliminate him as a suspect," Jackson said.

He set his mug down and leaned forward, with his elbows on his knees, as Amy told the story about how Paul had wooed her, tricked her into spontaneously eloping with him, then robbed her and abandoned her. Her voice was matter-of-fact, and more angry than sad. But as she talked, the pain in his core continued to grow until it felt like his entire body ached for her and what she'd gone through.

"When I first realized he'd left, my immediate instinct was to just try calling him over and over again," Amy said. "Which is ridiculous considering my number had been blocked, my bank account had been drained and every valuable gift he'd ever given me was gone. I was a total mess when Gemma came to get me. I don't know where I'd be without her."

Jackson silently thanked God that his sister had been there for Amy.

"Gemma insisted I call the cops," Amy said. "But there wasn't much they could do considering he was an American citizen and most of the stuff he'd taken were gifts he'd given me."

"Which I'm sure didn't do much to help the fact Gemma doesn't trust cops," Jackson said.

Amy glanced at him sharply. "How did you know Gemma doesn't trust cops?"

Right. Because he wasn't Gemma's brother. He was a stranger. But he was so exhausted and caught up in Amy's story, he'd momentarily forgotten his cover.

"You know that a few years ago, one of Gemma's college roommates disappeared near Manitoulin Island?" he asked.

"Yeah." Amy nodded. "Her name was Louise Roch. She'd been on a boat, and they believed she went overboard, but they never found her body."

"Well, Gemma apparently was really frustrated with how the police handled it," Jackson said. "She tried to contact the press and sent a lot of letters to different law enforcement agencies."

All of that was true, and he hoped she'd believe that any cop who was looking into Gemma's disappearance would've uncovered it.

"For all we know, Gemma's disappearance now could be connected to that cold case," Jackson said. "Not that law enforcement has found any evidence of that."

Amy nodded again. Then she picked up her mug and took another sip, even though he suspected the tea might be cold.

"Well, now you know the whole story about Paul," Amy said. "At least as far as I know it."

He wanted to envelop Amy in his arms. He wanted to hug her like she'd hugged him back at the camper, tell her that he was so sorry someone had treated her that way and that he'd do everything in his power to make sure no one ever hurt her again. Instead, he crossed his arms over his chest, mirroring her posture, and leaned even further back against the sofa, rooted there by the knowledge that he had no right to hug her. She didn't know who he was, she didn't like the guy he'd been when he was younger, and she'd dislike him even more in a few hours when she found out the truth.

"I'm so sorry," he said. "I wish there was something I could do."

She nodded, yawning, then said she was still planning on waking up early and getting to the bookstore to see about getting the power back on.

Jackson stood as she got up, took her mug and offered to tidy up the dishes.

He tracked her with his eyes as she slowly walked up the spiral staircase and down the hallway to the bedroom that had once been his. The door closed and the lock clicked. But still he stood there for a long moment staring at the closed door and wishing he knew what to say to take her pain away. Then finally he let out a long breath and started tidying the kitchen.

Hudson lay asleep on his blanket in front of the couch. But as Jackson approached, Hudson opened his eyes. The dog's eyebrows rose.

"It's okay, buddy," Jackson said. "Get some sleep while you can. I have a feeling that tomorrow is going to be a long day."

The dog closed his eyes and settled his head back down again. Within moments he could hear the gentle wheeze of Hudson snoring. Jackson wished he could fall asleep so easily.

Instead, he found himself stretching out on

the couch with blankets draped over his body and his eyes scanning the ceiling beams in the darkness. He drifted in and out of a fitful sleep, praying for answers that didn't come. Finally, the morning sun began to rise over the lake, casting the water below in pink and orange hues.

Soon afterward he heard the sound of Amy's footsteps as she made her way downstairs. He sat up and looked at his watch. It was quarter to seven.

"I hope I didn't wake you," she said. "Skye tends to rise with the sun and start kicking up a storm."

"Not a problem." Jackson swung his legs over the side of the couch.

Hudson leaped to his feet and ran over to greet Amy as soon as she reached the main floor. She smiled and ran her hand over the dog's head. "Good morning, Hudson."

"How did you sleep?" Jackson asked.

"Not too bad, all things considered," she said. She looked up at him. "How about you?"

"About as good as I could expect." He stood. "I should probably go take Hudson for a walk."

"I was planning on making French toast," Amy said. "Good by you?"

He smiled. "Good by me."

Her tone was friendly and polite, and a million miles away from the emotional closeness he'd felt with her the night before. Instinctively, he mirrored her tone and they stood there, smiling nicely at each other. He signaled Hudson to his side. Jackson and his partner walked out the front door across the porch and down toward the lake. The memory of how Amy had thrown her arms around him in a spontaneous hug the night before flickered at the back of his mind.

Had she regretted getting so close? Or being so vulnerable with Jackson when she'd opened up about her ex-husband?

Maybe Amy was intentionally putting distance between them, and if so maybe it was a good thing. It definitely wouldn't hurt for him to do the same.

When Amy found out the truth about him, she'd be understandably upset. And if watching the implosion of his parent's marriage had taught him anything it was that conflict lead to yelling, anger, insults and worse. There was no way he could imagine she'd ever forgive him for what he'd done. The best he could hope for now was to somehow lessen the blow.

He walked slowly down to the water, letting

Hudson run on ahead of him. He checked his phone. It was barely seven and the RCMP's Ontario K-9 Unit wouldn't open until nine. He needed to check in with Finnick and fill him in, but he also wasn't about to wake his boss up.

He could however wake up Caleb.

The phone rang four times. Then Caleb's voice was on the line, sounding slightly more alert than Jackson guessed he was. "Hey."

"Good morning," Jackson said.

"Is it really?" Caleb chuckled. "I'll take your word for it."

"Did I wake you up?" Jackson asked.

"Nah," Caleb said. "I was just staring at the coffee maker telling it to hurry up. How's your face?"

"Only slightly more haggard than usual."

"Ha." Caleb snorted.

Jackson quickly filled him in on everything that had happened in the night, including his suspicion that the intruder was a professional.

Caleb whistled. "Well, that woke me up fast. I'm going to meet with Finnick and Blake in the office in a bit. Then I should reach Clearwater around two thirty. Okay?"

"Sounds good," Jackson said. That would give him a few hours to figure out how to tell

Amy that he was Gemma's brother and apologize for being an idiot. "We're going to be heading to the bookstore in a little bit. The power was out yesterday and she really wants to get it open and running by nine. I figure it's as good a place to hunker down and wait for you guys as any. And it'll probably be good for Amy's health and sense of well-being to be focused on the store today."

"And Amy still doesn't know that Gemma's your sister, right?" Caleb checked.

"Nope," Jackson said. "But apparently our professional thief does."

"Wow. Okay." Caleb seemed to stretch the two words out into a few dozen syllables.

"By the way, thanks for covering for me when she called yesterday," Jackson said.

"No problem," Caleb said. "I hated doing it, though. I was so impressed she thought to verify your identity."

"Well, Amy's pretty smart." That was an understatement. "I'll see you at the bookstore this afternoon."

"See you then."

Jackson disconnected and called Hudson. Together they headed back into the cottage. Turned out Amy had made enough French toast to feed a small battalion, along with a fresh pot of coffee, which he knew was just for his benefit. She'd also opened one of the cans of dog food he'd set out on the counter the night before and scooped it into Hudson's food bowl. She'd even gotten the dog fresh water.

He let her know that his colleagues should be there after lunch and would meet them at the bookstore. They ate mostly in silence, punctuated by the kind of small talk about the weather that one might make with a stranger when stuck in a slow-moving checkout line. Although Amy smiled frequently and even generously, somehow her eyes never lit up the way they had the night before. When breakfast was done, they did the dishes side by side, with her washing and him drying.

Then the three of them headed to the store, this time taking his truck, with Amy in the passenger seat and Hudson spread out in the back. Finally, they pulled into the narrow alley behind the shop.

She got out of the truck, walked toward the door and paused. She turned back. Worry filled her eyes.

He opened the back door for Hudson. "What's wrong?"

"The door is ajar," she said. "It isn't locked and I'm positive I locked it."

"Get behind me," he said.

He pulled his weapon and signaled Hudson to his side. He crossed the alley, pushed the door open and stepped inside.

His heart sank. The lock had been busted. Shelves had been knocked over. Books covered the floor.

The store had been ransacked.

Chapter Six

"What's wrong?" Amy asked as she watched Jackson's body freeze.

"There's been a break-in," Jackson said. His voice was eerily calm and level, but that didn't stop her heart from plummeting into her gut. "Stay behind me."

She waited just outside the doorway as Jackson and Hudson moved through the shop.

"We're all clear," Jackson called from within, "but I've got to warn you, it's a mess."

She stepped through the doorway. Sorrow crushed her core as she scanned the wreckage of their precious little store. The power was still off but enough light streamed in through the large front windows to reveal that every single book had been knocked off the shelf. The bulletin board and her framed sketches had been torn down from the wall.

"Did Gemma have a bird?" Jackson asked.

"There's an empty cage in the other room, but no bird."

Oh no.

"Reepi!" She called the bird's name but didn't hear his cheerful chirping in response.

Where was Gemma's beloved parrot? Amy slid past him and ran into the side room. Her heart shattered. Reepi's empty cage was lying on the floor. The door was open. Green and gray feathers were scattered around the room.

The bird was gone.

Tears rushed to her eyes and she didn't fully succeed in blinking them back before Jackson saw them.

"Are you okay?" he asked, softly.

His comforting hand brushed her shoulder. Hudson's warm body pressed against her leg.

"Gemma had a conure parrot," she said. "His name was Reepi. He was only a few months old. But she loved him so much. I can't believe I lost him."

Hudson went over and sniffed the cage thoughtfully.

"Hey, it's okay," Jackson said. "He probably flew outside. The door was open a crack when we got here."

She ran her fingers over her eyes. "I don't know why I'm crying. He was only a bird."

"But he was family?" Jackson asked.

Amy nodded. "Yeah. Gemma really adored him and he kept me company after she was gone."

His hand ran along her back. It was comforting and supportive.

"Hudson's like family to me," Jackson said. "If anything ever happened to him, I'd be devastated."

How was it this man she barely knew sometimes seemed to know the exact right thing to say?

Jackson stepped away from her and went over to where Hudson was still poking around the cage. He ran both hands over the dog's head and a thoughtful look crossed his face. Jackson knelt down beside his partner, picked a feather up off the ground and held it up in front of Hudson's nose. The dog sniffed the feather obediently. A tiny ray of hope flickered in her chest.

"Search," Jackson ordered his partner. "Find Reepi."

Hudson's ears perked. The dog barked.

"Show me!" Jackson said.

Hudson woofed again, as if agreeing. The dog turned and trotted out into the main room.

"Is Hudson really able to track Reepi?" Amy asked.

"I don't know," Jackson said. "But he seems to think he can."

Hudson barked sharply as if telling them to hurry up. They walked through the main room and found him standing by the back door. Jackson and Amy followed the K-9 out of the store, through the narrow alleyway, past Jackson's vehicle, and then out into the thick and untamed woods. Trees hemmed in around them on all sides. The German shepherd confidently cut his own path through the forest.

"Reepi!" she called.

She glanced at Jackson. Deep lines creased his brow.

"Are you okay?" she asked.

"Honestly, I have no idea if this is going to work, and I'm worried about getting your hopes up. I don't want to let you down."

"Thank you for telling me that," she said. Instinctively, she reached for his fingers and squeezed them. "I appreciate your honesty."

She held his hand for a long moment before realizing what she was doing and letting go.

"Hey, Reepi!" Jackson cupped his hands around his mouth. "Little bird buddy! It's time for breakfast!"

He glanced at Amy and whispered, "It *is* time for his breakfast, right?"

"Yeah." She glanced at him gratefully. He met her eyes and smiled.

They reached a small clearing in the woods. The dog stopped suddenly. Amy held her breath and prayed. There was silence at first, and then something rustled in the branches above their heads.

As they watched, the parrot fluttered down from the trees in a magnificent display of gray and green. Amy's hand rose to her lips. The bird landed on the dog's head.

A laugh slipped through her fingers, mingled with a sob.

Jackson exhaled, and she wondered how long he'd been holding his breath.

"Thank You, God," Jackson prayed. Then he glanced down at his partner and ran his hand over his side. "Good job."

Amy reached out her hand for the bird, but Reepi bounced down onto Hudson's back and busied himself with cleaning his feathers.

"Well, he seems happy with his new perch," Jackson said. "Maybe he's tired from his adventures."

He chuckled, she did too, and then they turned and walked back through the woods to the store, with Reepi riding on Hudson.

It wasn't until they were back indoors that Reepi disembarked and flew through the main room back into the smaller side room. Within moments she heard his usual chirping as he bounced around the bookshelves. Jackson ran his hand silently over his partner's head and scratched him behind the ears. Amy followed the sound of the chirping bird into the other room.

For a moment, she'd been so elated about finding Reepi that she'd almost forgotten just how terrible a mess the place was. So many books were scattered on the floor there was barely anywhere to stand. She turned a small round table that had displayed large artistic picture books right side up again, and started stacking books on it.

Suddenly the lights flickered on above and she could hear the beep of the store's Wi-Fi router coming online.

"Eureka!" Jackson called. A moment later he appeared through the door. "Turns out our intruder cut a few electrical wires. Thankfully I'm handy enough with a pocketknife to splice them back together. Although, you're going to want to get an actual electrician in to do the job right."

"I'm guessing he wished he'd left the power on before he realized he'd have to come back to ransack the store," Amy said, wryly. "But my guess is our criminal hasn't been doing a lot of planning. He attacked me, thinking he'd get what he was after. When that didn't work, he tried searching the cottage. Then when that failed, he came back here."

"It's a good theory." Jackson looked around at the books on the floor. "How can I help?"

Something about the simple question warmed her heart. Cleaning up the store wasn't his responsibility. But he had her back without a second thought.

"Fiction goes on the right wall, alphabetically by author," she said. "Left wall is nonfiction and the back wall is for crime, cold cases and unsolved mysteries. There are a lot of those. Gemma loves them. I'll sort the children's and coffee-table books."

"Got it," Jackson said.

He started picking his way around the mess. For a long moment, she just stood there and watched him. She'd never met a man like him before. So strong and yet so kind and caring at the same time. She hadn't even realized she was staring until he stopped and looked up at her.

"What?" he asked. He straightened up and ran his hands down his legs.

Heat rose to her cheeks.

"I'm just really thankful that you're here," she admitted. "I know you told me you've made a lot of mistakes in the past and that you don't think you're cut out for family life. But from what I can see, you're a really amazing guy. I hope you're not being too hard on yourself."

She wasn't even sure why she was talking to him about this. But there was something incredible about him—something that drew her in and made her feel safe—and after everything he'd done for her, she hated the thought that he didn't see that in himself.

He swallowed hard.

"Thank you," he said. "But you wouldn't say that if you knew the real me. My parents' marriage was really toxic. And I was a terrible kid. I got into all kinds of trouble. I hate the idea of bringing a child into the world only for him or her to end up like me."

She reached her hand toward him. Her fingers brushed his arm.

"But you've grown since then, right?" she asked. "I don't know what you were like before, but the Jackson I know is helpful, funny, forgiving and kind. Maybe if you had a child, they'd turn out like the person you are now."

Something wavered in his eyes, like he was standing on the edge of a diving board afraid to jump. His mouth opened, and she thought he was about to say something important. Then he closed it again, stepped away and broke her gaze.

"Thank you," he said, after a long moment. He turned his attention back to the mess on the floor. "If your kid turns out anything like her mom, I'm sure she'll be pretty awesome too."

He scooped up a handful of books, turned his back to her and started arranging them onto the shelves. Why was he so uncomfortable receiving compliments?

Lord, whatever is hurting Jackson, and whatever lurks in his past, please help him see himself through Your eyes.

She went back to tidying the books and for a long while neither of them said anything.

"Our silent intruder was really careful when he searched the cottage," Jackson said, eventually. "But he was either angry, frustrated or in a hurry when he ransacked this place. I've never seen a place so thoroughly tossed."

"Maybe he's only quiet and methodical when he's afraid of being caught," Amy suggested. "I'm sure just throwing everything on the floor is a more efficient method of finding what you're after."

"Or maybe he's just really frustrated that this job has taken so long and has started to become more ruthless," Jackson suggested.

She bent down, picked up one of the brand-new picture books and looked at it. She ran her finger down the crisp, clean spine. A thought crossed her mind. "Remember I mentioned I wanted to search every book in this place for hidden messages? The state he left the store in practically confirms that he was looking for the laptop or at least something around that size."

Jackson's eyebrows rose. "How do you figure?"

"Well, he was clearly looking for something small enough to fit in a drawer but too big to fit in a book." Amy bent down and picked up two more coffee-table books. "He didn't flip the pages or look through these. Their spines are still pristine."

"Good point," Jackson said. "None of the children's books look leafed through either." He glanced back into the other room. "Also, he didn't open any of the VHS video or DVD cases. We can't assume it was a search for the laptop that caused all this chaos, but it's the likely culprit."

Reepi chirped loudly from somewhere above their heads, as if announcing that he knew the answer.

Jackson chuckled. "Why couldn't Gemma have gotten one of those talking parrots that solve crimes in adventure novels? It would be kind of nice if Reepi could just solve the crime for us."

She laughed. "Well, conures can be taught some words," Amy said. "But he's still pretty young."

Jackson looked up. "Where'd he go anyway? I can hear him, but I can't see him."

"Gemma just lets him fly around free range when the store's not busy," Amy said. "His favorite spot is the back wall. He likes to hide behind the books on the top shelf."

"Well, there are no books there now." Jackson stood on his tiptoes and looked up. "And I don't see him up there."

"Huh, well, I can definitely hear him."

Amy nudged a stool over to the back wall with her foot and stepped up on it.

"Be careful," Jackson said. "Let me steady you."

She felt his hand against the small of her back. "Thank you."

"Do you see him?"

"No," she said. She scanned the empty shelf, her confusion growing. "It's like he's vanished."

But she could hear the bird chirping as loudly and cheerfully as ever. Then she saw it, a dark gap in the wood on the back of the top shelf. "I think I've found a hole, though."

"A hole?" Jackson repeated. "Do you think we have a mouse?"

"I hope not. Hang on, I'm going to check it out." She walked her hands along the wood, then ran her fingers around it. "It's definitely a hole. It's perfectly round and smooth."

"How big?" Jackson asked.

"Maybe three inches?"

She slid her fingers into the hole and felt something move underneath her touch. There was a click. Then suddenly the entire wall of shelves gave way in front of her.

Jackson's jaw dropped as a huge section of the back wall swung open in front of them. Amy pitched forward as she lost her grip on the shelf. Quickly, Jackson wrapped his arms around her, just below her baby bump, and pulled her back against his chest. Darkness filled the space in front of him where the wall of books had been.

Reepi shot through the opening in the doorway and soared over their heads.

Jackson felt the gentle flutter of Amy's unborn baby against his palm, as if Skye was wondering who the unfamiliar hand belonged to.

"Are you okay?" he asked.

"Yeah," Amy said. "I just wasn't expecting that to happen."

"Neither was I," he said.

He held her steady as she stepped onto the floor.

"Thank you," Amy said. She stepped away from him and through the doorway that had opened in the wall.

"Be careful," he said.

She seemed to be feeling around for a light switch. An instant later a light flickered on with a gentle white glow.

"Wow." Amy exhaled and rocked back on her heels.

He followed her into the room and instantly saw what had taken her breath away.

A giant map of the country covered the wall, surrounded by dozens and dozens of newspaper clippings, sticky notes and computer printouts, many of which were connected to the map by thumbtacks and pieces of string.

"Well, I guess this answers the question of whether or not Gemma was hiding a secret," he said.

"Do you think this is what the intruder was looking for?" Amy said.

"Well, it's bigger than a book," Jackson said, "but doesn't explain why he was opening drawers or checking the cottage. I'm guessing this is where Gemma hid whatever it is he's looking for."

He took a step back and looked around, while Amy studied the wall. The room itself was long and narrow, about five feet deep, and stretched across the entire length of the adjacent room. He guessed it had once been intended as a storage room before Gemma had converted it into some kind of secret office. A small antique desk completely filled the space at the end of the room to his right. It was covered in even more papers, maps, and books on both law and criminology. A power bar lay on the floor with both laptop and phone cables plugged into it.

"We've got chargers but no laptop," Jackson said. "So, if I'm right in my guess that he was looking for Gemma's laptop, this might've been where she kept it."

Amy continued to scan the wall.

"These are all old crime stories," she said. "They're murders mostly, but also a few thefts and some missing people." She stepped back. "Some of them are ten, twenty, even fifty years old."

"They're all cold cases," Jackson said. Although he still had no idea why his sister had built herself a secret room dedicated to investigating them. "My boss, Inspector Finnick, is really interested in cases like these. He might be able to shed some light on all this."

"Finnick." Amy turned and her eyebrows rose. "Your boss has the same last name as you? Are you two related?"

Heat rose to the back of Jackson's neck. He broke her gaze. "No relation."

Finnick had warned him the night before that he was foolish to just wing his cover. And maybe he should've really sat down and done the work to develop a more solid backstory. Then again, he hadn't expected he'd need to. He'd been planning to hold her at arm's length. Instead, it seemed like with every conversation they somehow kept growing closer.

Amy didn't say anything for a long moment. When he glanced back, she had the same sharp look in her eyes that she'd had last night when he'd mentioned Gemma didn't like cops.

Help me, Lord. I made a big mistake yesterday and I don't know how to fix it.

He could feel something inside him prompting him to tell her the truth, immediately, without hesitation or even pausing to come up with the right words.

But he couldn't. Not yet. Not until backup arrived and he knew Amy was safe. Until then, he needed to make sure she trusted him to protect her.

She looked past him at the papers on the table.

"Hang on." She walked over. "It looks like Gemma was trying to get her private investigator's license."

"What?" Jackson turned. His sister was training to be a private detective?

"Look." Amy spread papers out across the desk. "These are all modules from the official Ontario Private Investigator Study Guide. This here is a practice copy of the test. She wasn't just interested in solving crime. She was actually going for it."

He sucked in a breath like he'd just been punched in the gut. His big sister was studying how to solve crime and had never breathed a word to him about it. Why? Didn't she trust him? He had chosen a career in official law enforcement, and here his own sister thought so little of cops like him that she'd decided to be a civilian detective...

He stopped and repented of the petty thought the moment he caught it crossing his mind. Maybe she'd tried to talk to him and he hadn't listened. Or maybe they'd sniped at each other so many times in the past, she hadn't even tried.

Lord, how did my relationship with my sister get so broken?

"I had no idea about any of this." Amy shook her head. "I can't believe she felt she had to hide something this important from me."

"I'm sure she was just trying to protect you," Jackson said. "She knew you were stressed and dealing with a lot. Maybe she just didn't want to worry you about this, especially if she wasn't even sure when she was going to take the test."

"She used to talk about wanting a career change or going back to school," Amy said. "But for the past year she's just been spending all her time at the bookstore. I had no idea this was the reason why. I don't understand."

Jackson reached out a hand to comfort her. But instead he stopped himself, pulled back and crossed his arms.

"I don't know either," he admitted. "But I'm pretty sure the last thing Gemma wanted to do was upset you, and she wouldn't want you to blame yourself now." He turned back to the wall. "But this puts Gemma's disappearance in a whole new light, doesn't it?"

"You think somebody connected to one of these cases has something to do with what happened to her?" Amy asked.

"Unfortunately, yeah," Jackson said. Here he'd suspected Gemma had kept looking into the petty conman who'd ruined Amy's life. But the array of murders, criminals and downright evil on display on the wall in front of him totally eclipsed all that.

What if his sister had gone after a cold-blooded killer who didn't want to be found?

He closed his eyes and prayed for her safety as his heart ached with the diminishing hope that his sister was still alive.

"I think I know where she was going when she disappeared!" Amy grabbed his arm as her voice suddenly cut through his fear.

He opened his eyes as she pointed at something on Gemma's desk.

"Look, this whole file is about these three mysterious deaths that happened at Pine Crest Retirement Home twelve years ago," she said. Hope shone in her eyes. "There was this string of thefts. People complained they were missing jewelry, money and war memorabilia. Then three different seniors died within a month of each other."

Jackson looked down at the pages. He felt Hudson's head buffet against the back of his knee. Jackson reached back to stroke the dog's head.

Three murders at a seniors' home that happened over a decade ago? How could that have anything to do with his sister's disappearance?

"Look." Amy laid a printed map in the center of the desk and pointed. "Pine Crest Retirement Home is less than a ten-minute drive from the place where Gemma's car was found. What if she found a lead? What if the killer discovered that Gemma was on his tail…and took her out before she could catch him?"

Half an hour later, they were back at the cottage. Jackson could tell that as much as

Amy wanted to open the store, both the scale of the cleanup job required and the discovery of the hidden room and Gemma's secret investigations had thrown her for too much of a loop. He'd taken pictures of every inch of the office and sent them to Finnick. He'd picked up everything he could find on the Pine Crest case, while Amy had coaxed Reepi back into his cage. Then Jackson had driven Amy, Reepi, Hudson and himself back to the cottage.

Now he sat on the couch and flipped through the Pine Crest file while he waited for Finnick to call him back. Reepi chirped happily in his cage from his new home on the dining room shelf. Hudson lay on the floor in front of the cage and watched his new friend bounce back and forth. Amy stood at the kitchen counter, eating crackers dipped in peanut butter and sketching something in a large pad.

Jackson spread the details of the case out on the coffee table. Twelve years ago, a retirement home near South River, Ontario, had experienced a series of petty thefts. At first, people had questioned whether items were just being misplaced, but as time went on it became pretty clear they had a thief on their hands. Then, within a few days of each other, three of the residents passed away—Mitsy Therwell, Angela Jeffries and Gordon Donnelly. All three deaths had seemed to be of natural causes at first, until the coroner found elevated amounts of painkillers in their systems. It seemed that someone had tampered with the doses on their IVs, maybe for no other reason than to put them to sleep so that someone could pilfer their belongings. All three families reported their loved ones had things stolen from them. Initially, suspicion had fallen on a maintenance man named Kenny Stanton. But police had cleared him and then hadn't been able to locate him when they wanted to do a follow-up interview.

Fresh hope fluttered in Jackson's chest. For the first time since he'd learned of his sister's disappearance, he had an actual idea of what she'd been up to and where she might've been going the day she vanished. This could be it. Somewhere in the pages laid out in front of him could be the answer to where his sister was and how to bring her home.

Jackson's phone began to ring. He glanced at the screen.

Finnick.

He looked from where Amy stood by the counter to where his partner lay.

"Just give me a second," he said. "I'm going to take this."

Hudson's ears twitched in Jackson's direction. Amy glanced up, smiled and went back to her sketching.

Jackson stepped out the sliding door onto the back porch and closed it behind him.

"Finnick!" he said. "I'm guessing you've seen the photos. What a surprise, eh? I guess we now know what Gemma's big secret was."

"Hi, Jackson," Finnick said, and something in his tone made the fledgling hope that Jackson had begun to feel start sinking like a lead balloon. "I've seen the pictures and we can talk about them in a moment, but first I'm afraid I have some bad news."

Jackson glanced behind him and double-checked Amy wasn't close enough to listen in. Then he leaned his elbows against the railing and looked out at the water.

"Hit me," he said.

"I'm sorry to inform you that Ontario Provincial Police think they've found your sister's body," Finnick said. "I'm sorry, but it seems Gemma might be gone."

Chapter Seven

It was like someone had punched their fist straight into Jackson's rib cage, grabbed ahold of his heart and crushed it. His legs went weak and he almost fell into the railing.

"There's not a lot I can tell you at this point," Finnick went on. His tone was direct but kind. "The body of a Jane Doe was found overnight in the water, downriver from where your sister's car crashed. She had no identification or personal items on her, and her body was badly decomposed. They're running DNA tests now. It'll be a few hours until we know anything for certain, and I can't authorize you to tell Amy Scout until we have more information. Again, I am so sorry."

The door slid open behind him.

"Jackson?" Amy called. "Is everything all right? Is there anything I can do to help?"

He turned. She was standing in the doorway,

her face awash with worry and her sketch pad clutched to her chest. He hadn't even realized she'd been watching him. He had no idea what his physical reaction to the news of his sister's potential death had looked like to an outside observer. But now here she was, just steps behind him, checking that he was okay and offering to be there for him.

A lump formed in his throat. He swallowed hard.

"One second," Jackson told Finnick. "I'll call you back."

He ended the call before Finnick responded.

Don't tell her the truth, not until you've got all the information. First get the facts, figure out what you're allowed to tell Amy and how you're going to break it to her, then sit her down and tell her the news.

And yet, at the same time he could hear a second voice, calling out from somewhere deep inside his heart, urging him to tell her everything. He wanted to confess that he was the boy she'd known as Ajay and beg her to forgive him. He wanted to pour out his fear that the body that had been found was Gemma's.

He wanted to pull Amy into his arms, hold her close and promise he'd never be anything but a hundred percent honest with her from now on. But if he did, would she ever be able to forgive him? And even if somehow she did, how could he let himself get close to her knowing that she deserved so much more than a man like him in her life?

"Yeah, I'm okay," Jackson said, hoping his voice sounded more convincing than he felt. "My boss was just warning me some big stuff has come in about a case I'm working on and it caught me off guard. I'm going to go for a walk and call him back." He watched as Amy's lips parted, and he was pretty sure he knew exactly what she was going to ask, so he quickly raised his hand. "If it's about Gemma, I'll fill you in when I can. But I can't tell you anything until I've talked to him. Okay?"

"Okay." Amy nodded.

He looked past her and watched as Hudson got to his feet and started toward him.

"What were you sketching?" Jackson gestured to the pad.

"Us," Amy said. Her face perked up slightly. "Well, me, Gemma and her brother. When we were kids."

She turned the notepad around. There in quick and precise pencil lines were Amy's and Gemma's smiling faces, back when they must've been around thirteen. And behind them, in shadow, he could see himself—Ajay—the boy he'd been and wished he could forget.

But the lines of his face were indistinct and vague, without clear features or form, like he was blending into the shadows around him. Was that how she'd remembered him? Out of focus and lurking in the darkness?

She turned the paper back around.

"I don't know," she said. "I feel like I'm missing something and sketching always helps. I think I'll go sit on the water for a bit while you make your call."

Amy shifted her sketch pad under her arm and pulled her hair back into a ponytail.

"You're going to go sit on the dock?" Jackson asked.

"No," Amy said. "We've got a canoe and I've made an anchor for it. I'm going to push out from shore a bit, anchor myself and sketch."

"You said the neighbors have a motorboat we can borrow," Jackson said. "Why don't you wait until I'm done my call and I'll take you out on the water? I don't like the idea of you going out alone on the lake right now."

"Thanks, but I do this every single day," Amy said. "I have for months. I really like the peace and quiet. Skye enjoys the gentle rocking of the water. And I think I need some time alone to think."

She darted back into the cottage and grabbed a set of pencil crayons. Then she held the door open long enough for Hudson to step through. The German shepherd looked up at Jackson with big, mournful eyes.

Jackson could tell that Hudson knew he was in pain.

"Don't worry," Amy said. "I'm just going to be floating peacefully in the canoe. I promise I'm not going to drift away. You'll have your eyes on me the entire time, Sergeant."

She pointed to her eyes with two fingers and pointed those fingers at him, as if to lightheartedly emphasize her point. Actually, it wasn't a bad idea. As long as Amy was out on the lake, she wouldn't be able to overhear his conversation with Finnick, and yet she wouldn't be out of view either like she would've been if he'd gone for a walk.

"Yeah, okay," he said. "Just stay where I can see you."

"Will do," she said. Then Amy hesitated. "But are you sure you're fine? You look a little sick."

Her lower lip quivered in apparent worry, even though he could tell by the way she pressed her lips together that she was trying to hide it. Could she tell that he was keeping something from her? Or was she just reeling from the knowledge that Gemma had been keeping such a big secret?

He wanted to pull her close and wrap his arms around her. He wanted to apologize for not admitting he was Gemma's brother sooner and tell her his heart was now breaking over the fact police believed they'd found her dead. Instead, he gave her what he hoped looked like a reassuring smile. "Have fun on the lake."

Amy turned and walked down to the water. She crossed the dock, slid on an oversize life jacket, got in the canoe and undid the rope. She picked up a paddle and pushed off into the water. Jackson's eyes never left her for a second. With slow and lazy strokes Amy paddled out until she was about two thirds of the way between the shore and the closest island. They all used to swim back and forth to that island as kids.

Amy dropped what looked like a laundry detergent jug full of sand tied to a rope over the edge of the canoe, where it landed with a splash in the water and sank. Then she eased herself down to a seated position on the bottom of the canoe, flipped to a new page and started sketching. And still he continued to watch her, somehow unwilling to break away from her face, as her dazzling eyes scanned the world, her lips tilted up and her fingers moved.

Lord, please bring peace and happiness into her life. Help her find someone who will love her and Skye the way they deserve to be loved. Protect her from all of her enemies.

Jackson swallowed hard.

Protect her from the pain I'm now feeling and from the foolish decisions I've made. Help me get justice for my sister and safety for Amy.

Then he dialed his boss.

"Jackson!" Finnick said. "How's Amy? Caleb just filled me in on what happened in the cottage last night."

Right, with everything else that had happened so far today, Jackson had forgotten to brief his boss on that part. Slowly Jackson started walking down the porch steps with Hudson by his side.

"She's okay," Jackson said. "Definitely a little rattled." Again, his eyes rose to the woman happily sketching in the canoe. "I didn't tell her that Gemma's body might've been found. And we have some privacy to talk without being overheard. Amy is incredibly strong, tough and brave. But I'm worried that she might be a little more shaken than she's letting on."

"Or maybe she's just pushing herself," his boss suggested, "and it'll all hit her later."

"Yeah, she's been hit with a lot." And now more bad news was coming. "I can't even remember what I've told you and what I haven't at this point."

"Well, let's go through everything now," Finnick said. "Top to bottom."

"It's a lot," Jackson said again. "Do you have the time?"

"I'll make time," his boss said. Jackson heard him get up from his chair, say a quick word to someone that Jackson couldn't quite make out and shut his office door. A moment later Finnick's chair squeaked again. "Okay, I'm back. Again, I wish there was more I could tell you about the body that authorities believe is Gemma's. But we won't know more until the DNA tests are complete. And while our hands are tied on that, we can make headway in finding justice by talking through the case."

"Thank you." Jackson wasn't sure what he

needed right now; he just knew that it didn't involve either staying still or being quiet.

He paced back and forth in front of the deck. He filled his boss in on the theory that whoever they were dealing with was a professional who had been clearly searching for something. He gave him a quick rundown of what had happened in the night and the mess they'd found when they got to the bookstore that morning.

"Sure, my immediate impression was that someone had trashed the shop," Jackson said. "But I don't think that he was intentionally trying to destroy the place. He didn't break anything. He just tossed it all on the floor, like he was looking for something."

"And you don't think he was looking for the hidden room?" Finnick asked.

"No," Jackson said. "Because he also opened drawers. But Amy pointed out that none of the books were rifled through, so whatever it was couldn't have been small either. I'm guessing it's gotta be Gemma's laptop. Maybe she discovered something the Pine Crest killer wanted to make sure never saw the light of day."

He looked out over the water. Amy had tossed her head back and was laughing at something. He wondered what it was.

"Not a bad theory," Finnick said, dragging Jackson's attention back to the call.

"What are your thoughts on Gemma's cold case investigations?" Jackson asked.

He could almost hear his boss leaning forward in the chair.

"I'm familiar with a lot of them," Finnick said. "I'm not overly up to speed on the Pine Crest murders, but I'll definitely be digging into them and seeing what I can find. I've seen a lot of amateur sleuths in my time and your sister is head and shoulders above the rest."

"Well, Gemma has always been pretty driven."

For better or for worse.

"You had no idea she was studying to get her private investigator's license?" Finnick asked.

"None at all," Jackson said. He could feel a touch of regret rising in his voice. He swallowed hard and tried to bite it back down. "I love my sister to bits, but we had very different personalities. As a teenager she found me annoying, in a really condescending way, and something about that made me want to annoy her more. Childish stuff, but we never worked through it. Because Gemma was the kind of person who avoided conflict."

"Like she'd give someone a fake name to avoid discussing the mistakes she made in the past?" Finnick said gently.

Touché.

"I think it's fair to assume that Gemma was heading to Pine Crest the day she disappeared," Jackson said. "I'm going to suggest I go there with Caleb to check it out, while Blake stays with Amy."

Not that he imagined Amy would be happy being left behind. But he wasn't about to take her into danger.

"What was Gemma's personal connection to the Pine Crest case?" Finnick asked.

"None." Jackson blinked. "Gemma didn't have any connection to that case."

He heard the sound of a small speedboat. A warning brushed the back of his spine. The masked intruder had escaped in a motorboat. Jackson scanned the lake but didn't see anything. He hadn't realized there was anyone else out on the lake. Not that the sound of a boat in itself was a reason to worry. He just hoped it wouldn't make waves and jostle Amy's canoe.

Just to be safe, he started toward the dock.

"It's just that normally when people are drawn so strongly to investigate a cold case like this, it's for a personal reason," Finnick said. "A lot of amateur detectives feel a very close relationship to their first case. Especially if it's one they're willing to risk their life for."

"Well, she does have a personal interest in a different cold case," Jackson said. "Her college roommate disappeared years ago and was never found. But that was a long time ago."

"And none of your family or friends were connected with Pine Crest?" Finnick pressed.

"Not that I can think of," Jackson said.

The sound of the boat drew closer. Instinctively, Jackson picked up his pace, readying himself to wave at whoever was driving and shout at them to slow down. A small speedboat raced past, cutting right in between the cottage and Amy, momentarily blocking her from view. A tall man stood at the wheel, his face hidden by a baseball cap. Then he was gone. The canoe rocked in his wake. Amy sat up straight and frowned.

"Nothing is ever truly random," Finnick said. "Like I said, I've heard of the Pine Crest case and I'll see what more I can find. But there has to be some reason she was heading there on that particular day. Maybe she found something specific, had a contact there or was meeting with someone."

The speedboat had turned around and was coming back again. Jackson hurried down the dock, with Hudson at his side. It was a long lake. Why come so close to the only other boat on the water?

Was it the same man from the night before?

"She hadn't completed her private investigator training or gotten her license yet, as far as we know," Finnick continued. "So, it's very improbable that she was hired by someone. She had a bookstore to run and a friend staying with her who's in need. And yet something pushed her to go there in person, without telling Amy. Why?"

The motorboat rushed back into view. Amy looked up. Her face paled. The boat was aimed straight toward her.

"One second," he told Finnick. "There's an aggressive boat out on the lake and he's hassling Amy. I'm worried he could be our intruder."

The driver took one hand off the wheel.

Then there was a flash of light, and a deafening bang shook the air.

Fear filled Jackson's core. The speedboat raced away. The smoke cleared.

The canoe had capsized—flipped over completely and lay upside down in the lake.

Amy was nowhere to be seen.

Amy surfaced under the feeble shelter of the overturned canoe and gasped for breath. White spots still blinded her vision and her ears rang from the flash bang. She furiously treaded water as her mind scrambled to process the past few seconds. The boat had drawn near again. She'd seen an unfamiliar man's chin and mouth underneath the brim of a hat that had been pulled down low. Then something long and cylindrical had glinted in his hands. Jackson's description of a stun grenade had flashed through her mind, and she'd thrown herself over the side of the canoe just as the man pulled the pin.

She closed her eyes and focused on trying to slow her shallow breathing and frantic strokes. Now what? She was still alive. Amy thanked God for that. The sound of the motorboat was fading in the distance. As it did, she could hear the faint sound of Jackson yelling her name, telling her to hold on and then commanding Hudson to help her. That was followed by what sounded like a splash.

Then she couldn't hear his voice anymore and

the sound of water lapping up against the side of the overturned canoe surrounded her again. Okay, she was a strong swimmer and Jackson would come for her. True, it might take him a while to swim out this far, but she had told him where to find the keys to the neighbor's boat. All she needed to do was hold on and wait.

Then the sound of the small speedboat rose. It had turned around. The man who'd set off the stun grenade was coming back.

Help me, Lord. I can't stay here. But I don't want to risk swimming all the way back to shore either.

She opened her eyes and took a deep breath. The slightly acrid smell of the stun grenade's smoke still hung in the air. There was a tiny little island not far away. No more than a pile of uneven rocks punctuated by a few trees. She'd swim there, hide among the rocks, and Jackson could pick her up from there.

Suddenly, she felt a hard and insistent cramp fill her belly. It was sharp and so overwhelming, she heard herself cry out as the pain seemed to block out every other thought from her mind.

Help me, God!

She had to get to safety. Now. For Skye. That was all she knew for certain and it was the only thing that mattered.

Amy slid out from under the canoe on the same side as the island, so that the overturned canoe hid her from the view of the man on the approaching motorboat. She couldn't hear Jackson or even see the shore.

I have to hold onto my faith that Jackson's out there, that I can trust him and that he's coming for me.

She fixed her eyes on the tiny island ahead of her and started swimming. Already her arms and legs were aching from the struggle of treading water, despite her life jacket. She'd always been a strong swimmer. But the added weight of carrying her unborn child seemed to drag her down and sap the strength from her body.

The sound of the boat roared closer. She was never going to make it in time. Would he hit her with another flash bang and cause her to drown? Did he have a gun? Would he run her over?

Amy swam on, pushing her pain-filled body through the water. Just a few more moments, just a few more strokes, and she'd feel solid ground beneath her again. But the island seemed to get farther away with every breath. A fresh cramp swept over her stomach. This one was stronger than the last, filling her body with such crippling pain she whimpered. It hurt to breathe. It hurt to move. She wasn't going to make it.

Then she felt a soft but insistent head buffeting against her arm. She looked over. Hudson was swimming beside her. Jackson must've sent the dog to help her while he ran for the neighbor's boat. The German shepherd pushed his snout against her hand repeatedly as if trying to get her to wrap her arm around his neck.

It's okay, his large brown eyes seemed to tell her. *Let me help you.*

She gasped a deep breath. Relief filled her core. She slid her arm around Hudson and grabbed ahold of his collar tightly. Together they swam for the island. She focused on the small patch of land ahead, trying to block out everything else but taking one strong kick after another.

Finally, she felt slippery rock underneath her feet. She climbed up onto the island on her hands and knees, with Hudson by her side. He licked her face. She hugged him. "Thank you."

She could hear the neighbor's larger boat now. The speedboat might take another pass at her, but she was safe on the island now and Jackson was on his way. It was going to be okay, no matter how many loud bangs and flashes of light the joker might unleash at her. Her palms pressed into the solid ground. She rolled over to a seated position and slowly inched her way up the rock. She could see the tiny speedboat on her left coming fast and beyond it, Jackson at the helm of their neighbor's stronger and more powerful watercraft.

Hudson positioned himself between Amy and the approaching speedboat. His hackles rose and his teeth bared. The man in the boat raised his hand again.

Her heart stopped. This time he wasn't holding another flash bang.

He was holding a gun. His boat slowed.

"You come with me or I shoot you!" the man shouted across the water toward her. "This isn't a game!"

The accent sounded even more fake than it had the day before. But his voice was no less menacing. His boat grew closer. So did Jackson's boat behind him, but he wouldn't reach her in time.

Hudson barked furiously. The criminal's boat drew so close it was only a few feet away. The man's finger brushed the trigger.

"You will get in the boat, Amy!" he shouted. "Now!"

With a growl, Hudson leaped at their attacker. The gun fired.

Chapter Eight

Time around Jackson seemed to move in slow motion, as he stood at the wheel of the neighbor's speedboat and watched as his faithful partner sprang through the air at the gunman, even as the criminal fired.

For a long, agonizing moment the sound of the bullet echoed around the lake, seeming to shake the air. Jackson heard the faint sound of Amy crying out in pain or terror.

Then Hudson landed in the gunman's boat. The bullet had gone wide and Hudson had escaped its path. The German shepherd clamped his jaw on the shooter's arm before he could fire again.

A prayer of thanksgiving rose in Jackson's heart, battling the sorrow and fear swirling within his chest. Gemma might already be gone. But he still had a fighting chance to get Amy and Hudson out of there alive.

His partner was now in the criminal's tiny boat, battling him. The gunman was wrestling with the dog, trying to force him to let him go. Amy was still nowhere to be seen, but still he could hear the plaintive sound of her crying. Jackson pushed the neighbor's speedboat as fast as it could go, but he was still so far away. Desperate prayers filled his heart.

Lord, please protect them. Keep Amy and Hudson safe.

Please help me reach them in time.

I might've already lost my sister. I can't lose anyone else today.

The rocky island lay ahead bare and empty. He watched as the criminal gave up trying to wrestle his hand free and started trying to use brute force and punch his partner in the face. But the German shepherd shook his head back and forth, dodging the blows. Jackson knew that Hudson wouldn't relinquish his grip until Jackson gave the order. Not as long as Hudson thought that Amy was still in danger and this man was going to hurt her. The attacker's small speedboat began to spin wildly in circles, threatening to capsize or run aground on top of the small island where Jackson could only hope Amy was sheltering.

Jackson's boat roared closer. He raised his hand, with the gun strong and steady in his grasp, knowing that unlike the man now fighting against Hudson, there was no way his shot would miss its mark.

"RCMP!" Jackson shouted at the top of his lungs. "Stop the boat now! Or I'll shoot!"

Suddenly the boat righted itself and began to speed away, taking Hudson along with it.

No, he was not about to allow this criminal to escape with his partner.

"Hudson!" Jackson shouted. "Release! Go! Swim to Amy!"

Immediately, the dog released his grip and leaped off the boat. Hudson began to swim back to the island. The small speedboat sped off and in a moment was gone from view. It seemed the man had seen Jackson coming and decided that dealing with both an RCMP officer and his K-9 partner was more than he'd bargained for. Relief filled Jackson's core.

Thank You, God.

Hudson reached the island just before Jackson did and scrambled up onto the rocks. Jackson slowed the boat to a crawl so he could stop safely without running aground.

"Amy!" he called. "Are you all right?"

"Jackson!" Her voice was faint and weaker than he'd ever heard it before. "I'm... I'm here."

Worry filled his core. She'd said "here." Not that she was okay.

Hudson disappeared behind an outcrop of rocks. Jackson cut the engine entirely, drifted up to the island and dropped anchor. Then he leapt off the boat and made his way across the slippery ground in the direction Hudson had gone. Finally he saw her. Amy was sitting on the ground, soaking wet and shivering. Her body was curled up in a protective ball, with her knees pulled up in front of her and her arms wrapped around them. Pain wracked her features. Her face was so pale, he thought she'd faint.

Hudson sat beside her, with his head held high, his ears alert and his body pressed up against her. The dog woofed softly in greeting but didn't leave Amy's side.

Good dog.

"Hey, Amy," he said, softly. "It's okay. I'm here now and I'm not going to let anything happen to you. Now, we need to get you in the boat and back to shore. Are you hurt? Can you walk?"

She looked up into his face. Anguish pooled in the depths of her eyes. Jackson's heart lurched.

"I think I'm in labor," she said. "The closest clinic is over an hour away…and Skye's coming now."

Time passed in a blur of fear and pain for Amy as Jackson gently helped her back into the boat and ferried her and Hudson to shore. He moored the boat at Gemma's dock. Then he scooped Amy up into his arms and slowly carried her back to the cottage as Hudson trailed them protectively. She wanted to protest that she was capable of walking on her own but then felt the pain of another contraction rip through her body. She clenched her teeth and did her best to hide it, but somehow Jackson knew immediately.

"How many contractions have you had so far?" he asked.

"Five," she said. "Thankfully, that one wasn't as bad or long as some of the others."

She could feel her heartbeat beginning to slow, and the painful anxiety that clutched like a fist inside her chest started to loosen its grip.

Jackson climbed up the back steps carefully.

Then he slid the back door open and they walked inside the cottage.

"Are they coming faster?" he asked. "Are the contractions getting longer?"

She shook her head. "No. They haven't been steady. Just painful and scary."

"Okay," he said, "right now we focus on keeping everything nice and calm, while I call 911."

Jackson laid her down gently on the couch, draped a blanket over her, and helped her out of her wet shoes and socks. Hudson parked himself on the floor in front of her defensively. Jackson pulled his phone from his pocket, and then carefully eased himself down on the couch under Amy's head so that she leaned back against his chest like a pillow. She hadn't even realized he'd grabbed a towel from his bag until she felt him gently running it over her sopping wet hair with one hand while he dialed with the other.

"Yes, hello." His voice was both steady and commanding. "My name is Jackson. I'm an RCMP sergeant." He rattled off a police badge number. "I have a twenty-eight-year-old civilian who's seven months pregnant—"

"Thirty-four weeks," Amy interjected weakly.

"Thirty-four weeks pregnant, with a history of high blood pressure and who's having painful and irregular contractions." He paused for a moment and seemed to be listening to the dispatcher. "We're in Clearwater, Ontario. Over an hour drive from the nearest medical clinic and a two-hour drive from the hospital in Huntsville."

Suddenly, pain swept over her again. She clenched Jackson's hand so tightly she could feel her nails digging into his skin. She'd have expected him to yelp in pain or push her away. But instead his thumb gently brushed against the back of her hand, as he glanced at the clock on the wall and counted the seconds as they ticked. Then the pain stopped and he filled in the dispatcher. There was a long pause as Jackson listened to whatever they were saying in response.

"We need to get in the truck and go," Amy said. "I'm not having my baby here."

"We don't want you having her on the side of the road either," Jackson said, softly. "Thankfully, your contractions are uneven and we still don't even know if you're in active labor. If Skye is going to come into the world today, we're a lot safer here, in a nice warm cottage with running water and professional help on the line, then if there was some kind of emergency on the side of the highway."

Jackson leaned forward and she felt his lips brush against her temple in a comforting kiss.

"What I need you to do right now is focus on taking slow, calming breaths and seeing if we can get your heart rate down," he said, his voice barely above a whisper. "The fact the contractions are erratic and seem to be slowing down is a very good sign that this might just be false labor. The dispatcher is arranging for emergency medical help, and it might take an hour for them to get here. But I've got a paramedic on the line right now who's not going anywhere until we're sure you're okay. Right now, all you've got to focus on is resting and breathing. You're not alone. Hudson and I are here, and we're with you every step of the way."

Hudson nuzzled her hand. Then the German shepherd laid his head on the couch beside her belly as if reassuring both her and Skye that he was there. Amy tried to pray but was unable to put words to the cries of her heart, beyond calling out to God for her and her baby's safety.

"How can I help you?" Jackson asked.

"Talk to me," she said.

"About what?"

"Anything," she said. "Something light-hearted. Just distract me with something."

"Okay." She felt Jackson shift beneath her as he reached over the back of the couch for something on the shelf behind him. There was the gentle rustle of pages. Then he began to read.

The book was one of Ajay's old adventure novels, featuring the same mystery-solving brothers as the book she'd found the note in back in the camper. In all the chaos that had happened in the past few hours, she hadn't really given herself time to think about the fact that Gemma's brother had had feelings for her when they were younger. But now she could feel the memory of it fluttering in the back of her mind.

Jackson's voice began to rise and fall in a soft melodic cadence as he read. She closed her eyes and rested in the comfort of his arms, as his words moved around her. Time ticked past, her breathing slowed, the pain stopped and then she began to feel the gentle flutter of Skye moving inside her.

Eventually Jackson stopped reading. "Have the contractions stopped?"

"Yes, and Skye's kicking."

"Thank You, God," he whispered.

He glanced at the clock on the wall, then he shifted the phone to his ear, and she remembered that there'd been someone waiting on the line the whole time.

"Okay, it's been half an hour since the last contraction," Jackson said. "The baby's kicking. I think we are good. Yup, okay, I'll get her to eat something and then will drive straight there. Thank you so much. I really, really appreciate everything. And if anything changes, I'll call right back. Thank you again."

He hung up and set the phone down on the table.

"She's called off the paramedics," he said, "which is good because there was a major accident on the highway north of Huntsville and they're short-staffed. We've got an appointment at a medical clinic in South River. They're the closest place that has the kind of facilities to make sure you and Skye are okay. It's about an hour from here, and I'll take you there as soon as you're ready."

South River was also only fifteen minutes away from the Pine Crest Retirement Home and near where Gemma's car had been found.

"Emergency services have already contacted the clinic and let them know to expect us,"

Jackson went on. He slowly eased himself up from the couch and set a large pillow behind Amy's head for her to lean back on. Then he stepped over Hudson and started for the kitchen. "I'll also text my colleagues Caleb and Blake and ask them to meet us there. They're probably delayed by the accident on the highway, so they should arrive there around the same time we do."

She stretched slowly.

"Are we going to stop in at Pine Crest Retirement Home while we're in South River?" she asked.

"I am," Jackson said. He stopped and looked back but didn't quite meet her eyes. "Hopefully, I'll be able to find out why Gemma was heading there and what her interest was in the case. I'll take Caleb with me. But I think it's better that you rest."

She couldn't argue with that, even though part of her really wanted to go. But she couldn't exactly rest and play detective at the same time.

But I don't want you to leave me alone at the clinic. I want you to stay there with me!

The thought crossed Amy's heart. But she pressed her lips together and stopped herself from saying it.

Jackson wasn't her boyfriend or her friend—let alone her husband or someone who'd stepped up to take any responsibility to care for her and Skye. No matter how safe and comfortable she'd felt in his arms, he wasn't a part of her life. He was just a stranger and police officer who'd happened to be there and stepped up to help her.

So what if she was drawn to him? And if she admired his kindness and generosity? Or how quick he was to leap in and help her, or how attentively he listened? After all, she'd married Paul and he'd turned out to be a liar who broke people's hearts and tossed them away like garbage.

How could she ever trust her own judgment ever again?

"The paramedic said it's important you eat something," he said. "Do you still have a hankering for crackers and peanut butter? Or are you craving something else? I make a mean scrambled eggs."

"No to the eggs, thank you," she said. "But I've got some leftover macaroni and cheese in the fridge if you don't mind reheating it."

"No problem, milady." The cop doffed an imaginary hat and gave a slightly goofy grin. "Your wish is my command."

She felt a weak smile cross her lips.

Jackson's legs twitched as if he was about to turn and walk away. But instead he stood there, just outside the kitchenette, looking at her. Somehow her own gaze was locked on his green eyes, and neither of them looked away. Something deep moved through her core. It was a feeling she'd never felt before. This man had protected, sheltered, calmed and comforted her. He'd helped her through the scariest moments she'd ever known and it hurt to know he was about to leave her life.

But she had a habit of leaping into things without paying attention to where she was going. And maybe that was fine when booking last-minute travel arrangements, but the growing life in her belly told her it was no way to make decisions about anything that really mattered.

No, she could not trust her feelings for Jackson—or any man—right now. And maybe she never would.

"Macaroni and cheese would be great," she called, realizing she was repeating herself but finding her brain lost for words.

She watched as Jackson busied himself in the kitchen, heating macaroni and cheese for her and making a peanut butter sandwich for himself. Odd how he always moved so comfortably around the cottage. Putting dishes away the night before and getting different ones out now. Grabbing a random book and reading it.

It was almost like he'd been there before.

Had he? It was also strange the way he sometimes surprised her by knowing just a little bit more about her and Gemma than she'd have expected. An unsettling feeling tickled the back of her neck. Just how long had he been investigating Gemma? Had he been watching them? Had he been lying to her?

She watched as he pulled the macaroni from the microwave, stirred it, then spooned it into a bowl. No, Jackson was a good man. A nice guy. He'd never given her any reason not to trust him. Her own broken heart and mind were just playing tricks on her.

She reached for the book he'd been reading, hoping the words would settle her mind just like it had when Jackson had been reading to her. Instead, her eyes caught the large blue letters scrawled inside the cover. They were in the same handwriting as the letter she'd found the night before.

Do not touch!
This means you!
This book is property of Ajay
aka Arthur Jackson Locke

Just like that she felt the blood freeze in her body, as a kaleidoscope of small random pieces that had been swirling around her mind suddenly coalesced into one solid picture.

Her gaze rose to the man behind the counter.

She looked past the beard, a nose that had once been broken and the green eyes no longer puffy with bear spray. She'd been both foolish and blind.

Jackson had been lying to her. Her heart hadn't learned a thing after Paul's betrayal but had instead led her astray again.

The man who had come to her rescue, kept her safe and promised to help her find her missing friend was Gemma's brother.

Chapter Nine

Jackson stepped around the kitchen counter holding a bowl of warmed macaroni and cheese in his hand and watched as the color drained from Amy's face.

"What happened?" He set the bowl down on the table in front of her. "Is everything okay?"

Oh no. Had she somehow figured out that Gemma might already be dead?

But Amy's lips curled as if she'd just tasted something wretched. She wasn't feeling a pain like the hollow one in his chest. She was angry.

"You're a real piece of work, you know that?" She pushed herself up to standing. Instinctively, he stepped forward to help her but the fury that glinted in her eyes like daggers told him to stay back. "You lied to me! This whole time!" Her voice rose. "You're Gemma's brother, Ajay!"

He opened his mouth to respond.

But she spoke before he could get the words out. "Don't you even dare deny it!"

"I'm not about to deny it!" Jackson said. His words flew out rapid-fire, in fear she'd run out of the room before he managed to get them all out. His heart was racing so quickly he almost felt dizzy. "You're right! I'm Gemma's brother. In all the chaos of the attempted kidnapping and bear spray, I momentarily forgot to tell you my name was Ajay, because everybody calls me Jackson now—"

"Ha! Jackson Finnick?" Sarcasm dripped in her tone.

"No, Jackson Locke," he said, "and I should've told you that the moment I ran into you behind the store yesterday."

"Yeah, you should have!"

"I know! But I panicked, and I've been winging it ever since," he admitted. "I was afraid that if you knew who I was, you wouldn't let me help you and you'd refuse to tell me anything about what happened to my sister. For all I knew, you might've bear sprayed me again and told me to get lost."

She pressed her lips together, as if she was about to fire back a retort and had barely managed to catch herself. Whatever she had been about to say, he was pretty sure it wouldn't have been good.

"Look, when I came up here to look into what happened to Gemma, I never expected to run into you," he said. His voice rose. But not like he was yelling. More like he was drowning and begging her to throw him a lifeline. "I didn't know you were living here and running the store for her. I paced back and forth in front of the store for ages trying to figure out what I was going to say when I walked in the door. Remember, the police officer who interviewed you initially thought you might be hiding something, and I was afraid you wouldn't tell me what I needed to know to find her."

"So, you lied to me because you were afraid I'd lie to you?" she asked. "You prejudged me and assumed I wouldn't forgive you for the dumb things you did when you were young, because you can't forgive yourself."

No. Maybe. That wasn't true, was it?

"I was afraid you'd feel like you had to choose sides between me and my sister," he replied, "and that as usual you'd choose her and that would keep me from finding her alive." And now it may be too late. "I always intended to tell you."

"When?" She crossed her arms. "When exactly were you going to tell me?"

He ran his hand over the back of his neck.

"Honestly? Just before we met up with Caleb and Blake, so you'd have somebody safe to leave with if you never wanted to see my face again."

She rocked back on her heels. Something softened in her gaze.

"You're so hard on yourself," she said. "All your talk earlier back in the bookstore about how you were such a terrible kid that you could never be a father is ridiculous. Yes, you were a troubled teenager, but I never thought you were irredeemable. Until I found out you lied to me, I was really impressed with who you were as a person. You were kind and thoughtful, and from what Caleb said, your colleagues think you're a really great cop." Then suddenly her words caught on her lips. Her eyes widened. "When I called your unit to verify your identity, Caleb lied to me about who you were, too!"

"Trust me—" Jackson raised his palms "—there's no big conspiracy here. Caleb was just trying to have my back."

"What about the other cop?" she said. "Blake?"

"Blake had no idea," he said. "She's a really wonderful officer. You can trust her."

Amy looked at him skeptically.

He searched her face and prayed that God would give him the right words to say. But Amy closed her eyes for a long moment as if trying to block him out.

"Thank you for heating the macaroni," she said. Her voice was so eerily calm, he almost wished she'd yell at him. "We need to get out of here and get to South River for my doctor's appointment. I assume Blake can bring me back here and fill me in on what you guys find out at Pine Crest?"

Jackson took a step forward. "Amy, you know you can't stay here anymore," he said. "Not after everything that's happened. I know the plan earlier was that Blake would bring you back here. But now, after the boat attack, it's pretty clear that it's not safe."

And the K-9 Unit didn't have the authority to grant round-the-clock protection to her indefinitely.

She opened her eyes.

"Maybe it's not safe here," she said. "Maybe I shouldn't come back here at all. But that's *my* problem to figure out, not yours."

He felt like thousands of words were floating unspoken in the air between them. Jackson wanted to apologize again and keep apologizing for as long as it took to get her to smile again. When he'd seen her through the bookstore window the day before, his heart had begun pounding just like it had back when he'd been a teenager. But what had started out as a crush had grown since then. He'd realized just how courageous, thoughtful and caring she was. He liked Amy—so much more than he'd ever liked anyone before. He wanted to tell her that he was nothing like Paul, the man who'd lied to her, hurt her, betrayed her and left her. He wanted to explain how embarrassed he was for his past and that she was the most incredible woman he'd ever met.

But instead, all he said was, "You're right, we need to get you to the doctor. I'll quickly pack up my stuff, take Hudson for a jog and meet you at my truck."

"Sounds good."

"Look, I know I made a lot of mistakes," he said, "and you have no reason to trust me. But I promise you that I will do everything in my power to protect you and keep you safe. And so will Hudson."

"I know." Amy nodded. "I honestly believe your heart is in the right place. For the record,

I've never thought you were a bad guy, Ajay. Just one who sometimes made really lousy decisions, and who now apparently can't forgive himself for them."

Jackson felt a sudden lump form in the back of his throat. He gathered up his stuff, signaled Hudson to his side, then went for a walk through the woods around the perimeter, being careful to never let the cottage out of his sight. When they got back, he found Amy waiting by the truck with an overnight bag in hand. They exchanged a few stilted words of small talk as each checked if the other was ready to go, then the three of them got in his vehicle and he began to drive.

It would take fifty-three minutes to get to the clinic, according to Jackson's GPS. That would give them plenty of time to talk and straighten out what needed to be said. Maybe he could even find a way to warn her that he had heard something about Gemma, and that while he wasn't authorized to give her all the details yet, it wasn't good news. Something inside him ached to ensure she got the news from somebody who genuinely cared about her and Gemma.

Instead, the two of them sat in silence as the

time on his GPS counted down like a slow and painful detonator to the moment that he would say goodbye to her, knowing he'd probably never see her again. He turned the radio on but didn't pay much attention to whatever was coming through the speakers. When that didn't help he prayed, feeling like he was the last person in the world to have the right to talk to God about anything, but not knowing what else to do.

When there was less than half an hour left on the GPS, he glanced over at Amy and realized she'd fallen asleep with her head against the window and her sweatshirt curled into the crook of her neck like a pillow. She didn't stir again until he pulled into the parking lot of the South River clinic. Blake was already there waiting for him.

She walked over and reached Amy's door, before Jackson could leap out of the vehicle, run around and open it for Amy. Blake had long, black hair pulled back into a French braid, the kind of distinct look that some called "stunning" and a confidence that put people at ease. Amy stirred slowly, as if waking from a dream far nicer than the reality they were in.

"Amy Scout?" Blake said. "I'm Constable Blake Murphy. Please, call me Blake."

Amy smiled. "Nice to meet you."

He watched as Blake helped Amy out of the car.

"Hi, Blake." He leaned forward. "Thanks for doing this."

"No problem," Blake replied. "Caleb will meet you at Pine Crest. He called ahead and they're expecting you. He says to tell you to stop and change into your uniform on the way. He thinks it'll help open doors."

"He's probably right."

She slid her arm around Amy and walked her to the door.

"Goodbye, Amy!" he called. "Take care."

But the words seemed so inadequate for what he was feeling, and when Amy didn't look back he realized that she probably hadn't even heard him.

Lord, please take care of her. Find someone to be her protector in the way I could never be.

Twenty-two minutes later, Jackson pulled up in front of the Pine Crest Retirement Home, having stopped at a gas station on the way to get both himself and Hudson dressed up in their navy blue RCMP K-9 Unit uniforms. Pine Crest was a large and sprawling brown building, with wings that branched out in multiple directions like an angular spider. It would've been completely unassuming, if not for the abundance of gardens that surrounded it, from well-tended flower beds to rosebushes and even vegetable allotments.

Caleb had parked his vehicle down at one end of the parking lot and stood beside it. His short blond hair and bright blue eyes gave the overall impression that he was more likely to be an actor portraying a rookie on some small-town television show than an actual cop. At least until people learned he ran on coffee and sarcasm.

"Good to see you," Caleb said, as Jackson stepped out of the car. "I've been here less than half an hour and I've already managed to start a commotion. I think every single resident in this place has spied on me through the window in the past half hour. They'll be relieved I'm finally stepping inside."

Jackson snorted, thankful that someone was giving him a feeble excuse to smile. He opened the back door of his truck, let Hudson out and then clipped his leash to the dog's official RCMP harness.

Caleb smiled at Hudson and ran his hand over the back of the dog's head.

"Well, look at you!" Caleb said to the German shepherd. "Just wait until they get a glimpse of you and they'll forget all about me and your grumpy human partner."

"Do I look grumpy?" Jackson asked.

"You look deflated," Caleb said. "I'm guessing you told Amy the truth?"

"No, she figured it out on her own."

Caleb blew out a breath. "You did say she was smart. Does she hate you now?"

"I think she hates us both, dude."

"Us?" Caleb's hand rose to his chest theatrically. "What did I do?"

"You covered for me," Jackson said. "Did Finnick tell you the news about my sister?"

Caleb's smile dropped in an instant as he clocked Jackson's face. Jackson had never been any good at hiding what he was feeling.

"No," Caleb said. "Did they find her?"

"Maybe," Jackson said. "External indicators of a Jane Doe match the known fact pattern, but DNA tests have not yet been run conclusively."

"Oh man, I am so sorry." Sorrow filled Caleb's face. "A close buddy of mine was murdered a couple of years ago, and they still haven't arrested the woman I know is responsible for it, for lack of evidence. It's rough."

"Thanks," Jackson said. "I can't really talk about it because I'm not authorized to brief anyone yet."

"Brief anyone on what?" Caleb ran his fingers across his lips to mime zippering them shut. Then he gave Jackson a quick hug.

"Come on." Caleb slapped him on the shoulder. "Let's go impress a bunch of senior citizens with our crime-fighting skills."

Jackson looped Hudson's leash around his wrist and the three of them walked to the front door. The door swung open automatically and they stepped into an open concept lobby. A large living room lay to their right, with every available chair filled with a silver-haired senior pretending not to watch them walk in.

A woman in a crisp tan blazer appeared and greeted them with a handshake.

"Nice to meet you, officers," she said. "I'm Marjorie Wilson, general manager of Pine Crest Retirement Home. How can I help you today?"

"Thank you for your time," Caleb said. "I'm Constable Caleb Perry. This is my colleague Sergeant Jackson Locke and his partner, Hudson."

"It's about time you guys showed up!" a male

voice called from somewhere within the audience watching from the lounge.

"Walter—" Marjorie directed her voice to a large, mustached man in a baseball cap who was sitting in a green armchair "—the officers are here to help, and we need to help them do their job."

Walter harrumphed and crossed his arms. "Over a decade too late."

"It's been twelve years since Angela, Mitsy and Gordon died!" another woman added.

"That's Captain Gordon Donnelly!" Walter corrected. "He served in the Canadian Air Force!"

Various other seniors leaped into the conversation, their voices blending into a chorus.

"In the Second World War!"

"Mitsy Therwell had six grandchildren and Angela Jeffries knitted everyone scarves!"

"It was crochet, not knitting!"

Marjorie turned toward them and raised a hand. "Everyone, I'm sure the officers appreciate that you have strong feelings about what happened to our friends and will be happy to talk to everyone in turn."

"Tell them it was Kenny!" Walter shouted. "Everybody knows it was him!"

"Kenny?" Caleb asked.

"Kenny Stanton was a maintenance man at the time," Jackson said, "and a lot of people suspect he had something to do with what happened."

"But you cleared him!" Walter added. "Because he was sweet, charming and had a smile like he couldn't hurt a fly."

"*You* liked him too!" a woman yelled at Walter.

Walter ignored her and turned back to Caleb and Jackson. "Did you know the police took DNA samples and never tested them?" the man asked.

"No," Jackson said. "I didn't know that."

He glanced at Caleb. His friend's eyebrows rose.

"Is that true?" Caleb asked him in a low voice. "Did police bungle the case?"

"I don't know," Jackson admitted. "But I'm sure Finnick won't be happy to hear it."

"You know what it's like to have your friends die and no one cares?" Walter went on. "I wrote dozens of letters to every politician and newspaper in the country, for years, and nobody tried to help. Until that girl Gemma saw our social media posts about it and started messaging us. And now she's probably dead too."

Pain twinged in Jackson's heart.

Caleb turned from Walter and the chorus of senior citizen onlookers back to Marjorie. "Did Gemma ever come here?"

"No," Marjorie said. "She just conducted some phone interviews and exchanged emails with some of our residents. She was planning on coming here to show us some pictures the day she disappeared."

"What kind of pictures?" Jackson asked.

"I don't know."

"Kenny probably killed Gemma too!" Walter called.

A chorus of voices agreed with him.

"I'm sorry about all this," Marjorie said. "As you can understand, there's a strong feeling here that police haven't investigated the deaths of Mitsy, Angela and Gordon as they should have."

He thought of the wall of victims' faces in Gemma's hidden office. Did every one of them have family and friends who felt the police had failed them too?

For the next two hours, Caleb and Jackson interviewed every resident and staff member who was willing to talk to them about the investigation. Thankfully, it all went faster and more smoothly than expected. Once they got past the initial and understandable frustration that many of the residents felt, it turned out that a lot of them were keen fans of mystery novels and crime shows. They were absolutely delighted to help in any way they could, especially if it meant getting a chance to pat Hudson and tell him what a good and handsome boy he was.

But the sad truth was that Jackson and Caleb left without much more information than they'd arrived with, except for the tip that police had taken DNA samples that might not have been tested. Nobody knew what Gemma had been heading to show them the day she disappeared, what had happened to her or why she'd been looking so intently into the case.

"Well, I've never felt so motivated to solve a case while simultaneously feeling completely and helplessly unequipped to do so," Caleb said, as he and Jackson got back to their vehicles.

"Agreed." Jackson unclipped Hudson's leash and opened the back door for him. Then he pulled out his phone and called Blake.

"Hey, we're just leaving Pine Crest now," he told her when she answered. "How are things with Amy?"

"Not good," Blake said. She blew out a hard breath. "I'm taking Amy to the South River

Motel to hopefully book her into a room. The doctor told her she can't leave town until they run more tests. Looks like there might be something wrong with the baby."

Amy looked out the passenger-side window as Blake pulled her RCMP cruiser up in front of the South River Motel. A sign in the front window said there were no vacancies, but she was under strict instructions from her doctor to rest and the next closest hotel was over an hour's drive away.

"Don't worry," Blake said. "I'll go inside, talk to them and explain the situation. I'm sure we'll find something. Do you want to come inside with me or do you want to wait in the car?"

Amy glanced up at the blue sky. The doctor's words swirled around her mind.

The test results are concerning. Rest up and try to relax. We'll run tests again tomorrow and then see where we're at.

"I'd like to sit outside, actually," Amy said. "If there's somewhere we can do that."

Blake paused for a moment. She had a serious face, framed by wisps of black hair that had escaped from her braid, and gray eyes with dark rings around the irises. She was beautiful in an unconventional way.

"Okay," Blake said. "I'll see what I can do."

The constable got out of the car and headed into the motel office. A quick moment later and Blake was back to let Amy know there was a large, secluded lawn out behind the motel, where Amy could stretch out and rest under the watchful eye of the security camera.

Blake pulled a soft, gray blanket from her trunk, Amy grabbed her bag and together they walked around to the back of the building, where they found a lush patch of green grass surrounded on three sides by dense forest.

"You going to be okay out here?" Blake asked.

"Absolutely," Amy said. "I need some time to think. Thankfully, I brought my sketch pad."

Blake spread the blanket on the grass and then offered her arm for support as Amy sat.

"Thank you." Amy stretched her legs out in front of her. "I'm sorry, I hate that I'm in this situation and I feel like I'm inconveniencing everyone."

"Don't worry," Blake said. "I've got a baby at home myself. He's turning one in the fall."

Yeah, but judging by the thin gold band on her finger, she wasn't facing it alone.

"My baby's father is a con artist who's run out on us," Amy said.

"I know," Blake said. Then she chuckled kindly and a different, warmer smile crossed her face. "And let me guess, you're beating yourself up about it?"

"Yeah," Amy admitted.

Blake laughed again and then crouched down beside her.

"Can I tell you a secret?" Blake asked. "My husband, Dustin, is currently AWOL from the Canadian military and there's a warrant for his arrest for desertion."

"You're kidding?" A sudden burst of sympathy flooded Amy's core. "I'm so, so sorry."

"Thanks," Blake said. She held up her phone and Amy looked down to see a picture of a clean-cut man with a big smile wearing a Canadian Army uniform. "I had no clue that Dustin had a drinking problem until after we were married. We got caught in this endless cycle of him apologizing and promising to never do it again, then I'd forgive him and it would happen again. Eventually, he joined the military, got deployed and told me it would be a fresh start." She sighed. "But he wandered off base, got drunk in a local bar and disappeared. So now I'm living with my mother, raising my kid alone and wondering if I'm ever going to see that sorry man again."

"I'm sorry," Amy said again, finding the words so inadequate for what she was feeling. Her heart twisted for Blake.

"Me too." Blake stood. "Just focus on that feeling of compassion in your chest right now, and practice directing that kind of love to yourself. We're all wounded by this world in different ways. So be kind to yourself and everybody else. I'll see you in a bit."

Blake turned and walked back around to the front of the motel. Amy sat in the sun and sketched. She hadn't been able to get the fleeting glimpses she'd seen of the intruder out of her mind. Maybe if she focused, she could find him on the page. Her fingers moved quickly. She hadn't been able to see the silent intruder's full face before he'd set off the flash bang back on the lake. But she'd been able to see his jawline and mouth. The day before, she'd seen his eyes through the holes in his mask and she could make a reasonable guess about the shape of his face. Maybe if she put it all together, someone would recognize him and know who he was.

Narrow eyes. Thin lips. Square jaw with an otherwise long face.

But even as the stranger began to come together on the page in front of her, the doctor's words still echoed in the back of her mind. Her blood pressure had spiked. He'd wanted her to rest locally overnight and come back in the morning for more tests. And if things still didn't look good, she might have to find a place close to the hospital in Huntsville and stay on complete bed rest until Skye arrived.

She set the sketch pad down in the grass beside her and ran her hands over her belly, feeling for the comforting contours of her daughter's tiny form. The baby stirred softly.

Help me, Lord. I've never felt so alone. I don't feel ready to be a mother and I'm terrified of failing her. Now my precious child may be in danger. I feel so alone and so completely helpless to protect her.

She heard the gentle jingling of dog tags. Amy opened her eyes to see Hudson trotting through the grass toward her in his official K-9 unit vest. She looked past him and didn't see Jackson anywhere, but she knew he wouldn't be far away. Hudson's tail wagged. He lowered his head as he reached her and nuzzled his nose against her arm.

"Hey, you." She ran her hand over his head. The dog licked her face gently then lay down beside her on the blanket. Amy buried her face in his fur and hugged him tightly.

Thank you, Jackson.

Somehow he'd known she didn't want to be alone right now, but had probably also figured that he was the last person she wanted to see. So, he'd sent Hudson to her on a solo mission. She lay down beside the dog for a long moment, feeling his heartbeat and resting in the comfort of having him there. Then after a while, Hudson's ears perked. The dog leaped to his feet. She sat up to see Jackson stepping around the side of the building.

He hesitated and seemed unsure whether to join them. Amy waved him over. Slowly, she sat up, cross-legged, resting her hands gently on her protruding belly.

"Blake told me I'd find you here," he said. "Caleb's with her now, waiting for the motel to sort out a room. Should be ready in a few minutes. They had someone leave early, they just hadn't cleaned the room yet."

"Well, I have something for you," she said. "I did a sketch of our silent intruder."

She nodded to the sketch pad that lay beside her in the grass. He sat down next to her and looked at it.

"This is incredible," he said. "How did you figure out what he looked like?"

"I put it together from glimpses of what I'd seen," she said. "I don't know how accurate it is, but it's my best guess."

"Well, it's really good," Jackson said. "I'm going to send it to Finnick. He can assign someone to search the database for a match."

He held up his phone and took a picture of it. She heard the swooshing sound of the email sending. Then they sat side by side for a long moment, without either of them speaking.

She wanted to tell him that while she was still angry at him and didn't think what he'd done was even remotely okay, she believed he meant well. And she was glad to know there was someone on the case who cared about Gemma as much as he did.

"Blake said the doctor told you that you needed to rest and come back for more tests tomorrow?" he asked.

Concern creased his forehead. A deeper sorrow than she'd ever seen before pooled in his eyes.

"Yeah," Amy said. "My blood pressure is still too high. He's worried about the impact my ongoing stress will have on the baby. It's too soon to know for sure if I'm facing a more serious problem. But if I don't get better results tomorrow, I might be looking at complete and total bed rest until Skye is born."

Her voice hitched with an unexpected sob.

"Hey, it's going to be okay," Jackson said.

His hand brushed over hers then quickly pulled away, as if he'd just caught himself. But Amy grabbed his hand, even as he was pulling it back, and squeezed it tightly.

"I can't let myself think about medical stuff right now," she said. "Or I might fall apart. Please, I need a distraction. Tell me how things went at Pine Crest."

"Okay," Jackson said. Slowly their hands pulled apart. "First of all, Hudson was a really big hit."

Although the dog's head didn't turn, Amy couldn't help but notice Hudson's ears twitch toward Jackson as he heard his name.

"Turns out Pine Crest is full of the most incredibly vibrant and opinionated seniors I've ever met," Jackson said. "They are also extremely disappointed that the cops have failed to solve the twelve-year-old cold case of the deaths of three of their friends."

"I can't blame them," she said.

"Police took DNA samples that they might have never even tested," Jackson said. "Did you know that we don't have a dedicated cold case unit in Ontario? Finnick—my boss, Inspector Ethan Finnick, head of the RCMP's Ontario K-9 Unit—has been fighting for years for the creation of a single, multidisciplinary unit dedicated to solving cold cases. Which is something that exists in other parts of North America. He's as passionate about unsolved crime as other people are about hockey or baseball. Now it looks like Gemma was too."

She thought of the wall of faces and names in her friend's hidden office.

"These are cases that were never closed," he went on. "In some, families have no idea if their relatives are dead or alive. In others, they know they're gone, but it was never even determined if someone was murdered, died by accident or of natural causes." He sighed and leaned back on his elbows. "Sorry, I'm rambling."

"No, I asked for a distraction," Amy said. She

lay back and looked up to the white clouds dotting a clear blue sky. "This is good."

"Well, I don't have any answers for the people at Pine Crest," he said. "Twelve years ago, there was a string of thefts. Then three elderly residents died of what may have been an accidental or intentional overdose of their pain medication IVs."

"What was stolen?" she asked.

"Umm…" He seemed to be thinking. "Well, first of all, money. Everybody started missing cash, big and small. Then there was a lot of jewelry of varying value. Some gold coins. And a bunch of memorabilia from when Gordon served in the Second World War."

"And there's a suspect," Amy said.

"Yup, Kenny Stanton," Jackson said. "Charming guy, with brown or blond hair, depending who you ask. Everybody loved him and police initially cleared him. But when he didn't show up for work and dropped off the map, everybody became suspicious."

She glanced down at the face she'd sketched on her notepad. "I don't know if I'd consider him charming."

Jackson's phone suddenly pinged with a text notification. He sat up.

"Whoa," he said. "Maybe not, but your sketch did the trick. We now know who our silent intruder is."

Chapter Ten

"Are you serious?" Amy asked. "That was incredibly fast."

"Well, your picture was really good," he said.

She sat up and looked at the mug shot on Jackson's phone. The face that stared back at her was so close to the composite sketch they might've been twins.

"His name is Reese Cyan," Jackson read. "Age thirty-eight. Born in Ireland but moved to Canada when he was two, so his accent is definitely exaggerated. Long criminal record and several outstanding warrants for theft, breaking and entering, grand larceny, and trafficking in stolen property."

"Wow."

"But besides one minor assault charge, there's nothing violent on his record. Nothing like kidnapping or murder. He just steals stuff, sells it and also sells stuff that other people have stolen. So, whatever's going on here is a complete break in his pattern."

"He looks vaguely familiar," Amy said, "but I don't know for sure if I've ever seen him before."

"Maybe he was hanging around outside the bookstore?" Jackson suggested.

"Maybe," Amy said. "So, we have one answer and even more questions. Is Reese Cyan also Kenny Stanton? Did Gemma figure out he was behind the murders at Pine Crest?"

"I don't know." Jackson sighed. "I just wish Gemma had confided in me about all this. Maybe I would have let her down, but I just wish she'd given me the opportunity to be there for her."

"Well, you two were never close," Amy said gently. "She never talked about you or even told me you were now a K-9 cop."

Was that because Gemma was ashamed of her brother? Or because Amy was deep in the middle of a crisis and Gemma was hiding her own secrets? It was hard to judge a person's true thoughts and feelings by what got talked about in the middle of a hurricane.

"We actually used to be really close," Jackson said. "We were best friends when we were kids.

People thought we were twins, because even though she was a grade above me, our classes were often combined."

"Really?" She'd had no idea.

"Everything changed when Gemma started grade seven and moved to a new school without me," Jackson said. "Suddenly she had this whole new life that I wasn't a part of and everything I did embarrassed her. She matured a lot faster than me. My parents were going through a divorce at the time, and I felt like everyone had forgotten I existed. So I got really loud and started doing stupid stuff to get attention. Figured being in trouble was better than being invisible." He ran his hand over his neck. "I'm not proud of it."

She thought of the note she'd found hidden in the camper. Part of her was glad he hadn't asked her out when they were teenagers, because she definitely hadn't been interested in romance back then. But maybe it would've been nice to be friends.

"I'm sorry," Amy said. "I never meant to take your best friend away from you. Everyone talked about how close Gemma and I were. Joined at the hip. Thick as thieves. I never intended for you to be left out."

"Well, it was pretty clear you hated me," Jackson said, quietly and without meeting her eyes. "Especially when you sent my letter back with 'I Hate You! Never Talk to Me Again!' written across it in huge block letters. Not that I blame you."

"I never did that!" Amy jolted upright. "You never sent me any letters!"

"Yes, I did," Jackson said. "I sent you one. When I was fifteen. After I crashed your grandmother's car into the lake at your birthday party, I got arrested."

"I remember," Amy said.

Gemma had been so embarrassed of her brother. There had been dozens of cops. It had been chaos.

"I got probation," Jackson said, "and ended up in this special group program for kids with behavioral problems. It probably saved my life, and there were a lot of great people working there. But that's also how I got this dent in my nose. Some other kids were bullying me when we were doing our public service hours cleaning up trash, and the incredibly terrible cops guarding us decided not to step in, for reasons I can only imagine."

"I'm so sorry." Amy's hand brushed his arm.

"Thanks," he said. "Something about seeing both the best and the worst from people in law enforcement inspired me to become a cop and pushed me to pursue justice and rescue people for a living. They also had service dogs there, and they were just incredible. But I also think watching what I went through was another one of the reasons my sister doesn't really trust police. Gemma never understood how I could just forgive and move on. Despite our differences, she was really protective of me. Anyway, one of the steps I took was writing apology letters to everyone I harmed. My parents were in charge of passing them out. I wrote you one. Are you telling me you never got it?"

"No." Amy shook her head. "There's no way I'd forgot that."

Had Gemma intercepted it, pretended to be Amy and sent it back? Why would her best friend do something like that? Frown lines creased Jackson's forehead, and she was pretty sure he was thinking the exact same thing. But neither of them said it.

"I didn't hate you," Amy said. She stared down at the grass. "I liked you. At least until you started doing stupid stuff. I thought you were really cool, adventurous and smart. Maybe

I even had a bit of a crush on you, and I wanted to get to know you better."

If she was honest, she had even more than a crush on him now. She was attracted to this man—for a dozen different incredible and wonderful reasons. But she couldn't even begin to trust what she was feeling, let alone act on it.

"Oh," Jackson said. "Well, I had a crush on you too."

"I know," she said. "I found a note you wrote hidden in one of your books in the camper."

"Wow." He brushed a hand through his hair.

"Just to be clear," she said, "I didn't like everything you did. I wasn't into people who pulled stupid antics. You became loud and obnoxious that summer you crashed the car. But I liked you before that. When you were the guy who carried adventure books around and were the only one brave enough to climb up onto the roof or jump off the highest rock in the lake. I liked that Ajay."

"So do I in retrospect," Jackson said. "I just wish I'd liked him back then."

His phone chimed with another text. Jackson glanced at it.

"Blake says your room is finally ready if you want to go lie down and nap," he said.

"Yeah, I probably should."

Jackson stood then reached for her hands; she took them and he helped her to her feet. They remained there a moment, face-to-face, with her fingers still linked in his.

"Again, I'm incredibly sorry for being stupid, both when I was younger and also yesterday," Jackson said. "But I hope you know that you're like a sister to Gemma. I know you're grateful for how she took care of you in the past few months. But if she were here right now, she'd tell you how thankful she is for everything you've done for her over the years. You were there for her when our parents were divorcing. And even though your lives took different paths, no matter where you are in the world, if she ever had a crisis—anytime, day or night—you'd answer the phone to be there for her. And she'd want to know that someone was taking care of you now."

He looked down at his hands enveloping hers. But somehow he didn't pull away, and Amy didn't either.

"I got some really bad news today when I was out on the porch talking to Finnick," he said. "I'm guessing you could tell."

"Yeah, you looked like you'd been shot," she said.

"Officially, I'm not allowed to brief you yet," he said. "Because we don't know anything for sure. But I don't want a stranger breaking bad news to you. And honestly, I'd rather get hit with a reprimand than hide something from you ever again."

She closed her eyes tightly as the worst thought she could imagine filled her heart. "Did they find Gemma? Is she dead?"

"Maybe," he said. "They don't know for sure, but they think it's possible. They found a Jane Doe they think is her."

Dread and pain washed over her in a cold, icy wave.

And he'd been keeping that news from her for hours? While he'd rescued her from the island, calmed her down when she was in labor and taken all the anger she'd unleashed at him when she'd found out he was Gemma's brother, he'd secretly been hiding the pain that his sister might be dead.

"Oh, Jackson. I'm so sorry."

She pulled her hands from his, wrapped them around his neck and hugged him tightly. He hesitated, then slowly embraced her.

"I want you to know that whatever you need, I'm here for you and Skye," Jackson said. "Just like Gemma would be if she were here. You are not alone. If you need me to help you find a place to stay until the baby is delivered, hire someone to live with you, or help cover your bills, I'm on it. If you want me to take time off work and drive you around, I will. Or if you want to avoid my grumpy mug altogether, we can find another way for me to help. It's up to you."

"Thank you." She hugged him tighter, as if they were both broken. Her head fell into the crook of his neck.

"You're not alone," Jackson said. "I care about you, I'm here for you and I've got your back. Whatever you need. I won't let you down."

She swallowed hard and gazed up into his handsome face. Sincerity filled his green eyes. Suddenly she wondered what their lives would've been like if they hadn't both made so many bad decisions.

His lips brushed against her forehead. Amy's heart raced. Warning bells clanged in the back of her mind, telling her not to make the same mistakes she'd made in the past.

But she found herself tilting her chin up toward him.

Softly and gently, their lips met in a kiss.

Jackson was kissing Amy Scout. The most beautiful woman he'd ever seen in his life was in his arms, despite the fact there wasn't a shadow of a doubt in his mind that he didn't deserve her. And yet, her fingers were brushing the back of his neck, and her lips pressed gently against his in a gesture that was so tender and sweet, it made him feel both stronger and weaker than he ever had in his life.

Hudson growled, then started to bark furiously. Jackson heard the snapping sound of a footstep in the woods behind them. They weren't alone. Someone was watching them! Jackson and Amy sprung apart. He glanced to the tree line just in time to see a figure in a dark hoodie take off through the forest.

"Get behind me!" he shouted to Amy. He yanked out his phone and dialed Caleb.

"Hello?" Caleb answered before it had even rung once.

"We have a hostile," Jackson said. "In the trees behind the motel. He's escaping on foot. I need you and Blake here now!"

"Copy that. On our way."

The criminal was running. But thankfully the woods weren't as thick as they were around Cedar Lake, and he could still catch a faint glimpse of the man between the trees.

Amy grabbed his arm. "You should go after him!"

"I'm not leaving you." Nor would he send Hudson without backup after someone who might be armed.

An instant later he saw Blake and Caleb sprinting around the corner of the motel, with their guns drawn.

"Blake, cover Amy!" Jackson yelled. "Get her to safety! Caleb, you're with me!"

He glanced at Hudson. His K-9 partner was standing at the ready.

"Go get him!" Jackson signaled his partner toward the departing figure. "Catch! Hold! Don't let him get away!"

Hudson dashed across the grass and into the trees.

Jackson glanced back at Amy, only to nearly be knocked back on his heels by the depth of emotion he saw in her eyes.

"Stay safe," she said.

"You too." Jackson turned and sprinted after

his partner, hearing Caleb just a few yards behind him. He ran through the woods, following the sound of Hudson barking as he pursued
his target.

*Lord, please help me catch him and finally bring
this nightmare to an end.*

Jackson pressed on, feeling fresh hope fill his
core. Hudson would catch the suspect. This
would all be over soon.

Sharp and furious barking rose ahead of him,
punctuated by loud and frustrated snarls from
Hudson that Jackson had never heard before
when in pursuit of a suspect. Then the trees
parted ahead of them and he saw why. Hudson
stood on his hind legs at the base of a large pine
tree. The dog's front paws hit the trunk again
and again, as if trying to shake it hard enough
to send his target tumbling to the ground. The
suspect may have been trying to hide, but there
was no way Hudson's keen senses were about to
be fooled. The K-9 had him trapped.

"Hudson!" Jackson called. "Come!"

Immediately, the dog relented and trotted
obediently back to his side.

"We have him cornered!" Jackson yelled back
toward Caleb as the constable's face appeared
through the trees. "Stay back and cover me!"

"Copy that!" Caleb shouted back.

Silence had fallen from the pine branches above. Jackson pulled his weapon, steadied it with both hands and raised it.

"I'm Sergeant Jackson Locke of the RCMP's Ontario K-9 Unit," he shouted. "Drop any weapons and come down with your hands up!"

The branches rustled. Then pine needles rained down as a slight figure in a black hoodie dropped from above and landed in a crouching position with his hands raised.

"I'm arresting you on the suspicion of involvement in the murder of Gemma Locke and the attempted kidnapping of Amy Scout."

"What? Someone tried to kidnap Amy?" The figure tossed her head back, the hood fell from her face and Jackson's heart suddenly stopped beating as fierce green eyes every bit as determined as his own met his gaze. Jackson reholstered his gun.

He raised a hand to signal to Caleb without turning around.

"Stand down and go back to the others," Jackson called. "The suspect is my sister, Gemma."

Chapter Eleven

Jackson stood in stunned silence with his eyes locked on his sister's face. She ran both hands through her dark hair, in a gesture he recognized as one he did all too often himself, when he was trying to get his brain to think. Gemma had cut her hair short and spiky since he'd seen her last. It suited her. Despite all the terrible fears that had filled his mind, she looked strong and healthy.

"Okay," Caleb's voice came from somewhere behind him. "I'll head back to the others and let you handle it."

"Don't brief them!" Jackson shouted, suddenly. "Keep this between us."

He didn't want Amy knowing that Gemma was still alive until he understood what was going on.

"Got it."

He heard the sound of Caleb retreating through the woods.

Jackson stood there, speechless, and looked at his sister.

"I thought you were dead," he said.

"I'm sorry," Gemma said. "What happened to Amy? You said someone tried to kidnap her."

"Yes," he said. "A very scary masked man we now know is named Reese Cyan. Amy got away and she's fine, except for some worries about how her blood pressure will impact the baby. Reese broke into both your store and the cottage. He was apparently looking for something. But, as important as all of that is, I've spent the last few hours believing you were dead! Police dredged up some body downriver from where your car was found. They thought it was you."

A dozen different feelings bounced around inside him like popcorn sizzling in hot oil— relief, frustration, confusion, anger, joy—and he didn't know which one would fly out of the pot first.

"Why were you hiding in a tree like that?" Not the most important question, he knew, but the top one on his mind. "Why did you run from me? Why would you let me keep believing you were dead?"

"I came here to talk to you!" Gemma said. Now they were both almost yelling. "I didn't know you thought I was dead."

"How did you know where I was?"

"The Pine Crest seniors were posting all over social media that you and your colleague were just there asking them about the cold case," she said. "I tracked your truck to the motel. I was hiding in the woods to make sure the coast was clear and that none of the other cops would see me, and next thing I know my brother is kissing my pregnant best friend!"

His big sister's hands snapped to her hips, as if she'd caught him doing something wrong. He crossed his arms in response. He still didn't know what he thought of his fleeting kiss with Amy. He suspected it had probably been a mistake. She was in a really vulnerable place and he couldn't let it happen again. But that didn't mean he was about to let his sister give him grief about it.

"I decided to make a hasty retreat and come back later when you were alone," Gemma went on, "then next thing I know you've ordered your big, scary dog to chase me and take me down. Plus, your colleague was running after me too. So, of course I ran."

He looked down at his partner. Hudson was sitting harmlessly by his side, with his head cocked as he was trying to figure out what Gemma was saying about him.

"Do you think we can trust Caleb?" Gemma asked.

"Do I think we can trust *Caleb*?" Jackson repeated. "Yes, he's a good cop, and I trust him with my life. In fact, I gotta say I trust him a lot more than I trust you right now. Why did you disappear and leave Amy all alone like that? She was in trouble. She needed you! Why haven't you reached out to anybody in weeks?"

Words tumbled out of his mouth so quickly he could barely contain them. But then he caught himself. *Forgive me, Lord.* It didn't matter how upset he was or how justified those feelings were. All he was doing now was repeating the same old patterns and pushing her away. Jackson held up both hands, palms up, in a sign of peace.

"I'm so sorry." His voice dropped. "That wasn't fair to barrage you like that. I was just really scared that I'd lost you and that I'd never see you again. I kept telling everyone that you

were so strong and tough, I was convinced you
were alive, but…"

His words trailed off as his voice broke.

He watched his sister's lips quiver and thick
tears fill her eyes. Wordlessly he opened his
arms and stepped toward his sister. She threw
her arms around him and hugged him hard. He
hugged her back just as fiercely.

"I'm sorry you thought I was dead," Gemma
said. "That sucks and I can't imagine how much
that hurt."

"It hurt a lot," Jackson said. "Are you okay?"

She nodded. Then Gemma pulled back and
he let her go.

"I thought I was doing what I needed to do
to save Amy's life," she said. "A stranger tried
to kill me. I figured as long as he thought I was
dead, I could hide out and figure out who he
was and get the evidence I needed to stop him."

"But if he thought you were still alive, he
might come after Amy?" Jackson asked.

"Yeah," Gemma said, "especially if I tried
to return to normal life back at the cottage. If
I was there with Amy, she'd be in the line of
fire and she had nowhere else to go. And considering how the cops bungled the Pine Crest
case, I couldn't dismiss the possibility there was

a corrupt cop involved. If so, maybe contacting you would put you in danger. So, I thought it was safer for everybody if I sorted it out on my own."

Okay, he got that to an extent. But didn't she see why that had been the wrong thing to do? She never should've tried dealing with this alone. As relieved as he was to see his sister again, he felt like he was at risk of falling into the same argument he'd had with her a dozen times before. He got the desire to protect Amy. But she still should have come to him for help, even if there had been a corrupt cop involved in the Pine Crest murders. It's not like he couldn't take care of himself...

Just like she was certain she could take care of herself.

Gemma was always a very private person. Amy's words from the night before filled his mind. *She was the kind who'd avoid conflict at all costs...* Then another thought crossed his mind. *Maybe we're more similar than I'd like to admit.*

He glanced at the trees above and prayed.

Lord, I lost my sister once. I don't want to lose her again. Help me break the cycle. Help me to stop being a brawler and start being the peacemaker she needs me to be.

He ran both hands through his hair, then caught himself and realized he'd just mirrored what she'd done earlier.

"Why did you go to Pine Crest today?" Gemma asked.

"We found your hidden office in the store," he said. "It's incredible, by the way. Amy saw the Pine Crest folder on your desk and figured out that might have been where you were going the day you vanished. I'm so proud of you for going for your private investigator's license. I'm sorry you felt like you needed to hide it from me."

"I wanted to wait until I'd actually passed my test and had my feet under me," she said. "I thought if you teased me or argued with me, I'd be too full of self-doubt to go for it. And I was afraid you'd take it personally, like I was deciding to go a civilian route to somehow spite you when you were in law enforcement."

He laughed as heat rose to his face. "Well, to be fair I did think something like that," he said. "But only for a moment, before I kicked myself for thinking it."

She laughed too. "I was hoping to take the test a few months ago, actually," she said, "but when Amy showed up she was so frazzled and upset. Then she got sick because her blood pressure was too high, and I didn't want to add to her stress levels."

"Yeah, I get that," Jackson said. "What happened to your car?"

"I was looking into the Pine Crest cold case," she replied. "I'd been doing a lot of online searches and sending emails, and I thought I had a potential lead. But while I was on my way there, a van ran me off the road. I barely managed to get out of the car before it went over the edge. It was terrifying. But thankfully I was able to escape with my bag and wallet."

She shuddered at the memory.

"I hid in the bushes for what felt like forever. The driver pulled over and started looking for me. He had a gun, and I was sure he was going to find me and put a bullet in me. But then he called someone, and I heard him tell them I was dead. I booked a nearby rental cottage, through an online app and under a false name, and have been hiding out there ever since."

He pulled his phone from his pocket and held up the picture of Reese Cyan. Gemma glanced at the screen, and before he could even ask the question, he watched as his sister's face turned ashen.

"That's him!" She pointed at the screen. Her finger shook. "That's the man who ran me off the road."

"He wasn't wearing a mask?" Jackson asked.

"No." She shook her head. "His van had tinted windows and when he was searching for my body, he didn't bother to hide his face, either because he figured I was dead or he was planning on killing me. Who is he? Is he the real Kenny Stanton?"

"I don't know if he's Kenny," Jackson said. "He might've changed his name or used an alias. His name is Reese Cyan, and he's a thief and fence with a history of trafficking in stolen goods. He may have robbed Pine Crest and accidentally killed Mitsy, Gordon and Angela. Or been working with an accomplice on the inside at Pine Crest, we really don't know. He's the one who tried to kidnap Amy."

"You said he was looking for something," Gemma said.

"Yup," Jackson said. "Something bigger than a book and smaller than a secret room. So, our best guess is that he's looking for your laptop with all your files and research on it."

"Well, then joke's on him," Gemma said. "It

was destroyed when my car went into the river. It might as well be a brick."

A cold breeze cut through the trees. The sun was beginning to dip lower on the horizon. He couldn't stand out in the forest talking to his sister forever. They had to figure out where to go from here.

"I'm sorry that we haven't had the kind of relationship where you felt safe coming to me with whatever you were going through," he said. "I know we haven't always seen eye to eye. But I love you, I respect you and I promise that I'm going to do a better job listening to you from now on."

"And you're not going to sideline me and take this over?" Gemma said.

"No way," Jackson said. "I'm just glad you're safe, and I promise that no matter what I'll do everything in my power to protect you."

"Ditto," Gemma said.

He chuckled.

"Come on," he said, "it's time for you to go talk to Amy."

The motel room that Blake had arranged for her was simple, but nicer than Amy had expected. There were soft blue-and-orange patchwork blankets on two twin beds and a large portrait of a waterfall on the opposite wall above the television.

Amy lay on the bed closest to the door, on top of the blankets. Her eyes traced patterns in the white stucco ceiling as she tried to relax and remind herself that Blake was standing guard outside her door. Yet, with every beat of her heart, her mind filled with questions about Jackson.

Was he okay? Was he safe? Why had Caleb come back without him? Why wouldn't he give her an answer about where Jackson was now?

And above all, why had she kissed Jackson like that? She'd gotten swept up in the emotion of the moment. She couldn't let herself act impulsively. Not like that. Ever again. Not after the mistakes she'd made.

Finally, after what felt like an eternity, there was a gentle knock on the door.

"Amy?" Jackson's voice was soft. Her heart leaped at the sound of it. "It's me."

She sat up. "Are you okay?"

"Yeah, I'm great," he said.

"Come in," she said. "Blake has a key."

"Okay," he said. "But I've got some pretty big news. It's good news, but still I don't want your heart rate skyrocketing. So, I need you to take a really deep breath and let it out slowly. Okay?"

"Okay." She did as he asked. "I'm good."

The door opened gradually and there stood Gemma.

A cry slipped from Amy's lips. Tears of joy filled her eyes. She swung her legs over the side of the bed as Gemma hurried across the room toward her. The two women hugged tightly, and Amy felt both relief and joy bubbling up inside her heart.

"I'm so sorry," Gemma whispered. "I never meant to scare you like that."

"I'm just glad you're still alive and that you're okay."

"Me too."

Finally, they pulled apart and Amy wiped her eyes. Tears shone in Gemma's eyes too, and although her friend's smile was wide, Amy couldn't help but notice the worry lines that creased Gemma's forehead.

"I never used to cry," Amy said, with a laugh, "but now it seems like I've been making up for a lifetime's worth of tears."

She glanced past Gemma to where Jackson and Hudson stood in the doorway.

"I'll leave you guys to it," Jackson said.

He started to close the door, but Amy reached out her hand toward him.

"Stay," Amy said, "and we can all talk this out together."

Jackson paused. He glanced at Gemma, and the siblings exchanged a long and indecipherable look.

"No," he said. "I've got to fill Blake and Caleb in on what Gemma told me, and also call Finnick and loop him in. I might be a while. You two will be fine on your own. One of us will be guarding the door at all times."

He left and closed the door behind him.

"Seems like you two have gotten really close," Gemma said.

She walked over to the bed beside Amy's and sat down.

"Well, he came up to Clearwater looking for you," Amy said, "and had my back when a really scary guy broke into the cottage and the store looking for something."

"While we were walking back through the woods, Jackson filled me in on everything that you've been going through in the past couple of days," Gemma said. "Reese Cyan is the man who ran my car off the road. I hid and let him think I was dead because I wanted to protect you. I'm so sorry. I never thought he'd come after you."

"He was looking for something," Amy said, "probably your laptop so he could erase any of the evidence you'd collected on him."

"Yeah, Jackson told me that too. But my laptop is useless, so whatever he's after is gone."

Amy wondered if Jackson had told Gemma how he'd hidden his identity at first, given Amy his boss's last name and how she'd caught him. Normally, it was the kind of juicy gossip she'd have been in a hurry to share with her best friend. But somehow, Amy found herself hoping that Jackson hadn't told Gemma. He'd made a mistake. And despite all the time she and Gemma has spent giggling over his mistakes when they were kids, she really didn't want to make fun of him now.

I guess I've forgiven him, Lord. Help me forgive myself for my own mistakes too.

Gemma leaned back against the headboard, pulled her knees up to her chest, wrapped her arms around them and looked at Amy, just like she had countless times before during sleepovers when they were kids. Amy leaned back against her own headboard, wedged a pillow behind the small of her back and crossed her legs.

"I know you must have a lot of questions," Gemma began. "There's so much I need to tell you, and I owe you a pretty big apology too. But I don't want to get your blood pressure up or cause any problems for you and the baby." Gemma waved one hand toward her. "Especially after Jackson told me about the medical tests and bed rest."

"It's okay," Amy said. "But when my heart was racing before, it really helped when Jackson just calmly talked to me."

"My brother talked to you calmly?" Gemma asked, skeptically.

"Yeah." Amy laughed. "He's not always loud, like he was when he was a kid. I mean, he shouts really loudly when he needs to. But he's a really chill and cool person, actually. Did he tell you I went into false labor earlier today?"

"No." Gemma's eyes widened. "Are you okay?"

"It was pretty scary," Amy said. "But he held me and calmed me down, and then he read to me for half an hour. I think as long as our voices are calm and we're taking things in bite-size chunks, it would be good to hear everything you've been going through."

Gemma shook her head as if she had water

in her ears. "Okay… I'll take your word for it. Just let me know if it gets too much."

"I will," Amy said. "Let's take it nice and slow."

Amy leaned back and listened as Gemma filled her in on her dreams of becoming a private investigator—how she'd gotten interested in cold cases when her college roommate Louise had disappeared, how that case had made her realize just how many unsolved crimes were at risk of being forgotten, how she'd set up the hidden office and started looking into the Pine Crest murders.

Even though Amy had the impression her friend was still hiding things from her—maybe to help keep her stress level down—there was something comforting about lying there and listening to her friend's voice rise and fall as if they were telling stories back in the cottage when they'd been kids. Gemma explained that she'd been studying to be a private investigator and setting up her office before she invited Amy to stay. But she didn't tell her because she hadn't wanted Amy to think she was being a burden or feel any additional stress or guilt.

"I didn't want you to think that you were getting in the way of my dreams," Gemma said.

"You were already dealing with so much, you felt like you had nowhere else to go, and I didn't want to add anything onto your plate."

She kept talking, skimming over the details of being run off the road by Reese Cyan as lightly as a rock skipping over the surface of the lake.

"When I realized that Reese thought I was dead," Gemma went on, "I thought it would be much safer for you if I let him believe he'd killed me and then I could try to investigate this on my own."

"You were wrong," Amy said.

"Yeah, I see that now." Gemma sighed. "I honestly thought I was protecting you."

Amy didn't know what to say to that. For a long moment, both friends stared forward at the picture of the waterfall in silence. Maybe their friendship was always heading to a point like this. Obviously, Amy hadn't predicted something this dangerous and dramatic. But maybe this was what happened when everybody was so busy trying to protect each other and avoid conflict, they let things build up for weeks, months or years. Until finally, things blew up, just because they'd been afraid of hurting each other.

"I want you to know that whatever happens

next, you and your baby can count on me,"
Gemma said. "We'll make whatever modifica-
tions needed so that the cottage is a safe place
to rest and recuperate. Or if the doctor thinks
the cottage is too far away from the hospital, I'll
close the store and we'll rent a place together in
Huntsville. Whatever it takes, it's going to be
okay. You and me are in this together."

And where would that leave Jackson? Would
he be shut out again, like they'd shut him out
when they were younger?

"Thank you," Amy said. "I love and appreciate you more than I have words to say. But
we're not kids anymore, right? We're not going
to freeze your brother out this time?"

Gemma broke her gaze and didn't answer.

"Jackson and I figured out that you must've
intercepted the apology letter he sent me when
we were teenagers," Amy went on. "You scrib-
bled on it that I hated him and never wanted
to see him again."

Now a flush rose to Gemma's face. "Yeah,
I'm sorry."

"I know you tried really hard in the past to
protect me from Jackson," Amy said. "I know
that you pushed him away when we were kids
and didn't let him hang out with us, because

he was obnoxious and loud. But your brother has grown into a different man since then. He's a good guy with a great heart and he means well—"

"I know." Gemma crossed her legs in front of her and leaned back in a posture mirroring Amy's. "I love my brother. But the reason I didn't talk about him when you moved back in with me, and the reason I sent his letter to you back like that, wasn't because I was trying to protect you from him. It's because I was trying to protect my brother from you."

Amy felt her eyes widen. "You were trying to protect your brother from *me*? Whatever made you think you needed to protect Jackson from me?"

"Because my brother might've had some problems as a kid," Gemma said. "But he also has a really soft heart—the biggest of anyone I know." She waved her hands in the air as if summoning a chorus of memories. "He cares deeply about people, and he's always had feelings for you."

She ran both her hands through her hair.

"And, Amy, you know how much I love you and value you," Gemma went on. "But you're spontaneous and a risk-taker. I like that about you. But I've always been afraid that my brother would give you his heart and you would trample over it on the way to your next adventure. I saw you kiss him today. I just hope you guys aren't making a big mistake getting close."

"You saw that?" Amy asked.

Of course, she should have realized that Gemma had been the one eavesdropping on them from the trees. But she'd been so distracted by having her long-lost friend suddenly turn up, she'd momentarily forgotten. Maybe the kiss had been a mistake and Jackson deserved somebody more steady and less impulsive than she had a history of being.

"Yeah, I was eavesdropping on you," Gemma said. "I was trying to figure out who all was at the motel with you and when I could risk coming out without being seen. For all I knew, one of the cops you were with was involved in covering something up in the Pine Crest case." She paused, then said, "Or maybe, if I'm being incredibly honest, maybe that's how I was rationalizing the fact I was thrown by seeing the tenderness between you two, and I was feeling frozen by indecision."

Gemma changed the subject and went on to tell Amy about the cottage she'd been staying in for the past few weeks and her failed attempt to figure out who Reese was. She explained that while she had never planned to hide so long, the more the days ticked past, the harder it was for her to figure out what to do.

After a while, Amy felt her eyes begin to close, and she realized she was drifting. Gemma gave her another hug and slipped out, promising she was going to talk to Jackson, but she'd return soon. Gemma locked the door behind her and Amy heard her say hello to Caleb, who she assumed must be standing guard.

Amy didn't expect to fall asleep, but somehow she felt her eyelids grow heavy. She lay back on the bed against the pillow, wrapped a blanket around her and closed her eyes.

She started to pray, thanking God that Gemma had been found alive and safe, and asking God to keep Skye strong. Then she started to tell God how thankful she was for Jackson. She fell asleep with the memory of his face filling her mind.

She awoke to the sound of a high-pitched beeping. She sat up and swung her legs over the side of the bed, feeling suddenly lightheaded. The sun had set outside the window.

The motel door clicked and swung open, and Caleb rushed in.

"We've got to go!" Caleb said. "Somebody's set off the fire alarm."

She gasped. "I don't smell smoke."

"It might be an attempt to either lure you out or get to you in the chaos." He reached his hand toward her. "Come on, any second now and the parking lot is going to be full of people and emergency vehicles."

She shoved her feet into her shoes and crossed over toward the door.

"Where are Jackson and Gemma?" she asked.

"They're on their way to Pine Crest with Hudson," he said, "to show everyone the picture of Reese and see if anyone recognizes or identifies him as Kenny.

"Blake had to go back to Toronto," he added, "so it's just me for now." Caleb held up his phone. "But I'm calling Jackson right now."

Caleb put the phone on speaker and pressed it into her hands. She stepped outside. The fire alarm seemed even louder out in the parking lot. Motel guests streamed out of their rooms. Sirens wailed in the distance.

"Hey, Caleb," Jackson's voice came on the line. "Just on our way to Pine Crest."

"Jackson," she said. "It's me."

Caleb took her arm gently and steered her through the busy parking lot to the end of the building.

"Amy!" His casual tone shifted to concerned in an instant. "Are you okay? Where's Caleb?"

"I'm here!" Caleb called. "Someone set off the fire alarm so I'm evacuating Amy to safety."

"I'm fine," Amy said. "This place is turning kind of chaotic right now."

"Gemma and I are on our way," Jackson said. She could hear the tires screech through the phone. "We're turning around now and should be there soon. You there, Caleb?"

People kept streaming into the parking lot. Amy handed Caleb the phone. They pushed through the crowd, like fish trying to swim against the current.

"I'm here!" Caleb confirmed.

"Get Amy out of there," Jackson said. "Put her in your car and drive north. We'll meet up with you en route and find a quiet place we can touch base away from the chaos. Keep the line open."

"Will do!" Caleb said. He dropped the phone to his side, but she noticed he didn't end the call. "My vehicle is parked around the side. I didn't want the fact an RCMP SUV was parked in front of the motel to alert anyone to your location."

But maybe someone had found her anyway.

Fire trucks and ambulances began to pull into the front lot. He led her around the side of the building where a lone white police vehicle sat beside a thick wall of trees.

Caleb opened the side door for her.

"Don't worry." He smiled. "Everything is going to be okay."

She heard the sound of the gunshot before she could even determine where it was coming from. Caleb's face went ashen; he clutched his chest, then crumpled to the ground in front of her. His phone fell. Blood seeped from the wound between his fingers.

Amy screamed.

"Caleb!" Jackson shouted. "Amy!"

Then a masked man stepped out from the trees. He aimed a gun directly between her eyes.

"Don't move," Reese said. "Don't move a muscle! You are going to get in the car and we're going to take a little ride. Otherwise, I will kill you and your baby."

Chapter Twelve

"Amy!" Jackson shouted her name into the cell phone that was mounted on his truck's dashboard. "Caleb! Update!"

But all he could hear was the muffled sound of a man shouting, a door slamming and then an engine revving.

"That sounded like a gunshot," Gemma said.

He glanced over at his sister, who was sitting in the passenger seat of his truck. All the color had drained from her face.

Then the call went dead. The highway stretched long and endless ahead of them. They were still a good fifteen minutes away from the motel.

Dear Lord, please help me get there in time. Please keep Amy, Caleb and the baby safe!

Hudson whined in the backseat, and Gemma reached back to comfort him.

Jackson dialed 911.

"Emergency services." The male voice that answered sounded confident.

"This is Sergeant Jackson Locke of the RC-MP's Ontario K-9 Unit. Reporting sound of a gunshot at the South River Motel. Possible officer down, named Constable Caleb Perry. Potential injury or abduction of a pregnant civilian named Amy Scout."

"Are you on the scene?" the dispatcher asked.

"Negative," Jackson said. "I'm on the road about fifteen minutes away. I was on the line with Constable Perry when it happened."

"Are you still?"

"No," Jackson said. "Call went dead."

He heard the sound of a keyboard clacking down the line. Gemma sat back in her seat, leaned over and squeezed Jackson's arm for a long moment.

"The sound of gunfire was called in by several people on the scene," the dispatcher told him. "Police are converging. Search and rescue helicopters are being deployed. Constable Perry was found alive with a gunshot to the chest and is being tended to. But the civilian, Amy Scout, was not found. It is believed she was abducted by the gunman in the officer's vehicle. The vehicle was last seen headed west. Officers are mobilizing roadblocks."

He glanced quickly at Gemma because it sounded like she was struggling to breathe. He knew it was caused by her worry. He knew the feeling. Fear seized Jackson's heart so tightly his head felt dizzy. But he took a deep breath and prayed.

Lord, help me focus. Amy needs me to think like a cop right now.

Not like a man who could lose a woman and child that his foolish heart longed to hold.

"The suspect may be a man named Reese Cyan," Jackson said. "RCMP Ontario can provide officers with a picture. He is a suspect in a crime that we're investigating."

More keyboard clicks and clacks. Jackson wondered how many people the 911 dispatcher was coordinating with right now.

"The suspect won't stay in the RCMP vehicle for long," Jackson said. "He'll have some alternative getaway car hidden out of sight that he'll switch the hostage into."

But he probably hadn't been expecting to come up against an officer who knew the rural roads of Northern Ontario like the back of his own hand, as Jackson did.

"I'm going to keep the line open and try to cut him off," he added.

"I can't advise that," the dispatcher said.

"I know," Jackson replied. "Huge thanks to you and everyone else working to get her back safely."

Then Jackson glanced at Gemma. His sister's worried eyes met his.

"Hold on tight," he told her. "I'm going to go off-road, do a bit of fancy driving and see if I can cut Reese off. You might want to grab the phone in case it goes flying."

Then his eyes cut to the rearview mirror and he glanced at Hudson in the backseat.

"Sorry, buddy," he said. "I know how much you hate wearing your seatbelt. But if you'll be patient with Gemma, I'm going to get her to buckle you in."

Thankfully the dog was still in his K-9 vest and harness. Jackson glanced at his sister.

"On it." She'd already taken her seatbelt off and was squeezing her torso between the two front seats to reach the dog.

"It's the long, gray seatbelt to the right," he said. "Just feed it through the thick loop at the front of his harness, and buckle it in."

"I got it!" she called. He heard a click. Then

Gemma refastened her seatbelt and grabbed his phone off the front console.

"Ready?" he asked.

Gemma took a deep breath. Then she gritted her teeth. "Ready."

His sister sounded even more determined than he was.

Thank You, God, for Gemma.

A farm loomed ahead. A narrow and unpaved service road lay beyond it. That would do just fine.

"Here we go."

He gripped the steering wheel tightly and gunned the engine toward the farm. The truck flew across the field, jolting and bumping across the uneven ground so severely the entire vehicle seemed to shake down to its bolts. They hit the drainage ditch, bounced up on the other side and swerved onto the unpaved road. It wasn't much more than a thin dirt track. The tires spun on the loose soil, threatening to send the truck flying right back off into the ditch again. Then the wheels caught traction. Jackson whispered a prayer of thanksgiving to God and kept driving.

The dirt track gave way to another one, heading southwest. He cut down it, weaving down country roads and any track through the woods he could find. Tree branches scraped against the vehicle. Police chatter filtered through his radio letting him keep track of where Caleb's stolen SUV had last been spotted.

Reese was like a rat in a maze with a dozen talented cats searching for him at once from multiple different angles. It was only a matter of time before someone caught him, Jackson told himself. He just prayed that both Amy and her unborn child would be alive and safe when that happened.

They'd been driving southwest for almost twenty minutes when they crested a narrow bridge over a rural highway surrounded by forest.

"There he is!" Gemma shouted and pointed toward Jackson's window. He glanced to the left just in time to see an RCMP vehicle fly under the bridge and down the highway behind them, with Reese at the wheel and Amy looking petrified but alive in the passenger seat.

"Hold on!" Jackson smashed the brakes and yanked the wheel hard. The truck spun on the narrow bridge. He could hear his sister praying to God that they wouldn't break through the barrier, fly off the overpass and crash down onto the road below. Trees and sky flew past the window. Then finally, with a jarring crash the front of his truck smacked into the barrier fence. They shuttered to a stop.

He leaped out, pulled his weapon, spun toward the departing vehicle and fired, praying his aim would be steady and sure.

Please, Lord, protect Amy and the baby! His bullet caught the back-right tire. It exploded with a bang. The vehicle swerved into a tree and crashed.

He turned to release Hudson from the backseat, but Gemma was already out of the truck and unbuckling his partner. Hudson bounded onto the road.

"Grab the phone!" he told her. The line with the dispatcher remained open.

"On it!" Gemma shouted.

He signaled Hudson to his side, ran to the end of the bridge, jumped a narrow fence and scrambled down an incline to the steep road below. Ahead of him, he could see Reese dragging Amy out of the car and into the woods.

"Stop! Police!" Jackson shouted.

He raised his gun to fire, but he didn't take the shot. He didn't have a clean line of sight and wouldn't risk hurting Amy and Skye.

"We have eyes on the suspect and hostage!" Gemma hurried after him and ran down the road just a few steps behind, yelling into the phone. "Single vehicle collision. We need paramedics and backup."

Jackson and Hudson reached Caleb's smashed-up vehicle. It was empty.

The forest lay dark and quiet ahead of him. He couldn't even see Amy.

"They're sending everyone!" Gemma called. "Police, helicopters, you name it. I gave them both our GPS coordinates and our intersection."

"Well done."

"Thanks." She reached his side and bent over, panting. "But apparently, I don't just need to practice running but also shouting while doing so."

They turned toward the trees. Silence fell. He couldn't see or hear them anywhere. Reese had a head start and was an expert at being silent and staying hidden.

"How do we find them?" Gemma whispered.

"We don't," Jackson said. "But Hudson will."

He looked down at his faithful partner. Hudson was standing at attention, ready for orders.

Gemma's chin rose. "I'm coming with you."

"I have an obligation to order you to remain on the road and stay with the vehicle," he said. "But since I know you won't do that, I'm going to say that however far you think you should hang back, double it. He's got a gun. I just got you back and I don't want to lose my big sister."

His hands clasped hers for a moment. Then he yanked a ski mask from within the vehicle and held it in front of Hudson's nose. The dog sniffed it, then sniffed the ground. His ears perked.

"Search!" Jackson ordered. "Find him! Take him down!"

The dog barked like a general calling them to battle. Then Hudson took off running through the trees, with Jackson on his tail. Jackson was running blind, unable to either see or hear his target, but he trusted in his partner with every step he took.

Hudson's tail was straight, his head was high and his nose sniffed the air as he confidently charged through the trees.

Suddenly a gunshot pierced the forest. Jackson signaled Hudson and stopped. His body froze as Hudson ran back to his side. Then he glanced through the trees and saw them.

Amy was crouched at the base of a tree. Reese stood over her, with one hand cruelly holding her by the arm. The other hand aimed a gun at her temple. Amy's hands rose and tears streaked her cheeks, but as she glanced at Jackson, he could see the depth of faith and strength shining in her eyes.

"Not another step!" Reese shouted. "Or I will kill her!"

Pain wracked Amy's body. The contractions had started again, stronger, harder and more relentless than they'd been before. Reese gripped her left arm tightly. His violent threats filled her ears. And yet, as she fixed her eyes on Jackson's brave form and the loyal K-9 partner standing by his side, she could feel a fresh strength moving through her.

She was going to survive. She would not let herself die here in these woods.

"Drop your weapon!" Jackson shouted. "Get down on the ground now!"

Hudson barked furiously. The dog's hackles rose.

Reese dug the barrel of the gun painfully into her temple.

"You have no leverage here!" Reese shouted. "Turn around and leave now, or I will shoot her!"

"Take me instead!" Gemma shouted. Suddenly her best friend was running through the trees several feet to the right of Jackson. She stopped, panting, and raised her hands. "I'm the one you want! Not Amy! I'm the one who was looking into the Pine Crest murders. It's my store and home you broke into. I'll give you my laptop and all my research. She doesn't know anything and I'm willing to trade my life for hers!"

Gemma pulled in a deep breath. Then a defiant twinkle shone in her eyes.

"Oh, and surprise, I'm still alive," Gemma shouted. "You didn't actually manage to kill me."

For a moment, Reese didn't move; instead, he looked from Amy, to Jackson, to Gemma, as if they were three different points of the same triangle.

Then Amy felt the barrel of the weapon move away from her head as he turned toward Gemma and set her friend in his sights. And Amy knew she was no longer in the line of fire.

She glanced at Jackson. A warning flashed in his eyes as if he could read her mind. But Amy didn't hesitate. She'd always been impulsive. She'd never been one to do what was expected.

And now, Amy hoped, that part of who she was would save everyone's lives.

Her right hand balled into a fist. She spun toward Reese, throwing a punch right into his gut with every ounce of strength she could summon.

He grunted and let go of her arm. She turned to run, only to be sent sprawling forward as Reese grabbed her leg. Amy landed on her hands and knees, then kicked up hard, catching him in the face with a satisfying crack. He dropped his grip again and she scrambled back across the ground, as she heard Jackson shout, "Hudson! Take him down!"

The German shepherd's majestic black-and-tan form leaped over Amy, caught Reese by the shoulder and brought him to the ground. Jackson ran for Reese and wrestled the gun from his grip. He flipped the criminal over and cuffed his hands behind his back.

"Reese Cyan," Jackson said, "I am arresting you for the offense of kidnapping and attempted murder. You have the right to retain and instruct counsel without delay."

Gemma reached Amy's side as Jackson continued to arrest Reese.

"Please tell me you were bluffing to cause a distraction and not actually offering to let him take you," Amy said to her best friend through gritted teeth.

"Sure, let's say that." Gemma crouched down beside her. "Are you okay?"

Amy tried to nod, only a sudden burst of pain swept over her again. She grabbed her belly as suddenly her eyes met Jackson's. "I think Skye is coming now!"

For a moment, she thought Jackson was about to leave the prisoner on the ground and rush to her side.

Instead, he turned to Gemma. "Stay with her. Tell dispatch we need an airlift to the nearest hospital."

Then his green eyes focused on her face again.

"Amy," he called. "Just keep breathing. It's going to be okay. I promise."

Time blurred through waves of pain, as Jackson hurriedly marched Reese back to Caleb's damaged vehicle, locked him in the back, and then ran back through the woods to join Gemma and Amy. Together, the siblings helped Amy to her feet and slowly walked her through the woods.

Then suddenly she heard the sound of sirens filling the air and the thrum of helicopter rotors overhead.

"Over here!" Jackson shouted. "We need paramedics here now!"

Suddenly law enforcement was rushing through the woods toward them. Paramedics helped Amy onto a stretcher and carried her the rest of the way through the trees, asking her questions about how she was feeling and how far apart her contractions were. Jackson and Gemma flanked her on either side. She looked to her left and saw police taking Reese into custody. Then wind whipped the air around her as a bright orange air ambulance helicopter landed a few yards to their right.

A flight paramedic in a fluorescent yellow jacket ran toward them. He glanced at the siblings. "Which one of you is coming with her?"

Amy glanced at Jackson. His deep and fathomless eyes met hers.

I want it to be you. I don't know why, but I want you by my side.

But he broke her gaze and looked at his sister. "You should go with Amy," he said. "I'll wrap things up here."

Amy felt herself whisked onto the helicopter. Paramedics were checking her vitals. An oxygen mask was placed over her face to help slow her breathing.

She looked back to see Jackson and Hudson standing alone on the road.

Then the helicopter door closed, blocking Jackson from her view, and she felt the air ambulance begin to rise.

Chapter Thirteen

Jackson paced circles around the Huntsville hospital waiting room. It had been over four hours since Amy had been airlifted from the forest just outside South River and two and a half hours since Jackson and Hudson had arrived there in his truck. Thankfully, despite a dented front bumper, it still drove just fine. According to his sister, Amy had been rushed into surgery as soon as she'd arrived. Since then, there had been nothing to do but wait, pace and pray.

Now Gemma sat curled up on a plastic chair furiously typing something into her phone, and Hudson lay spread out under her seat. The German shepherd's eyes followed Jackson's path around the room.

Gemma sighed and ran one hand through her hair, so that it stuck up between her fingers.

"What are you doing?" Jackson asked.

"I'm trying to find a missing person's report that matches our Jane Doe," Gemma said.

She frowned at the screen.

Jackson sat down beside her. "What Jane Doe?"

Gemma glanced up at him. "You told me that a female body was found washed up downriver from where my car crashed."

"Yes," he said. "But the only reason Finnick alerted me to that is because local police thought it was you."

"I know," Gemma said. "But just because she wasn't me, and isn't related to the Pine Crest case, doesn't mean she isn't somebody. She was a person with a life that's now over. Someone loved her and is wondering where she is."

She fixed her bright green eyes on her brother's face.

"Now, we know police think the body was female," Gemma said. "She was found in the river, she didn't have any identifying belongings on her and police didn't ask you to do a visual identification but were relying on DNA. That means that either she was dead so long that she had significantly decomposed, which doesn't seem probable considering they thought it was me—"

"Or that she was a victim of the kind of severe attack that doesn't leave belongings and makes the victim hard to identify," Jackson finished.

"Right," Gemma said, "so it's unlikely to be an accidental death. It's more probable that someone killed her and then tried to destroy the body and any trace of who she was."

Jackson leaned over and kissed his sister on the top of her head.

"I like who you are and how your mind works," he said.

She laughed. "So, you'll help me make sure that she doesn't become a cold case?"

"Absolutely."

It definitely beat pacing. Jackson and Gemma sat side by side, typing on their phones and searching various missing person's reports. Eventually, after about an hour they identified a young woman who had gone missing a few weeks prior. Police had dismissed it as a runaway. Her family had been convinced her ex-boyfriend murdered her.

"I'll flag this to all the right people," Jackson said. "Hopefully they have her DNA on file and can check Jane Doe against it. It may not be good news for the family."

"But it will be closure," Gemma said.

A tired-looking male nurse with a trim beard and pale blue scrubs appeared in the doorway.

"I'm looking for the friends and family of Amy Scout," he called.

Jackson leaped to his feet. So did Gemma, and Hudson wriggled out from under the seat to join them.

"That's us," Jackson said.

Gemma squeezed her brother's arm and he patted her hand reassuringly.

"I'm happy to tell you that Skye Elizabeth Scout was born at 2:15 a.m.," he said. The nurse's smile was tired but genuine. "She weighed in at five pounds, six ounces. Both mother and baby are doing fine and recovering well."

"Oh, thank You, God." Jackson breathed a prayer.

For a moment he felt his knees threaten to buckle out from under him. But then his sister grabbed him and hugged him tightly.

"They're okay," Gemma said, tears choking her voice. "Amy and the baby are okay."

Relief and joy cascaded through Jackson's heart like thunderous waves.

"They're being moved into a recovery room

now," the nurse went on. "They will be free to see visitors soon."

Gemma and Jackson released each other and turned back toward the nurse.

"Thank you," Jackson said.

"I take it you're the father?" the nurse asked Jackson. "You're welcome to come see her and meet your baby now."

Jackson felt his mouth go dry.

"No," he said. "Thank you, but I'm not the father. I'm... I'm her best friend's brother."

"Oh, I'm sorry," the nurse said. He blinked. "I thought Mrs. Scout's husband was here to see the baby."

The nurse nodded and disappeared back down the hallway.

"I seriously doubt Paul has somehow rushed to small-town Canada to check in on Amy," Gemma said, dryly. "I can assume Amy told you what a nasty piece of work he is?"

"Yeah," Jackson said. He dropped back into his chair, suddenly feeling deflated. Hudson lay down on his feet. Something about the nurse's well-meaning and maybe predictable misunderstanding had left him spent.

Who was Jackson to Amy? What was Amy to him?

Were they even friends? Or just acquaintances?

He wasn't her boyfriend, her husband or the father of her child. Not someone who had stepped up and promised to be there for her and have a role in her future.

Despite the fact he wanted to be everything to her, he was nothing to her at all.

"What would you say to popping outside and getting some fresh air?" his sister said, cutting through his thoughts.

"Yeah," he answered and stood up again. That wasn't a bad idea and maybe it would help him clear his mind. "I'm sure Hudson would really appreciate getting a walk."

The dog's tail thumped in agreement. He clipped Hudson's leash onto his harness and the three of them headed out of the maternity ward, down the hall and into the main lobby. Suddenly, Hudson woofed happily and his tail started wagging. A moment later Jackson saw why. A tall man with silver-gray hair, wearing blue jeans and a blazer, was standing by the front desk, with a black Labrador retriever sitting at his feet. Jackson blinked.

"Inspector Finnick!" he exclaimed. "What are you doing here?"

Jackson rushed over to his boss as Finnick

turned, stepped away from the desk and smiled. Hudson and the black Lab wagged their tails and nuzzled each other in greeting.

"Gemma," Jackson said. "I'd like to introduce you to my boss, Inspector Ethan Finnick, head of the RCMP's Ontario K-9 Unit and his K-9 partner, Nippy."

"Short for Nipissing," Finnick said, with a smile. "All of the dogs in our unit are named after major Ontario lakes and rivers."

"This is my sister," Jackson added. "Gemma Locke."

"It's very nice to meet you," Finnick said, smiling at Gemma. "I'm glad to see you're alive and well."

"Nice to meet you too," Gemma said. She shook his hand. "Thank you for giving my brother time to come up here and look for me."

"What are you doing here?" Jackson asked.

"I'd driven up to the area to check in on Caleb," Finnick said. "He's doing great, by the way. He's got a few stitches and an impressive-looking scar, but nothing serious to worry about. He'll be released tomorrow. Since I was driving all the way up to South River, I figured I'd also swing by here on the way back for an update."

"Did you hear Amy had the baby?" Jackson asked. "Five pounds something. Baby and mother are both doing well."

Finnick's smile widened. "That's really awesome to hear."

"We were just about to go for a walk," Jackson said. "Do you want to join us?"

"Absolutely," Finnick said.

The five of them stepped through the automatic doors and out into the parking lot. The sky was inky black and dotted with hundreds more stars than Jackson would ever see back in the city. He stepped back and turned to his sister.

"Gemma's been busy trying to identify the Jane Doe that was mistaken for her and thinks it could be a young missing woman who was identified as a runaway," Jackson told Finnick, as they made their way through the parking lot. "Those seniors at Pine Crest really opened my eyes to how frustrating it is when cops don't solve a case and get justice for your loved ones."

True, he'd known intellectually that Gemma had been frustrated with how police had handled the disappearance of her friend Louise. But being confronted head-on by the seniors had hit him with that reality in a new and deeper way.

Or maybe something inside himself had changed.

"Well, loop me in on what you've got and I'll see what I can do," Finnick said.

They followed a path down the side of the hospital. Slowly the noise of vehicles and people coming in and out of the parking lot faded, until they were completely alone. Finnick glanced around as if ensuring no one would be able to overhear them.

"So, as you know, Reese Cyan has been arrested," Finnick said. "He's being charged with kidnapping and attempted murder. He will be arraigned in the morning. We're already hearing reports from jurisdictions across the country where he's wanted on charges of both theft and trafficking in stolen property. Thankfully pawnshops are required to keep meticulous records and it now appears some pieces of jewelry he pawned in Toronto over a decade ago matched some of the items stolen from the Pine Crest Retirement Home. I'll make sure we test his DNA against the DNA collected from the Pine Crest scene. I'll also suggest opening an internal investigation into what went wrong with the initial investigation of these murders."

"Do you think there was corruption or some kind of police criminality involved?" Gemma asked.

"No," Finnick said. "Just really sloppy police work. More should've been done at the time to check to see if anything had been pawned and that DNA should've been tested years ago. No promises that we'll be able to pin the murders on Reese too, but we'll be investigating."

"I can't believe we're so close to giving those people at Pine Crest closure," Gemma said, "and yet we're still not quite there."

"Don't worry," Finnick said. "We're not about to give up just because it's hard."

"You'd be hard-pressed to find anybody who cares about solving cold cases more than Finnick here," Jackson said.

Finnick chuckled wryly. "Yeah, I've been fighting for us to get our own dedicated cold case unit for a long time."

A narrow park lay to their right with trees and benches. Streetlamps flickered on overhead as they approached, sending gentle pools of light down at their feet.

Jackson let Gemma and Finnick walk on

ahead while he fell into step behind them. They let their K-9 partners off their leashes. Hudson and Nippy ran around the park, charging at each other, rolling in the grass, but never straying too far from their humans.

"Your brother sent me pictures of your office wall," Finnick said with what sounded like genuine admiration. "I have to say I'm impressed. Your investigative work on half a dozen of those cases is absolutely incredible. I think it's a shame that you're not pursuing a career in police work."

"Thanks, but I don't," Gemma said, and Jackson could hear the smile in her voice. "Some people don't like talking to cops, sometimes for good reasons and other times for stupid reasons. A private investigator can get leads that police can't. Also, there are procedures in place that impact what cases you go after, and private investigators don't have those limitations."

"All true," Finnick said, "but we have a lot more resources. Which is why we need a dedicated unit."

"That works in cooperation with civilian investigators?" Gemma asked.

Finnick chuckled then glanced back at Jackson. "I can see why you told me your sister is relentless and tenacious."

Jackson listened a moment longer as Gemma and Finnick talked back and forth about various cold cases Gemma had been investigating and their theories on each. Jackson was almost jealous. He'd never felt like he was completely on the same wavelength as either his sister or his boss—as much as he genuinely admired both—and yet they were clearly cut from the same cloth.

"You and Caleb created a bit of a stir when you visited Pine Crest," Finnick told Jackson. "Several of the seniors posted on social media." He glanced over to where Hudson was play-fighting with Nippy. "Apparently, although they had mixed feelings on what the police were doing about the case, they all thought Hudson was absolutely adorable and should star in his own series of crime movies."

Jackson laughed. "Yeah, well, I'm glad I got to meet them," he said. "When all this blows over, I'm happy to help push for this unit you want to set up to anyone who'll listen."

A sudden wave of pride filled his core.

"Also, I hope you and my sister stay in touch," Jackson added. "Because if you want members of the public pushing for this, there is no better person in your corner than Gemma. She genuinely cares about the little guy and will be relentless in doing what it takes to help them."

Gemma laughed. "Thank you, bro."

"You're welcome," he said, "and while I'm sorry I wasn't there for you earlier, sis, I'm completely behind you now."

"I have to ask you something…" Finnick glanced at Gemma. "What was it about the Pine Crest case that got your attention? Why that case?"

Gemma ran both hands through her hair and laughed. "I had a theory," she said, "which I now realize is ridiculous, now that we know about Reese Cyan."

"And what was that?" Finnick asked.

"I thought Kenny Stanton might possibly be Amy's ex-husband, Paul Keebles."

She laughed, but Jackson didn't. He felt his whole body stiffen.

"What do you mean you thought Amy's ex-husband could be the Pine Crest killer?" Jackson asked, so sharply that Gemma stopped walking suddenly and turned back to face him. So did Finnick. He noticed his boss wasn't smiling and hadn't seemed to find the thought funny either.

"Okay," Gemma said, "so it turned out Paul had a lot of pseudonyms, including Paul Kent and Stanley Paul. And I thought if you put Ken and Stan together…"

"You get Kenny Stanton," Jackson said. "I get the link, but it's weak."

"I know," Gemma said and shrugged. "And after Reese tried to murder me, I realized I wasn't dealing with some two-bit conman after all but someone much more dangerous. The idea that Paul could be Kenny just got stuck in my mind and I couldn't shake it, especially after Amy told me Paul loved showing off these medals that his grandfather supposedly won in the Second World War. Which got me thinking, what if Paul had once lived in Canada? What if while he'd been here, he worked at a seniors' residence and messed around with some senior citizens' pain IVs when he was younger and accidentally killed them?"

"It's very tenuous," Jackson said, slowly. "But not impossible. After all, Reese Cyan only has a record of theft and trafficking in stolen property, and we had no problem jumping to the conclusion that he was capable of murder."

"Right," Gemma said. "But I couldn't find any evidence that Paul had ever even been up here."

Just like they hadn't thought it was possible that he was up here now.

Suddenly a thought washed over him, jolting his system like freezing-cold water.

He summoned Hudson, turned and started running back to the front door.

"Where are you going?" Gemma called.

"The nurse told us he thought Skye's father was here in the hospital!" Jackson shouted. "We assumed it was a misunderstanding. What if it's not? What if Paul was working with Reese Cyan and thinks Amy has unknowingly seen evidence that could put him away for three murders?"

Amy lay in her hospital bed and looked over at the tiny bundle lying in the cot beside her. Her eyes traced her daughter's sleeping form. Skye's tiny fingers were curled into fists. Her eyes were closed and her little button nose was scrunched in sleep.

A joy deeper than any happiness Amy had ever known welled up inside her.

"You're perfect," she whispered to her tiny child. "You're safe, you're here and you're so very, very loved. I will do everything in my power to take care of you."

"Knock-knock," a female voice called from the doorway. Amy looked up to see an elderly nurse pop her head around the corner.

"I was wondering if you were up for visitors?" the nurse said. "I've got somebody special here who's been dying to meet the little one."

Jackson.

Amy smiled. "Yes, please send him in."

A giant bouquet of red roses came through the door along with the largest teddy bear Amy had ever seen, completely blocking the face and body of the person carrying them.

"I'm so sorry I didn't make it here sooner, darling, but I had a nightmare of a time getting here." The voice was male but definitely not Jackson's. "Why did you choose to have our child somewhere so many hours' drive away from an airport?"

Her fingers grabbed ahold of the blanket and held it tightly.

No, no, it can't be...

Through a haze of painkillers and exhaustion, she watched as Paul set the abundance of flowers and the teddy bear down on a table. He looked older than she remembered. Something about his expensive-looking suit and tie made her think of somebody wearing a "rich man" costume in a low-budget play. The lines on his face seemed deeper too, making the huge, broad grin that he flashed seem more like a grimace.

He thanked the nurse, closed the door and pulled the curtains shut.

"There," Paul said. "That's better. Now we're alone."

"How…how did you find me?" Her words felt slow and sluggish. "How did you know I was here?"

Paul chortled. He walked toward her, barely even glancing at the tiny baby in the cot on the other side of her bed.

"Don't start thinking silly thoughts," he said. "Of course I was going to know where you are. I have a whole team of lawyers for things like that. I've got people up here keeping an eye on you, and when you checked in to the hospital, they called and alerted me that my wife was having my child."

He had people up in Northern Ontario? And were these the same "lawyers" that had told Gemma he was getting a restraining order against both of them? No, he had to be lying. What he was saying wasn't making sense.

"I don't believe you," Amy said. "That's not

a thing that lawyers do, and hospitals don't give out information like that."

"You're just confused because you're tired." He leaned over and patted her hand, pressing it firmly into the mattress. Then he picked up the emergency call button the nurse had left her with and moved it onto the dresser behind him. "Trust me, sweetie, you're not thinking straight. Your horrible friend Gemma tried to poison your mind with all sorts of ridiculous lies about me. And now you're just so tired and confused that you don't know your up from your down."

His voice was soothing, sweet and gentle. Paul had always been charming, and everybody had always loved him. But his million-watt grin didn't work on her anymore. Paul had fooled her once and wouldn't trick her again.

Charming guy…everybody loved him…

The words started kicking insistently at the back of her mind, like they were trying to get her attention. Where had she heard them recently?

She pulled her hand away from his, dug both palms into the hospital bed and pushed herself up to sitting.

"Everything you told me was a lie," Amy

said. Her voice sounded weak to her own ears, and yet she felt it growing stronger with every word. "You have other wives and other kids. You had multiple fake names and identities! You broke my heart and you shattered my trust, and I don't want anything to do with you now. I want you to get out of my room. I don't know who you really are and I don't care. Our relationship was a lie, our marriage was a fake and I'm going to do everything in my power to keep you out of Skye's life. So go ahead and call your team of imaginary lawyers on me. I'm never going to let you hurt me again."

Paul stepped back as if she'd slapped him. His face paled. "Honey, you're being silly and you're getting emotional."

"You're right I'm emotional!" Amy said. "I have every right to be. In fact, my heart is absolutely full to the brim with deeper emotions than a shallow conman like you could ever dream of. Like determination and pride. I'm feeling gratitude for my friends, and I'm feeling love for my child. When you met me I didn't know who I was or where I was going. You took advantage of that. Now I know who I am and what I'm capable of."

Paul leaned over her. His face loomed just inches above hers.

"Keep your voice down, sweetie," he hissed.

"Or you'll do what?" Amy said. "I'm not impressed by you anymore, and you definitely don't scare me. You have any idea how strong I am? Or how much courage it took for me to go through what I lived through in the past few months or the last couple of days? I'm stronger than you could ever possibly imagine. You might say you come from a long line of military veterans and your grandfather might've served in the Air Force—or whatever other lies you tell to make yourself seem big—but you're so weak all you can do is try to make yourself feel big by waving around somebody else's medals and memorabilia..."

Her words trailed off as she suddenly realized what she'd said.

Paul had shown her the Second World War Air Force medals and memorabilia...

Like the ones stolen from the Pine Crest victim...

By the charming man everyone had loved, but who'd disappeared...

In a case Gemma had been looking into

without telling her but had been so invested in, she'd nearly died to chase a lead.

Amy felt her face pale and the truth began to dawn.

"What military did your grandfather serve in again?" she asked.

Paul snorted. "Good old U. S. of A., of course."

Right, she knew Paul was American. But she remembered the medals he'd shown her had a crown in the insignia. She thought of Blake's story about her AWOL husband. The American military's insignia didn't have a crown on it. But Canada's did.

"And how did you know I was here and then get here so quickly?" she pressed. "It would take hours to get here from the States."

He chuckled again, and it sounded even more forced. "I told you, I've got people up here."

"But what people?" she asked. "Where are they? And who did you have keeping tabs on me? And why me? I can't imagine you have people keeping tabs on all the women you've hurt and abandoned."

He didn't answer right away. She had no doubt his mind was swirling for an answer. But her mind was working faster. Too many things weren't adding up. She'd thought she'd seen Reese Cyan somewhere before. What if Reese had been the business contact Paul kept flying up to Canada to see...? What if he was the fence who Paul had used to sell the stuff he stole from the various people he conned? That would explain how Paul knew where she was living and what hospital she'd gone to. Maybe he'd been using Reese to keep tabs on her for weeks.

Amy had told Jackson that Paul never cared about her enough to try to hurt her. But it would be a whole lot different if Paul thought her friend Gemma could prove that he'd committed murder.

"You're Kenny Stanton." Her voice barely rose above a whisper. "Aren't you?"

She half expected him to laugh and deny it. Like he'd lied to her face so many times before. But instead, for the first time since she'd met him, fear filled Paul's face. He recoiled.

"That's... I'm... It's not... How do you know that name?"

He stammered as his usually golden tongue struggled for words. Amy's gaze darted from the tiny child in the cot beside her to the emergency button he'd placed behind him.

What would Paul do if she reached for the

call button? What would happen if she shouted for help? Would anyone even hear her over the hustle and bustle of the maternity ward?

Lord, I need Your help now. Protect me and my child.

"Help!" Amy yelled as loudly as she could. "I need security in here now!"

Suddenly, Paul's face went red. The mask of civility fell from his eyes. He lunged at her. With one hand, he grabbed her by the throat and pinned her down against the bed. She pushed him back as hard as she could.

But she was still weak from giving birth, and he had the upper hand.

Paul clamped his fingers around her throat and squeezed, blocking the air from her lungs. With the other he pushed the button on her IV to increase the amount of medication swamping her system.

"Now, I told you not to get any silly ideas in your head," he whispered. "You're not thinking straight. Once we get out of here and go somewhere quiet, I'll explain everything. You will listen and then I'll fix this mess and everything will be okay."

No.

But she could feel herself getting weaker.

Blackness was seeping into the corners of her eyes. Any moment now she was going to pass out. She was at the mercy of a killer. One who wouldn't hesitate to snuff out her life.

Help me, Lord! Save my child!

Darkness swept in and the world went black.

Chapter Fourteen

"Where is Amy Scout's room?" Jackson stood at the reception desk and showed his badge to the same male nurse he'd spoken to before. "I need someone to take us there, immediately. I have reason to believe she could be in danger."

"This way, officer." The nurse leapt to his feet immediately and gestured to a woman in scrubs to come take over his post.

The nurse led Jackson quickly down a maze of hallways. Jackson had Hudson by his side, and Finnick, Nippy and Gemma followed close behind. He'd rarely been so well reinforced, and yet he'd never felt more lost and terrified.

He had to be wrong. Amy and Skye had to be okay...

Lord, I need them to be safe, like I need the air that I breathe.

Jackson heard the plaintive sound of a tiny

baby wailing. His chest ached and somehow he knew that it was Skye.

The nurse's footsteps quickened. Jackson's heart pounded so hard he could feel it in his chest. The nurse reached a closed door, knocked twice and then opened it. "Excuse me, ma'am, but you've got the police here to see you."

The words froze on the nurse's tongue and a second later Jackson saw why. The bed was empty. Amy was gone. Skye was alone in her crib. Instantly, Gemma slipped past them into the room and swept Skye up into her arms, comforting her and holding her to her chest.

Jackson turned to the nurse. "Where is Amy?"

"I don't know," the nurse said, gravely. "But I will find out."

The nurse ran to the nearest internal phone and called in a missing patient report. Jackson could only hear his side of the conversation, but it was clear the hospital would be going into lockdown until she could be found.

Jackson prayed it wasn't too late. Hudson whimpered and pressed his snout into Jackson's hand. Skye had begun to settle down in Gemma's arms.

His sister's large, worried eyes met his. "What's happening?"

"I don't know," Jackson said.

He stood by Gemma and Skye, as Finnick ran down the hallway, stopping person after person, flashing his badge and asking if anyone knew where the patient in room 812 had gone. The nurse ended his call and turned toward Jackson. His face was so pale it was almost gray.

"Apparently, someone spotted her leaving the maternity ward a few moments ago," he said. "She was in a wheelchair and being pushed by a balding man who identified himself as her husband and said he was taking her for fresh air."

"He's not her husband!" Jackson shouted. A cold, near paralyzing fear filled his gut. "He's a suspect in a triple homicide."

"I'll get to the security office and coordinate the response," Finnick called. "Jackson, go find Amy."

"I've got Skye!" Gemma added. "I'll keep her safe. You go!"

Jackson silently thanked God for them, then he looked down at his partner. The dog was standing at attention. Jackson looped the dog's leash tightly around his hand.

"Hudson," he ordered, "find Amy!"

His partner barked and then took off running down the hospital hallways, dragging Jackson behind them. They pushed past startled staff and visitors, running as fast as Jackson's legs would allow, even as he could feel his partner pulling him to go even faster. Hudson led him through a maze of back corridors and service hallways, into the quieter and more isolated areas of the hospital. They ran through a large laundry room and the sound of sheets and towels rolling and tumbling rose around them.

An emergency exit loomed ahead. Hudson's barks echoed around them as the dog practically threw himself at the door. Jackson pushed it open and they burst through into an alley behind the hospital. It was empty. Hudson's snout rose. He sniffed the air. Then he barked again, turned and led Jackson down to the end of the alley. An even narrower laneway lay ahead. They turned into it. There was an empty wheelchair lying on its side. One wheel still spun in the air.

Then Jackson saw them. Paul was trying to drag a semiconscious Amy into the back of a white delivery van, while she fought and struggled against him.

Jackson turned to his partner and unclipped Hudson's leash.

"Go get him!" he called. "Take him down! Save Amy!"

Hudson charged toward Paul, with Jackson running a few steps behind. Startled, the criminal dropped Amy onto the ground, where she crumpled like a rag doll, and took off running. In a moment, Jackson had reached her, lifted her up and cradled her into his arms.

"Jackson?" Her voice was weak. Amy's head fell against his shoulder. "Is that really you?"

"Yeah, it's really me," he whispered. "It's okay. I've got you, and Gemma's got Skye. You're safe."

Paul sprinted down the alley, but he was no match for Hudson's strength and speed. With a triumphant howl, Hudson launched himself at Paul. His strong paws hit him in the back and knocked him to the pavement, pinning him there. A door clanged open behind them. Jackson looked back to see uniformed security officers and police spilling out into the alleyway.

"You found her?" a man in a dark blue uniform shouted at Jackson.

"Yup, she's safe!" Jackson called. "I've got her."

Officers ran past him. Jackson ordered Hudson to release Paul as the officers stepped in to arrest him. Hudson returned to Jackson's side, leaned his paws against Jackson's leg and licked Amy's fingers. She ran her hand over the dog's head.

"It's all over," Jackson said. "Paul's being taken into custody right now. Hudson took him down."

Amy smiled. Her eyes fluttered open and then closed again. "Good dog."

"Very good dog," he said.

But it seemed he'd spoken too soon as a flurry of shouting and activity rose from the end of the alley behind him. He turned. Somehow Paul had managed to wriggle free from his arresting officer. Paul had taken off running again down another alley in the direction of the parking lot, with a half dozen people on his trail shouting at him to stop.

"They underestimated him," Amy said weakly. "Like I did."

"Don't worry," Jackson said. "He won't get away this time."

A gunshot sounded somewhere out of view. More shouts rose and Amy pushed herself closer into Jackson's chest. Hudson growled toward the departing group and glanced up at Jackson. He could read the question in his partner's eyes.

"No, buddy," Jackson told Hudson, and his voice sounded gruff to his ears. "Not this time. We're going to let somebody else deal with bringing the bad guy to justice right now. Our job is protecting Amy."

He turned and walked back toward the open hospital door, with Amy in his arms and Hudson by his side. As he stepped through the doorway, a nurse offered to take Amy, but Jackson shook his head. "It's okay, I've got her."

Jackson carried Amy in his arms all the way back to her hospital room where Gemma waited, still holding the sleeping infant. A soft cry escaped Amy's beautiful lips as her eyes alighted on her baby girl.

"Skye's safe," Gemma said. Happy tears filled her eyes. Hudson's ears perked as he sniffed in the direction of the tiny, sleeping child as if memorizing her scent. Gemma laid the baby back to rest in her cot. "She's perfect, Amy."

Gently and tenderly, Jackson set Amy down on the bed.

"It's all going to be okay now," he whispered. He eased his arms out from under her. "I won't let anything happen to you or Skye, I promise."

A fleet of medical staff in uniform filled the

doorway. Gemma slipped past them and out of the room. Jackson turned to follow.

But Amy grabbed his hand. "Stay with me. Please."

He swallowed hard.

"I'm going to have to give the doctors and nurses some space to do their thing," he said. "But I'll be right outside the door and I'll come back in as soon as they give me permission. Okay?"

Amy nodded weakly. "Okay."

He signaled Hudson to his side. They stepped out of Amy's room. The nurse they'd spoken to before nodded to Jackson and closed the door behind them.

Gemma was standing a few feet away in the hallway.

"You okay?" Gemma asked. "You look exhausted. You want to go grab a quick bite or even just a drink of water?"

"No, I'm staying," Jackson said. He wasn't surprised he looked tired, and he was sure fatigue would hit him like a ton of bricks later. But for now, he stood up straight and crossed his arms. Hudson sat at attention by his side. "Amy asked me to stay and I promised her I wouldn't leave."

His sister's green eyes searched his face for a long moment, as if Gemma was seeing him for the first time. Finally she nodded.

"Well, I'm going to go get a drink of water for you and one for Hudson too," she said. Gemma turned as if to go, then she hesitated, turned back and gave him a hug. "I'm really proud of you, brother."

He opened his mouth to thank her, only to find a lump in his throat so large he couldn't get the words out. Instead, he nodded to his sister, she nodded back, then Gemma turned and started down the hallway.

Time ticked by slowly, punctuated only by the round clock on the wall and his own worried thoughts. After a few minutes, Finnick and Nippy appeared around the corner and started down the hallway toward them.

"I hear you've got our girl safe and sound," Finnick said, but Jackson couldn't help but notice he was frowning. "Well done."

Jackson felt his spine straighten even further.

"Yes, sir," he said. "Doctors are just checking her over now."

"That's good," Finnick said. The frown lines in his forehead grew even deeper. "It looks like we've lost our main suspect."

Jackson blinked. "Paul got away?"

"No, he's dead." Finnick ran his hand over the back of his head. "It was a stupid, senseless death. He ran into the parking lot, with cops barely three feet behind him, tried to pull a gun on a motorist and hijack her vehicle. She grabbed the gun in self-defense, they fought for it and it went off. They tried to rush him into surgery, but it was too late. He's gone."

Jackson sucked in a breath. "How's the woman?"

"In shock," Finnick said. "But thankfully she's fine." He shook his head. "This whole situation is so infuriating. If he is the man behind the Pine Crest murders, and investigators had done their job in the first place, so much pain and suffering could've been avoided."

The hospital door opened behind him, and medical staff filed out again. A nurse informed Jackson that Amy was ready for him to come back in. She was groggy and would probably sleep for a while, due to the large dose of meds that Paul had hit her with, but that thankfully she'd be okay.

Jackson thanked him, and Finnick excused himself. Then Jackson took Hudson back into Amy's room, closing the door behind them.

She was sitting up in bed. The pink had already begun to return to her cheeks and her face was a little less pale than it had been when he'd left her. But her eyes widened as she clocked his expression.

"What happened?" she asked. "Is everything okay?"

"Am I that transparent?" Jackson asked.

"To me you are."

He crossed the room and crouched down beside her bed.

"I don't know how to tell you this," he said. "But Paul has died."

A sob choked in her throat as he filled Amy in on everything that Finnick had told him. He reached for her and hugged her tightly as she buried her face in his shoulder for a long moment. When she pulled back and he let her go, he noticed that while tears filled her beautiful eyes, they'd stopped before they could even fall.

"Such a waste of a life," she said, bitterly. "He was so talented, smart and charming. But he used those talents to lie, cheat, steal, con, swindle and even kill. Up until the very last moments of his life, he was trying to take advantage of some poor woman." She closed her eyes and prayed. "Thank You, God, that he's finally been stopped."

"Amen."

They talked about the case for a few more minutes, but soon Amy's eyelids fluttered and then closed. So, Jackson settled himself down in a chair opposite the bed, with Hudson by his feet. And that's where he stayed for the next few hours, as Amy slept. Gemma came back with water and some snacks for him and Hudson. She sat with them in silence for a while, and then after an hour told him she was going to get hotel rooms for them both in the area in case Amy and Skye needed to stay a few days. Finnick popped back in too, to let Jackson know he was heading back to the city. Medical staff came in and out to check vitals on the machine by Amy's bed. Skye woke briefly and fussed but settled back into sleep when Jackson scooped the tiny baby into his arms and rocked her gently.

Still Amy slept and Jackson stayed. He wasn't about to leave her side or risk her waking up to find he'd left her.

He was going to be there for Amy as long as she needed him. And then when Amy no longer needed him and could stand on her own two feet again, then what? He didn't know. All he knew was that what had started as a youthful crush so many years ago had grown into something so much deeper and stronger than he ever could've possibly imagined.

He loved Amy Scout and her newborn baby. He wanted to be there for them always, take care of them and keep them safe, in whatever way Amy wanted, for the rest of their lives.

He hadn't even realized he'd dozed off while sitting in the uncomfortable chair until he heard Amy calling his name and looked up to see the rising sun filtering through the windows.

"Jackson?" She whispered his name like music.

He looked over. She was sitting up in bed, with Skye tucked peacefully in the crook of her arm fast asleep.

He swallowed hard, as an unfamiliar lump formed in his throat.

"I'm here," he said, softly. He walked over and knelt beside the bed. "How are you feeling?"

"I'm good." Her free hand reached for his. He looped his fingers through hers. She held his hand tightly.

"She's amazing, isn't she?" Amy whispered.

Love filled her hazel eyes as she looked down at the baby in her arms. Something fierce and protective moved through his core.

"She's incredible," he said.

He looked from the tiny sleeping child to Amy's radiant face and knew that he'd never seen anything more beautiful in his life.

"*You're* incredible, Amy," Jackson said softly. "You're brilliant, brave and incredibly strong. I meant every word I said yesterday about being there for you and Skye. Whatever you need and whatever comes next, you can count on me. I promise, because—"

I love you, Amy.

The words crossed his heart, but before he could speak them, Amy pulled her hand from his and pressed her fingers against his lips.

"Don't say it," she said. "I know what you're going to say. And I feel it too. You're the most incredible man I've ever met. You're amazing and kind. You apologize for your mistakes and you're committed to growth… But we can't say those words to each other. Not yet. Not now."

He nodded to tell her he understood. She took his hand again.

"All my life I've been impulsive," she said. "I've rushed headlong into things without considering the consequences. And you deserve better than that. We both do. So I can't let myself rush into this. Not until I know for certain that I'm ready."

Jackson swallowed hard.

But what if she was never ready? What if the time never came?

Lord, please give me the strength I need to wait for her and be patient.

"Okay," he said.

"Thank you."

Amy leaned toward him, he bent down toward her, and their lips met in a kiss that was sweet and tender. Yet somehow it also felt as if they were both glancing through an open door before closing it again.

Then Amy leaned back against the pillow and fell asleep, holding his hand.

Chapter Fifteen

The early November air was crisp with the promise of winter, as Amy stepped through the sliding doors of the South River Medical Center following Skye's checkup. She moved across the parking lot, with a diaper bag slung over her shoulder and her daughter nestled safely on her hip. On the other side of the road, she could see forest stretched out to the horizon in a maze of orange, red and gold leaves.

She scanned the lot. Where was Gemma?

"Anybody need a taxi?" Jackson's warm voice rang out from among the parked cars.

A moment later she saw him striding toward her. A lopsided grin crossed his handsome face. Joy shone in his eyes. Amy felt her heart skip a beat. Skye squealed and waved her chubby arms in greeting.

"What are you doing here?" She rushed toward him. "I thought Gemma was coming to get me."

"She had to rush back to the cottage for an unexpected thing," he said. "And I had an errand up here anyway, so it all worked out. I hope this is an okay surprise. Gemma said there was no cell phone reception inside the clinic."

"It's a great surprise."

He opened his arms for her, and she stepped into the warmth of his chest. She felt his beard brush against her cheek.

Jackson had become like a part of the family in the months since Skye had been born. He'd taken a two-week vacation from work immediately after her birth to help Amy, Gemma and the baby get settled in the cottage. And then he'd come up to visit almost every weekend since, to bring groceries, help with Skye, cook, clean, babysit and rebuild his friendship with his sister. Not to mention the countless hours Amy and Jackson had spent together walking, talking, reading, boating, doing the dishes or just being together in comfortable silence.

They pulled apart again.

"What kind of errand and what kind of thing?" she asked.

"My errand is at Pine Crest," he said, "and

I'll let Gemma tell you her own thing back at the cottage. It's nothing bad, I promise."

"Okay." She smiled and said, "I trust you."

And she did. He stretched out his hand for the diaper bag and she let him take it. Then he reached for Skye, and the little girl practically launched herself into his arms.

Jackson chuckled and wrapped his arms around Skye, and she reached up and patted his face.

"Hello, princess," he said. Then he glanced at Amy. "How did her checkup go? It's her six-month one, right?"

"Yup," she said. They walked through the parking lot toward his vehicle. "Just routine."

"And how is she?" Jackson's eyes were still on Skye.

"Absolutely perfect."

"Ha! I could've told you that."

As they reached Jackson's truck, she could see Hudson's head sticking out the front window. But as they approached, Hudson leaped into the backseat and curled up beside Skye's car seat. Jackson opened the back door and buckled her in.

"Goggy!" Sky shouted as she flopped her

head sideways onto Hudson with a giggle. He licked her cheek.

"Yes, sweetie," Amy said. "Hudson is a big fluffy doggy."

Jackson's eyebrows rose. "Is that her first word?"

"Doggy?" Amy translated, with a laugh. "It might be. Are you jealous?"

"Of Hudson?" Jackson asked. "Always. He's everybody's favorite."

"Not mine," she said.

His eyes met hers and held them for a long moment. Then he opened her door for her. Once she was inside, he walked around to his side, stepped in, and they started driving.

"Do you have an update on the investigation?" she asked.

"Not this time," Jackson said. "I just need to drop something off quickly to a friend."

Jackson and Hudson had made several visits to Pine Crest Retirement Home in the past few months to fill them in on the case as it developed, sometimes with Gemma, Amy and Skye in tow. After Paul's death, his DNA had come back as a match to Kenny Stanton's. Several seniors had also made a positive photo identification, and military medals found in Paul's home had turned out to belong to murdered veteran Gordon Donnelly.

While Paul died before he saw justice, Amy knew it had given the residents a degree of peace to know the case had finally been solved. Thanks to some firm pushing from Finnick, an investigation had been opened into how the original case had been bungled too, with several current and retired officers being brought in for questioning. Thankfully, Reese had pled guilty to the kidnapping and working with Paul to fence stolen items, saving Amy the ordeal of having to testify against him at trial. Investigators across Canada and the United States were still unraveling the mystery of the man who'd called himself Paul Keebles, his multiple aliases, and the many people he'd lied to and stolen from. His legal name had turned out to be Kenneth Paul Stanley, he was eight years older than he'd told Amy he was, and officers were currently investigating his suspected involvement in various other jurisdictions for multiple other cold case crimes and murders.

As they pulled up in front of Pine Crest, Amy could see Walter sitting on a bench in front of the home, arms crossed and hands covered in large woolen mittens. Jackson pulled the car to a stop. But as he and Amy got out, Walter stood and waved both of them off.

"Stay there," he called. He ambled toward them. Despite the fact he was trying his best to frown, Amy could see the unmistakable twinkle of joy in the old man's eyes. "No need to get yourself out. I'll come to you."

"Yes, sir," Jackson said with a smile. He went around to the back door, opened it and pulled out a wooden box from under the driver's seat.

Amy gave Walter a warm hug.

"How are you doing?" Walter asked. "Jackson taking care of you all?"

"He is," Amy said.

Jackson stood back and waited as Walter stuck his head in the open backseat and said hello to Skye and Hudson in turn. Then the older man turned to Jackson.

"So, what's all this about?" he asked. "You called and said you had something for me?"

"Yes, sir." Jackson handed him the wooden box. "Police released Gordon Donnelly's possessions from the evidence locker today, and when they contacted his granddaughter, she said the family wanted you to have these."

Walter took off his mittens and opened the box. His eyes misted as he looked down at the collection of Second World War medals nestled in the blue velvet inside. He wiped his hand over the back of his eyes, opened his mouth, then closed it again and patted Jackson on the back.

"Thank you," Walter said.

"You're welcome," Jackson replied. "Thank you for being so relentless in making sure this case wasn't forgotten."

Walter nodded. Then he glanced at Amy.

"This man is a good man, you know," Walter told her and pointed at Amy.

Amy's eyes searched the strong and tender lines of Jackson's face. "I know."

Jackson and Amy drove in comfortable silence back to the cottage. Jackson laid his hand in the space between them. She took it and their fingers linked so naturally it was as if their hands had been made to hold each other. She'd lost track of how many times she and Jackson had held hands, hugged or gently kissed goodbye over the past few months. All she knew is that there was something safe and comforting about having him near. She'd never felt this before.

When they reached the cottage, there was an unfamiliar truck parked in the driveway. She carried Skye to the house, and Jackson held open the door for her. She quickly realized who the pickup belonged to as Nippy made a beeline toward them. The two dogs greeted each other in a flurry of enthusiastically wagging tails. Thankfully, Gemma had made peace with having the K-9s around, although Amy knew that in Gemma's heart, no dog could ever hold a candle to her Reepi. Amy could hear the parrot chirping cheerfully from his perch in the living room. He'd been traveling with Gemma to and from the store since the break-in, and was no longer there alone overnight. They found Finnick and Gemma sitting at the dining table. When Jackson had told her that something important had come up for Gemma, she hadn't imagined it involved Jackson's boss. Gemma and Finnick stood.

"How did everything go with the doctor and with Walter?" Gemma asked.

"Wonderfully." Amy gave her a one-armed hug and slipped Skye into Gemma's outstretched hands. Then she turned to Finnick.

"It's nice to see you again, Inspector," Amy said. "To what do we owe the pleasure?"

"I'm here to offer Gemma a job," Finnick said.

And the huge smile and slightly overwhelmed

look on Gemma's face told Amy that she'd said yes.

"I've finally got permission to launch a dedicated Cold Case Task Force," Finnick went on. "I'm planning to pull in officers from across the province and around the country to tackle many of the cases that have gone unsolved for far too long. I'm hoping to not only bring justice to a lot of families who've been waiting for it, but also to help restore confidence in our commitment that no victim of crime will be forgotten."

Amy turned to Gemma. "You're going to become a cop?"

"No way," Gemma said, with a laugh. "I'm very happy to be a private investigator. I'm going to join the task force as a civilian consultant and family liaison."

"As Gemma rightly pointed out, there are a lot of people who have lost confidence in police," Finnick said. "So, Gemma's going to be an integral part of building trust, and I'm going to be partnering her with law enforcement officers on some cases. I've already got plans to talk to Blake and Caleb about the team, as well as to try roping in Jackson here. But I wanted to talk with Gemma first."

Joy filled Amy's heart as she looked from one shining face to the next. "That's incredible."

"Yeah, and an answer to a whole lot of prayers," Gemma said. "But this does mean I'm going to need your help more than ever to keep the store running."

"You can count on me," Amy said. Already the small turquoise barn full of books and artwork was beginning to feel like home. Amy had been helping at the bookstore on and off over the past few months as she was able, and had designated a special space on the wall in the main room to be a roving display for local artists—including some incredibly talented children, teenagers, senior citizens, painters, sketch artists and photographers to display and sell their art. "We'll work it all out, and it'll be amazing."

Thanksgiving filled her heart for the immeasurable prayers that had been answered in the past few months, and yet an odd aching in her heart told her that there was one thing still missing.

"Do you mind watching Skye for a moment?" she asked Gemma. "I need to talk to your brother about something."

"Absolutely," Gemma said. "No problem."

Jackson leaned toward Amy. "Everything okay?" he asked softly.

"Not quite yet," she said. "But it will be."

Together they walked out the sliding glass door onto the back porch, down the steps and out toward the water until they reached the end of the dock. There they stood, side by side. A crisp autumn breeze cut through her jacket. She leaned her shoulder against Jackson and he put his arm around her.

"So, are you going to join the cold case team?" Amy asked.

Jackson grinned. "Probably, if it doesn't get in the way of me being around here to help give you guys backup when you need it."

Lord, I was so worried of wasting my own life that I just recklessly threw myself into every adventure I could find. I never even stopped to look and see if there was a path that You'd laid out for me or think about what I wanted for my life. But since my life was forced to slow down, I've finally been able to see what I want and where I want to be.

She glanced at the incredible man beside her.

"I'm ready," she said.

Jackson turned. Confusion crossed his face, then amazement and finally hope.

"Are you saying what I think you're saying?" he asked.

She turned to face him.

"I'm ready to start the next chapter of my life," she said, "and I don't want to waste a single moment of it." She took both of his hands in hers and looked up at the strong, handsome man she knew, without a shadow of a doubt, that she wanted to see for the rest of her life. "I wake up every morning thinking of your face and I fall asleep every night grateful that you are in my life. For once, I'm not leaping blindly. I love you, Jackson. I've known it deep in my heart every day for months. And I want to spend the rest of my life with you."

"I love you too," Jackson said. "I always have and I always will."

Slowly, he pulled his hands from hers. Then he reached into his jacket pocket, pulled out a small box and opened it. There, lay a simple gold and diamond engagement ring.

She laughed. "How long have you been carrying that around?"

"Months," Jackson said. "Ever since the moment I knew that, more than anything else in the world, I wanted to marry you, Amy Scout. I love you."

"I love you too."

"And you'll be my wife?"

"Absolutely."

He slid the ring onto her finger. She wound her hands around his neck. He wrapped his arms around her and held her close.

"Are you sure about this?" Jackson asked.

"As confident as I am in the ground beneath our feet, the sky above us and the air we breathe."

"Me too," Jackson said.

He kissed her deeply. She kissed him back and knew with every part of her that she was where she was meant to be.

★ ★ ★ ★ ★

Her Duty Bound Defender

Sharee Stover

MILLS & BOON

Colorado native **Sharee Stover** lives in the Midwest with her real-life-hero husband, youngest child and her obnoxiously lovable German shepherd. A self-proclaimed word nerd, she loves the power of words to transform, ignite and restore. She writes Christian romantic suspense combining heart-racing, nail-biting suspense and the delight of falling in love all in one. Connect with her at www.shareestover.com.

Visit the Author Profile page
at millsandboon.com.au.

For God shall bring every work into judgment,
with every secret thing, whether it be good,
or whether it be evil.
    —*Ecclesiastes* 12:14

DEDICATION

For all the dedicated law enforcement K-9s
and their handlers. Thank you for your service.

Chapter One

A tragic murder in a blissful setting.

That's how the Denver media sensational-
ized Peter Windham's horrifying Valentine's
Day murder. An involuntary shiver passed over
Naomi Carr-Cavanaugh. Peter Windham and
Henry Mulder—both Naomi's high school
classmates—died of gunshot wounds. Additionally, the killer left a malicious note stabbed
into their chests, claiming they'd gotten what
they deserved. Worse, the crimes mimicked the
demise of three other Elk Valley High School
classmates and fellow Young Ranchers Club
members in Wyoming a decade prior. Her
gaze remained fixated on Peter's barn, looming
ahead in the distance with the gorgeous Colorado landscape for a backdrop. The same place
where law enforcement discovered his body two
months prior.

Why had the murderer returned now?

Why Peter?

Tears filled Naomi's eyes, blurring her vision.

Unlike her teen crush, Trevor Gage, and his friends, Peter—the quintessential nice guy—was Naomi's friend.

Naomi's connection to all the murder victims and the prank they'd played on her at the YRC dance ten years prior remained one undeniable fact. Memories of the horrible night rushed at her, dragging Naomi back to the painful moment with Trevor and his friends—including Peter.

She shoved the unpleasant thoughts away.

Did Peter move to Colorado intending to flee their hometown and the painful reminders, just as she'd done?

The last rays of the April evening sun prepared to set behind the majestic Colorado mountains bordering the deserted Windham Ranch. The headlights of Naomi's Ford Transit Connect van illuminated her path. She drove slowly, navigating past the outbuilding, stable and farmhouse to the barn doors, where she parked and shut off the engine.

Why am I here? Naomi had no suitable answer for the pestering question. She'd contemplated her motives since the last of her tour bus customers disembarked tonight. As the owner operator of her small business, Friends of Foothills Tours, she provided guided tours to common attractions around Denver and the bordering foothills. This night, she felt compelled to visit Peter's property, and she'd driven straight here.

Again.

Months earlier, just after Valentine's Day, when the news first reported the incident, Naomi made this same trip. Due to the heavy law enforcement personnel presence, she'd known better than to intrude.

But tonight, no other people milled along the property.

No coroner's van drove Peter's body to the morgue.

No crime scene technicians collected evidence.

She released her seat belt and opened her door, then paused. The trills of the birds faded as they nestled in the trees that bordered the pasture—void of the horses Peter loved to train. A swift kick under her ribs gained her attention, and Naomi caressed her swollen belly where her active baby boy moved. "We're here, little man. I might as well look around."

She awkwardly scooted out of the driver's

seat, reminded that no movement was easy at the advanced stage of her pregnancy.

Time was running out, though.

Soon she'd be a busy single mommy.

It was now or never.

Her ballet slipper flats crunched softly on the gravel road. Gravity pulled on her aching muscles, and she braced her palms against the small of her back, then leaned to stretch. Sprouts of overgrown grass and weeds peeked sporadically through the ground. A soft breeze fluttered the tendrils of hair that had escaped her French braid, tickling her neck. Goose bumps rose on her bare arms. She reached in and grabbed her favorite blue cardigan from the seat, donning the sweater. Then she withdrew her cell phone from her purse and activated the flashlight app, mentally chastising herself for not bringing a real one. Of course, she reasoned, she'd not anticipated coming to the ranch.

Naomi stood motionless, surrounded by inky darkness, and serenaded by chirruping crickets. With one last glance at her van, she started toward the barn.

Rusty red paint covered the wooden structure and a side door stood ajar. The motion sensor light overhead activated at her approach.

Naomi jumped back, startled, and pressed her hand against her racing heart. Grateful for the extra light, she chuckled nervously and surveyed the grounds. Long rows of evergreens bordered the lane where she'd driven. Weeds and tall grass had overgrown the landscape. Shadows stretched out in all directions, bathing everything in an eerie veil, juxtaposing Denver's nighttime ambient glow.

Her legs and back ached from the long day of sitting and driving. A walk would relieve the tension. Besides, since her husband Ted's accidental death six months prior, she had no one to go home to. Not that he'd been around much before the mishap.

Naomi inhaled a fortifying breath, passed the barn and headed for the pasture separated by a split-rail fence. Sweet memories of her high school rodeo performance days trickled into her mind, and she smiled. All of it seemed a lifetime ago.

Naomi faced west, where the last glimpses of the sunset disappeared behind the craggy landscape. She inhaled the fresh air. Away from the busyness of the city, she relished the quiet, though it reminded her of Elk Valley.

Her baby shifted again, refocusing Naomi to her purpose.

She turned and walked toward the barn.

A rustling in the foliage behind her had Naomi pivoting. She scanned the row of evergreens bordering the lane, then her gaze roved the prairie.

Was it her imagination or did something move in the distance?

"Hello?" Naomi's voice hitched, revealing her fear.

No response.

This was a huge mistake. She had no right to be on private property.

But there might not be another opportunity.

She approached the barn door, placed her hand on the iron handle and tugged it open. It creaked, though she'd expected nothing less. She stepped over the threshold and entered the darkened space.

Something rushed at her.

Naomi gasped and stumbled back into the opened door as a form whipped into the space between her and the outdoors. Her cell phone light captured the rabbit's white tail as it darted into the pasture.

Naomi's heart thudded so hard against her

ribs it vibrated through her body. "Stop it," she admonished before sweeping the light across the vacant barn.

Childhood and teen memories of her friendship with Peter fluttered to mind. They'd had such fun, and Naomi considered him one of her closest friends. They'd lost touch after the night of the semiformal dance, except for a single meeting after she'd left their hometown in Wyoming and moved to Colorado. However, she'd not entertained reviving their friendship. Between the loss of her parents, her husband and now Peter, life was too short to embitter herself by dwelling on thoughts of past hurts.

"If only things had been different." Her words echoed in the empty barn, where the scent of hay and copper mingled. She proceeded farther inside, hesitating beside a large circular stain marring the hardwood floor.

Realization hit Naomi with the force of a tsunami.

Peter's murder scene.

What was she doing here? Naomi again surveyed the space, unable to shake the strange sensation that someone watched her.

An icy shiver traced down her spine, and the urge to escape the area overwhelmed her.

She spun on her heel, hurrying for the door.

Gravel crunched outside the barn, and she peered out, still hidden behind the open door.

Would she be arrested for trespassing on private property?

Headlights bounced on the single lane, approaching the ranch.

There was no way to escape without being seen.

She glanced over her shoulder again, glimpsing the stained floor, and sucked in a breath.

Terror gripped her heart.

Had Peter's killer returned?

Revenge nursed an insatiable hunger. The saying couldn't be truer as Detective Bennett Ford watched through the binoculars. "Now you're behaving like a serial killer, returning to the scene of the crime—possibly to meet up with your accomplices." The sedan approaching Peter's barn slowed.

He lowered the binoculars. If the situation were different, he might find the petite woman with chestnut brown hair and bright hazel eyes attractive. That part of the case file didn't jive. How had anyone considered her a plain Jane? Regardless, the endless string of boring surveillance days following the Mountain Country K-9 Task Force's number one murder suspect, Naomi Carr-Cavanaugh, had finally paid off.

Bennett exchanged the binoculars for his service weapon and tactical flashlight, gaining his K-9 partner Spike's attention. "This is it! The truth always comes out."

His beagle's tail thumped the front seat, conveying his readiness to work.

Bennett didn't have the heart to tell his partner that his unprecedented narcotic detection skills—a valuable asset to the MCK9 task force—might not be required on this case. The fifteen-person team headquartered in Wyoming was comprised of skilled law enforcement professionals, including local police, US Marshals, FBI agents, state troopers and sheriff's deputies. However, the task force leader had asked Bennett to trail Naomi because Denver was his hometown. He was very familiar with the city and the surrounding area—including the Windham Ranch location. Plus, Spike's nose could always come in handy for tracking. No matter. They were part of the elite group's unified mission. Specifically, taking down the Rocky Mountain Killer or RMK, who was responsible for the heinous murders of five young men across Rocky Mountain states—Colorado, Montana and Wyoming—spanning ten years with the threat of more to come.

"Sorry, Spike. Wait here," Bennett whispered.

The beagle harrumphed his displeasure and curled up on the seat.

For the first time since trailing Naomi, she'd deviated from her normal, predictable routine. Her daily schedule never strayed. She left her Roxborough apartment at the break of dawn and picked up six to eight tour customers at her small downtown storefront. Then she escorted them all over Denver, ending at Red Rocks Amphitheater, and dropped them off where they'd begun. Naomi drove straight home, turned out the lights early and repeated it the next day. Evidently, she'd planned to work right up to the baby's birth. If Bennett didn't know otherwise, he'd assume Naomi used boredom as her weapon of choice. He snorted at his sarcastic thought.

Tonight, she'd finally provided a twist from her norm by driving south of Denver to the Windham Ranch in Ridge. No doubt, to relish in her latest crime and, Bennett also hoped, to retrieve the 9 mm pistol used in all the murders. The weapon—which the authorities had yet to find—would give him the coup de grâce when he closed the RMK case.

The unexpected arrival of the second vehicle, however, provided the ultimate icing on the investigation cake. It explained how a woman in her final pregnancy trimester killed two grown men in different states—Peter Windham in Colorado and Henry Mulder in Montana. Additionally, the accomplices expounded on Naomi's dire financial straits. She'd paid hired assassins to exact her revenge on the ones who humiliated her ten years prior.

The updated case file now shared the undeniably sad story of golden-boy Trevor Gage inviting Naomi to the YRC semiformal dance as a prank. When she arrived, all Trevor's friends, except Peter, had laughed at her. Now, five of those young men were dead. Peter was the one anomaly, as he hadn't participated in humiliating Naomi. The prank revealed Trevor had only asked her out as a joke. Devastated, she'd bolted from the dance in tears. A month later, on Valentine's Day, authorities discovered three of the teens murdered in an Elk Valley barn. The start of Naomi's reign of terror.

Not that Bennett condoned the young men's

unacceptable bullying behavior. What they'd done to her was beyond cruel, and someone should've held them accountable. Naomi's illegal vigilante actions solidified her motive and thwarted any hope of the young men's recompense. In an ironic twist, it turned the tables, offering those same instigators warranted justice.

Peter's friendship with Naomi didn't fit with the other victims' intentions. Though the MCK9 team argued a better friend would've protected her from the start.

Peter's adult life included a spotless reputation. He was an active churchgoer and well-respected horse trainer. Why kill him on the ten-year anniversary of the first three murders?

Unless the death of Naomi's husband and her pregnancy triggered the killer inside? Were they the catalyst for her latest acts of revenge? She'd moved to Denver shortly after Peter Windham did. Stalking him, perhaps? Assuming she'd be far from her hometown of Elk Valley, Wyoming, and no one would piece the cold case murders together?

Bennett's experience with liars, both professionally and personally, had taught him outward appearances didn't reveal a person's real underlying motives. He'd never again under-estimate the mind of a criminal, thanks to Delaney Huxley—con woman, drug dealer extraordinaire and Bennett's ex-fiancée.

Everything pointed to Naomi, and she might've gotten away undetected with the prior victims' cases going cold. But she had to satisfy her insatiable appetite for revenge by killing Peter and Henry. Both were found bearing the same fatal gunshot wounds and vicious notes stabbed into their chests with a knife. *They got what they deserved. More to come across the Rock-ies. And I'm saving the best for last.*

This time, Naomi wouldn't get away with murder. She'd pay for the five innocent lives she'd taken. Women serial killers were less common than their male counterparts, but were certainly not unheard of. Although, in Naomi's case, if they added in her deceased husband who "accidentally" fell off a cliff hiking six months prior, the body count rose to six. Bennett scru-tinized that a smarter killer would've purchased life insurance on the victim before shoving him to his death. However, if Ted Cavanaugh had discovered his wife's murderous secrets, that was motive enough for her to eliminate him.

Bennett closed his truck door and crept

through the brush toward the barn. He kept to the shadows, then hid behind Naomi's small bright turquoise transit van with massive daisies painted in primary colors, covering the vehicle's exterior. Magnetic signs in a shade of purple Bennett's grandmother called wisteria advertised *Friends of Foothills Tours* in flowery lettering, with several catchy hashtags and contact information. After spending days surveilling her vehicle, he'd see daisies in his dreams for months after he closed the case.

Bennett double-checked the magazine in his gun. Arresting Naomi as the Rocky Mountain Killer and her accomplices would propel his career to new levels. Not that he'd minded his past service with the Denver Police Department Narcotics Unit, but his position with the MCK9 task force was a step up. After his ex-fiancée's betrayal, Bennett was ready for more than chasing down local drug dealers like Roderick Jones. The criminal he'd started his narcotics career pursuing. Jones had eluded police at every turn. Now Bennett wanted more.

Contentious voices rose, growing louder.

Bennett scurried for the cover of a massive lilac bush and ducked down. Two large men, one wielding a gun and both wearing ski masks over their faces, walked behind Naomi.

Why would her accomplices hide their identities?

Something wasn't right.

Bennett dropped low, remaining out of sight.

"Don't move!" one of the guys shouted at her. "Turn around."

Naomi slowly faced the men, giving Bennett a perfect visual of the fear etched in her expression.

"Stop playing games!" the gun-wielding man hollered. "Where is it?"

"I... I don't know what you mean," she stammered, her eyes widened to the size of dinner plates. She kept her arms low, covering her pregnant belly.

By the sounds of it, her accomplices' arrival was unfriendly. She'd apparently made enemies in her revenge pursuit. No honor among criminals and all that. A twinge of conscience interfered with Bennett's judgmental thoughts. Still, he couldn't help but pity her unborn baby.

The two hoodlums threatening Naomi might buy her innocent act, but Bennett's skepticism argued otherwise. What was the *it* they wanted? Money? Drugs? Guns? He needed more information. Balance and timing were imperative. Closing in too soon risked stifling the creeps from unknowingly handing him the evidence to arrest the trio. Not moving fast enough could cost Naomi her life. Bennett refused to allow that to happen.

The other man stalked closer to Naomi, cracking his knuckles in an intimidation stance.

She backed up, cowering. She must be unarmed, or she'd surely brandish her weapon.

Bennett ground his teeth. Indignation at the ignorant brute's tactics overrode his curiosity at the situation. He would not tolerate watching two idiots hurt a woman.

Even if she was a killer.

But from his position, he wouldn't be able to get a clean shot without endangering Naomi.

"You're going to give it to us one way or the other," the gun-wielding man said.

"Please, you have me confused with someone else," Naomi pleaded.

"Where. Is. It?" he insisted in staccato grunts.

"I don't know what you're talking about!" Naomi cried.

Bennett trained his sights on the gun-wielding man while maintaining visual on the other. They stood too far apart for him to take them both out in a single shot. He had to make it count.

The other shifted as though uncomfortable with the action. "Maybe she doesn't know."

That surprised Bennett. *Hmm.* Unless he was trying to gain Naomi's trust. The tactic wasn't unheard of. Bad cop, good cop, or in this case, bad criminal, worse criminal.

"I promise I don't know what you're talking about," she said.

The man lifted his weapon.

Naomi shrieked and squatted.

Bennett moved forward.

Several consecutive blasts echoed across the open land as the man shot out the tour van's back window and rear tires. A flock of birds nesting in the tree above Bennett burst into flight, startling him.

"No!" Naomi screamed, ducking her head. "I'm nine months pregnant. If I knew, I'd give you whatever you want. Don't hurt me. For my baby's sake."

Her sincere concern for her unborn baby triggered Bennett's instincts. She truly either didn't know what the man wanted or couldn't tell him.

The situation had gotten out of control too

fast. "Police!" Bennett bolted from the tree line. "Put down your weapon!"

The men spun in a synchronized effort, facing Bennett, and the first fired at him.

Bennett dodged to the right, avoiding the hit, which spewed bark near his head. He rolled behind a large bramble and returned fire. The shooter's accomplice bellowed, indicating Bennett's bullet found its mark, though he couldn't be certain in the dark. The two ducked into the shadows between the barn and stable, disappearing from sight.

Bennett's gaze bounced between the fleeing men and Naomi—who was still his chief priority as the murder mastermind. She got to her feet and hurried off in the opposite direction.

Catching her and getting her to safety overrode the need to chase down her accomplices. The sound of an engine roared from behind Bennett as the men sped from the property.

"Stop!" Bennett sprinted after Naomi. "Police!"

Chapter Two

Naomi glanced over her shoulder. The stranger with a gun was getting closer. He claimed to be the police, but she couldn't believe anything after what had just happened.

She tried to increase her pace, but her body refused to cooperate.

He would catch her.

No. No. Her feet were heavy, sluggish, as though she moved through quicksand. She pushed through the trees, branches slapping at her face. Searching for a place to hide, she stepped over a log and her ankle twisted on the uneven ground, causing Naomi to stumble.

Like a bird taking flight, her widespread arms grasped for something to stop her fall and she landed hard against a prickly tree trunk. Her cheek scraped the rough bark, and she pushed back, attempting to right herself. Her breaths came out in short pants, and she visually sought her pursuer.

Where had he gone?

A glimmer ahead caught her attention, and she bolted forward. Drawing nearer, she spotted a Silverado, and she prayed the keys were inside.

Naomi hurried as fast as her feet and current state allowed. She reached the driver's side door and turned to see the man appear from the foliage.

"Stop! Police!"

Naomi slowed to catch her breath, though her mind screamed to keep moving. Regardless, her body was done. Unable to take another step, she leaned against the vehicle.

"Naomi! Don't move!" The man was at her side within seconds. "Why did you run?"

Her eyes roved from his hand to his face. "Because. You. Have a gun," she panted, then blinked. "How do you know my name?"

"I'm a cop," he said, still holding the pistol. He didn't elaborate on his comment, as though his title explained everything. "Don't move."

"Couldn't...if I...wanted," she replied.

He lowered the weapon but didn't put it away. With his other hand, he reached into his shirt neckline and withdrew a chain holding a leather pouch with a shiny badge. "Aside from being on the task force, I'm with the Denver

Police Department. Detective Bennett Ford."
He stepped back, and a sharp bark from inside
the pickup startled Naomi. "Are you okay?"

She turned, coming face-to-face with the
narrow snout and wide eyes of a small dog peering out from the driver's side window.

"That's Spike, my K-9," the detective explained. She looked up at a tall man with short
blond hair. His brown eyes were unreadable.

"Yes." She took a deep breath. "Just a little
shook up."

"Understandably so. Who were those men?"

"I have no idea." She shrugged. "Are they
gone?"

He seemed to study her. "Yes, but who knows
for how long. Before I put you into my truck,
I need to make sure Spike and I aren't in any
danger of you riding with us. Are you armed?"

"Of course not." She tugged the edges of her
pale blue cardigan around her belly.

"I have to pat you down—for your safety
and mine."

"What?" She narrowed her eyes, then gestured wide with her arms. "Is that really necessary?" As though she could hide anything under
her long tunic, sweater, and leggings.

"Yes, ma'am, it's protocol."

"Fine," she exhaled.

"You're not carrying any bazookas or flame throwers, are you?"

Despite the seriousness, a grin tugged at Naomi's lips at the silly question. "No, sir, just a baby boy. But he's also unarmed."

"Good. Please lift your hands above your head."

"I understand." Naomi complied, assuming the position she'd seen on TV. For a moment, she contemplated if that was a mistake. Would he assume she was familiar with the arrest process?

He respectfully patted her down and seemed satisfied she was unarmed. "Okay, let me help you up into the truck, and we'll drive over to check on your van."

Relieved he'd not associated her as one of the criminals, she said, "Thank you for saving my life, by the way."

"Glad I could help." He nodded curtly while offering a tight grin. "If those men return, we're exposed out here in the open."

Naomi hesitated, then inhaled deeply, finally catching her breath. "This doesn't look like a cop vehicle."

The pathetic argument provided her the opportunity to stall. What if he wasn't who he claimed to be? In a side glance, she spotted the badge still hanging around his neck.

"It's my personal truck. Hard to do surveillance in a patrol vehicle." He held out a key fob and pressed a button. Headlights beamed through the brush.

In the light, Naomi studied him. Tall, handsome, dressed in jeans, running shoes, and a long-sleeved T-shirt. Yet suspicion hovered in her mind. Except for the badge and gun, not much about Detective Ford appeared cop-like. She hesitated, determined to gather more information. "Wait, you said Denver PD? Why are you here?"

"That's what I'm hoping to talk to you about." He spoke calmly in a matter-of-fact manner.

"You're a little out of your jurisdiction," Naomi countered.

"Actually, I'm not." He stood, arms crossed, and she didn't miss the way his pose accentuated his biceps. "I'm a member of the Mountain Country K-9 Task Force."

Naomi tilted her head. "And what's that?"

"MCK9 is a special task force with a mission to take down the Rocky Mountain Killer, who has claimed the lives of innocent men from Elk

Valley." He spoke the words as though throwing down a gauntlet.

The effect worked, and she gasped. "Elk Valley?"

A glimmer in his eyes indicated his satisfaction, and she instantly regretted her reaction. "Familiar with the area?"

"Yes. I grew up there." A wave of nausea swirled in her stomach, and she swallowed hard. Desperate to steady herself and the ground spinning beneath her, she reached for the pickup.

"You look a little green. Let me help you."

She acquiesced, and he led her to the passenger side. The dog barked again, and she hesitated, unsure what to expect. Would an attack K-9 come lunging at her? Didn't cops have those German shepherds or Malinois-type dogs?

"First, I have to relocate Spike."

She stepped aside while he opened the passenger door. He turned, holding a beagle, who watched her with a curious expression. Totally not what she'd expected. "Aw, he's cute."

"He thinks so," the detective chuckled. "Spike, kennel."

Without hesitation, the beagle hopped into the steel kennel positioned in the back seat. Detective Ford offered his hand to help Naomi into the truck, then closed the door.

At least he hadn't handcuffed her.

He slid behind the wheel seconds later, speed-cleaning the set of folders and takeout bags on the floor. "Mind if I ask a few questions before I drive you to your van?" Detective Ford started the engine.

"First, I need more information. Like why you were here to begin with?" She glanced from him to the windshield, wondering how long he'd been there. "Were you watching me?"

"Yes." His answer came without hesitation or resignation. "It's a good thing I was here, or that incident might've had a much different ending."

"True." She couldn't argue with that logic. "Detective Ford, what's going on? Am I in trouble? I apologize for trespassing on private property. I came out of the barn when I heard the vehicle approaching. If they were family members of Peter—" *or the killer returning* "—I didn't want them assuming I was stealing or bothering anything." Aware of her rambling, Naomi searched for a justifiable reason to visit a murder scene. Although, learning the detective watched her explained the strange sensation she'd had earlier. Her mother always said, *Trust your instincts.*

"Those men are determined to get something from you," the detective said, refocusing her attention.

"I don't know what they wanted or what they were even talking about."

He quirked a disbelieving brow. "Let's start with why you're here?" He met her gaze, unrelenting.

Her neck warmed with embarrassment. "It's complicated."

"This is an active murder scene. Not exactly a tourist attraction. But then you're aware of that, right, Naomi?"

"You still haven't answered how you know my name."

He didn't respond.

Naomi surmised he'd ran her license plate, confirming the van was registered to her. A small measure of relief reassured her. "I assumed law enforcement had cleared the area since the yellow tape wasn't on anything. I apologize. I meant no harm." Naomi's ears warmed with embarrassment. "Is that why you're here?"

His expression remained stoic.

"Oh, wait." Naomi's hand flew to her mouth,

and she whispered, "Are you watching to see if the murderer returns?"

"Something like that."

She nodded.

"Let's head to your van." He drove out from the tree cover and approached the main road, then turned onto the Windham property.

"Do you think those men killed Peter?"

"I'm not sure." He shrugged. "What can you tell me about them?"

"Nothing." Naomi shifted in the seat, eager to go home and forget the terror of the night's events.

"Did you notify anyone you'd be here?"

Sadness swooped down on her. Who cared where Naomi went any day? "No, sir. No one else was aware I was coming here. Until I started heading home tonight, I didn't even know."

"It appeared like a last-minute move."

His words landed in her mind, slowly taking root, and she gaped at him. "How long have you followed me?"

"It's my job."

"How did I become your job?"

"Answer my questions first, and we can talk about the rest."

What a frustrating man! "I came here because Peter Windham was an old friend of mine, though we'd fallen out of touch over the years. Today, one of my tourist customers talked about how short life is, and I immediately thought of him."

"Are you having regrets?" He turned onto the lane leading to her van.

"No, not really." She glanced down at her hands. "I wish things had been different between us, though."

Why was he asking so many questions?

"Any idea why someone would hurt Peter?"

"No. He was a good guy. Peter always understood me," Naomi continued. "When I moved out here, Peter visited me, but I made it clear I wasn't interested in any reunions. I distanced myself from Elk Valley for a reason." She paused, pondering. "That was the great thing about Peter. He didn't press me or get offended. My husband was all I needed."

"My uncle says we all have enemies, and they're usually those closest to us."

Naomi shrugged. "I suppose."

"Did Peter have enemies?"

"I couldn't tell you."

"I disagree." He pulled up next to her van,

shifted into Park, then pierced her with a stare. "Tell me what happened. Did he say something to remind you of that horrible prank at the Young Ranchers Club dance ten years ago? If so, I understand why you did it."

"What are you saying?" Her brows knit together as she processed the information. "Are you implying I'm a suspect?"

"Should I be?"

"Of course not!"

"Aren't you tired of carrying all that weight? Talking to me is the only way I can help you."

"Help me what?" She leaned into the seat, pulse racing.

"Understand why you returned to the scene of the crime. Your crime."

"What?" Naomi blinked. "No. Peter was my friend. I was thinking about him and just came to…to… I can't explain why I'm here. I made a mistake."

"Let's end this game. Why did you kill him?" His question alluded to the confidence of already knowing the answer.

If not for the pain radiating up her back, Naomi might not have had the courage to snap at the detective, but her patience waned. "That's ludicrous!"

"Okay. Tell you what. Let's get out of here and see what damage they did."

Was he baiting her? She reached for the door handle. "Fine."

"Spike's been cooped up in here for a while. Mind if he takes a quick break with us?"

Whatever hurried this along. "Not at all." She climbed out before he reconsidered and continued interrogating her.

Detective Ford walked around the hood, approaching on her side. He opened the back door, snapped on a leash for the beagle, and then gently placed the dog on the ground. He left the engine running, headlights illuminating the area. "How about it, Spike? Ready for cookies?"

The beagle barked and wagged his tail.

Naomi watched the team, intrigued.

With a flashlight in hand, the detective and his dog surveyed the van's perimeter, inspecting the damage. Naomi trailed them. The beagle roamed to the full extent of his leash, sniffing the vehicle. Naomi paused at the rear of the van, gaping at the flat tires and shattered windows. What a disaster!

"This will cost me a fortune to fix." She

groaned, fighting back tears. "Not to mention, what do I drive in the meantime?"

"I'll call a tow truck and have it transferred to a repair shop." He watched his dog. "Do I have your permission to check your vehicle and the contents?"

His words traveled to her as though she were underwater, filtered and thick. She nodded, unable to speak beyond the lump in her throat. Besides, she had nothing to hide.

Spike turned, aiming for the rear tires.

"Where's he going?"

"Good question. Maybe looking for cookies." Bennett chuckled.

The beagle stopped next to the driver's side rear fender, barked twice, paused, and then barked once more.

Naomi blinked. What did that mean?

An expression clouded the detective's face, and her pulse quickened. "What's wrong?"

Detective Ford faced her, eyes dark. "My dog just alerted to the narcotics you hid in your van."

Bennett laser-focused on Naomi. She'd almost convinced him with her innocent act. The idea that the van held drugs seemed far-fetched at first, but his skepticism had won again. He'd surreptitiously instructed Spike to search for drugs, using the keyword *cookie* in their conversation. When he recognized his dog's heightened sniffer action near the van, Bennett was thrilled.

"You might've fooled me, but you won't fool him." He gestured toward Spike, who sat, tail wagging, anticipating his reward. "Good job." Bennett reached into his back pocket and withdrew the stuffed taco dog toy, tossing it to the beagle. Spike snatched it in midair, chomping gratefully.

"I'm telling you, I don't have any drugs," Naomi insisted. "You've checked me. Look through my purse in the van! You won't find anything!"

"Spike says otherwise."

"Well, no offense to your dog, but he's wrong."

"Negative." Bennett snorted. "Spike is never wrong. Let's start at the beginning. Are the narcotics what those thugs were after? Is that how you paid them to kill Peter?"

"What? No!" Naomi shook her head. "For the last time, I don't have any drugs on me. I'm not using them. I'm pregnant."

"I've seen too many drug-addicted mothers-to-be. Pregnancy doesn't exclude you. What are you dealing? Pills? Marijuana?"

"I don't know how else to say this. I'm not doing anything!" Naomi placed a hand against her back. She looked exhausted and worn out, but Bennett couldn't let her go now.

"Naomi, I am a narcotics detective, and my K-9 has the best certified nose in Denver. He alerted for a reason."

She spun on her heel, teetering a little off-balance.

"Careful." Bennett reached out a hand to steady her.

She glared at him as though she intended to refuse his help, but her skin had blanched, and she clung to his arm. He'd seen people faint when Spike found their drugs. The blood rushing through their system and the need to lie sometimes turned their legs into noodles.

"Now you'll accuse me of being high," she snapped. "But for your information, I didn't eat much today, so I'm sure it's just low blood sugar."

That might be true. She'd not stopped to have lunch in between tours. "Let's have you sit here while we figure this out." He helped her to a crate near the stable door. Bennett gazed at her tour bus. "Spike and I are going to search inside your van."

"I didn't agree to a second search."

"Don't need it. Once he's alerted I have probable cause."

Naomi sighed, saying nothing more.

"Please remain here until we're finished," Bennett instructed, keeping her in his visual but at a close enough proximity should she try to escape. "Normally, I'd handcuff you. I'm going to trust you'll stay there. Don't push me by doing something foolish."

She harrumphed, crossing her arms over her chest.

Bennett and Spike entered the van, and he spotted her purse on the passenger seat. He searched the bag, finding her wallet, two ten-dollar bills, a tube of lip balm, tissues and a package of peanut butter crackers. It was a long shot that she'd keep the 9 mm murder weapon linked to all the cases there, but hope reigned eternal.

Bennett knelt beside Spike. "I need your taco, buddy." The dog dropped the soggy toy to the ground. Bennett spoke in an excited tone. "Time to work! Find the cookies."

The beagle barked and wagged his tail.

"Okay, find the cookies!"

Spike sniffed the interior and alerted again by the rear fender.

Confirmation of the first signal.

He exited the van, meeting Naomi's curious gaze, then ordered Spike, "Stay. Guard."

The beagle took his position facing Naomi. He wasn't an apprehension or a guard dog, but she didn't know that.

Bennett rushed to his truck, withdrew a pair of latex gloves and donned them, then returned to the van. Lying face up, he examined the underside, sweeping his flashlight beam. He probed around the fender liner of the rear driver's side wheel and knocked. The resounding thud signified the normally empty space held something solid inside. Bennett felt around the undercarriage and liner until he located a small door. He lifted the well-disguised latch and found a hidden compartment. Adjusting the light, he inched closer and smiled at the box shape masquerading as part of the van's understructure. He'd seen a lot of narcotic hiding places in his enforcement years, but this was elaborate.

Bennett inserted his hand into the fender

well and withdrew two thick plastic bags. He scooted out from the vehicle and got to his feet, holding the object in his hands.

Naomi's mouth formed a perfect O, vehemently shaking her head as though that nullified his find. Satisfied, Bennett strode toward her, determined and angry. He'd almost bought her lies! He held up the bags. "Care to explain? This time, try the truth."

"I can't. That's not mine. I never put anything there."

Bennett illuminated the bags with his flashlight. Both contained a white crystal–like substance that he recognized as fentanyl. Likely illicitly manufactured and deadly.

He struggled to reconcile the evidence. The thugs had threatened Naomi, demanding their product. She could've used the drugs as payment for the hits on Peter and Henry. But why hide them? If she wasn't using the fentanyl as currency to pay off the men, was she dealing? Like his ex-fiancée, street distribution was the goal. Unless…she was muling it for someone else? He needed to get to the bottom of the mess, but it was a big detour from the RMK. "Let's finish this discussion at the PD. You'll have to come with me."

"What about my van?"

"Douglas County PD will impound it at their lot."

"Great." Naomi groaned. "How am I supposed to work, then?"

She either had a complete disconnect from what he'd just found, or she was in denial. He was about to arrest her, and she was worried about how she'd fulfill her commitments? Bennett stared at her, gathering his thoughts. She was probably due any day now, but she hadn't slowed down, based on her fourteen-hour, seven-days-a-week tours. Normally, Bennett would've viewed her tenacity as a strong work ethic.

But Naomi wasn't a sweet first-time mother-to-be.

She was a cold-blooded killer.

"Detective Ford, I realize you have no reason to believe me, but I promise you that the drugs aren't mine. I didn't even know they were in there." Naomi maintained her stunned response. "What is it? Cocaine?"

He exhaled an incredulous breath and assumed the cop pose—standing tall, feet shoulder width apart, arms crossed over his chest. "Don't insult my intelligence and yours by playing games with me. You're fully aware a crystal of fentanyl the size of a grain of salt is lethal!"

Naomi gasped, clamping a hand over her mouth. "How did it get under my tour bus? Am I in danger? Is your dog at risk from sniffing it?"

She seemed genuinely concerned. Would a heartless drug dealer be able to fake that?

"No, it's packaged well. Right?"

"I've got no idea."

"We won't take any chances." He moved to his vehicle and withdrew an evidence bag from the toolbox and placed the drugs inside. Bennett secured the evidence in the safe, removed his gloves and returned to where Naomi sat on the crate, holding her head in her hands.

"Naomi, this is your last chance to tell me the truth about it all."

"I can't."

Bennett had assumed she was a serial killer, not a drug dealer. Once more, he berated himself for almost falling for the lies of a beautiful woman. Were the drugs Naomi's actual source of income? Under-the-table dealings that made it appear she was broke on paper? Disdain flowed through him. The familiar situation reminding him of his drug-dealing ex-fiancée,

Delaney. "We'll have to finish this discussion at the PD." He reached out a hand, helping her to stand.

Her solemn expression combined with her slumped shoulders, and the exhaustion apparent on her attractive face tugged at a hidden part of Bennett's heart. A stray lock of her thick chestnut brown hair escaped her braid, and she tucked it behind her ear. She paused, placing a hand on the small of her back, clearly worn out. A twinge of sympathy threatened to expose Bennett, and he grunted, actively shoving it away. Sympathy was a weakness in his character that had cost him dearly with Delaney. He'd never go down that road again.

Not now.

Not ever.

Naomi Carr-Cavanaugh was a drug-dealing murderer.

Still, Bennett wondered if the guilt of her crimes weighed on her shoulders. Maybe she wasn't a complete psychopath. Regret for her actions might give her life in prison instead of the alternative. For the sake of her unborn baby, Bennett hoped that was true.

She gasped, gripping her belly. "This can't be happening."

Was she faking labor? Fat chance he'd buy that ruse. "Naomi, I need to read you your rights. You're being arrested for possession of a deadly, controlled substance."

"No. Wait." Her head snapped up, and her skin blanched. "It's not mine."

"Naomi Carr-Cavanaugh, you have the right to remain silent."

She gasped again, crying out in pain. Her knees buckled, and she plunged, digging her nails into his forearm. Her eyes pleaded with him. "Please take me." She heaved. "To the hospital." Another gasp. "I think I'm in labor."

Chapter Three

Naomi inspected the IV line that drooped from her arm. She watched the monitor, relishing the rhythmic beeps and lines reflecting her baby's fetal heart rate. Grateful for the private room, she closed her eyes and prayed for help from the mess that had become her life.

Two raps on the slightly open door preceded Bennett's entrance, ending her prayer time.

"Hey, how're you doing?"

If she wasn't mistaken, he almost appeared uncertain as he entered. Under any other circumstances, that might be touching. Except tonight, she was a suspect, and he was a cop.

"Better." She sat up and Detective Ford hurried to her side, helping to adjust the pillows behind her head. "The contractions are still strong. The doctor said I'm not effaced and only a centimeter dilated."

"It's been a long time since I did obstetric training. Dilate, I remember..." The confused expression on the handsome detective's face implied he needed clarification.

"I have a long way to go before delivery."

He blew out a long breath and pulled a chair closer to her. "Oh."

"They said they'd like to keep me for a while just to make sure. Oh." She gripped the handrails and breathed through the contraction.

He looked a bit overwhelmed and slightly helpless as she practiced her Lamaze breathing technique.

When it finally passed, she exhaled. "Whew!"

He lifted a plastic cup of water, handing it to her. "Has this happened before?"

"Contractions?"

He nodded.

"Nope, this was my first time. Of course, I'm also new to this pregnancy thing, so every event sort of happens unexpectedly." She took a sip, considering the personal feel of their conversation. If only she could forget she was a suspect. Facing him, she addressed why he sat beside her. "You have no reason to believe me, and I have no way to prove my innocence. I've never used—" she glanced past him to make sure the door was closed and whispered "—drugs."

He looked over his shoulder. "Why are you whispering?"

Her cheeks warmed. "It's embarrassing to have this discussion."

The corner of his lips tilted upward. Did she amuse him?

"Anyway, nor do I associate with anyone who uses them." She sniffed. "Who am I kidding? I don't associate with anyone outside of my tour customers, period."

"No friends?"

"Acquaintances, but nothing beyond that. After Ted's death, I buried myself in my job. I have bigger fish to fry, as they say." She rubbed her belly for emphasis. "This little man is my biggest and most important priority. I'd never endanger or risk losing him. Especially not for something like that."

"I don't say this lightly. I want to believe you, but your word isn't enough."

Naomi glanced past the detective, refusing to let her emotions take hold of her again.

"You're in possession of illegal narcotics. I cannot ignore that." He leaned back in the chair. "It's against protocol."

Naomi opened her mouth to protest, then closed it. "I understand." Wasn't the saying possession was nine-tenths of the law?

He tilted his head.

"Why are you looking at me that way?"

"Rarely do people surprise me, Naomi." He met her gaze, and for the first time, she noticed the light brown color of his eyes. "I expected a knock-down-drag-out fight with you."

"Sorry." She lifted her hands in mock surrender. "I'm too tired. The hits just keep on coming, and I'm running out of energy to battle the world, Detective Ford."

"At this point, let's shift to a first-name basis," he said. "Please call me Bennett."

"Bennett." She tried the name, concluding it fit him well. "Is that protocol?" she quipped.

"No, definitely not. Having my suspect go into labor while I'm trying to arrest her is new for me."

She offered him a slight grin. "Where is Spike?"

"They wouldn't let him in with me, so one of the hospital security guards was kind enough to take him until we're released."

"Oh, that was nice. But you don't have to stay here."

He guffawed. "Um, yes, I do. We have un-finished business."

"Right." She slid further down in the bed, warring with the urge to pull the blankets over her head and hide from her waking nightmare.

"I also called the Douglas County Sheriff's Department and requested they pick up your van. It'll be in their impound lot."

"Great." She rolled her eyes. "One more thing to pay for and deal with."

"Since we're killing time—" Bennett lifted one foot, resting it on his knee in a figure-four position "—let's discuss you and Peter."

"I was shocked and brokenhearted to learn of his...death." Naomi fidgeted with the blanket. "Sad too that we didn't talk more. He came to see me when I first moved here."

"Is he the reason you relocated to Denver?"

"No, this was my husband Ted's hometown." Naomi glanced at the baby monitor again. "When he brought me here to research ideas for our tour business, I fell in love with Colorado."

"I get that. I've seen beautiful places, but I was glad to be back on my home turf for this case." Bennett took another cup, pouring water from the plastic pitcher. "Kind of makes me protective of it."

Naomi nodded, unsure what he meant by the comment.

"You returned to Peter's ranch to reminisce about him?" Something in his question told Naomi he was fishing for more.

When she'd apparently taken too long to respond, he said, "I have assumptions, but I'd prefer your side of the story." His posture softened. "Naomi, I explained I'm with the MCK9 task force. We're searching for the Rocky Mountain Killer. The person responsible for the deaths of Seth Jenkins, Brad Kingsley, Aaron Anderson, Peter Windham and Henry Mulder."

"I still can't believe a serial killer murdered my former classmates."

"I'm sure you understand there are several common factors linking the cases. You were recent graduates of Elk Valley High School involved in the Young Ranchers Club, and you all attended the semiformal ten years ago."

"We weren't the only people fitting that criterion."

"Except you're the one cohesive portion."

"What?" Naomi's head whipped upward. "Why? I knew all the victims—past and present. That's no secret to anyone."

"Hey, I get why someone would think those

young men had it coming to them. What they did to you at the dance was incomprehensible. I can't even imagine the pain they caused you. The humiliation." Something in his eyes conveyed honesty in the statement.

"What they did was horrible and mean, but to retaliate by killing the people who bullied them?"

"Happens more than you'd believe."

"That was ages ago. I don't cling to the past."

"But they define us." Bennett leaned forward, elbows on his knees. "Experiences good and bad change us. Mine did."

What did that mean? "Experiences don't define our identity. They help us grow and learn. If we're willing. Are you a man of faith, Bennett?"

He hesitated. Was he reluctant to answer her or not willing to share anything about himself? Finally, he said, "Yes. But my faith has changed over the years, too."

"As it should. I believe God uses everything—good, bad, and indifferent—to mold our character. I trust Him to redeem even the bad stuff. I can't spend valuable time and effort nursing grudges and holding on to past anger."

"I suppose that's true. Except five of the individuals who were connected to the prank are dead. That goes beyond coincidence."

Unable to rebut that, she remained silent.

"How did you find out about Peter and Henry's murders?"

"I don't live in a cave," she said, tilting her head. "News travels fast with the internet, and my brother, Evan, still lives and owns a business in Elk Valley. He told me." She swallowed hard. "I was sad to hear about Henry. Nobody deserves to die the way they did. But Peter's demise hurt me the most. He was always kind to me."

"He wasn't on the night of the prank. A friend would've warned or protected."

Naomi looked down. "He didn't participate in the prank."

"That's a compassionate attitude."

"Peter and his friends went everywhere together. Acted like they're invincible, and all had reputations for dating multiple girls. Have you considered the possibility that they played pranks on other students, too?" Naomi's question seemed to hit home.

"It's possible," Bennett replied.

"Be assured, I've had more than enough excitement and difficulty over the past year that I don't need to invite trouble."

"Are you speaking of your husband's death?"

Naomi hesitated, momentarily taken aback by his obvious research into her life. "Yes. Losing Ted—" her voice cracked, but she quickly recovered "—and trying to keep up with the bills and our tour company while growing another human being is a lot."

He nodded. "Financial pressure is a reason for many crimes."

"I'm surviving."

"Here's my take on what happened. Those young men had to pay for what they did to you. The first three murders happened on Valentine's Day a year ago. You sent them the message, asking to meet at the barn, then took them out one by one."

"I did not!" Naomi bolted upright in the bed. "I don't own a gun. Check my alibi! I wasn't anywhere near the barn the night of Seth's, Brad's and Aaron's deaths."

"Hmm." He appeared nonplussed. Was he listening?

"Evan will vouch for me. I was home on Valentine's Day. He was there comforting me while I bawled my eyes out. I felt stupid for falling for the prank. I had a huge crush on Trevor Gage, and I was giddy when he asked me out.

I'd watched all the teen romance movies and naively assumed the dance would be the beginning of something wonderful between us. Evan stayed with me until he left to pick up his girlfriend, Paulina."

"Paulina Potter?" Bennett clarified.

"Yes, and they went on their big night out."

"That leaves a gap where you could've committed the murders."

Naomi fisted her hands. "I worked the late shift at the hospice in Elk Valley."

He withdrew a notepad from his shirt pocket. "What time was that?"

"Nine p.m. to two a.m. I was in a building full of nurses and patients that night. Check the records."

"That's helpful. Thank you."

His willingness to consider her alibi prompted Naomi to continue. "I was in ninety-nine-year-old Annie Perkin's room from eleven p.m. to one fifteen a.m." Naomi hadn't reminisced about Annie in ages. "Such a sweet lady." The details returned, motivating her to speak faster. "Her nurse came in at midnight to check her vitals. Annie pleaded for me to stay with her. She was dying and didn't want to be alone."

"What was her nurse's name?" Bennett's pen hovered over his notepad.

Naomi traversed her recollections. "Yvette Jacobsen. Annie had dozed off and Yvette stayed with me for a while. We talked about her son and his recent move to San Diego for college. Feel free to call her, too."

"Okay. We'll dig into that."

"See, that clears me and proves I didn't kill anyone."

"Well, it's an alibi for the first three murders, but not for those of Henry Mulder and Peter Windham." He tapped his pen against the notebook paper.

Several seconds ticked by before Naomi gaped at him. "Wait. Are you still implying that I killed Peter and Henry?" She gestured at her belly. "In my current condition? You must be kidding. Look at me!" She swept her arms wide. "I'm nine months pregnant. I'm a human duck waddling around. How would I murder two grown men?"

Bennett's tone remained calm. "You had cause, arguably justifiable cause for revenge, and realistically, physical strength isn't required to fire a gun."

"Again, I don't own a gun, nor do I know

how to use one." She fought to maintain a controlled persona. She'd not give the detective the satisfaction of seeing her fall apart at his questioning.

Bennett exhaled.

Naomi's heart thudded against her chest in frustration, and another contraction hit. She repeated the breathing exercises until it passed.

"I'm not here to upset you, Naomi. But without facts, like the alibi at the hospice, I have nowhere to look." He leaned forward again.

"Detective, I assume you've followed me for a while. Otherwise, I'm not sure how you found me at Peter's."

He held his place, one hand on the bed. "Yes."

"Then you're aware I work from sunrise to sunset. Once I finish my tours, I'm exhausted and every part of my body hurts. Hauling and growing another human requires substantial effort." Naomi wrapped her hands over her belly.

"I can't argue those facts."

"Not that I'd expect you to understand. I don't have the time, energy or inclination to hunt down people from my past." Naomi sat up. "Check my tour bus records. I use a computer application." She spelled the name of the program, providing the login and password for him.

Bennett wrote the details in his notebook.

"You'll see I've had a full schedule for months. I don't get time off, and even if I did, I can't afford to take it." She sucked in a breath and paused.

He met her gaze, concern etching his forehead.

"My husband cleaned out my bank accounts, and I have yet to find the money. I must work for a living, which impedes on my opportunities to commit murder. Therefore, I am not the serial killer you're seeking."

"I appreciate your candidness." Bennett pocketed the notepad and sat back. Was he finished interrogating her? "Should I call someone to let them know you're here?"

"You mean as in my one phone call when you book me?" She'd meant the statement sarcastically, but it fell flat.

If she hadn't imagined it, he almost seemed to cringe.

"I'll save it for calling my brother if and or when that becomes necessary."

He nodded. "Tell me about your brother, Evan? Does he visit often?"

Apparently not. "He comes to visit me twice a year." Naomi shrugged. "Evan's the best. Every little sister probably says that. We've never been especially close. Since the death of our folks, even seeing him is hard on me. Without those connections to my past, I can forget parts of the pain and loss. But each of those reminders makes it all fresh."

"Did you receive the invitation to the Elk Valley High reunion?"

"Yes. Why?"

"I imagine receiving that brought back those old memories. Created the catalyst for finishing off the men who hurt you. You were all graduates of Elk Valley High."

Naomi's patience waned. "As I explained, Detective, I have bigger things on my mind than taking revenge for a stupid prank at a dance." She turned away. "It's been a long day and I'm exhausted. I'd like to rest."

"Sure." He stood. "I'll play it straight with you, Mrs. Carr-Cavanaugh. You had motive, opportunity and means. The MOM method, as we'd say."

The acronym seemed especially cruel now. "Detective, that's true of a lot of people. If you had evidence, you wouldn't waste time following me. Now, with all due respect, sir, either arrest me or let me sleep." She didn't wait for him to respond. She rolled over, facing the baby monitor machine, and closed her eyes.

Bennett shut Naomi's door softly behind him and walked toward the waiting room at the far end of the hall. Relieved to enter the empty space, he sat positioned with a good visual of Naomi's door.

"Might as well make some more calls," he mumbled, glancing down, half expecting to see Spike. Talking to himself appeared less strange when his K-9 partner accompanied him. Bennett chuckled, withdrew his phone and dialed the MCK9 teammate tech specialist, Isla Jimenez.

She answered on the second ring. "Hey, Bennett."

"How's it going?"

"Depends on what we're discussing."

Bennett assumed Isla referenced the foster parent approval process she was enduring. At their last discussion, she'd told him there was an infant they were placing with her. "Any word on when you'll get the baby?"

"Not yet. I'm grateful for the busyness of

this case to keep me occupied. Otherwise, I'd spend every waking moment biting my nails and walking on pins and super-excited-can't-wait-for-the-phone-to-ring needles."

"I'm sure it'll happen soon." Bennett grinned at the enthusiasm in her voice. "You must be their poster child candidate for what a great foster parent should be."

"I pray you're right." Isla laughed. "What's up?"

"So much I'm not sure where to start. I have interesting information to share about Naomi Carr-Cavanaugh." He paused, considering how differently her name sounded on his lips than it had in the beginning. The one-dimensional cardboard Naomi had become three dimensional. When had that happened?

Knock it off, Ford. He shook off the thoughts. No. She remained a suspect until they confirmed or destroyed her alibis for the murders. Thus, the need to involve Isla.

"Ready when you are." Her voice prompted him, reminding Bennett he'd stalled too long.

"Here's the rundown." He withdrew the notebook where he'd written the details Naomi provided.

"Bring it on."

Bennett conveyed Naomi's story about sitting with the hospice patient on the night of the first murders. "I could be wrong, but it seems plausible. She was confident Yvette Jacobsen would corroborate her alibi."

"Should be easy to verify that information," she replied, and tapping filled the line. "I'll check the hospice facility records and get back to you."

"There's more," Bennett replied. "She claimed to run a full tour bus schedule since before Ted's death. If that's true, she also has an alibi for the last two homicides."

"Hmm, any chance she told you which online scheduling program she uses?"

"Yes." Bennett read off the details.

"That's an older app. Stand by." More tapping. "I'll dig into the calendar and contact her customers to verify they were on her tours at the times of the homicides," Isla confirmed. "I'll be in touch."

After they'd disconnected, Bennett called FBI Wyoming Bureau supervisory special agent Chase Rawlston, the appointed leader to the task force. "Hey, Bennett."

"It's been an adventurous night." Bennett launched into a detailed but concise synopsis of the evening, including the shooting, Spike's drug find and the events leading up to the hospital visit.

"You went from zero to sixty in a single night," Chase replied. "How is Naomi doing?"

"They have her in a private room, monitoring the contractions. Apparently, she's not effaced or dilated, which means she won't deliver soon. The doctor wants to keep her for a while to make sure."

Chase chuckled. "You're getting an education in obstetrics."

"Affirmative." Bennett dropped into a chair. "I planned to cite and arrest her for possession, but then she started having contractions, and now we're at the hospital."

"Understandable," Chase said.

"There's more. She has reasonable alibis for all the murders. Isla's checking out the details, but I've got doubts about her involvement as the RMK."

"Put a pin in that until Isla contacts you," Chase replied. "Regardless, her alibis don't explain the drugs."

"Agreed, and I'm not inclined to just let that go, but I'm struggling to reconcile the chain of events."

"You're doubtful the drugs belong to Naomi?" Chase asked.

"I don't know." Bennett leaned back in the seat and ran a hand over his hair. Chase knew his history with Delaney, so he was grateful he didn't need to explain that or his hesitancy to trust his instincts. "I can't tell you how many times someone's claimed they're holding drugs for a friend or relative. Or they plead ignorance. Something is different about her."

"Talk it out with me."

"If she's the RMK, why drive to the crime scene with narcotics? That's a risky move all by itself."

"Or Naomi drove there to heighten the thrill of getting away with murder. She celebrated by meeting her accomplices to deliver the fentanyl."

"True." Bennett paused. "Why not meet them in a clandestine place? For the record, I'm not convinced those men were working for or with her. They both wore ski masks. Why hide their identities?"

"Yeah," Chase grunted. "That's strange."

"Exactly. And get this, she blushed and whispered the word *drug* as though she was worried someone might overhear her."

"That's easily explained. She is in the hospital, pregnant and close to delivery," Chase responded. "She's right to worry a nurse would eavesdrop on the conversation, putting her in danger of losing custody of her baby."

"I hate when you're logical," Bennett said. Once more, he'd lost focus. Another perfect example of why he needed his team to keep him unbiased.

"Nah, you're in the thick of the investigation. Helps to talk it out and gain some perspective," Chase replied. "Sometimes the logic is right in front of us. Other times, it's masked by circumstances."

Or Bennett's inability to read through the lies spoken by a beautiful woman. "I'd feel better if more of the details added up, especially regarding the drugs."

"Unless the shooters trailed you trailing Naomi. Doubtful since they didn't try to take you out before attacking her. How'd they know she'd be there?"

"Can't argue that." Even though he wanted to. "There's something more going on here. If she is the RMK, the drugs are important but not the goal." Bennett ran a hand over his head. "Would you allow me to release her for medical reasons with the citation for possession while we run the bags for DNA and fingerprints?"

"Approved. I don't see Naomi as a flight risk."

Bennett exhaled relief, though he wasn't sure why. Didn't he want to arrest Naomi? No, he wanted to take down the RMK. Stopping any distribution of fentanyl was important, but not the goal. Either way, he wouldn't fall for another innocent woman act. She remained a suspect he was keeping a close eye on. That was all. "Thanks."

"Get the evidence transferred to Isla ASAP, and we'll find out what's going on," Chase said.

"With your permission, to expedite results, I respectfully request utilizing local resources to process the evidence. I've got a great contact at a Colorado lab here that the Denver PD uses."

"As long as your highest priority is maintaining a tight chain of custody," Chase replied. "And include Isla in all communication."

"Roger that. Douglas County is the responding agency for the Windham Ranch incident. I'll follow up with them as soon as we disconnect. I want Spike to go through Naomi's vehicle again to confirm we didn't miss anything the first time." Bennett couldn't shake his skepticism that Naomi faked the contractions to prevent him from finding more drugs.

"Good plan. Keep me updated."

Talking with Chase triggered something in the back of his mind about Naomi's involvement. Once Denver PD tested the bags for DNA or fingerprints, he'd feel better. If she'd hidden the fentanyl, he doubted she'd bothered to do so wearing gloves. Additionally, if they found her fingerprints on the bags, he'd have more evidence to prove she was dealing drugs.

"Is that everything you needed to tell me?"

"I think so," Bennett replied.

"My turn," Chase said. "Should've looped you in sooner, but things are hectic on this end, too."

Bennett's full attention shifted to his boss.

"Cowgirl is missing."

"Say again?" Bennett gaped at the phone, unsure he'd understood Chase. The cute Labradoodle had been gifted to the task force to train as an emotional support dog for their investigation.

"Liana was outside with Cowgirl in the training center. She thought she heard gunfire and turned to look for a shooter. Liana called for backup, and when she finished talking to the dispatcher, Cowgirl was gone. She saw a man in black running away, but he vanished into the woods."

"Unbelievable. Why take her?" Bennett muttered. "Didn't Liana hear her barking?"

"We're not sure exactly what happened. Liana's taking full responsibility. There's no way she could've predicted this would happen. Cowgirl never barked, at least not to Liana's recollection. But that's not a surprise. She loves everyone."

"Oh, wow." Bennett thought about his teammate, Ashley Hanson, a cop in Elk Valley and the youngest member of the MCK9 task force. An emotional support dog had been Ashley's great idea, and her dad, an FBI bigwig in DC, had gifted her to the team. "How's Ashley holding up?"

"She's determined to find Cowgirl, like the rest of us."

"Is there anything I can do?" Why hadn't they told him sooner? Team communication was essential.

"We've searched the area and have feelers out for any sightings to be reported straight to the MCK9 task force. It's a local job, and that's part of the reason I didn't race to tell you." Chase's comment answered Bennett's unspoken question. "I need your undivided attention focused on Naomi and the investigation there. Selena and Kyle are returning to Colorado to assist in the investigation. They'll be in touch soon. Between all of you, I'm hoping we'll find what we need to stop the RMK from taking any more lives."

"Affirmative."

Once they'd disconnected, Bennett glanced down at his phone and sent a silent prayer for Cowgirl's quick and safe return. He called the Douglas County Sheriff's Department. The dispatcher provided him a case number and connected him directly to the deputy assigned to Naomi's van.

"Deputy McClintock," she answered on the second ring.

"This is Detective Bennett Ford with the Mountain Country K-9 Task Force. I was advised you're handling the processing of evidence from the Windham shooting incident."

"Yes, sir. Sorry for the delay in getting out there. It's been a busy day."

"Understandable. I'm at the hospital with the owner of the van," he said. "Would it be possible to get an update?"

"Not much to share. I handled the transportation and impounding of Mrs. Carr-Cavanaugh's vehicle. The shooter did quite a number on it. Other than severe cosmetic damage, strangely, it's still running. We've also collected casings."

"I appreciate that." The deputy's response sounded a little dramatic compared to what he'd seen, but then maybe she'd not had as much experience with shootings as he had over the years. "Would you please transfer the evidence to my contact at Denver PD? He'll handle the processing for our team."

"Absolutely."

Bennett provided Deputy McClintock DPD's crime lab technician Eduardo Gomez's information. "I'd also like to have my K-9 go through the van again once the doctor releases Mrs. Carr-Cavanaugh."

"Not a problem. Just advise the case number and show your credentials to the guard at the entrance if I'm not here."

"Thank you."

Bennett disconnected and got to his feet. He strolled through the hallway, where cheerful baby decorations filled the space. When he reached Naomi's door, he rapped softly. He got no response and gently pushed open the door.

Naomi lay on her side, eyes closed, breathing evenly.

He retreated and walked back to the empty waiting room. His cell phone vibrated as he sat down.

Isla's contact information popped up on his screen.

The moment of truth.

Bennett swiped to answer. "What do you have for me?"

Chapter Four

Naomi glanced around the hospital room, relieved she was alone, then checked her cell phone on the bed table. She'd napped for more than an hour. No sign of the detective. Good. Maybe Bennett Ford had gone home and given her a reprieve from his incessant interrogation.

Ted's appreciation for nonstop crime shows made her wary of the detective's antics. He'd been tough with her, then befriended her, intending to bait Naomi into confessing she'd killed Peter and the others. She'd recognized his unrelenting determination, etched like the rigid lines in his expression. He believed Naomi was a murderer. After the fact, the urge to remain silent and contact a lawyer had occurred to her. She'd probably talked too much in her resolve to set the record straight.

How did I get into this mess, Lord?

Tears threatened. She'd faked sleep in a cowardly effort not to face her accuser when the detective had returned to her room. After all she'd endured in the past six months, this was one more thing to deal with, and she didn't have the energy.

The fetal heart rate monitor chimed softly, filling Naomi with worry. If Ford arrested her, what would happen to her son?

As soon as the detective mentioned the Elk Valley High School reunion, Naomi discerned what had drawn her to Peter's ranch. Zoe Jenkins's invitation. A part of Naomi wanted to attend, but only as an observer. The greater temptation was to light the invitation on fire and pretend she'd never received it.

Without her consent, Naomi's thoughts traveled to the night of the dance and the incident Detective Bennett claimed gave her the motive to kill. She'd fallen prey to Trevor Gage by her own childish, impossible crush. How ridiculous to believe the town's golden boy would want anything to do with someone like her. But when Trevor asked her to the dance, she'd practically jumped out of her skin with delight. She'd spent all day getting ready and arrived with stars in her eyes. Until Trevor's pack humiliated her and she'd run home crying. Her only happy memory of that night was Evan's attempts to console her.

She thought about the note the killer had left stabbed in their chests. Didn't it say something about how they deserved it? Trevor's despicable friends had triggered someone's murderous hatred. Except sweet, thoughtful Peter wasn't like them. Whether he'd participated in the prank to any degree, and she doubted he had, he was her friend. She'd preferred his company over the snobby girls who befriended her, only to reject her on a dime.

Naomi caught her reflection in the fetal monitor, revealing the rat's nest her hair had become. She pushed herself upright in the bed, tugged off her hair tie and then finger-combed the strands. Another unwelcome memory returned, reminding Naomi of an incident in the school bathroom. She normally avoided going in when the cheerleaders were there, but they'd come in after her, and she was cornered. One of them, whose name escaped Naomi's mind, had rudely suggested Naomi color her hair to get rid of the "mousy bland brown" to blond or red. Until that moment, Naomi had liked her hair. When she told her mother about the comment, she'd brushed her long locks, cooing about the color, soft and tawny, like a fawn. Sorrow constricted Naomi's heart.

She gasped at little man's impatient kick to the ribs. "You're right. That was a long time ago." Her hand gently stroked the place where her infant's foot pressed against her skin. "Thank you for the reminder, Lord," she prayed aloud.

Talking with the detective reactivated too many buried memories that refused to be ignored. She'd never regretted moving away from Wyoming and starting a life in Colorado with Ted. Even with the assortment of abundant troubles toward the end of their marriage, she was grateful for the pleasant years they'd had before things spiraled downhill. She'd cling to those and not the sad parts. As Daddy would've said, *Too much hindsight masks the future in could've-beens.*

Her thoughts shifted to the last couple from her evening tour. They were kind, as Naomi imagined her parents would've been, had the car accident not cut their lives short. They'd regaled her with tales of their eight children and fifteen grandchildren. The woman had shared excruciating details of delivering each of her babies. Naomi grinned. She could have done without that.

It happened more often than not. Strangers found it necessary to share their gruesome birthing experiences and attempted to rub her belly while she was standing in line at the store. As though she wore a giant sign with Pet Me on it.

Naomi chuckled softly. She loved talking with her customers. Since Ted's absences were masked as busyness at first, then marital separation and subsequent death, the silence in her home was deafening. "You'll fix that, though. Won't you, sweetie?" She cooed, rubbing her taut belly.

Her son wriggled in agreement with two quick kicks. "Come on, little man, I know you're squished in there but that's not fun for mommy."

Soon, the months of loneliness would end, and she'd hold her precious gift from God. Tears stung her eyes. Unless Detective Ford arrested her for murder and charged her with possessing illegal narcotics.

Why would someone hide drugs in her van? If she couldn't get the detective to listen to her and search for the truth, how would she convince him of her innocence? Would the charges alone cost Naomi her baby? The tour bus company? Would she lose her license?

Naomi's pulse increased, and the fetal monitor beeped, reminding her of the urgency.

Her life had spun out of control.

The door opened, jolting her to the moment. An unfamiliar man entered, then pushed the door closed. He was tall, and the white doctor's jacket he wore over blue scrubs seemed too tight against his husky stature. He wore bulky, dark-rimmed glasses. A surgical mask covered the lower half of his face, but the menacing look in his dark eyes bore through Naomi. A small scar trailed over his left eyebrow, deep and thick.

Her instincts blared. This was no doctor.

Naomi gasped, leaning hard against the pillow. Her hand slapped at the bed coverings, seeking the call button remote.

At last, her fingers grazed the thick cord.

The device hung on the side of her bed.

Out of reach.

Naomi maintained eye contact with the intruder while inching the remote closer. It thwacked the bed rails, demanding his attention.

"I wouldn't do that if I were you." He closed the distance between them in two long strides.

"What…what…do you want?" Naomi's stammered question exposed her fear.

"Only what belongs to me." The man's voice was a deep growl, vicious and terrifying. He stepped closer, blocking her escape, and lifted his hand. The light bounced off the large blade he produced from his doctor's jacket. "Scream, and it'll be the last sound you ever make."

Naomi swallowed hard, instinctively moving her hands to cover her belly.

A rapping on the door caught their attention. The man spun as though unsure what to do. He backed up, placed a finger against his lips and ducked into the bathroom, hidden from sight.

Naomi was certain he was watching.

Another rap on the door.

"Come in," she squeaked.

The kind nurse who had spent most of the visit attending to Naomi entered, leaving the door ajar. "Time for another check. If you haven't made any progress, the doctor will release you. Then you can chalk this adventure up to Braxton-Hicks contractions."

Naomi's throat went dry. How could she warn the nurse without endangering them both?

In response to her unspoken question, she spotted the man surreptitiously slipping out of the room, undetected.

★ ★ ★

Bennett exited the restroom and dodged to the right to avoid colliding with a young man sprinting around the corner. "Whoa," Bennett said.

"Sorry. I'm looking for room 242. They admitted my wife already and it's our first baby and I'm all turned around." The man's rapid-fire speech paused for a second.

"It's behind you. The numbers go up from here. You want the other hallway." Bennett gestured to the closed double doors separating the hospital's new wing.

"Great. Thanks." The man spun on his heel and hurried past Bennett.

After making a ridiculous number of laps around the waiting area to force himself to stay awake, Bennett had the hospital layout memorized.

He walked toward Naomi's room. He'd done his best to give her the rest she'd needed. The last thing he wanted was to be the reason she went into early labor. He reached Naomi's door, nearly colliding with the on-call female doctor approaching from the hallway to his left. "Hi there. I'm headed in to examine Mrs. Carr-Cavanaugh."

Bennett wasn't sure what that entailed, but he felt confident Naomi wouldn't appreciate him intruding in on that moment. "Oh, I uh…" Words failed him.

"You can come in with me or wait until she's finished, whichever you're more comfortable with," the doctor said.

Grateful for the excuse, he replied, "I'll wait out here."

"No problem. I'll wave you in when I'm done."

Bennett took the opportunity to call Isla while observing Naomi's door. Not that he'd expected the shooters to follow them to the hospital, but instincts said to remain vigilant.

He dialed Isla's number. "What's up, Bennett?"

"I'm killing time and thought I'd check in. Any progress on confirming the alibis?"

"I'm close. So far, she checks out, but I should have it completed by this evening," Isla replied. "Just waiting for the hospice records to come through. Talk soon."

The line disconnected before Bennett responded. He glanced at the phone. That wasn't like Isla, but he'd swamped her with information. Add that to the RMK investigation and

Cowgirl's missing status, and Isla's shortness was explainable.

From the end of the hall, Bennett spotted the doctor waving him over. "All finished."

He rose and went to Naomi's room, rapping on the door.

"Come in," Naomi called.

He entered to find her fully dressed except for her shoes. "They're springing you, huh?" As soon as the words escaped his lips, he longed to erase them.

Naomi's eyes widened, and she swallowed hard. She looked as though she wanted to respond, but the nurse returned with discharge orders in her hand. "You're a free woman."

Ugh. They'd both chosen the wrong words.

Naomi averted her gaze. "I'm embarrassed."

"Don't be, honey. I had awful Braxton-Hicks contractions with my first. They'll tell you they're just uncomfortable." The nurse grunted good-naturedly. "Not hardly. Enough to bring me to my knees." She winked at Naomi, then addressed Bennett. "Make sure she drinks lots of water and gets plenty of rest." She patted him on the shoulder. "I'm sure you'll be wonderful parents." She exited the room.

Bennett's face warmed.

"Sorry," Naomi whispered. "I didn't know what to say when they assumed you were my husband."

Husband. It had been a long time since he'd even entertained the thought of sharing his life with someone. He studied Naomi, and though he had reason to be irritated, he wasn't. What was wrong with him? "It's fine. Easier than saying I'm your arresting officer."

"Right."

He helped her with her shoes. "I have good news and bad news."

Fear complicated her inquisitive expression. "Okay."

"Good news first, my commander has authorized me to cite you for possession with a medical release."

"Guess that's better than going to jail."

"I'll give you a ride home." He wasn't taking any chances she'd try to get into her van.

"What about my van?" she asked as though reading this mind.

"That's the bad news. Douglas County Sheriff's Department impounded it, and it's too late to get in there tonight."

"I'll cancel my tours for tomorrow." Naomi

hung her head. "I'll have to refund everyone's money unless I can get Addy to cover for me."

"Who is that?"

"Adeline Everett owns Mile High Town Tours." Naomi exhaled. "My competitor."

Bennett wrote the name on his notepad, intending to ask Isla to follow up on it later. "Are you friends?"

"Sort of," Naomi replied. "More like frenemies. It's a complicated relationship."

"How so?"

"We offer the same services and comparable prices, which puts us on opposite ends of the competitive spectrum." She tilted her head. "At the same time, she's the perfect one to help in situations like this. And we've worked out an agreement for when the baby comes."

Bennett considered the information. Would Addy have reason to eliminate Naomi's business? "Does she get all the profit? She'll be doing the work, but she's also getting your customers."

"Most of the profit. We agreed on an eighty-twenty split." Naomi shrugged. "It's better than nothing when I'm unable to work."

The agreement didn't seem fair to Bennett. Addy was taking advantage of Naomi's vulnerability, especially if she'd booked the tours prior. But what did he know about the tour business? He quirked a brow and tucked the notepad into his pocket.

Bennett might sympathize with Naomi, except he wasn't the one who'd hidden illegal drugs. "I need to pick up Spike," he said, diverting the conversation before he offered to comfort a possible criminal. He held open the door, allowing her to exit first.

Then he led her down the hallway to the elevators.

"Can I go with you?" Naomi's demeanor had changed. She seemed skittish, hugging her purse close to her body.

"Of course. Is something wrong?"

"What? Why?" She spun to look behind her.

"Because you're a little jumpy."

What had happened in the time she'd spent in her room? Had she had nightmares? Did the person she was holding the drugs for contact her? Irritation wove through him. He'd considered the possibility of her innocence in this mess. Once more, he was wrong.

They wordlessly walked to the security office on the main level. A large sign posted on the closed door instructed them to push the buzzer for assistance. Bennett depressed the button, which emitted a horrendous buzz that must've startled Naomi, because she jerked and bumped into him with an apologetic grimace.

A speaker beside the door crackled to life. "Security."

"Detective Bennett Ford."

A click announced the lock had released. Bennett turned the knob and pushed the heavy door open. Naomi shifted close behind him. Spike lounged on the loveseat at the far side of the office. At Bennett's entrance, the beagle jumped up on all fours, wagging his whole body.

Bennett couldn't contain his smile. "Hey, buddy."

"Detective," the security officer greeted from his seat in front of a series of computer monitors.

Bennett struggled to remember the guy's name. Ben? Bert? He shifted to the side, glimpsing the badge. Bill Nolice. "Thanks again."

"It was a joy." Nolice smiled broadly.

Spike rushed and jumped into Bennett's outstretched arms.

Nolice chuckled. "He's happy to see you."

"The feeling's mutual." Bennett set Spike down and snapped on his leash.

The stout man rose, keeping one hand on the chair. "I enjoyed his company."

"He's great if you don't have drugs on you." Bennett ruffled the dog's fur, catching Naomi's wince in his peripheral vision. Stuck between feeling like a heel and the satisfaction of reestablishing their roles, he averted his eyes. "Let's get going."

"Have a good night." Nolice offered Naomi a nod.

She returned a tired half smile.

They exited the security office and walked silently to where his pickup was parked.

Once they'd driven away from the hospital, Naomi said, "I need to tell you something."

At last, she'd confess. "Okay." Bennett slowed and pulled the truck over to the side of the road.

"No! Keep going!" Naomi twisted around to look behind them. "He might follow us."

"Who?"

"Drive and I'll talk."

Bennett accelerated.

"A man threatened me in my room."

Bennett slammed on the brakes, stretching his right arm to cover Naomi in an involuntary protective maneuver. "What?" He searched the parking lot and road for any approaching vehicles.

"Not here. It was before the doctor released me." Naomi waved her arms. "Go!"

Against his better judgment, Bennett continued driving from the hospital. "You should've told me sooner!"

"Why didn't you stop him from getting into my room?"

Bennett's head snapped back from the verbal slap. "I watched your room the entire time we were there. The only distraction I'd had was almost getting run over by a soon-to-be-dad."

Understanding poured over Naomi's face, illuminated by the truck's interior dashboard lights.

"Please start from the beginning."

"I awoke right before a man entered my room. He wore scrubs and a doctor's coat, and a mask covered his mouth. There was a big thick scar over his left eye. I didn't suspect anything until he got closer. I could feel hate rolling off him in waves." Naomi exhaled. "He held a knife. He warned me not to make a sound and demanded I give him 'what belongs to him.' Then the nurse knocked on the door. He hid in the attached bathroom. I was terrified he'd burst out and stab her!" Naomi's words ended on a quivering note.

Bennett reached a hand to comfort her. She'd put someone else's life ahead of her own?

"I'm sorry." Her voice trembled. "I wasn't sure if he'd stayed at the hospital watching us. I wanted to get out of there alive."

"We'll need to review the hospital security footage." Bennett pulled over and called Isla.

"I don't know if we've ever talked this many times in one day," Isla said, but the teasing words didn't match her sharp tone.

"Hey, is everything okay?"

"No. We'll talk later. What's up?"

Concern for his teammate had Bennett pausing, but he wouldn't press her with Naomi freaking out beside him. "I need to get access to the security footage from the hospital." He relayed the information Naomi had shared, including the description of the intruder. "Also add Adeline Everett to your background search. She's a colleague of Naomi's."

"On it."

"Thanks."

They disconnected, and Bennett shifted

into Drive. "I wish you'd told me all of this at the hospital."

"I was scared and seriously considered running away, except you'd have labeled me a fugitive serial killer slash drug dealer." She gave him a weak smile.

"I'm glad you didn't run. And this explains why you were so jumpy."

Naomi didn't cease to surprise him, but anger at his ineptness in missing the intruder's appearance boiled his blood.

Naomi's voice trembled. "He threatened to kill me and demanded his stuff."

Bennett wanted to reprimand her for withholding the information, but her justification made sense. "Wait, what did you say?"

"He said he wanted what belongs to him."

"Do you think he meant the drugs in your van or something else?" An icy shiver trickled down Bennett's back. Had he recovered everything from the van? Or was there something more hidden there? And if so, what?

"That's what I'm assuming."

Bennett checked the dashboard clock. The impound lot was closed. Surely, someone guarded the premises. One look at Naomi, and the exhaustion she wore concerned Bennett. He couldn't drag her out there at this hour, anyway. "Naomi, please use my phone to call Deputy McClintock and put it on speakerphone."

She did as he asked. The deputy answered on the third ring, sounding less than pleased with his late-night interruption. "Deputy Mc-Clintock."

"I apologize for calling at this time of night, but there's been a recent development in the case I'm working on. Does the impound lot have twenty-four-hour security?"

"Yes, both a full-time guard and security cameras."

"My K-9 and I will go over the van first thing in the morning."

"I'll notify the guard."

"Thank you," Bennett said.

Naomi took the phone and swiped to hang up. "What're you thinking?"

"I want to find anything left in the van before they do."

Chapter Five

The ride to Naomi's home was silent for many reasons. None of which helped her current predicament if she bothered striking up a conversation.

"It's the end building." Before Naomi finished speaking the words, Bennett had already headed in the direction where she'd pointed. Of course, he was familiar with the area if he'd followed her. Irritation rose within her at the realization.

He parked in front of her two-story townhome. A bright colorful wreath decorated with plastic Easter eggs hung askew on the front door. As if seeing the decoration for the first time, Naomi realized the holiday had passed two weeks ago. She'd come and gone, scarcely noticing it or the fact that a detective had surveilled her. Her extended work hours had melted into one continuous day, making them indistinguishable from one another.

Bennett shut off the engine and faced her. "I need to leash Spike before we head inside."

Naomi didn't argue. It was pointless to do so. More than likely, he wanted the beagle to search for narcotics. Whatever. She didn't have any drugs in her house beyond ibuprofen and prenatal vitamins. Let him look to his heart's content.

Until he'd found the bags stashed in her van, the possibility that someone would hide them there had never crossed her mind. However, she didn't have a garage, so she parked her vehicle in front of her house. Anyone could've accessed it. Right? Her home was different. It was a safe place. Her solace. Nobody would put drugs there for safekeeping.

Bennett slid from the driver's seat and released Spike while Naomi exited the vehicle. The contractions had stopped, but her exhaustion was tenfold from before the shootout at Peter's ranch.

She exhaled in relief at finally being home. Might as well enjoy the freedom until Detective Ford arrested her. As Naomi strode toward the front door, the baby resumed his ninja moves. She chuckled, relishing how it grounded her.

Naomi placed her hand over her son's tiny foot, which was still kicking. *Thank you, Lord, for this beautiful reminder of Your presence in my life.*

Bennett and Spike caught up with her. "Are you okay?"

"Yes, little man was on the move again."

"Good to hear." Bennett offered her a hand as she stepped onto the sidewalk from the parking lot.

To an outsider, the duo might appear protective. Instead, she recognized Bennett's motives for keeping her close. Sadness hovered like a fog. How could he think she'd kill Peter and the others? Her eyes welled with tears. She blinked them away, unwilling to show Detective Ford anything but quiet calmness. She was tired and her emotions were raw, balancing on the edge. The last thing she needed was to come apart at the seams in front of the man determined to arrest her for a murder—strike that, *murders*—she hadn't committed.

Eager to get inside and take a relaxing bath before bed, Naomi walked faster. She started to insert her key into the lock when the door opened.

She turned and caught Bennett's eye.

"Step to the side." He moved an arm defensively in front of her in a sweeping motion, one hand brandishing his gun. "Wait here until I clear the apartment." His tone was barely a whisper, but it held a firmness that left no room for argument.

Naomi flattened herself against the stone wall exterior.

"Spike, stay. Guard." Bennett removed the leash.

Clearly oblivious that his slight stature intimidated no one, the little beagle maneuvered in front of her in a solid stance.

Naomi shifted, attempting to peer around Bennett, earning her a warning look. Too exhausted to outrun another shooter, she retreated to her original position. The maternal instinct to protect her unborn child prevailed, and she inhaled a fortifying breath for courage.

Bennett entered her apartment, leaving the door ajar.

She glanced down at Spike, his compassionate eyes meeting hers. "It won't take long," she whispered, speaking more to herself than the dog. With two bedrooms and one bathroom, her cozy townhome was far from extravagant.

Bennett returned within minutes, holstering

his gun, and snapped on Spike's leash. The look on his face compelled her to push past him.

Naomi stepped over the threshold and gasped at the destruction. With her hand over her mouth, containing the cry that threatened to escape, she slowly walked through her home.

The once lovely burgundy faux leather couch she and Ted had saved up to buy sat maliciously gutted. Slash marks ravaged the fabric and stuffing spewed from the inflicted wounds. She pivoted toward the bookcase where the mess continued with her belongings haplessly strewn across the carpet.

Pages from her favorite leather-bound classic books littered the floor and coffee table. The only framed picture she'd kept of her and Ted lay amid the shards of glass. The broken image contrasted Naomi's dreams of a happy family with their failed marriage. Her throat constricted as she knelt.

"No." Bennett's command and his hand on her arm halted Naomi in place.

Empathy filled his light brown eyes.

"You can't touch anything until the evidence technicians have documented the scene."

Naomi averted her gaze, everything within her aching physically and emotionally. Before she could stop it, the tears welled again, filling her eyes and blurring her vision. Bennett helped her to stand, supporting her lower back with one hand, and offered a light squeeze of her arm. Though she would normally resist his touch, her resolve had fled, leaving her vulnerable.

"I've called for assistance." His response offered no comfort.

Great, more cops. "My life is falling apart, and I don't understand why. What did I do to deserve this? Why now?" The questions tumbled out like the tears streaming down her face.

Naomi didn't look at Bennett. She also didn't withdraw from his touch, but she was grateful he didn't pull her into an embrace. The slight distancing helped her to remember their roles.

They weren't friends.

She walked to the bedrooms, where the destruction continued. Her heart dropped to the floor at the sight of her baby's crib shattered, his nursery destroyed. Naomi gasped and leaned against the door.

"It'll be okay," Bennett said, coming up behind her.

"How is it going to be okay?" she snapped, swiping the moisture from her face.

If she wasn't mistaken, Bennett seemed to wince at her reproach.

She didn't have the luxury of falling apart. Not now. There was no one to help her or lean on. Her baby shifted. He was all that mattered. This was just stuff. Naomi lifted her chin in a quiet resolve to fight, if not for herself, for her unborn son.

"It's not safe for you to stay here." He released his hold. "I'll help you gather whatever you need for a couple of days' stay."

"And where am I supposed to go?" She planted her fists on her hips. "It's not like I can sleep in my van."

"I live about twenty minutes from here." Bennett hoisted Spike into his arms. "You're welcome to stay with me."

Naomi shook her head. "No way."

"I realize it's a little unorthodox. However, I have a spare room."

"I'll be fine." She crossed her arms.

"Let me word this another way. You're still my prime suspect, like it or not—"

"As though I get an opinion?" It wasn't fair to unleash her emotions on Bennett, but he was the closest recipient. Even the sweet little beagle in his arms didn't prevent her from targeting him with her frustration.

"Of course you do." Bennett stroked the dog's fur. "Until I have more information on the drugs and the most recent events from tonight, I can't let you out of my sight. The offer to stay with me remains. If not, your alternative is for me to book you into the county jail."

Naomi gaped. Surely, he was joking. "On what charges?" She immediately regretted the question.

"Possession with intent to distribute, for starters." He answered matter-of-factly, like a glass of cold water in her face. "I don't want to do that, Naomi. But whoever did this—" he swept his arm wide as if reinforcing his point "—might not stop. Prison is full of criminals willing to kill for money. If they get wind you're incarcerated…"

Naomi swallowed hard. "Why would someone want me dead?"

"Good question."

A knock sounded. "Naomi?"

Naomi jerked upright, recognizing Addy's voice. Bennett stood with gun in hand. "It's Addy," she whispered. "The one who has the competitive tour company. Coming," she called, then swiped at her eyes and hurried to the stairs.

Addy stood in the living room, eyes wide. "What happened?"

"Someone broke into my home."

Bennett quickly descended behind her, gun poised.

Addy gasped.

"He's a cop," Naomi explained.

"Oh." Addy visibly relaxed. "I stopped by to bring you this." She passed Naomi a stack of fliers. "I'm starting hiking tours and thought you could give them to your customers."

"Sure," Naomi said absently.

"This is an active scene, you'll have to leave," Bennett replied.

Addy crossed her arms. "You're a real charmer." She addressed Naomi. "Maybe you should go somewhere safe. Whoever did this—" she gestured toward the destroyed room "—might return."

Bennett stared at Addy. "Would you know anything about who that person might be?"

"Of course not! Probably one of her husband's deadbeat friends," Addy snapped.

"What did you know about Ted?" Bennett asked.

"Nothing more than he was a loser who

should've helped his wife instead of abandoning her."

Naomi gaped at Addy. She'd never spoken about Ted that way before. Instead of feeling protected, the comment made her feel vulnerable.

"Shouldn't you be asking for backup or collecting evidence instead of interrogating an innocent citizen like me?" Addy challenged.

"I haven't interrogated you, ma'am," Bennett's eyes narrowed. "Perhaps we should start there."

"Thanks for stopping by, Addy." Naomi inserted herself. "I'll add these to my handout packet and send you any referrals."

"You're too close to your delivery date. You shouldn't be working this late into your pregnancy, anyway. Get some rest." Addy held Bennett's gaze for several seconds. "Let me know if you need anything." She spun on her heel and stomped away.

Bennett moved to the door, apparently confirming Addy had departed. "That's your friend?"

"She's nice when you get to know her."

He snorted, closing the door.

"Let me get my stuff together." Naomi

moved past him and gathered an overnight bag, tossing in essentials, a couple of changes of clothes and a second pair of shoes.

She returned to where Bennett and Spike searched the room. "Looking for drugs?" The inquiry came out a little snarkier than she'd intended, but her politeness had evaporated.

"Yes." His quick reply should've shocked Naomi, but it didn't.

"Find any?"

"No."

"I could've told you that, but I'm glad you figured it out on your own." Naomi slung the bag over her shoulder.

"Until we're able to verify your alibi, you must remain close to me."

"You've made that clear." She softened her response while maintaining her distance. Better to be in his care than alone when whoever had destroyed her apartment returned. The men at Peter's ranch didn't believe her when she'd proclaimed no knowledge of the drugs. They would invoke whatever means necessary to threaten her. Naomi shivered at the implications. When she confessed the police had the drugs, what would they do then?

Why had someone targeted her? Were they

using her van to mule? She'd read about criminals choosing an unsuspecting person, usually a teenager or a woman, and planting drugs on them.

Even if Bennett accepted Naomi wasn't involved, it didn't help her with the murder charges. How could he possibly suspect her of being a murderer? It was ludicrous.

"Do you need anything else?" Bennett glanced around the room.

"Proof I'm not a drug-dealing serial killer?" She made no effort to hide her sarcastic response. If Naomi failed to prove her innocence, her life would take a horrible turn of events.

Two hours later, Naomi clung to her backpack for dear life, treating the bag like a security blanket. Bennett had insisted on dropping off the drugs at the Denver Police Department before they drove to his downtown condo. That took longer than she'd expected, but waiting for him to finish processing the evidence gave her time to reschedule her tours with Addy, who was all too willing to take the extra business. Most of her customers were gracious, but the few that weren't stressed out Naomi. Still, she was grateful for Addy's help in the last-minute situation.

The burdens clung to her like a stone-filled sack. Losing Ted months prior had destroyed her dreams of a loving marriage. Now, she faced the loss of their business. Everything was being stripped from her, tearing at her heart one piece at a time.

"Coming?" Bennett called, jolting her from her thoughts.

Naomi hurried to catch up to him and Spike while surveying the high-rise building. Bennett held the glass entry door open, and they walked into the foyer, which was decorated in minimalist fashion. They rode the elevator to the eleventh floor, then exited and strolled down the long hallway. How did Bennett afford to live in a place like this? She shoved away the thoughts. What business was that of hers?

"Bennett, I appreciate this."

"No problem." He smiled, and unless Naomi was mistaken, it seemed genuine.

Spike trotted ahead as much as his long leash allowed. He rounded the corner and paused beside a door. Bennett inserted his key and pushed open the door, allowing Naomi to enter first. She stepped over the threshold, and he released Spike from his leash. The dog gave a thorough shake of his fur and strolled past her, obviously comfortable in his surroundings.

The open floor plan with a kitchen to her right and living area to the left was decorated in modest, neutral colors. A cozy dining space with a rectangular table divided the two rooms. The powerful aroma of teakwood filled her senses, and she fought not to wrinkle her nose at the smell. She spotted the plug-in diffuser in the hallway.

As though sensing her thoughts, Bennett explained, "The lady at the store recommended this scent, and I haven't gotten used to it."

"It's got a strong masculine undertone," Naomi replied, sounding like a salesperson.

"That's one way to put it." He chuckled and hung Spike's leash on a small hook by the door. "Let me show you to your room."

Naomi trailed mutely behind him down a short hallway, her gaze roving for any inside information on Bennett Ford. No personal decor covered the walls, adding to her curiosity.

He gestured toward an open door, revealing a bathroom on one side and a bedroom on the other. A white wedding ring quilt covered the queen-sized bed, and the only other piece of furniture was a side table and lamp. "Make yourself comfortable."

She entered the space, instantly liking it. "Do you treat all your prisoners this nicely?"

"You're my first, to be fair," he teased.

"Thank you for giving me a place to stay that didn't involve orange jumpsuits."

"I'll let you get some rest."

"I wish I could." Naomi set her bag on the floor beside the bed. "Considering everything that's happened tonight, you'd think I'd pass out cold. But my mind won't stop racing. There's no way I can fall asleep right now." Her stomach rumbled, and she averted her eyes, cheeks warming with embarrassment. Food hadn't been on her mind, but apparently little man had other ideas.

Bennett's eyes widened. "I didn't even consider that you'd be hungry. It's close to midnight, but you must be starving. Is there anything you'd like? I could whip up something." Bennett turned toward the hallway. "I'm not home much, so it's hard to say what's in my fridge, but we'll figure it out."

"I am a little hungry." She shrugged. The incredible urge for chocolate cereal made her mouth water. No way was she asking for that.

But once the thought entered her mind, it took on a life of its own. The craving was strong. Little man always got his way. "Whatever you want to do is fine. I'm not picky. Would you mind if I freshened up first?"

"Sure." Bennett tilted his head. "I'll put together something to eat."

"Thanks."

He blocked the doorway. "My experience with pregnant women is limited. Do you have any cravings?"

Naomi shifted from one foot to the other. "I do, but it's embarrassing."

"Why?" Bennett leaned back, crossing his muscular arms over his chest. "I don't have pickles, but there might be ice cream."

She laughed. "Um, no. Neither of those. I kind of crave…cereal."

"Like granola, shredded wheat?"

"Nothing healthy." She rubbed her belly, making circles with her hands. "He likes… chocolate puffs."

Bennett grinned. "Now that's a craving I can get on board with." He spun on his heel and hurried down the hallway.

Naomi stayed planted, surveying the space. The slam of a cabinet carried to her, and Bennett returned, carrying a box of her favorite breakfast cereal. "Like this?"

She stared, and it took all her self-control not to rip the box out of his hands. She envisioned herself tearing into the packaging and shoveling handfuls of the chocolaty delights into her mouth. "Yes," she chuckled, trying to maintain control. He grinned and turned back toward the kitchen.

Naomi hurried to the bathroom with her bag and closed the door.

When she emerged, the scent of bacon and toast filled the air, drawing Naomi to the kitchen. Bennett cut a sandwich in half. "BLTs with a side of cereal?"

"That sounds amazing." She grinned. "How can I help?"

"Grab the cereal and milk." Bennett gestured to the end of the counter. He carried the sandwiches on plates, placing them in front of two of the dining room chairs.

Naomi wasted no time sitting down and fixing a bowl of cereal.

After several satisfying bites, she reached for the BLT. Naomi bit into the sandwich, relishing the perfect blend of bacon, lettuce and tomato. They ate in silence and when she'd cleaned her bowl and plate, Naomi wiped her mouth. "I was hungrier than I thought. I inhaled that."

"Me too." Bennett leaned back. "Is great taste in cereal the only craving you've had?"

"No." Naomi picked at a piece of lettuce on her plate. "At first, I wanted baked potatoes, which is comical, considering I don't like them."

"I'll try not to hold that against you," Bennett teased.

She laughed. "I do like French fries."

"Well, it's a start." His conversational tone didn't match the tension evident in his posture.

Naomi couldn't help but notice Bennett's handsomeness. His blond hair reminded her of a model's, perfectly styled with that just-out-of-bed look that only attractive men could pull off. His light brown eyes held a hardness that spoke of experience and pain, but beyond that, laugh lines testified of better days when he must've smiled a lot. She wondered what had taken those away. She understood experiences that wounded a soul to the point of eliminating joy.

"After the great potato aversion, what happened?" He reengaged her in the discussion.

"That only lasted for the first month, then in

the past six weeks, all I want is chocolate puff cereal." She groaned. "Not exactly low-calorie nutrition."

"I'm far from judgmental regarding nutritional food. Cops learn to live on whatever is available when we have time to eat."

Bennett's financial status lingered in her mind. Who was she dealing with? "I apologize, but I have to ask something."

"Shoot."

"This is none of my business, but how do you afford to live in a downtown Denver condo this nice?" Her gaze roved the space.

"Beg your pardon?" His quizzical frown conveyed disapproval.

Naomi's ears warmed, but after all she'd endured, her politeness waned. "I haven't a clue what a cop's salary is, but it can't be enough to afford a place so nice. Not in this area." She fixed her gaze on Bennett, unwilling to relent in her challenge.

"Fair enough." Bennett leaned back in his chair. "It belonged to my grandmother in the days before this became the yuppie hot spot."

Relief coursed through her. "I apologize for the invasive question."

"You shouldn't. I'm a skeptic at heart, so I appreciate your willingness to call me out on anything you see as questionable." Sincerity hung in his features.

"Thank you." A subtle reminder of their roles sobered Naomi. "Did you always want to be a police officer?" She caught herself. "Sorry—detective."

"Yeah, pretty much." He sat up straighter and took a sip from his water glass. "My uncle was a DPD officer for over thirty years. In fact, I'm named after him."

"That's kind of cool." She tilted her head, silently pondering what her little boy would want to do when he grew up.

"I always looked up to him. He's a great guy." Present tense meant the man was alive. Unexpectedly, Naomi's throat tightened with emotion. All she had left was her brother, whom she barely saw. She studied her belly a little too hard, focused on the T-shirt fabric.

Spike trotted out from the kitchen and paused beside her, allowing Naomi to run her fingers through his velvety fur. Strange, even after he'd found drugs in her vehicle, he didn't hold a grudge. If only humans were the same. "He's sweet."

At her declaration, Spike licked her hand and

offered her a compassionate gaze before moving to a round dog bed near the sofa.

"He's an exceptional partner."

"Evan and I spoiled our family dog, Rusty. We always snuck him dinner treats." Naomi sighed. "Daddy would pretend to admonish us, but he was just as bad. Mama used to wag her finger, but then we'd catch her fixing Rusty his own plate of leftovers when she thought no one was looking."

Bennett grinned. "What kind of dog?"

"A purebred mutt." She smiled at the memories. "He had the fur of a golden retriever but the coloring of a black Lab. And, if you can picture this, the body of a Great Dane."

As she'd expected, Bennett's eyes widened.

"Right?" Naomi chuckled. "He was the gentlest creature. We had him for over fifteen years before he passed away. That hit us all hard. Rusty wasn't just a dog, he was a part of our family."

Bennett nodded, glancing at Spike. "I get that. Did you and Ted have dogs?"

"No, we worked long hours and agreed it wouldn't be fair to the animal." Fond memories of her deceased husband returned. "In our dating years, we hiked a lot." She glanced down at her belly. "I'm sure that's hard to picture given my current state."

"Not really. I can see you being outdoorsy."

"I love it."

He shifted forward, placing his elbows on his knees. "I'm not in the practice of speaking ill of the dead, but I'd like to ask you about Ted."

"Okay." Naomi hadn't missed the way his disposition had softened toward her. His emotional distance remained, but his tone was less accusatory and more inquisitive.

"Tell me about your marriage?"

She cringed. Of all the topics on the planet, talking about her failed relationship was the last on her list. Naomi hoped to divert. "We had our trials like most folks." She focused too hard on the wilting piece of lettuce on her plate, wishing she had more to eat to avoid the discussion.

"Were there any extenuating circumstances, especially toward the end?"

"You mean was my husband cheating on me? Or hurting me?"

"Yes, but also about Ted's behavior. Addy didn't seem to hold him in high regard."

Naomi considered his question. "Things were good in the beginning. We had fun together.

He was my best friend and greatest confidant. I trusted him more than I'd ever depended on anyone before."

Her heart constricted at the memories of Ted's kindness and tenderness. But she couldn't ignore the painful memories of how he'd transformed toward the end.

"What changed?" Bennett probed, no doubt able to read her expression.

"It was like he had a complete personality exchange. Where he'd been thoughtful, he became distant and elusive. He quit holding my hand, something I cherished, like touching me repulsed him."

"Was the baby planned?" Bennett's cheeks reddened. "I'm sorry. I don't mean to—"

"As much as any baby, I suppose. He was a welcome surprise, but we weren't actively trying to have a child." She felt her own cheeks warm and averted her gaze. "We'd talked about having a family in the beginning. I hoped Ted would revert to those kinder years when I told him we were expecting."

"Did he?"

"At first, Ted was involved and excited, but money was a constant stressor. We had steady tours, which kept our heads above the financial waves, but he worried about the additional costs the baby brought to our lives. I reminded him that our trust wasn't in anything other than God. Ted wasn't a man of faith." She didn't add how he'd mocked her beliefs as flimsy and childish.

"Financial stress is common in young marriages." He tapped his fingers against his water glass. "Can't speak from personal experience, but that's what I've heard."

Naomi jumped on the opportunity to divert the discussion. "Never married or come close?"

"Close." Bennett's jaw hardened. "Dodged a fatal bullet there." She didn't have long to ponder because Bennett returned to interrogating her. "How did Ted handle the financial worries?"

"He started coming home late, if he bothered to at all, and making ridiculous excuses."

"You questioned his behavior?"

"At first, but once he moved out, I gave up. And then…he was gone." Naomi pushed back from the table and rose, collecting the dishes.

The confession solidified what Bennett already knew from his research into Naomi's life. "Leave it. I'll do them."

"Thank you. I'm tired. I'd like to go to bed."

"Absolutely." His eyes held a tenderness. "If you need anything, holler at me."

"Thanks." Naomi headed to the spare bedroom without looking back. The depressing past and pressure of the present hung heavy on her shoulders with an unbearable weight. Worse, her confusing emotions about Bennett intermingled with the mess. His kindness refreshed her heart after the desert dry loneliness she'd experienced. However, she reminded herself, it didn't negate his mission to arrest her for a crime she hadn't committed.

Naomi couldn't risk losing focus. Her life was on the line. Falling for someone like Bennett wasn't feasible, now or in the future.

And none of it would keep her out of prison.

Chapter Six

After cleaning the kitchen, Bennett moved to the sofa, considering all that Naomi had shared. He studied her behavior as much as her words, and she didn't bear the usual evidence of a liar. She spoke with confidence and a certain grace. However, many psychopaths used their manipulative and charismatic personalities to lure their victims to their deaths.

She'd held his gaze, unrelenting. Not in defiance, more with a calm assurance. Nothing about her demeanor conveyed deception. But he wouldn't relax his suspicious nature until Isla had confirmed or destroyed her alibi.

Naomi had looked exhausted, and once more, the twinge of sympathy for the mother-to-be battled with his cynical views. She'd get plenty of rest in prison. Still, he was at the point of deciding whether to arrest her or let her go. For now. He knew where to find her, and she hardly posed a flight risk. Her explanation was plausible. Could Naomi be innocent of the drugs and the murders? But if she wasn't the RMK, who was?

A text from Isla chimed on his phone. Still up?

He quickly dialed, and she answered on the first ring. "You're working late."

"I figured you'd want an update ASAP."

"I do, thanks."

Naomi approached, wearing a pensive expression.

Bennett spoke into the phone. "Isla, can you hold one second?"

"No problem."

He pressed the cell against his chest. "Everything okay?"

"I'm sorry, I just remembered something." Naomi stood clinging to her small cosmetic bag. "I hate to ask this, but I have an OB appointment tomorrow morning. I'm so close to my due date, and after the hospital visit today, I'd really like to see my doctor."

"Uh, sure." Bennett processed the request, realizing the implications. "What time?"

"Ten forty-five in Littleton." Naomi referred to the suburb south of Denver.

"Sounds good."

"Thank you." Relief swept over her face.

She must have a million things to think about. Taking her to the doctor wasn't a big deal. Plus, it kept her near him, and he wouldn't have to worry about her trying to break into her van.

"Good night." She turned and headed for the bedroom, closing the door with a soft click.

Not that Naomi couldn't overhear his discussion, but he preferred to talk to his teammate privately. Placing the phone against his ear, he said, "Sorry about that, Isla. What do you know?"

"First, I got nothing on the hospital security footage. The man skillfully eluded the cameras."

"Great. That means he had knowledge of their location."

"Exactly."

Bill Nolice's cheerful face bounced to the forefront of Bennett's mind. "Dig into the security guard, Bill Nolice. He watched Spike for me when Naomi was admitted to the hospital."

"Will do." Isla continued. "Second, Naomi's alibi checks out with the hospice unit time sheet records. I also spoke to the nurse she mentioned, Yvette Jacobsen. She corroborated Naomi's claim that she was working at midnight."

"The same time the murders occurred ten years ago," Bennett concluded.

"Yep." Typing on Isla's end filtered through the line. "There's more. Naomi's tour bus records substantiate she was driving during the most recent murders of Peter Windham and Henry Mulder."

The sense of relief shocked Bennett, and for the first time since he'd confronted Naomi, he could breathe. "That's great news."

"Yeah, just one thing that struck me as strange. I contacted random passengers from Naomi's rosters to verify they rode with her on the scheduled days and times. Of course, I provided my creds right off the bat." Isla referenced her professional credentials as a member of the MCK9 team. "One woman felt compelled to reiterate how sweet Naomi was."

"Why was that strange?" Bennett asked.

"Just a feeling, ya know?" Isla paused. "She tried too hard to convince me of Naomi's innocence."

"Did you tell her why you were calling?"

"Of course not. But she made the law enforcement connection, and I'm telling you it was strange."

"What's her name?"

"Hazel Houston."

Bennett snorted. "Sounds like a made-up name."

"It is. Already ran a background and came up blank."

"So, why use a fake name and proclaim Naomi's innocence?"

"The line is disconnected, too, so I can't follow up," Isla said. "Also pulled Adeline Everett. She has a tour bus business that offers the same features as Naomi, including nature hikes coming in the summer. She's clean, other than a few parking tickets."

"Okay, thanks," Bennett replied. "Have you notified the team?"

"Was just about to."

"Let's do a quick group call. I have updates, too."

"I'll set it up and send the video conference link."

"Thanks." He'd never spoken truer words. He hadn't dined with a killer after all.

The link popped up on his phone, and Bennett connected with the team. Not surprisingly, the rest of them were also still awake and working. "Sorry for the late-night check-in," Bennett began.

"Justice never sleeps," Elk Valley PD Officer Ashley Hanson replied, appearing wide awake. A benefit no doubt of being the youngest member.

"Exactly." Bennett leaned back. "So, we have an update." He launched into an explanation of the events at Peter's ranch, the break-in at Naomi's apartment and the attack at the hospital.

"I've confirmed Naomi isn't our killer," Isla added, pulling back her long brown hair with one hand. "Her alibis check out for the past murders and present kills."

"Wow." Task force leader Chase Rawlston leaned closer, revealing shadows on his face that spoke of worry and the weight of leading the team.

"I dropped off the drug bags at DPD and requested a rush for fingerprint and DNA testing," Bennett advised. "We'll have data soon."

"Does someone owe you big?" Teasing flickered in Idaho Deputy Selena Smith's green eyes and a grin played on her lips.

"Something like that." Bennett chuckled. "Never underestimate the power of connections."

"True." New Mexico Bureau FBI agent Kyle West joined the discussion.

Bennett had heard people describe him as intense with his dark hair and eyes, but Bennett failed to see him that way.

"Until we have the results from the bags, we cannot completely discount Naomi's involvement with the drugs," Chase reminded the group. "And just because she wasn't the one who pulled the trigger, it doesn't exclude her from being involved with the RMK."

"Everyone has enemies, even if they're unaware," Bennett replied. Though he wanted to argue, Chase's comment was a reality check for him. He doubted Naomi was the RMK, but he'd been wrong before in trusting a woman he shouldn't. He shifted his focus on the commander and told himself to remain professional and impartial. "Any word on Cowgirl?"

"Not a thing," Isla responded with a long exhale. No wonder she'd cut Bennett off earlier. She was juggling a hundred different things at the same time.

"If she was dognapped, did the thief have great coordination skills?" Elk Valley PD Officer Rocco Manelli strode closer, revealing his tall, slender frame.

"Yep," Utah Highway Patrol State Trooper Hannah Scott replied while simultaneously whipping her long red hair into a clip.

"She'll attract attention in town," Bennett said.

"Her markings will help," Selena agreed. "Though Labradoodles are a common breed, the telltale dark brown splotch on her right ear gives us a unique feature to give the public."

"Liana has posters around town." US Marshal Meadow Ames sat close to her camera, filling the frame with her contrasting dark hair and green eyes. "And she's blasting social media with information and pictures of Cowgirl, too."

"We have SAR dogs," Bennett said, referring to the team's dedicated search and rescue K-9s.

"We're doing everything to find her," Chase assured them.

Bennett clamped his mouth shut. Doubtful the boss appreciated his implication that he'd not allocated resources adequately.

"I've authorized Bennett to hold off on citing Naomi for drug possession and arresting her until we get the results from the fentanyl bags," Chase advised, turning the discussion back to Naomi.

Bennett got to his feet and glanced at the

spare room where Naomi roomed. The door was closed, but he lowered his voice and moved to the furthest end of the living room. "I could be wrong, but I don't think Naomi's involved with this. Unless she's one exceptional actress, she's shaken up by the cascading events. I propose we go over the suspects, those with motives, enemies, etcetera, and expand our search."

"Agreed. However, in the meantime, I'd like to see what results we get with the fingerprint analysis," Chase replied. "Everyone, get a good night's rest and let's do a briefing tomorrow evening." With that, the team ended the call.

Bennett dropped onto the recliner and leaned forward, head in his hands. He prayed silently for wisdom to view Naomi through the eyes of an investigator. If Delaney had taught him anything, it was that the best deceptive wolves dressed in convincing sheep's clothing. A nudge to his hand reverted his attention to where Spike sat. Bennett stroked the dog's fur. "I wish you talked."

Spike gave a soft sigh.

"What do you think?" Bennett glanced toward the hallway. He recalled the conversation and Naomi's request to drive her to the doctor. Unsure what that entailed, a sudden rush of nerves got a hold of him. Recalling how the hospital personnel treated him as though he was the father-to-be, he groaned. *Ugh*.

Bennett leaned his head against the sofa cushions, still stroking Spike, who offered no wisdom. However, the beagle's interactions with Naomi said a lot. He was no Belgian Malinois, like Selena's K-9, Scout. Spike didn't have the intimidation factor, but he had good dog sense about people. He'd accepted Naomi from the start, separating her from the drugs. Bennett considered his training, reminding himself that psychopaths were skilled at manipulation. He met Spike's soulful gaze.

Dogs weren't easily fooled. Wouldn't Spike see through her lies? He'd never liked Delaney. That should've been a bright red flag from the start.

If he was wrong, he'd provided Naomi every opportunity to finish him in the middle of the night. Had he invited a serial killer to sleep under his roof?

Bennett jerked upright from his deep sleep, instinctively snagging his duty weapon and aiming it at his locked bedroom door. Spike sat up beside him with an annoyed expression.

He yawned with an accompanying squeak as the phone rang a second time. Bennett lowered the gun and glanced at the cell, shaking his head to awaken himself.

He reached for the device and hurriedly swiped the screen after seeing DPD crime lab technician Eduardo Gomez's contact information.

"Hey, Eduardo," he croaked, hating the way his voice confirmed he'd just woken up.

"Rise and shine, Clementine." Eduardo chuckled.

"It was a late night." Bennett scrubbed a hand across his face.

"Not sure what you're hoping for on the outcome, but I got a fingerprint match on the bags of fentanyl."

That got Bennett's full attention. "And?"

"Ted Cavanaugh, based off a concealed carry permit application."

"No kidding," Bennett mumbled under his breath.

"Yep."

"Outstanding work. Thanks again for the rush."

"No problem, but this makes us even, right?"

"Right." Bennett chuckled.

"Cool. Later." Eduardo disconnected.

The running joke between him and Eduardo about who owed who never ended. But this was important, and he'd not waste the request on anything trivial. Bennett understood it was a big ask to rush the results, and he appreciated Eduardo's friendship.

The drug case added to Bennett's already full investigative plate of apprehending the RMK. But he had to follow every lead, and if Naomi was connected to the drugs, he'd do whatever it took, even if it meant arresting her. Thanks to Eduardo's information, he wouldn't have to do that today.

Bennett threw off the blankets and stepped into a pair of running pants and shoes, then leashed Spike. He unlocked his door, feeling silly for his overreaction the prior night, and tugged it open. After scribbling a message on a sticky note to Naomi, advising he'd taken Spike out for a walk, he activated the motion sensor camera on his doorbell. Then they exited the condo, took the stairs to incorporate extra exercise, and pushed through the stairwell door to the empty foyer.

They strolled in front of the condo's entrance. While Spike sniffed and did his business, Bennett monitored his door video. Once Spike finished, they quickly hurried back.

Sounds from inside Naomi's room indicated she was awake. He sent a quick group text to the team, advising them of the findings and notifying them Eduardo would forward the report to Isla.

His phone lit up with their responses and Chase's order for a short video conference in ten minutes.

Bennett freshened up and rushed to the kitchen for a bottled water, prepared to join the chat three minutes prior to the scheduled time when Naomi emerged from her room.

"Good morning," Bennett said.

"Mornin'." Her bedraggled hair and rumpled, oversized T-shirt enhanced her adorableness.

Bennett blinked. What was wrong with him? "Uh, I have a task force meeting shortly."

"I'll get ready." Naomi turned and headed for the bathroom.

In the excitement of Eduardo's call, Bennett had forgotten about the OB appointment. Visions of sitting in a waiting room packed with pregnant women collided into him.

Where are you? Isla's text bounced over the chiming phone and redirected his attention.

Great.

He quickly signed into the video conference. "Good morning. Sorry I'm late."

The comment earned him quizzical looks from his teammates.

"Why are you so cheerful?" Hannah groused.

"Eduardo's results point to Ted Cavanaugh?" Rocco asked. "That's a plot twist."

Bennett nodded. "It's clear Naomi's husband was responsible for the drugs. And I believe the thugs who attacked us at Windham Ranch were in cahoots with him."

"Why wait to confiscate them? Were they aware Cavanaugh hid the drugs in her van?" Selena asked. "And how does that fit with the murder of Peter Windham?"

"Maybe it doesn't," Hannah said. "Could be two different and unrelated cases."

"All excellent discussion," Chase said. "But for this call, let's focus on the RMK investigation. Review the victims again, searching specifically for any enemies. There must be a connection tying them together."

"We already had that with Naomi," Rocco added. "She was the victim of a prank they'd played on her. She *is* the common denominator."

"There's obviously more to the story," Hannah said. "We need to find it."

"Peter Windham had no enemies," Kyle reminded the group.

"Everyone's got enemies," Chase argued. "Old Peter just might not have known it."

"I agree. Naomi is still our link to the victims, and it's clear she remains in danger based on the attacks at the ranch and hospital," Selena said.

"But the evidence doesn't support her as the RMK," Bennett reiterated. "However, the fentanyl and her deceased husband's involvement might give us something. Doubtful the men who attacked her at the ranch chose that location by accident."

"Agreed," Ashley said. "Still, there are that many connections to Naomi without them tying into the murders. Elk Valley is the relative point, so the RMK lived there or nearby."

"The YRC is also a factor," Hannah said. "I'll dig into past memberships."

"Hmm, or rejected potential members," Ashley added.

"Definitely," Rocco said.

"Were there other young women that experienced what Naomi did?" Meadow asked.

"It's possible," Isla said. "They were quite the group."

"Good. Dig into anyone else who fits the profile," Chase advised.

"I'll take Spike back to the impound lot to scour Naomi's van in the daylight." Bennett hesitated, then said, "First, though, I, uh, have to take Naomi for her obstetrician appointment this morning."

His coworkers' expressions conveyed more than the accompanying quiet. If he didn't miss it or misjudge it, Ashley stifled a smirk.

"I'll keep her close until we get this figured out," Bennett continued, aware he had overjustified his actions. "Whoever is after her won't stop until they get what they want."

"True, and if they want those drugs, it'll get ugly when she can't produce them," Selena added. "Kyle and I are headed to the Windham murder site. If the thugs followed Naomi there, perhaps we'll find evidence tying them to the crimes."

"Keep us updated," Chase said.

"We'll also hunt through the evidence files," Kyle said. "Selena and I requested the lab results from both Windham and Mulder's crime scenes."

"Are there updates on Cowgirl?" Bennett glanced where Spike sat waiting for his breakfast.

"None," Chase replied.

A momentary silence conveyed the team's worry and sadness for Cowgirl's situation.

"I'll also send you lists of any recent murders in the surrounding states," Isla said.

"Yes, let's wrap this up," Chase inserted. "Search for links, connections and common or related repetitive things."

A collective response of "Roger that" and "Affirmative" sounded from each of the members before they disconnected. Relieved that Naomi was no longer a suspect warred with Bennett's uncomfortableness at having to accompany her to the appointment. But the beautiful, scared, pregnant woman needed someone to watch her back.

Bennett couldn't shake the question that remained. Who was the RMK?

By the time he'd finished putting away his laptop and walked out of his bedroom, Naomi was sitting on the sofa, scrolling on her phone. "Hey, I'm still working out a few details for my rescheduled tours. I called the dealership, and they'll repair the windows once the impound lot releases my van." She met his eyes with expectation and hope.

"We should be able to get that handled soon." Unless Spike found more drugs.

"Okay." She reverted her attention to her phone again. She'd tied her hair back into a loose ponytail with tendrils framing her face. If she wore makeup, it was lightly applied. Her long, dark lashes emphasized her hazel eyes. In the morning light, Bennett noticed they held splashes of deep green. Naomi was truly beautiful.

What? No. He shook off the thoughts with a grunt.

"Why are you looking at me like that? Is something wrong?"

"No, no. It's good. Fine. Everything is okay. In fact, I have good news. Your alibis checked out for the five murders. And you're no longer a suspect in the drug case."

"Really? Why?"

He couldn't share the confidential details of an ongoing investigation. He'd offer limited information. Strangely, at the moment, he didn't want to explain everything to her…at least, not yet. Though he wasn't sure why. He'd tell her more if the situation presented itself. "Evidence excludes you from the drugs I confiscated from your van, so I won't have to charge you with possession."

"That's fantastic news!" She pushed herself to her feet and walked to the kitchen. "I didn't want to eat breakfast without you. But little man is starving. I'm merely his transportation."

Bennett chuckled. *Stop it.* How could he feel so right around her while fully aware of his own emotional walls? Nothing could come from their interactions. "Does the name Hazel Houston mean anything to you?"

"No." Naomi shook her head. "Sounds like a movie star or singer. Why?"

"She's listed in your travel manifest and seemed compelled to proclaim your innocence."

"Hmm. Maybe we bonded during a trip? I talk to my customers a lot while we're driving. Though I don't remember her, maybe she remembers me? I am innocent, after all." She grinned.

"Right." He snorted. "How about if I whip up eggs?"

"Actually, if you don't mind, I'm craving cereal again. Little man pretty much wakes me with his menu requests." She flashed him a smile that nearly buckled his knees.

He needed coffee urgently, before he did something he'd regret.

"I suppose he gets the final say." Bennett hurried to gather bowls and spoons while Naomi pulled out the milk and cereal, placing them on the table.

"Yep, he runs my life and my schedule, along with my tours." She poured herself cereal and passed the box to him.

"I'm sorry about the customers you lost with all this."

"Me too, but most were understanding." She dipped her spoon into the bowl. "Honestly, this is the first day off I've had in eight months."

"In that case, I don't feel too bad." He crunched away at the sugary treat. "What does it say about me that my grocery preferences are the same as a child?"

"No judgment here." Naomi winked good-naturedly.

"I'd like to run to the impound lot before we go to your appointment." A glance at the clock confirmed they had time.

"Works for me."

They finished breakfast and cleaned the dishes, moving around the condo in a comfortable synchronicity. He struggled with the strange connection they had, as though they'd always known one another. It was too easy being with Naomi.

Bennett realized how much he enjoyed it.

Spending time with Naomi was far too dangerous.

Chapter Seven

Naomi settled into the passenger seat in Bennett's pickup. After years of driving others around, she appreciated the ease of riding. Traffic was light due to the early morning hours, making for a short commute to the impound lot.

"Because of the recent evidence, I'd like to revisit the topic of your marriage," Bennett said, "since we never finished the discussion."

Naomi did a double take. "What're you talking about?"

He hesitated, as though debating what to tell her. Was he withholding information?

"If you've found something, I have a right to hear about it."

"Yes and no." He focused on the road.

"That's a cop out."

"But it's valid." Bennett shrugged. "Did Ted own a personal gun?"

The shift had Naomi lingering in order to traverse back to their early relationship years. "I think so. And that was a lousy way to dodge my question."

"I promise there's a connection to my incessant interrogations."

"In that case—" Naomi acquiesced "—he had a pistol before we were married. I wouldn't allow him to keep any weapons in our home." She tried to remember where Ted had put the gun. "Now that you mention it, I have no clue if or where he kept it."

"That's a long answer to a short question."

"I'm not trying to be difficult. It just didn't cross my mind. Why?"

"His fingerprints are on file with the state for a concealed carry permit."

Naomi shrugged. "Okay…"

"Ted's prints were on the bags of drugs I confiscated from your van."

She twisted to face him. Had she heard him correctly?

"As I explained before, I don't like speaking ill of the deceased," Bennett began. "However, it's the reason I have to ask you a lot of questions."

"I…" She hesitated, fidgeting with her tunic

fabric. "He…" Why couldn't she get any words out that made sense? "Ted was dealing drugs?"

"Until I have more information, I can't answer that. His fingerprints were on the bags, which alludes to the possibility that he placed them in the fender liner prior to his death."

Naomi rubbed her temple. "It's too early in the morning to learn my deceased husband was a drug dealer."

"Was he a user?"

"Not that I am aware of. He was as strait-laced as they come." In the beginning. Except she couldn't deny how Ted's mannerisms had changed drastically from their dating days until his death. He'd started by evading her. Then he'd ignored her questions about his whereabouts, making ridiculous excuses for why he chose to sleep in the spare room. Until eventually, he stopped coming home all together.

"You're awfully quiet."

"Sharing this is humiliating."

"That's not my goal at all." Bennett reached over and gently squeezed her hand.

The kind gesture touched her heart.

"I need a better picture of your daily lives."

"I understand." Naomi considered her next words. She exhaled. Remembering Ted used to hurt. Now, it was like telling someone else's story. "He'd left me emotionally before his horrible accident. You're probably already aware he drained our bank accounts, leaving me penniless except for the tour bus business, which barely makes ends meet."

"What did he do with the money?"

"Not a clue." Would it make any difference? Doubtful, but the unknowns left worse images than hearing the truth.

"Was your brother aware of your marital issues?"

"I never saw the necessity of involving Evan. I keep to myself." With the loss of her parents, and the rare times she got to spend with Evan, loneliness had become a normal way of life.

"Did you know Ted's friends?"

"He didn't have many."

"So, you're not sure if Ted was involved with anyone shady or new?"

Naomi sighed, focusing out her window. "It would be easy to say yes, putting all the blame for the drugs you found on my tour bus on Ted."

"True."

"I'd prefer denying it all to preserve his memory, but truthfully, I don't know. He apparently lived another life in the last part of our marriage. I already explained how I'd hoped the baby would give Ted more of a stake in our life together. Instead, the news pushed him further away emotionally...physically." She didn't want to look at Bennett, so she kept her gaze on the landscape passing by. "My parents were happily married, so I had a good example. Not that I'm oblivious to the hardship of relationships or the fact that they take work. And at first, I figured that's all that was happening with him when he started coming home late and lying about where he'd been."

"What clued you into his deception?"

"Ted was no Jason Bourne." Naomi snorted, her ears warming at the unladylike sound. "He didn't have the greatest excuses. The lies I'd caught him in broke my heart, and each one separated us a little further apart."

"Did you call him out?"

Naomi winced. This is where he'd judge her for weakness because she'd not walked out on Ted. Compelled to justify her reasons, she said, "I believe in the sanctity of marriage. I took a vow before God, and that meant something to me."

"I understand."

"You think I'm naive for not leaving him." She lifted her chin, defensiveness rising.

"Not at all. If I ever got married, I'd want it to be forever."

At his heartfelt confession, Naomi's wariness deflated, and she turned to look at Bennett. Everything within her hollered to keep her distance and watch what she said, so he wouldn't use it against her. Yet something about him tore through her heart armor.

A part of Naomi trusted Bennett, which made no sense. Except she couldn't shake that phenomenon of comfort, as though she'd known him forever. And that was wrong on so many levels. Before today, Detective Bennett Ford had considered the possibility that she was a drug-dealing serial killer.

"He stopped loving me a long time ago." The words escaped before Naomi realized she'd spoken aloud. Still, it was the truth, not a ploy for sympathy, just the reality of her life. "I tried everything to save our marriage. Counseling. Praying harder." She glanced down at her belly. "Even hoped that this little blessing would change his heart and draw us together. Sounds ridiculous, but my heart was desperate."

"Not at all."

"Ted wasn't the same guy I'd married. He moved out a month before his death, claiming he needed space. I didn't argue, praying he'd return. He never did." Admitting the truth eased some of her stress. "He spent a lot of nights at our tour bus office, and we worked together. In fact, he was checking out locations for nature hikes when he died. We wanted to stay competitive by adding those options."

Bennett's gaze remained on the road ahead. Several long beats passed before he said, "Naomi, what if Ted's death wasn't an accident?"

"Ted was a skilled hiker."

"Yet he fell down a steep cliff." A statement, not a question.

"Even professional outdoorsmen can't avoid accidents. It's not like someone ran him off the road." Naomi studied the handsome detective.

Silence hung between them. She appreciated that he didn't push her. Instead, he remained quiet, allowing Naomi to think.

Images of the past twenty-four hours slammed into her, along with the realization that Ted had hidden the drugs in the van. "Although, until yesterday, I accepted the coroner's report at face value."

"There are some twists in the narrative." Bennett pulled into the impound facility.

Naomi struggled to process all the information. Why would Ted put her and the baby at such risk?

Bennett showed his credentials to the officer working the gate, and they passed through, traveling to the far side of the lot.

When they neared the van, Naomi stared in disbelief at the mutilated vehicle. Surely the mass of metal Swiss cheese wasn't hers. The distinctive flower paint decoration and her business number said otherwise.

Bennett shut off the engine, but Naomi didn't wait for him. She threw open her door and got out of the truck, set on inspecting the damage.

Numerable bullet holes pierced the exterior, and all the windows were gone.

"What happened to my van?" Naomi cried.

Bennett moved to her side with Spike. "How did this happen?" His jaw tightened and his narrowed eyes spoke of confusion and fury at the sight. His reaction offered some comfort.

"How did they get in here?" Naomi surveyed the chain-link fence that surrounded the property.

Bennett withdrew his phone. "Give me a second."

She listened as he made a call.

"Deputy McClintock, this is Detective Ford. I'm here with Naomi Carr-Cavanaugh—the owner of the van—at the impound lot." A pause. "Yes, I'm confused how anyone got in here, let alone inflicted this much damage."

Naomi continued surveying the vehicle, remaining close enough to eavesdrop on the call.

"Um, no. The shooters had blasted out the back window and tires." Bennett ran a hand over his head, agitation clear in his expression. "No, ma'am. How long did it take to get it impounded?"

That got Naomi's attention, and she moved closer.

"Yes, I'd love to see pictures. Thank you." He disconnected and faced her. "Apparently, when Deputy McClintock arrived to get the van, it had already sustained this damage. She's texting photos for us to compare."

Within seconds Bennett's phone pinged, and he held it out, allowing Naomi to examine the pictures. True to the deputy's account, bullets pulverized her van prior to the impounding.

"Those goons watched us leave?" Naomi surmised, placing a hand over her mouth.

"That's what I'm thinking." Bennett sighed, pocketing the phone. "Deputy McClintock got called out to an incident on the highway after receiving orders to impound your van. She got there as soon as she could."

"Why didn't they send someone else?"

"Staffing is always an issue. Too many incidents, not enough responders. An impounded vehicle takes lower precedent over a vehicular accident. Worse, they're lengthy to process."

"Which provided the shooters plenty of uninterrupted time to destroy my van." Although Naomi understood the logic, she couldn't help but wonder what would've happened if the deputy had arrived sooner.

He moved closer, inspecting the damage. "These guys are bold."

Bennett's voice faded behind her as Naomi walked to the driver's side and peered through the shattered window. She had nothing left. Without the van, she couldn't conduct her business. "Oh God, what am I going to do?" She whispered the desperate prayer. Hopelessness weighed on her with such force she wanted to collapse.

The thugs who'd done this wouldn't accept her word, and she shuddered to think what they'd do to her.

She glanced at Bennett.

The handsome detective had worked hard to protect her, but one man against two or more crazed killers weren't great odds.

Another survey of her van confirmed Naomi's fear.

There wasn't a person in the world strong enough to save her. *God, I need You.*

Bennett raged at the sight, mentally berating himself for not ordering security at the ranch. He recalled the earlier conversation with Deputy McClintock. Her confusion about safeguarding the van in the impound lot made sense now. Why protect this mess?

The shooters had waited for them to leave, then returned to search for the drugs. The cowards probably assumed Bennett had called for backup. Whatever the reason, he sent a silent prayer of gratitude that Naomi hadn't been one of their casualties.

He approached her. "Deputy McClintock and her team collected ballistic evidence from the scene, and it's already on its way to my contact at DPD for processing." The words tasted like a betrayal. Platitudes weren't helpful.

She looked at him, face crumpling. Tears

streamed down her cheeks, and helplessness consumed him.

"Why?" The single question carried with it the desperation of her heart and situation.

Against the voice in Bennett's head reminding him of their respective roles, he pulled Naomi's body, racked with sobs, into his arms. Even Spike moved closer to her. The beagle sensed her hurt and offered comfort. Bennett rubbed Naomi's back, unsure what to do. He feared for the baby. "Shh, Naomi, it'll be fine. Somehow. Focus on your son. Calm down for him."

She surprised him by releasing her hold and swiping at her face. "Right. I'm okay."

"Liar." His mouth quirked in a half smile.

"Guilty as charged, but I need to see the rest of the damage."

"Are you sure?"

"Yeah, no point in pretending it's not horrendous."

Together, they inspected the interior, where the destruction reminded him of Naomi's apartment—vicious and unrelenting.

Bennett led her away from the vehicle. "Naomi, I'd like Spike to inspect everything once more. I doubt we'll find anything." He jerked his chin toward the van. "They most likely didn't either. That kind of mutilation speaks to pure fury or a warning."

Her eyes widened.

He winced. "Sorry, I guess I should've phrased that better."

"I'd rather hear the ugly truth." She shook her head. "Ted must've used the van to hide drugs. How could I have been blind to his activities? Why would he put me and the baby in danger?"

"This is not your fault. You are not responsible for Ted's actions." The comment washed over Bennett. Was his callous skepticism a product of blaming himself for Delaney's deceit? He'd taken in the humiliation, accepting responsibility for her crimes. He was no more accountable for her decisions than Naomi was for Ted's.

She nodded, swiping again at her cheeks with a tissue she'd produced from her purse. Bennett squeezed her shoulder, resisting the urge to pull her close. It had felt so right to hold her, but that wasn't fair to her or him. He should've come alone. Still, this was a first for him.

His cell phone chimed with a text from Isla. The hospital security footage wasn't altered by Bill Nolice. The perp just avoided cameras. Nolice's background is clean. Ex-military, awarded several medals.

He responded. Thanks.

The information didn't preclude Nolice from assisting the intruder in Naomi's room, but it didn't point to him as an accomplice.

Naomi's continuing sobs drew his attention. She fell apart, crying to the extent of full hiccups between her words. "He. Shouldn't. Have."

Bennett placed a hand on her shoulder. "Breathe. Calm down. Think of your baby."

Naomi inhaled, hiccupping.

"Good. Take deep breaths," he encouraged.

She exhaled and blew her nose on the tissue. "You're right." She hiccupped. "It's just… a van."

"We won't let them get away with it. Let's shift into offensive mode."

She tilted her head. "Now is not the time to play football."

The seriousness of her comment exploded a guffaw from him, which made her laugh. "No, I meant instead of us being on the defensive, taking the hits as they dish them, let's get ahead of them."

Their chuckling quieted, and he elaborated,

"For all of this to happen six months after Ted's death raises questions." Bennett scoured his mind for information and landed on the possibility that Ted wasn't alone in the drug business.

"I'm not following you."

"What if one of your 'customers'—" Bennett made air quotes with his fingers "—hid the drugs?" Had someone followed Naomi, using her van to transport the drugs? Had Ted done that all along?

If Ted had an accomplice, it explained the time delay between his death and the arrival of the thugs at the ranch. However, it didn't expound on why.

"I suppose anything is possible."

"Let Spike and I search. Are you all right waiting here?"

She nodded and produced another tissue.

Bennett rushed to his truck, retrieved the stuffed taco, and placed it in his pocket. He knelt beside the beagle and used his voice inflection to inspire the dog. "Okay, Spike, ready to work?"

The beagle's white-tipped tail wagged excitedly.

"Let's find some cookies. Find the cookies!"

Spike took off toward the van, running to

the full extension of his lead. Bennett trailed as the dog made his way, nose in full force. Spike aimed for the rear tires where the intruders had torn out some of the flooring.

He barked twice, paused and barked again, then lay down.

Bennett scanned the area with his flashlight, finding nothing. The alert meant Spike detected the scent of narcotics. Though none were currently present, the drugs left a lingering odor or residue. The location correlated to the hidden compartment under the van's rear fender well where he'd found the fentanyl inside the liner. Whoever was involved with Ted Cavanaugh assumed he'd placed the drugs there or had placed them there to retrieve later. Based on the destruction they'd left behind, they were resolute to hurt Naomi.

He glanced out the shattered window where she stood, head held high, exuding confidence and grace. In that moment, Bennett decided he'd do whatever it took to protect her and her baby. He wouldn't let her out of his sight until he found the villains responsible.

Bennett surveyed the area, then glanced at his watch. They had to get on the road if they planned to make Naomi's doctor appointment.

Leading Spike from the van, Bennett walked to her.

"We'd better go."

She nodded, and he helped her into the truck before loading Spike.

A Douglas County Sheriff's cruiser pulled up beside his pickup.

"I'll be right back." Bennett walked to the patrol unit as the deputy exited.

"Again, Detective, I apologize for the miscommunication. I assumed you were aware of the damage."

"They returned after we'd left." He gestured to his truck. "We're late for an appointment. If you find anything that might help in the investigation, please contact me immediately."

"Understood."

"I appreciate it." Bennett strode to his pickup and slid behind the wheel. He texted the team with pictures of the van and a quick update, then started the engine and exited the property.

Once they were on the road, Naomi said, "Thank you for helping me to put things into perspective."

"How did I do that?"

"You reminded me of what's important. I must keep calm for the sake of my baby. The last thing I want is to spend another day at the hospital with Braxton-Hicks contractions." She leaned back in the seat. "The next time I show up there, it'll be to deliver."

"Sounds like a solid plan to me." Bennett reached over and squeezed her hand. "I am truly sorry for all you're going through."

"Thank you. Me too."

Bennett merged onto the highway.

"I'm baffled at the overkill damage to my van."

"Yeah." He gritted his teeth as images of what would've happened to Naomi if he hadn't been at Windham Ranch when the men showed up.

Both had their windows down, and a light breeze filtered through the cab.

Bennett traveled Santa Fe Drive, taking a route that paralleled Interstate 25, avoiding the rush hour traffic. They'd gone several miles when he noticed a large truck speeding from behind.

"Do not panic. We have unwanted company. Please scoot down as much as your seat belt allows." Then he shouted, "Spike, kennel!"

The dog disappeared into the steel box and a click sounded, confirming the automatic lock had fallen into place.

"What's going on?" Naomi twisted to look behind her.

"I'm not sure yet." Bennett's gaze bounced between the rearview mirror and the road ahead. "But I'm certain we don't want them getting too close to us."

A revving engine behind them nearly muted his statement. Bennett reached for his weapon, steadying the vehicle. There was no place to turn off the road that wouldn't put them at worse risk. He had to keep moving and get to highway C-470.

The truck sped up on Bennett's side.

He glanced at Naomi just as she cried, "Gun!"

"Stay down!" Bennett ducked and jerked the wheel.

His pickup slammed into the other vehicle.

Gunshots exploded through the cab, missing them while shattering Naomi's side mirror.

She squealed, covering her head with her arms.

Undeterred, their pursuers rammed into her door, attempting to force Bennett's truck into the heavy guardrail.

He fought to maintain control against the bullies. The cab filled with the grinding of metal on metal.

Finally, Bennett forced his way out of the battle, accelerating ahead. "Naomi, can you reach into the console? There's a lockbox. Enter the code four two zero five and get my backup weapon."

"Yes, I think so." She turned from her position on the floor. In an awkward twist, she retrieved the Sig Sauer. Naomi held out the pistol with both hands, clearly uncomfortable handling the gun.

"Tell me you've shot before." Even as Bennett spoke, he knew the response.

"No." She shook her head vehemently. "It's heavy."

"Two days ago, it would've thrilled me to hear that." Bennett groaned. "At the moment, I was hoping you'd say otherwise."

"I mean, I can try." She lifted the gun with both hands, whipping the barrel to face him.

He ducked. "Keep the weapon downward at all times unless you're firing it."

"Sorry." She winced, turning the gun downward, uncertainty still written on her face.

The truck drew closer again.

Bennett maneuvered his Silverado unsuccessfully to avoid the hit.

The shooters nudged his bumper, completing

the tactical maneuver, sending Bennett's pickup fishtailing. He gripped the wheel, recovering quickly, and pulled out of the skid.

Naomi clenched the seat with both hands. "Is Spike safe back there?"

"Yes." Bennett didn't elaborate. The fully enclosed kennel secured Spike from the gunfire, and he prayed it would also protect him from the jostling.

Several vehicles approached in the oncoming lane.

Naomi screamed.

Gunshots erupted from the pursuer's passenger window as they sped past, nearly colliding head-on with a semi before swerving in front of Bennett.

The steering wheel tugged to the right. "They hit a tire!" Bennett slowed, still fighting for control.

Ahead, the shooters swerved all over the road, then turned off at the next exit, disappearing from sight.

Chapter Eight

"Is it over?" Naomi's fingers dug into the seat cushion, eyes squeezed shut.

"For now."

She opened her eyes and released her hold.

Bennett extended his hand, helping her get into her seat. "Are you okay?"

"Uh-huh." Honestly, her muscles were strained and aching. Her gaze roved the road, occupied with morning travelers. "If only they'd been there a little while ago," she mused.

"Yep, that's what scared them off."

The truck rode awkwardly and a *womp-womp* sound carried from the rear.

"What is that?"

"A flat tire courtesy of those creeps. Based on the way my gas gauge is looking, they also hit the fuel line, so I don't want to stop anywhere on this road." Bennett focused ahead.

Naomi glanced out the windshield, spotting

several vehicles approaching from behind them and in the oncoming lane.

"Please use my phone and text my teammates, Selena Smith and Kyle West. Tell them where we are and ask them to meet us." He jerked his chin downward, where his cell peeked from his shirt pocket.

Naomi withdrew the device and held it out, allowing Bennett to hold his thumb over the reader to unlock it. Once the device came to life, she opened a new message.

"Tell them we have the partial Colorado license plate number of our assailants," Bennett instructed. "Advise 'K, seven, ten.' That's all I read off of it. We'll meet at the Linkhalter Steel parking lot just off Titan Road."

The truck's tire continued making the *womp-womp* sound.

"I need to pull over soon before I ruin the rim." Bennett pointed ahead, where Naomi spotted a large sign high above a warehouse building.

"Got it." She sent the message and within seconds received their chimed responses. "They're on their way," Naomi reported. "ETA ten minutes."

"Good. Hey, Spike, how're you doing?"

A sharp bark emitted from behind Naomi, and she twisted in her seat as much as possible. She spotted the white tip of Spike's tail wagging inside his kennel.

Bennett drove to a expansive, populated parking lot, and a sign overhead read Linkhalter Steel. He parked at the far side of the lot, farthest from the building, near a wide strip of grass. "Are you sure you're okay?"

Naomi's insides were wound tight as a crocheted knot. "Honestly, I'm a little shook up. Can you give me a few minutes to gather my wits?"

Bennett shut off the engine. "No problem. I'll check on Spike." He reached for the handle and shoved hard, but the driver's door refused to budge. After several shoulder thrusts, he surrendered. "It's stuck."

Several awkward seconds ticked by. Naomi realized Bennett couldn't get out until she did so that he could slide across the front seat. Unsure if her legs would hold her, Naomi exited the truck and leaned against the side panel. Her heart pounded hard against her chest.

Bennett released Spike from his steel kennel. "Great job, buddy." Bennett cradled the beagle in his arms, then gently set him on the ground.

He ran his hands over the animal's body. "Not a mark on you."

Spike barked and wagged his tail in appreciation. He strode to Naomi and nudged her leg. She leaned over. "I'm okay, too. Thank you for asking," she teased, stroking his fur.

Bennett offered his arm for support in a gentlemanly fashion. The concern in his eyes and Spike's sweet disposition reduced her racing pulse to a normal rhythm. She linked her arm in his, grateful to have him steady her shakiness.

They strolled the perimeter of the pickup, stopping to inspect the driver's side where the guardrail had dented it with a massive crease.

"That explains why I couldn't open the door." Bennett's narration did nothing to enhance the sight. "Let's keep walking."

Sunshine warmed their skin as they sauntered the perimeter of the property. Naomi breathed deeply, filling her lungs with oxygen. Spike led the way to a grassy island, pausing to sniff the surroundings.

In less than the predicted time, two black SUVs pulled into the lot and parked on either side of Bennett's vehicle. Both marked units bore the same logo Bennett wore on his uniform shirt.

"There's Selena and Kyle," he announced.

Nervous, Naomi strode beside him as they approached the vehicles. A fit man wearing a gray shirt with the same MCK9 logo exited the first SUV. His thick, dark hair was cut short. Naomi didn't miss the way his brown eyes pierced her with unspoken questions, even from a distance. He moved to the rear door of his SUV and released a large dog with long, floppy ears. He snapped on a leash, and the animal strolled beside him, tongue lolling to the side as he paused, waiting for the woman also exiting her vehicle.

"What kind of dog is that?" Naomi whispered to Bennett. "Sort of resembles a bloodhound."

"Close," Bennett said. "That's Rocky. He's a coonhound trained in cadaver detection."

Naomi shivered at the thought of the animal finding a body. Had Rocky found Peter? Sadness mingled with the unpleasant images in her mind.

From the other vehicle, an attractive woman with auburn hair emerged. She turned, fixing her green eyes on Naomi for a second before moving to the rear door. A brown blur bolted out of the SUV, then pranced around her. At her command, the dog sat, allowing her to secure a leash.

"That's Selena Smith and her Belgian Malinois, Scout," Bennett explained.

Naomi stiffened at the sight of the intimidating dog. "And his specialty?"

"Suspect apprehension."

"Great," Naomi muttered.

The team closed the distance between her and Bennett. Naomi realized they must've all considered her a drug-dealing serial killer, if they didn't still. "Um, do they think...?"

"That you're a murderer?" Bennett winked at her. "No, we've had meetings where I've updated everyone."

Naomi exhaled relief, yet she couldn't shake the sense they were sizing her up.

"Hi, Naomi. I'm Deputy Selena Smith." The woman extended her hand first. "This is my K-9, Scout." She gestured toward the Malinois.

Scout met Naomi's eyes in a silent warning. *Apprehension* meant if she tried running, she wouldn't get far. She swallowed hard. Duly noted. Naomi forced a shaky smile. "He's gorgeous."

"Don't tell him that." Selena grinned. "He's already got a big head."

The dog barked once and whined. The moment lightened the tension, and Naomi relaxed a little.

"See?" Selena rolled her eyes in a teasing reply.

"Rocky's biggest focus is food," the strange man replied.

At the mention of his name, the coonhound glanced up with soulful desperation.

"He looks hungry," Naomi commented.

"Nah, that's a total act. He just finished breakfast an hour ago." The man quirked a brow, feigning irritation, but a sparkle in his brown irises implied otherwise. "Hi, Naomi. I'm FBI Agent Kyle West." He didn't offer a hand to her. His daunting demeanor and title established their respective roles.

"It's a pleasure to meet you both, although I wish it were for other reasons," Naomi replied, suddenly cognizant of her arms hanging limply at her sides. Where was she supposed to put her hands?

The team engaged in discussion, using police terms, while Naomi focused on the animals.

The coonhound harrumphed, fluttering his long jowls, and glanced passively in her direction. Surely a cadaver dog was disinterested in the living. As opposed to his intimating friend, who looked like he could have her for lunch. The dog sighed and reverted his attention to Spike, offering a customary sniffing. He then sidled up to Naomi, as though confirming she was safe to be around while somehow defusing her nervousness. A grin tugged at her lips.

"Thanks for meeting us so quickly," Bennett said.

"Good thing we were close at the Windham Ranch when you called."

Naomi glanced up, catching Selena's gaze. She saw no challenge in Selena's eyes, but Naomi felt the weight of her curiosity.

"Let me catch you up." Bennett offered the team a synopsis of what had happened earlier, including the surprise of finding Naomi's van pulverized with bullet holes.

"Wow." Selena shook her head.

"Spike detected narcotics inside the vehicle near the same place where I found the two bags of fentanyl," Bennett continued. "Whoever did that to her van expected to retrieve their stash."

"Are there more?" Kyle asked.

"At this point, anything is possible," Bennett replied. "But the shooters drove a sedan. The truck that attacked us today was older, probably a seventies model, set high with a lift kit, push bumper and faded red paint. Doubtful you'll find them."

"Yep, your text offered that information," Kyle said.

Bennett shot Naomi a confused glance, and she shrugged. "I figured the additional description would help."

"Well done," Bennett replied. "You continue to surprise me."

Naomi's knees weakened at his approval.

"I reported the shooters to the local and state police. They've issued a BOLO for the vehicle." Kyle glanced down at his phone. "Speaking of. Just got a lead on the truck." He addressed his dog. "Rocky, let's go. We'll be in touch." The duo hurried back to their SUV and quickly departed the parking lot, leaving a dust cloud in their wake.

"We should probably go if we want to make your doctor's appointment." Bennett jerked his chin at Naomi, then addressed Selena, "I'll meet up with you and Kyle at my condo when we're done."

"Sounds good."

A contraction tightened around Naomi's middle, and she sucked in a breath.

Selena reached to support her. "What's wrong?"

Clearly, she'd not hidden anything from her expression. She waved off the deputy's concern with a forced smile. "Nothing more than Braxton-Hicks contractions." Naomi wrapped her hands protectively around her belly. "This little man is very busy." Not a lie, but she refused to draw attention to herself. The last thing Naomi wanted was returning to the hospital only to hear it was another false alarm.

Bennett moved closer, speaking to Selena, but standing nearer to Naomi. "They struck us on the driver and rear sides. She could have injuries."

"No. I mean. I'm fine," Naomi stammered as a case of uncontrollable shivers overtook her body. "I'm a little…shook up is all." Aware she was rambling but unable to control the erratic shaking, she said, "I'm sorry. It's just… I haven't…the hit."

"Shh, it's okay. Don't apologize. You're in the middle of an adrenaline dump, no doubt. Totally understandable. Just breathe deep." Selena spoke in a gentle tone, placing a hand at the small of Naomi's back. "Let's get you examined."

Though Naomi wanted to object, she feared

her legs wouldn't hold her much longer. The last thing she needed was to fall.

"Spike can hang with Scout and me," Selena offered. She glanced at his pickup, pockmarked with bullet holes and dents. "Not sure that's safe to drive. I'll call for a tow truck and take you to the appointment."

"I can rent a car while we're at the doctor's office," Bennett said.

"I'll report it for you," Selena said. "You focus on Naomi."

"Thanks." They started toward Selena's SUV, and Naomi gave her a grateful nod. "Bennett?"

He turned to face her. "Yeah?"

"Maybe use a different impound lot," she teased.

"Roger that." He chuckled.

"And…" That was the last thing Naomi remembered before everything went black.

Bennett flipped through the same magazine he'd held since arriving at the obstetrician's office. The paper was a curled mess from his nervous twisting. He tried focusing on the case and contemplating potential leads. But his thoughts revolved around his concern for Naomi. She'd been in the examination room for an hour.

Was that normal? She'd passed out after the car attack and quickly regained consciousness, for which he was eternally grateful. However, without discovering the reason she'd passed out, he couldn't relax. A brain injury? Internal injuries? His overactive imagination was stressing him out.

He'd utilized the time by pacing the waiting room, demanding updates from the cranky receptionist—who simply ignored him other than to say Naomi was fine and to please take a seat—and praying like he'd never prayed before that she and the baby were okay. At last, the door to the examination rooms opened, and he jumped to his feet as Naomi emerged. He tossed the magazine he'd pretended to read for the past hour.

"Are you all right?" His voice echoed, gaining him the attention of two women sitting nearby.

"I'm fine," she reassured in a whisper.

Her quiet rebuke reminded him he'd spoken louder than he'd intended.

Naomi checked out with the receptionist, and they exited the office.

Before Bennett burst, he blurted, "What did the doctor say? Is everything okay?" He led the way to the rental car—a white sedan—using the key fob to unlock the doors. "Did he explain why you fainted? Do you need to go to the hospital?"

"I told you it's good. I'm sorry I scared you." Naomi placed a hand over his forearm. If he wasn't so stressed about her condition, he might've focused on the way her touch sent his heart into an arrhythmia.

"What did the *doctor* say? Did he agree?" Bennett repeated, opening the passenger door and helping Naomi inside.

"*She*, Dr. Pankratz, did all the tests and monitored the baby's heartbeat. She confirmed I'm fine." Naomi withdrew her hand, and he missed it instantly. "Sometimes I pass out if my blood sugar gets too low, which is totally on me. I know better than to just eat cereal and not protein first thing in the morning." Naomi snapped on her seat belt, and he gently closed the door, then scurried to the driver's side and slid behind the wheel.

"Did the car attack hurt the baby?" Bennett asked, continuing the conversation. His stomach roiled.

"No, the baby's heart rate is normal. Little man ratted me out on my lack of nutrition. No more giving in to junk food cravings...at least not without adding something healthy."

Bennett exhaled relief. "Thank you, Lord." Being worried about Naomi and the baby reminded him how out of touch he'd been with God lately. He'd just met her, and she had too big an impact on him—he'd explore that another time.

Regardless, he had to guard Naomi. Though his teammates could handle her protective detail, they'd more than proven themselves trustworthy, the idea of transferring her care to someone else was unbearable. Not with killer thugs relentlessly pursuing her.

Bennett merged away from the doctor's office and onto C-470 east and Interstate 25 northbound.

"Me too. I've had more excitement in the past two days than my entire life."

"The receptionist was close to tossing me out. I kept asking her if everything was okay. Like every five minutes. Toward the end, I expected her to call security."

"I'm touched by your attentiveness." Naomi chuckled, then the smile fell away. "I've been on this pregnancy journey alone from the start. It was nice to have the company today."

Bennett considered Naomi's strength and position. Even after facing the harsh realities of her husband's nefarious deeds, she maintained her kind disposition. In contrast, he'd grown bitter after Delaney Huxley, whom he'd shamelessly touted as the perfect woman to his coworkers and subsequently his fiancée, turned out to be the major drug dealer he hunted. That had changed him.

"I'm glad the receptionist didn't call the cops or have you thrown out. Though explaining why my arresting detective—who no longer held me as suspect—was having a conniption fit in the waiting room might've been awkward."

At the implication, Bennett grinned. "True." He loved Naomi's personality, her quick wit and teasing manner. *Stop that! She's off-limits!* He ran one hand over his head, squelching the thoughts.

"I'm unsure how this will play out with the men who are determined to kill me, but the doctor said I need to rest until the baby is born." Her hands caressed her belly. "I had a full schedule of tours. I can't afford to take the time off this close to the delivery date, but she said another incident or high stressor could bring on early labor."

"Didn't you leave open dates on your calendar in case you delivered sooner?"

"Unfortunately, that wasn't an option with no sick leave." She shook her head. "I scheduled up to my due date. My mom always talked about Evan and I being late arrivals. I don't expect to deliver early." Naomi shrugged. "I guess the truth is I didn't want to be sitting home alone twiddling my thumbs until little man arrives."

"I don't do well with idle time, either." Bennett's opinion of Naomi only grew better, but the poor woman needed to rest. "I'll help cancel your remaining tours."

"I'd appreciate that. Addy offered to handle my tours while I'm recovering from delivery. We'd talked about that as a backup plan in case little man came early."

"Smart! We'll tackle that first thing. Considering all that's happened, I'd prefer if you stayed at my condo. Selena and Kyle will assist in your protection detail."

"Thank you." Naomi seemed to relax slightly at his offer.

"I hate to drag us back to unpleasant topics, but can you think of any place the thugs might look for the drugs?"

"I have no clue." She grunted. "I was oblivious to my husband's activities." Naomi twisted in the seat slightly to face him. "Isn't it funny how you think you know someone so well, then discover you didn't know them at all?"

Bennett blinked several times. Thoughts of Delaney infiltrated his discussion like an unwelcomed visitor. The perfect timing also reiterated why he shouldn't have feelings for Naomi.

The realization hit him. He had feelings for her.

When had he lowered his heart shield? The emerging emotions weren't appropriate. Not only because she was his charge, but because of all that he'd endured with Delaney. "Yeah. It does. Are you angry?" He had no intention of blurting the question, but since the discussion was open, he pressed on, "Doesn't it make you want to distrust people and refuse to take them at face value?"

"Are you talking about Ted?"

Bennett shrugged. "In general."

"I'm angry that he put our lives at risk with his poor choices. It's hard to be on the receiving end of someone else's mistakes." She shook her head. "To answer your question, I can't live like that. Suspecting everyone all the time.

That's exhausting. As my mother would've said, it puts you in prison."

"I'm not following you."

"If you hold on to bitterness and unforgiveness, withdraw from everyone and stay skeptical of people, you're putting yourself in a personal prison. The person who hurt you isn't suffering at all. Yet you live alone in the name of self-preservation. Ted owns his mistakes. They don't belong to me or those who enter my life after him."

Bennett swallowed hard. Naomi's words were like a splash of ice-cold water drenching his face. What she said made sense, but he bristled. He'd suffered at Delaney's choices. And until that moment, he'd never considered himself unrealistic. Since her betrayal, he didn't extend trust until the person had proven themselves first. That wasn't prison; it was wisdom. "I see it differently. Once you learn how untrustworthy folks are, you shouldn't be naive. You're required to make calculated decisions."

"Hmm, that's justifiable, too." Naomi shifted in the seat. "I'm sure in your profession, you can't take people at their word."

"Precisely."

"I'm a hopeless optimist, and Ted's bad choices won't change that. My baby deserves the opportunity to have a positive life outlook. I don't want to turn into one of those grumpy types who looks like she drinks lemon juice all the time. My mother said staying positive keeps the wrinkles away."

He chuckled. "Sounds like something my mom would say, too."

The highway was busy, and flashing lights ahead warned of an accident. They came to a stop, and Bennett glanced at Naomi. Her creamy skin and brilliant hazel eyes with gold flecks behind the green were enrapturing. He could get lost in them. Thankfully, she didn't seem to notice him staring as she leaned forward, peering out the windshield. "Wow, looks like a multi-car accident up there."

Bennett returned his focus to the road. "Yeah, it'll get uglier in rush hour."

She sat back in her seat. "Thank you for all you've done to help me and for willingly reviewing the evidence and proving the drugs weren't mine. I'm truly grateful. Without you watching over me, I'd probably be dead by now. But I would understand if you needed to transfer me to someone else's care. You've got better things to do than babysit me."

He sat speechless. He'd assumed the worst of her while she held him in high regard. Now she was offering him an out, and he wouldn't dare take it. His feelings for Naomi entered dangerous emotional territory.

Naomi's cell phone rang, and she reached to answer it. "Hey, Addy." A pause. She frowned. "Uh, yeah. I guess so. It's just temporary. But I'll be back at work soon. Right. Thanks." She disconnected. "Addy's a little pushy about sharing the proceeds of the tours she's handling for me. She's asking for a bigger share with an 85/15 split."

"Do you think she's involved with any of this? She stands to profit if you're no longer in business."

"I doubt it. You've checked into her, right?"

"Yes."

"See?" She yawned and covered her mouth. "Sorry, I'm tired."

"Rest. It might be a long drive with the accident up there."

"You don't have to tell me twice." Naomi leaned back and closed her eyes.

Bennett flicked a glance her direction, then

focused on the road as traffic loosened and bot-tlenecked around the multi-car collision. Naomi's words pelted him with conviction, yet he clung to his strategy. Optimism was dangerous.

Chapter Nine

Naomi was contagious—at least her upbeat personality and kindness were. Bennett had distanced himself, opting to work on his laptop from his couch. The location provided a clear visual of the women seated at his dining room table. Their easy conversation and occasional laughter filled his lifeless condo with an unfamiliar lightness.

Based on Selena's demeanor and obvious ease around Naomi, Bennett wasn't the only one who enjoyed spending time with her. From where he sat, it was evident Naomi had won over Selena. She had a talent for endearing herself. Selena's guarded side had given way to a cautious but friendly attitude in the short time she'd hung out with him and Naomi.

The cursor on his internet search engine blinked, mocking his inability to focus. For the past hour, he'd pretended to busy himself, looking for updates pertinent to the RMK case and Ted Cavanaugh's death. He'd distance himself from Naomi in hopes of reigning in his bizarre and unwelcomed feelings.

So far, nothing had worked. His thoughts were on an endless reel, revolving around the beautiful mother-to-be sitting a few feet from him.

Bennett gazed over the top of his screen, studying Naomi. She fit in so well with his team, Spike and him. Even Scout had taken a liking to her. And all of it couldn't be more wonderful and horribly wrong. He didn't want, nor was he actively seeking, a relationship with anyone. Not that she'd demonstrated any interest in him. At nine months pregnant, her biggest focus was her baby. As it should be. What right did he have to entertain any romantic thoughts at this point in his life or hers? She deserved the best. That wasn't Bennett Ford. He was a broken, jaded, bitter workaholic. Crimes evolved and persisted without lessening, which allowed him to transition from one investigation to another. Never slowing down. He had plenty to deal with in the present regarding the identification and apprehension of the RMK. If they failed to find the killer, someone else—

like Trevor Gage or any of his other friends—remained in danger.

If only Naomi's words hadn't created a fog of emotions around his mind and heart. She oozed encouragement, kindness and optimism. Her strong faith inspired him while making him question his cop sense. No one since Delaney had affected him the way Naomi did. And until he'd met her, Bennett was satisfied being alone.

Bennett caught Selena's disapproving frown in his peripheral vision and averted his eyes. Spike came to his rescue, bouncing at his feet. His whole back end wagged, thumping K-9 Scout's face with his tail. The Malinois lounged next to Bennett and gave Spike an annoyed harrumph.

"Sorry about that, Scout." Bennett hoisted Spike onto the sofa, lavishing affection on the beagle.

"Someone missed you," Selena said.

"It's not like I was gone for days." Bennett grinned. "He's not used to being away from me."

"Scout's the same way." Selena pushed away from the table and joined him in the living room.

Naomi did the same and slid into the recliner.

"It must be wonderful to come home and have someone excited to see you."

Bennett caught the hint of sorrow in her tone, and he fought the urge to comfort her.

She leaned back and blew out a long breath. "Little man is growing like a weed and taking up all the space where my lungs are trying to work."

"I take it you know the baby is a boy?" Selena sipped a soda.

"Yes, but I'm keeping his name a secret until he gives his grand appearance. For now, I call him 'little man.'"

"That's cute," Selena replied. "Hopefully, you can rest until you deliver with no more galli-vanting into wild car chases."

"No arguments here." Naomi chuckled. "You talked me into it."

"With all we've learned so far," Bennett said, taking the opportunity to launch into the inves-tigation, "let's review the facts. It might spark a burst of brilliance and new leads."

"Agreed." Selena retrieved her laptop from her backpack and settled it onto her legs.

"How about brainstorming?" Bennett's gaze flitted between the women, and he noticed Naomi's slight wince. She averted her eyes. Not wanting to ask her the question he'd repeated ad nauseam, he opted for a fresh approach. "Before we get started, Naomi, do you need anything?"

At the mention of her name, Naomi looked up, lip quivering. Tears shimmered, and a blush covered her face.

"What's wrong?" Bennett tossed the laptop to the side and rushed to her. "Are you hurting? In pain?"

Naomi waved him off. "Ugh, stupid hormones. I'm fine. Just tired. Honestly." Her attempt to laugh emitted a forced grunt.

Selena passed her a tissue.

"Thank you. I never know when I'll start crying. It's super annoying." She dabbed at her eyes. "I'm grateful for the kindness you two have shown."

"I can't imagine all you've been through." Selena set a bottle of water on the coffee table nearest Naomi. She dropped onto the seat across from her, leaning forward.

Though he longed to comfort her, Bennett returned to the sofa.

"Others have endured worse. I'm not complaining," Naomi said. "God has seen me through the hard stuff. I'm never alone with

Him. And as my mother would say, troubles keep me clinging to my faith, right?"

Troubles hadn't done that for him.

"Let's talk about the case. How can I help?"

"We should wait." Bennett glanced at Selena. She responded with an understanding jerk of her chin. "The doctor warned about stress," Bennett reminded Naomi.

"Pah. This isn't stressful. We're just talking." Naomi leaned back, adjusting herself on the recliner.

Spike hopped down from the couch and strolled to Naomi. "Well, hello there." She patted her leg. He sprung up, settling beside her.

"That's new," Bennett said. The dog's attention to Naomi and the warmness of the animal's compassionate gaze touched his heart. "As we discussed earlier, forensics confirmed Ted's fingerprints on the bags of fentanyl based on his concealed carry license permit."

"I can't believe I'd forgotten he had a gun." She blinked and shook her head. "I guess that shouldn't have surprised me. I try to think the best of everyone, especially those closest to me. His betrayal hurts."

Selena met Bennett's eyes as understanding of

the Delaney debacle and her own experiences with her ex-boyfriend passed between them.

"On a positive note…" Bennett began.

"What? You're looking at the positive?" Naomi teased.

"Just this once. Don't get used to it," he quipped.

"Right." She grinned.

"Anyway, the forensic confirmations helped us to clear you from the possession charge," Bennett reminded Naomi.

"True. I appreciate that." She tilted her head in that endearing way Bennett had come to expect.

Selena inserted, "I'd like to talk about Ted."

"More?" Naomi blew out a breath. "What else can I share with you that you aren't already aware of? In fact, you guys find things I'm oblivious to."

"You'd be surprised," Selena replied. "Our image or impression of Ted is based on what we learn through our documents and internet searches. Basically, boring one-dimensional Ted. You can offer us a view of his personality. The real Ted beyond his crimes."

"Yes," Bennett inserted. "What you share will help build his entire profile with nuances we weren't able to consider."

"That's logical." Naomi readjusted, but Spike didn't move. "Ted was outgoing, extroverted. We balanced each other well in that respect. He excelled at sales, so he did our promotional stuff. I preferred driving the van and connecting with the customers." Naomi resumed petting Spike, and he sighed contentedly.

Bennett wondered if his dog had dumped him. He grinned. Spike wasn't leaving Naomi's side anytime soon.

"What about before the business?" Selena asked.

"He was supportive of my rodeo-cowgirl performer career dreams. Riding was a big part of the reason I became a member of the YRC."

Bennett recalled Evan mentioning it in the interview he and Ashley had with him the month prior.

"No offense, Naomi," Selena said, "but after spending time with you, that's a big contrast to your personality."

Naomi chuckled. "Yeah, shy girls don't normally choose a spotlight career. Riding was different, though. Being on a beautiful horse gave me courage. I was in my own world."

"What changed those ambitions?" Selena asked.

"Ted and I began new dreams," Naomi said. "We wanted a business we could do together."

"That's understandable. A person's daily habits are telling, too," Bennett said. "Did Ted have any?"

Naomi took a few seconds before answering. "He loved to jog in the morning—weather permitting. I was never a runner, so I didn't go with him. Not that he'd invited me to."

"Did that bother you?" Bennett asked.

"Nope. I appreciated our relationship independence." Naomi tucked a stray tendril behind her ear. "We had separate and collective interests. We wanted to be our own person instead of becoming one of those couples who cannot function without each other."

Bennett had once believed independent lives were healthy until Delany took advantage of him. Was it just another thing she'd exploited?

Selena regained his attention. "Were there any particular trails or areas he preferred?"

"His favorites were the foothills closest to our townhome."

Bennett made notes on his computer. "You mentioned that toward the end of his life, Ted had changed?"

"We'd talked about adding in nature trail hikes to our tour company, as I explained before," Naomi said. "A few weeks before his death, he spent a lot of time testing out trails. In retrospect, I have no idea if that was true."

"Addy just added nature hikes to her business," Bennett said. "That's sure coincidental. Was she aware you and Ted were also adding the feature before his death?"

Naomi didn't respond.

"You didn't go with him?" Selena asked.

"No, we had a full schedule. We used the divide-and-conquer method. Besides, I couldn't stop the tours to join him."

Naomi had trusted Ted implicitly. A common mistake Bennett recognized in marriage. Except, when did one take off their skeptical glasses?

Had Ted abused her trust by pretending to need time alone to hike? Or had the excuse provided him the perfect reason to get away by himself and conduct his nefarious drug dealings?

As though reading his unspoken question, Selena inserted, "Don't most hikers use smartwatches and GPS apps on their phones?"

Naomi nodded. "Yes, Ted wore a smartwatch, and on the day he died—" Her voice hitched.

Neither pushed. They waited patiently as Naomi collected herself. "I provided the police with the recorded coordinates. They recovered his body nearby."

The details confirmed Bennett's assumption of her innocence. If Naomi had killed Ted, why deliver the location to the authorities? "Naomi, do you think Ted hid the rest of the stash or that he had something else they want—like records of deals or suppliers?"

She shrugged. "I suppose?"

"If he was hiding the drugs, the mountain trails provide endless places," Selena surmised.

"Are you saying he stashed them in the place where he died?" Naomi sat uprightly.

"I'd argue Ted did exactly that." Bennett activated a map on his computer, locating the site where law enforcement had recovered Ted's body.

"If he was in the process when the thugs showed up, he might've panicked," Selena said. "Or they tried to kill him, and he was running away—"

"As much as a person can while standing on the side of a mountain," Bennett interrupted.

"Then, in his haste to escape, lost his footing," Selena concluded.

Curiosity and questions lingered in Naomi's expression.

Excitement built within Bennett, and he jumped to his feet. "Selena, would you and Scout stay here with Naomi while Spike and I do some narcotic detection work?"

"Absolutely."

Naomi settled onto the sofa. "I wish Bennett would call, although I'm not sure how that'll affect the next course of events."

"Every lead draws us closer to catching the bad guys," Selena said. "Which in your case, means you can stop dodging drug-dealing enforcers."

"Right." Naomi reached for the bottle of water and took a sip. "I'm ready to disembark from the emotional and physical danger roller coaster."

"No one volunteers for that unwelcomed adrenaline rush."

Naomi tucked a throw pillow behind her back. "I'm beyond grateful Bennett didn't toss me in jail."

"Normally, he would've. He had sufficient

evidence, too. Totally unlike him." Selena met her gaze. "Not gonna lie. I'd have arrested you and sorted out the details later."

Once more, she offered a silent petition of thanks. "Why didn't he treat me that way?"

"Bennett's not a spontaneous person. He weighed the situation, then acted applicably."

"He's an enigma," Naomi said.

Selena laughed. "That's one way to put it."

"Have you and Bennett known each other a long time?" The question escaped Naomi's lips before she'd processed how strange it might sound to Selena. At the deputy's quirked brow, Naomi quickly added, "I don't mean to pry."

Selena studied her for several uncomfortable seconds.

Had she overstepped some invisible discussion boundary? "Forget I asked. It's none of my business."

Selena closed the laptop and set it on the coffee table. "Bennett and I worked for different agencies, so the task force brought us together. We've sort of bonded over the shared experience of having our love interests betray our trust." Selena sipped from a bottled water. "I fell in love with a man who was later convicted of murder and sent to prison."

Another long pause overrode Naomi's quiet curiosity. "Was he guilty?"

"I don't know for sure." She crisscrossed her legs on the recliner. "I trust the judicial system. It's my life and how I make my living. To say I don't depend on it makes me a hypocrite."

"Yeah, but like most systems, there are flaws," Naomi reasoned.

"True." Selena sighed. "Part of me hopes—no—believes he's innocent. If he is, then I wasn't a fool to trust him."

"Self-preservation is understandable."

Selena grunted. "I'm a deputy. Trained to detect deception. Not seeing that in the person closest to me makes me either foolish or bad at my job."

"I disagree. Everyone has secrets." Naomi considered her statement. What had she withheld from Ted? The answer was easy. She'd never told him about the murders in Elk Valley. "Ted was the adventurous one. I happen to be in the jet wash of his choices."

"Been there, done that," Selena said.

"That sounds like experience talking."

Selena looked down, studying the water bottle. "I fell hard for Finn—that's his name—at the ripe old age of twenty-two. Of course, I thought I knew everything about him... Boy, was I wrong."

"Was there some part of you that questioned him?" Naomi shifted on the sofa. "I wonder if I missed signs?"

"I asked that same question."

Compassion for the deputy welled within Naomi. Scout strolled to the kitchen and sounds of him lapping water carried to them.

"Ugh, he's probably making a puddle." Selena set down her laptop and pushed out of the recliner.

Naomi watched as she entered the kitchen and groaned.

"Nice, Scout. Try to get some of the water in your mouth next time." Her teasing admonishment brought a grin to Naomi's lips. Selena gathered paper towels and bent to mop up the mess. "It's like having a furry child." Selena chuckled, resuming her position on the recliner.

"I understand. The beauty of loving someone is getting to be ourselves and not questioning everything?"

"That's the dream," Selena agreed. "If you could do it over again, would you still marry Ted?"

"Yes." Naomi answered without hesitation.

"Really?" Disbelief clouded Selena's face.

"Each experience is training for the next level of our journey." She rubbed her belly. Little man offered a thump of agreement. "Without Ted, this little guy wouldn't exist. And I wouldn't trade being his mama for anything in the world."

Naomi rose and walked to the sliding glass door, stepping onto the small deck. Bennett's condo sat on the outskirts of downtown Denver near the state capitol building. From her vantage point, she spotted a woman standing near the stoplight across the street. She glanced up as though sensing Naomi was watching her. The stranger didn't move, her position was almost a challenge.

From the height of the deck, Naomi had no chance of making out any details about the woman. Yet gooseflesh rose on Naomi's arms that had nothing to do with the spring breeze that fluttered her hair.

Something about her demeanor and stance seemed familiar. Naomi stepped closer to the railing, hoping to gain a better look.

A large delivery truck pulled up, waiting for the light to change. The woman disappeared into the building's shadow.

"Stop being silly," Naomi said aloud, then turned and reentered the condo. Selena had her computer open again, so Naomi strolled through Bennett's open-concept home, saddened by the sterile decor. All of it screamed *temporary*. Aside from the essential furniture and accents like lamps and blinds, there were no paintings on the walls. No family pictures. No memorabilia or personal belongings. Bennett lived as though he could pack up and leave any day. Why? Did he fear putting down roots? Did his job not allow it? Naomi realized how little she knew about him.

"Is Bennett not planning on staying here?" Naomi moved to the sofa.

"Our positions with the Mountain Country K-9 Task Force mean we go where we're needed, though Denver is his hometown." Selena shrugged. "We're headquartered in Elk Valley, and our members are scattered across several states."

"I don't remember hearing about a task force when I lived there."

"We were brought together recently for the purpose of tracking down the Rocky Mountain Killer."

An involuntary shiver ran through Naomi's

body. Her thoughts circled the overthinking drain. The future she'd once expected and planned for was gone. She looked around, realizing she also lived in the land of temporary. Would she ever go home again?

Chapter Ten

By the time Bennett and Spike arrived at Beaver Brook Trailhead outside the city of Golden, Colorado, Bennett was crawling out of his skin with eagerness. Though it was a weekday, visitors packed the place, forcing him to park a quarter mile from the trailhead. He'd expected nothing less. People flooded into Colorado from other states, overpopulating the beautiful grounds, in his humble opinion. Additionally, the number of passersby didn't bode with their initial thoughts of Ted concealing drugs here. Why not venture to a more private setting where multiple hikers weren't milling around?

Bennett used his phone to study the online trail map. Unless Ted had ventured deeper into the woods?

He turned slightly in his seat, utilizing his laptop set in the vehicle's docking station. Bennett surveyed Ted Cavanaugh's digital case file.

A pair of hikers corroborated Naomi's account of Ted's GPS last known location when they advised seeing what appeared to be a human at the bottom of a deep ravine. Law enforcement had scoured the area and discovered Ted's body in the early morning hours of October 3. The medical examiner deemed Ted's fatality as accidental—a fall from the cliff. The autopsy listed Ted's cause of death as a severed spinal cord and noted several other injuries, including broken vertebrae, multiple lacerations, contusions and numerous fractured bones—the largest of which ascribed to his right arm and left leg.

Bennett's mind whirled. Had someone shoved Ted off the cliff after beating and possibly torturing him? The ME had requested no further investigation. He'd had no cause to.

Not until now.

He needed to survey the crime scene.

Bennett closed the laptop and exited his patrol unit. He released Spike from his kennel in the back seat, then snapped on the dog's harness and leash. He spotted a man standing close by, watching them. Based on the curiosity in his demeanor, Bennett anticipated his approach.

Sure enough, he stepped forward. "Cute dog," he said.

"Thanks," Bennett replied, tugging on his backpack and locking his SUV.

"You a cop?"

"Something like that," Bennett remarked.

"Cool. Is he like a search dog?" the man asked.

Bennett was used to inquisitive strangers. Spike got people's attention. "Yep, he's amazing. I just hold the leash."

"Whatcha searching for?"

"Today is a little different," Bennett said, diverting the discussion. "Out for a little R&R." Reconnaissance and Recovery, he thought, forcing away a grin.

"Cool." The guy lingered for a second. "Enjoy. It's a great day to be out," he said, walking away.

Bennett and Spike trekked the curvy road to the trailhead entrance. A posted sign designated Beaver Brook's trail level as moderate to advanced.

Bennett glanced down at his MCK9 uniform short-sleeved shirt and pants. He'd changed into hiking boots, but even Spike's MCK9 harness caught the attention of hikers as they passed. Bennett made light conversation but didn't linger. Other than a few nosy questions—which he tactfully avoided answering—he continued without stopping. When he neared the location where Ted's body was found, Bennett stepped from the trail into the forested area. He sought a better place to survey from, journeying deeper into the thick grove of trees bordered by craggy walls steeped high to one side.

From his position, the foliage provided concealment from hikers on the path. Bennett shifted his gaze to a flattened space where a gigantic boulder perched on the edge of the steep cliff. After double-checking his GPS coordinates on his cell phone to confirm he was in the correct place, he withdrew binoculars from his backpack. Bennett spotted an outcrop where the landscape leveled off slightly.

With Spike's leash snapped to his belt, Bennett hiked closer to inspect the area. The land transitioned, plummeting down a tapered ravine where sharp rocks and tree shrubs peaked up from the uneven gravel and dirt walls. Narrow, but not unpassable for a skilled hiker like Ted. The leverage also allowed him to remain hidden from witnesses. A surreptitious location to hide his stash.

Bennett surveyed the landscape, ensuring no one approached before he knelt beside Spike.

He adjusted the K-9's harness, double-checking the leads were secured. "All right, Spike. Ready to search for some cookies?"

The beagle's thin tail swished with excitement.

"Let's find the cookies!"

With Spike in the lead, they carefully traversed the treacherous landscape. Bennett angled his feet to strengthen his stride as they descended the precipice. When they reached a space dotted with spiny plants and boulders in varying sizes, Spike tugged harder, aiming for a colossal stone. Bennett cautiously edged closer around the rough ground, vigilant to give Spike the leash length he needed.

To his surprise, Spike continued forward, descending the ravine and into a wooded area.

When they were fully concealed behind the foliage, Spike moved to a sizable rock. He barked twice in the distinct beagle sound, paused, and then barked once more. Just as Bennett had suspected.

Ted had buried the narcotics.

Bennett rushed closer and knelt. He glanced up, confirming their location was hidden from the hikers above. It took Bennett several tries before he rolled away the stone, exposing a soft dirt section. Withdrawing a small trowel from his backpack, Bennett dug into the rocky earth. After several minutes, the tip of the tool halted, tinging against something hard. Bennett dropped it. Using his hands, he brushed away the loose soil, revealing a metal box.

"Good job, Spike!" Bennett yanked the stuffed taco dog toy from his pocket and tossed it to the beagle.

While Spike enjoyed his reward, Bennett unearthed the container.

Voices drew closer. The beagle's ears perked up. Bennett lifted the binoculars. A pair of hikers passed on the path above, oblivious to him and Spike. Once they were out of sight, Bennett looped the binocular cord over his neck, letting them hang there. He donned latex gloves and opened the box.

Tiny amounts of familiar white crystals—fentanyl—littered the bottom, along with a folded piece of paper and a thick wad of cash. He lifted it, flipping through and counting. Mostly hundreds. The drugs were gone. Stolen? Moved? If so, why leave behind the money? Bennett carefully unfolded the paper. Messy script, indicative of a man's handwriting, centered the document.

I'm sorry, N.
To you and the baby. I got in over my head and
they know I want out. If anything happens to
me, the dealer after me is Roderick Jones and
his henchmen.

I love you,
T

Beneath the letter, Ted had scrawled *Ecclesiastes 12:14.* Bennett grew up going to church but hadn't memorized his Bible that well. He'd have to follow up later.

Thunder rolled in the distance, and Bennett surveyed the darkening sky as rain clouds slowly stirred overhead. A soft breeze passed over him and a chill slithered down his back. Roderick Jones was a local criminal, a most-wanted celebrity. All the Denver metro area and surrounding law enforcement agencies kept Jones on their radar. Taking him down was akin to lassoing the golden goose.

Like one of those Plinko games, the pieces started falling into place. Ted had tried hiding the drugs, though his motive remained unclear. Either he'd intended to go to the police with the information, or he foolishly believed he'd outsmart Jones. He'd underestimated his enemy, and he'd paid with his life.

If Bennett didn't stop Jones, Ted's mistakes would cost Naomi and the baby's lives, too.

He used his cell phone to capture a picture of the note.

A rustling got his attention, and he looked up. Another roll of thunder warned of the impending storm.

Bennett returned the contents to the box and closed the lid, then placed it inside a plastic evidence bag along with his gloves, ensuring the fentanyl didn't contaminate his supplies. He sealed the bag before securing it inside his backpack, then added his trowel. Not wanting to waste a single second with the possibility of getting caught in the storm, he determined to call Selena on the way to DPD. He'd have to stop there first to drop off and log the evidence.

"Sorry, Spike, but you have to give me your taco."

With a few more quick squeaks, Spike relinquished the soggy toy into Bennett's hand. He tucked it into his pants pocket.

They hiked up from the ledge and started through the deep, forested trees to the hiking path. Bennett's new goal expanded. Not only would he take down the RMK, but he would finally get Roderick Jones and his cronies.

First, he'd have to break Naomi's heart with news of her deceased husband's deeds.

That elevated his blood pressure more than a hundred gunfights.

They'd reached a thicketed area when Spike stopped and barked, tail and hackles raised.

What had sent the beagle into a frenzy?

Bennett turned just as a slam to the back of his head thrust him into darkness.

Four hours had passed since Bennett's departure. Naomi's gaze flitted to the clock on the mantel. "Should we be worried that Bennett hasn't called yet?"

"No. The commute to Golden with traffic is lengthy by itself," Selena replied. "If he's hiking the area, that'll take time."

"But it's nearly dark out."

"Naomi." Selena's one-word admonition had her slinking into the kitchen, desperate to busy herself.

Naomi grabbed a dishrag and wiped the counter, mulling over the situation. She had no right to feel the strange emotions she did for Bennett. They'd just met. He'd planned to arrest her for being a serial killer. Yet she couldn't deny her concern for his safety and well-being. She'd lost Ted in those mountains. She couldn't bear to lose someone else she cared for.

She continued her contemplations while wiping down every inch of the small room when Selena's cell phone rang.

"Is it Bennett?" Naomi hurried to sit beside her.

"Yes."

Naomi leaned closer, making no attempt to hide her efforts to eavesdrop.

"Hey, what did you find?" Selena listened for several seconds, brow furrowing. "What? Are you or Spike injured?"

Naomi strained to hear. "What happened?"

"I think you should call for an ambulance, Bennett. Sounds like he hit you hard." Selena shook her head. "Fine, but I disagree."

"What's wrong?" Naomi blurted, heart racing.

"Bennett has an update for us." Selena set the device on the table between them and pressed the speakerphone option. "Go ahead."

"Can you hear me?" Bennett asked.

"What's wrong?" Naomi blurted. "Are you hurt?"

"I'll explain when I get there," Bennett responded. "Spike and I are fine."

"Now," Selena mumbled.

Naomi leaned closer to the phone. "Please tell me what happened."

"We're getting ready to leave Beaver Brook Trail."

"You've been there all this time?" Naomi asked.

"Yeah, our trip had a minor detour when someone attacked me. Before you flip out, I'm fine. Just a hard knock upside my head."

"At least you didn't hurt anything important," Selena teased, though Naomi noticed the worry in her green irises.

"Anyway—" Bennett dragged out the word for emphasis "—the best I can tell, I was out for about five minutes. It was long enough for the perp to get away," he grunted. "Apparently, Spike's barking got the attention of a hiker. He rushed to help us. Thankfully, the assailant didn't hurt Spike."

"Go straight to the hospital," Naomi blurted.

"Seriously, I'm fine. I need to tell you what we found."

Several seconds passed without another word. Naomi inched closer to the phone. Were they still connected?

"Now's not the time for suspense, Ford," Selena remarked.

"I had a nosy passerby when I first arrived. I didn't think much of it at the time, though looking back, he hesitated a little too long and asked questions about Spike and I." Bennett exhaled into the receiver. "Spike found a metal box buried near where Ted died."

"What was inside?" Naomi blinked, unsure what the discovery had to do with her. "I'm confused."

"About a hundred thousand dollars cash—smaller bills—and a handwritten letter addressed to you," Bennett replied. "I'm texting Selena a picture of it. It's faded and might be hard to read. Whoever attacked me took the box."

"I could see them stealing the money, but why the letter?" Selena asked.

"It wasn't a random mugging. Someone followed me here, anticipating that I'd look for it and would find it with Spike's help. They'll be disappointed, though."

"Why?" Naomi asked.

"There were remnants of fentanyl, same cut as what I found in your van, Naomi," Bennett explained. "That's how Spike triggered on it to begin with. I think Ted buried the box and removed the drugs. I believe the money was intended for you."

"I'm struggling to grasp all of this," Naomi said. "Where would Ted get that kind of money?" Though even as she spoke the words, she knew the answer.

"The find adds to our suspicions that Ted was dealing," Bennett explained.

"It's a lot to absorb," Selena replied.

"Not sure I can handle much more," Naomi said.

Selena frowned. "I'm sorry you had to find out this way."

"Naomi, normally I would show this to you privately," Bennett said. "Because the information is imperative for us to work the case, I felt it was best to read it aloud. Selena must hear it, too."

Naomi inhaled a fortifying breath, bracing herself for what it would say. "How bad is it?"

"Selena, can you open the picture for Naomi?"

She raised the phone and swiped at the screen, gently placing it in Naomi's palm. A compassion she hadn't seen before in the deputy's face nearly undid her.

With a deep breath for courage, Naomi adjusted the device. Immediately, she recognized

Ted's familiar scrawl. Like a voice from the grave, his words stretched out to her. Naomi's eyes welled with tears, blurring her vision.

"Naomi, does the handwriting look like Ted's?" Bennett asked.

"Yes." Her voice cracked.

Selena reached over and offered a light touch to Naomi's shoulder as she read the letter aloud. When she finished, silence hung in the air.

Naomi pressed her fingers against her trembling lips, trying to remember the scripture Ted had referenced at the bottom of his letter, and came up blank.

Selena swiped at her phone. "For God shall bring every work into judgment, with every secret thing, whether it be good, or whether it be evil."

"Hmm," Bennett said. "Confession?"

"Maybe. Roderick Jones!" Selena's enthusiasm confused Naomi.

"Who is that?"

"A big-time drug dealer," Bennett advised. "Someone I've chased most of my career. He's got long arms with a wide reach and escapes conviction."

"He's also extremely dangerous. No wonder you've been running for your lives," Selena added, cringing at the harsh reply. "Sorry, I didn't mean to put it that bluntly."

"But why come after me?"

"That's harder to explain. Ted must've moved the drugs that were in the box. I can't yet rationalize why. Unless it's the fentanyl from inside your van," Bennett clarified.

Naomi placed Selena's phone on the coffee table.

"Surely, Jones is aware you confiscated the drugs," Selena commented.

"Right. Or there are more that Ted hid somewhere else," Bennett said. "Naomi, can you think of any place we should consider?"

"He stayed at our storefront a few times, but that's nothing more than a tiny cube of an office."

Selena paced beside her. "Where did he live after moving out?"

Humiliation swarmed over Naomi. "I don't know. I tried to give him room, hoping that would help him find whatever space he searched for. I was so naive."

"No, you trusted your husband and took him at his word," Selena said.

"Keep brainstorming," Bennett said. "Jones wouldn't love losing his money, but it's not enough for him to come after you, Naomi. It's minnows in his ocean of crime."

"Ted intended to do something with the drugs he hid," Selena surmised. "Sell them?"

"Negative. His reasoning isn't clear, but maybe he planned to hand them over to the authorities. If Jones figured out he'd lost Ted's devotion, he'd take whatever means necessary to eliminate him," Bennett explained. "Ted's death wasn't an accident. He premeditatedly buried this box. It took time and planning to find the right place. Jones or his henchmen probably followed or traced Ted to the location. If he refused to give up the information, they may have tortured him, then thrown him off the cliff."

Naomi's stomach roiled at the images. "I'm not sure if I'm angry that he was involved in such a mess or confused why he didn't go straight to the authorities. Worse, why not come to me and tell me the truth? We could've worked through it together," Naomi said. "But why are Jones and his cronies still coming after me?"

"Jones's henchmen may have thought Ted told you where he'd hidden the drugs or that you knew of Ted's plan," Selena replied.

"So why wait six months after his death?"

"In line with Selena's rationale, they've probably watched you for a while. Which means they've watched me watching you, so they had to be careful and tread wisely," Bennett explained. "They figured—as we had—that if they gave you space and let you take the lead, you'd show them what they wanted. Your predictable schedule baffled them. You weren't buying expensive things or acting any differently than you had since before Ted's death. They waited to see what you'd do." Bennett's voice grew softer. "When you went to Peter's ranch, it was outside of your normal routine."

"They assumed I had the drugs with me, or that I'd hidden them on the property or in my van," Naomi concluded. "Is the stress getting to me, or is that logical?"

"You're reasoning like a cop." Selena patted her hand. "It makes sense."

"I still don't understand why or how Ted got involved in this." Naomi sighed.

"You mentioned his concerns about finances," Bennett began. "If he connected with Jones or any of his low-life cronies, they probably promised Ted he'd bring in more money than he'd ever make in the tour business."

Naomi bristled. Was he seriously justifying Ted's crimes?

"Drugs lure lots of unsuspecting people into a world beyond their control," Selena agreed. "They make tiny compromises, and before they know it, they're in deep."

"Selena is dead-on accurate. I've watched it happen many times in my career, Naomi. Money is that lying voice that promises things it can never deliver." Bennett's comment spoke of experience, along with a deeper knowledge she couldn't quite put her finger on.

With countless thoughts bouncing around in her head, she could scarcely think straight.

"Worse, once Ted was in Jones's inner circle, there was no way out," Bennett expounded. "Jones isn't someone you want to mess with. I'm sure Ted feared for his life and yours. He was coming to a dead end—sorry, no pun intended."

"Or he hid them in advance, then Jones and his henchmen demanded the return. They take him back to the site, but Ted is uncertain where he buried them. Or he lied," Selena offered. "Maybe he tried running, they pursued, and he fell. That's still not an accident, though."

"Yes, that's plausible, too. Whatever the case,

they're responsible for Ted's death. I intend to add that to their long list of accumulating charges," Bennett said. "It's pure speculation, since we don't have evidence of what happened that day. Ted hiding the fentanyl says to me he was trying to get out of the mess he'd gotten into."

"Wow." Naomi put her head in her hands, trying to contain the absurd amount of information. "This is a living nightmare of a true crime show. Whose life looks like this?"

"It's a lot to process," Bennett said. "Ted clearly wanted you to have the note and the money. Obviously, something stopped him from telling you where it was, but he must've regretted his actions."

Was that a comfort? "What happens now?"

"We work on the case," Selena replied. "You rest and deliver a healthy baby."

"While we keep you safe," Bennett answered. "I need to stop at Denver PD, so I'll update the rest of the team from there. It'll take me a while, but I'll be back ASAP."

"Roger that." Selena exhaled. "I'll type up the details in the case file."

"See you soon." Bennett disconnected.

Naomi jumped to her feet and paced the

small living room, catching the attention of Scout and Spike. The dogs both sat in sphinx poses, watching her. "Excuse me."

She walked to the bathroom, desperate for a few moments alone to process the mess of her life. She closed the door and stood with her hands flat on the countertop and studied her reflection in the mirror.

Every single part of her marriage with Ted floated in an abyss of unexplained questions. Naomi wept as the sting of betrayal infiltrated her heart. While she'd planned a future for their baby, in a loving home where she'd dedicated herself to being a wife and mother, Ted had looked her in the eye and deceived her. Not just once, but over the course of months, years maybe—so many times that she wondered if he'd ever told the truth.

Chapter Eleven

After praying, peace had settled over Naomi. God would take care of her.

She returned to the living room, where Selena worked on her laptop. "Hanging in there?"

"Yes. I had a good cry. At least this time it's not just hormones." Naomi crossed her arms. "Once Jones gets the drugs Ted hid, he'll kill me."

"We won't let that happen."

"Someone attacked Bennett!" Naomi snapped. "If they got to him, how will you protect me?"

"The MCK9 task force is good. We'll get justice for Ted and for you. I can't promise when, but we won't stop until you're safe."

"I appreciate it, but I'm also enough of a realist to accept that Jones has eluded capture all this time for a reason."

To her credit, Selena didn't argue.

Images of someone shoving Ted off a cliff ratcheted her pulse.

Naomi walked to the dining room and sat down. Placing both elbows on the tabletop, she steepled her fingers. "Selena, I'm aware your team can't protect me indefinitely."

"Correct, as much as I hate to agree."

"I need practical advice on where to go from here. Do I move away, change my name? How do I protect myself and my baby?"

"Let's take one step at a time. If we're forced to consider other options, we'll deal with it then."

Naomi stared at the table's pattern.

How clueless was she to miss Ted's transgressions? The man she'd married wouldn't use or deal drugs. What changed?

Images of Ted's desperate state of mind brought on a wave of sorrow over Naomi. She couldn't help but pity him. If he'd let her into his troubled world, things could've been different.

Naomi bowed her head. "Lord, I don't know what to do with all of this. It's too much of a weight for me to bear by myself."

"Amen." Selena rested a hand on her shoulder. "You're not alone."

Naomi swallowed the emotion clogging her throat. Her stomach tightened. How was she supposed to avoid stress with the never-ending barrage of unbelievable facts thrown her way? She inhaled deeply, calming herself against her rising emotions. Little man kicked, fully engaged in his daily round of baby aerobics. All that mattered was ensuring she stayed healthy for the sake of her child. Ted was gone. Regardless of what he'd done, or his reasons, nothing had changed.

Naomi offered a prayer of thanks for Bennett and Selena. They'd worked hard to help her find the truth. She had to trust someone. For now, that meant trusting them.

Her thoughts returned to Bennett. The mysterious detective. She replayed Selena's comments about how differently he'd treated Naomi.

Selena walked back to the recliner.

Naomi walked to the kitchen, opened the cabinet, withdrew the box of cereal, and then poured some in a small bowl. She headed for the living room.

"Snack time?" Selena smiled.

"Nervous energy."

She took a bite, trying to distract herself from her racing thoughts. "I wonder if I'll be enough for this little man," Naomi admitted, rubbing her belly. "He will need a father, and I can't be that for him. My brother is wonderful, but he works a ton, and I'd never ask him to shoulder that responsibility."

Selena met her gaze.

"I assumed we were headed in the right direction. He was going in another. Turns out, Ted and I had no future. I was the last one to realize it."

Scout strolled into the room and dropped beside Selena. "I guess we never really know the people in our lives. We imagine we do, but they can sure surprise us. You're not the only woman to be blindsided by her significant other."

Naomi snorted. "Nobody is as oblivious to their spouse's activities as I was."

"Remember, I was in love with a convicted murderer." Selena tilted her head. "Bennett had a similar experience with his ex-fiancée."

Naomi nearly choked on the cereal at the word *fiancée*.

At her stunned silence, Selena's eyes went wide. "Or…did he not mention that?"

"No. He didn't." Naomi gaped, hoping she wouldn't clam up.

"Guess that wasn't my story to share," Selena mumbled. "I just assumed...with the three of us having such similar experiences..."

"I don't want you to violate any confidential information, but would you be willing to tell me some of his story?"

Selena paused. "I'll only tell what's in the court documents. Bennett found out Delaney was the drug dealer he was tracking."

Whoa. Naomi pondered Ted's betrayal. "I can't imagine how that hurt Bennett."

"Yeah, it made a huge impact. Bennett's more guarded and jaded than I am. And that's saying a lot." Selena exhaled. "He doesn't trust easily. However, the experience also gives him understanding of your position."

Naomi nodded mutely.

"Now that I've revealed stuff I had no business sharing, is it too much to ask that you forget everything I said?" Selena joked.

"I have a lot going on in my life at the moment, so it's possible." Naomi chuckled. "Bennett seems like a private person. I'm that way, too. Not that I have a lot of folks to share my life with." In the years she'd lived in Colorado and prior in Elk Valley, Naomi hadn't had many friends besides Peter. "I had a hard time making friends as a kid. It's worse as an adult. Especially when you find you don't want to tell anyone details about your life."

"I get that."

"I keep to myself, although in this case, that's beneficial. How would I explain that my husband died hiding drugs from a lethal dealer?" Naomi gave a bitter laugh.

"Might be a great icebreaker for new friendships," Selena teased.

Naomi giggled despite the seriousness of the topic. "Right? I probably shouldn't bring it up in mother-and-baby groups. I'm not sure they'd invite me again if I blurted that."

Selena guffawed. "I'm sorry. I don't mean to minimize your situation, but thank you for making me laugh."

"Laugh or cry. I figure those are our only options here."

"True." Selena blew out a long breath and took a sip of water. "Well, sadly Bennett and I both understand."

"You realize that's abnormal?"

"I'm submersed in law enforcement life. I forget the rest of the world isn't like us. On the other hand, as you see, you're not the only one." Selena gestured in a ta-da manner from her chair. "We've had exes who weren't who we thought they were."

"Maybe there's still hope for us optimistic romantics."

"I'm not sure I'd classify myself as optimistic or romantic. At least not anymore." A sadness appeared in Selena's green eyes.

Naomi surveyed Bennett's condo again. The lack of personal adornments and pictures made sense now. When Ted had moved out, then died, she'd kept only the single picture of them together. Everything else brought back painful memories.

"Bennett's a great guy, but he's committed to the job," Selena added.

Naomi heard the hint, but it didn't stop her from speaking the next words. "Most definitely. He's easy to be around, protective, comforting, engaging in conversation. His sweet disposition reminds me what it's like to be cared for in ways I'd forgotten were possible. It's as though we've known one another forever."

"Dangerous events can influence romantic thoughts. It's that need to survive that comes with facing trauma. Emotional transference."

Naomi averted her gaze. "And he's devoted to his career."

Why had she revealed her crush on Bennett? Her cheeks flushed. "I'm sure taking on an already established family—" she gestured toward her belly "—isn't on his agenda." Naomi realized her comment sounded like she was baiting Selena for information. "Not that any man would be interested," she blurted.

"Who knows?" Selena lifted her hands in mock surrender. "Just keep your expectations low."

Naomi nodded, disappointment clouding her heart. She caressed her belly, reminded again that God had given her a precious baby to care for.

He was her biggest priority.

Her only priority...besides staying alive.

Selena's cell rang. "Yep," she answered, rushing to the front door.

Naomi sat up straighter, unsure what was happening.

The familiar coonhound entered, panting softly beside his FBI agent partner, who carried a large pizza box. He also balanced a cardboard drink holder containing cups of ice cream on top.

Naomi struggled to remember both his and the dog's names.

Selena rescued her from embarrassment. "Kyle, I've never been more grateful to see you." She lifted the ice cream container.

"Rocky, go chill by Scout," Kyle said. "Hey, Naomi." He walked to the dining table and set down the pizza box.

"Hi." Unsure if she needed to use his title, first or last name, she stuck with the single-syllable greeting and rose to join them.

Girl talk with Selena had ended, but Naomi's disappointment faded with the aroma of food and the affirmation that Bennett Ford was off-limits.

Night had fallen when Bennett arrived at his condo. For the first time since returning to Denver in pursuit of the RMK, they'd made progress. Granted, it wasn't toward that case, but he'd take the lead on Roderick Jones as a win.

Bennett released Spike from the vehicle and snapped on his leash, giving him a short walk before they headed upstairs. Selena had texted Bennett, advising Naomi was already in bed so he wouldn't wake her.

Disappointed, Bennett strolled to his front

door. The strange emotions swirled in his mind. Why did it matter that he wouldn't get to talk to Naomi tonight? She was nothing more than his charge.

Yet he had looked forward to seeing her.

"Get a grip, Ford," he mumbled, punching the elevator button.

Spike sat and turned, glancing at him.

"Don't say it. I already chastised myself."

The beagle snorted, and they entered the elevator. By the time the doors opened again, releasing him to his floor, exhaustion settled in. Maybe he'd finally get a good night's rest.

Bennett unlocked the door and walked into his condo.

"Hey." Selena looked up from where she sat on the sofa, working on her laptop. "That took longer than expected, huh?"

"Happens every time I go into the DPD lab. Eduardo—"

"The crime tech lab guy?" Selena asked.

"Yeah, he and I got to talking. How'd the evening go?"

"Good. Naomi and I chatted, and Kyle brought pizza and ice cream."

"Please tell me there are leftovers." Bennett's mouth watered. "I haven't eaten tonight."

"Yep. There's plenty in the fridge and freezer, respectively."

Bennett walked to the kitchen to wash his hands. "Where is Kyle?"

"He returned to the hotel to work out before crashing for the night." Selena closed her laptop and got to her feet. "I've spent most of the evening going through the lab results from Peter Windham's crime scene. Just like Henry Mulder's Montana barn, there's nothing substantial. No fingerprints. No strange plants or things that are out of the ordinary for the area. The RMK was careful not to leave any trace behind."

"If only that shocked me," Bennett replied sarcastically, pulling out the pizza box from the fridge and setting it on the counter. He opened the lid. "What's all the green stuff on it?" He wrinkled his nose.

Selena approached with a grin. "Uh, those are called vegetables, Detective."

"Ha ha. What kind is it?"

"Veggie with a light crust." Selena closed her laptop.

"What's the point?" Bennett lifted a slice, inspecting it. "That's not pizza. Where are the layers of cheese and pepperoni?"

Selena chuckled. "Welcome to grown-up pizza."

Bennett took a bite, and though he had to admit it tasted good, he wasn't giving in easily. "Catch me up on the evening."

He strode to the living room and dropped into the chair opposite Selena.

"Here's where I need to apologize. I may have stuck my foot in my mouth."

Bennett chewed while Selena provided a short rundown of the discussion she and Naomi had regarding Delaney. Bennett paused, picking at a stray olive. Though he'd prefer not to share the intimate details of his personal life, it was better Naomi knew the truth.

"I assured her you're not in the market for romance," Selena concluded.

"Why? Was she implying she was interested in me?"

A sparkle in Selena's eyes said she'd picked up on his not-so-subtle way of fishing for information.

"I mean, if she was, you heading that off was smart," he said between bites of pizza. Did he really believe that?

"Are you sure?"

"Yes. Yeah. Most definitely." He infused appreciation into his tone while silently questioning the strange sense of disappointment. Naomi was off-limits for too many reasons. "The last thing I need is another failed relationship."

"That's what I figured you'd say."

"Kinda preferred Naomi didn't hear my pathetic history for getting buffaloed by a heartless wonder of a criminal." He swallowed and took a sip of soda. "But it's fine."

Selena winced. "Again, I'm sorry for overstepping. Just remember, you're in good company. It seems the three of us have a common connection in that department." She patted his shoulder. "And I'd say we are all intelligent, competent people, so it's not a personal defect."

"You're just saying that to make me feel better," Bennett grumbled, but he appreciated it anyway.

"Nope. It's as true for me as for you." Selena sighed. "I'm going to head out for the night. We should touch base first thing in the morning with the team. I haven't heard from anyone since notifying them about your mountain adventure, so I'm guessing there are no updates on the RMK or Cowgirl."

He nodded. "Good night." Bennett walked

her and Scout out, locking the door behind her. Spike trailed them, tail wagging. "Hungry, buddy? Yep, you want dinner, too."

He led the way to the kitchen, pulling out Spike's food. After filling his bowls and washing his hands again, Bennett finished the last piece of pizza.

He glanced at the clock. It wasn't that late. Would Isla still be working? Bennett sent her a text, and she quickly responded, agreeing to a video chat. Bennett carried his laptop to his dining table and logged in, inserting his EarPods to prevent waking Naomi.

"Hey, sounds like you had a busy day," Isla said once they were connected.

"It's satisfying to have something to move forward with. Even though this isn't where we were headed."

"Yeah, unbelievable Roderick Jones is involved. What're the chances?"

"In this area, decent. He's been running drugs hard here for a while."

Isla leaned back in her seat. She looked calmer than when they'd last spoken.

Bennett took the opportunity. "When we spoke earlier, you seemed a little distracted. Everything all right?"

"Sorry about that," Isla said. "This whole foster parenting thing is complicated."

"How're things going with the placement?"

"I expect to hear any day about when they'll bring me the newborn. I cannot wait to be an official foster mother!" Isla beamed from the other side of the screen.

Bennett smiled at her enthusiasm. She'd make a great parent. Images of Naomi and Isla talking about their children's first milestones bounced to mind. He blinked and shook off the strange thoughts. Where had that come from?

"I promise I had a reason for pestering you at this time of night," Bennett began.

"Aw, now I'm hurt. It wasn't just a friendly chat?" Isla teased.

Bennett grinned. "Well, that too. I really did want to check in and see how you're doing. I also hoped you'd work your mad tech skills for me."

"Always."

"In talking with my pal Eduardo down at the DPD lab, I kept circling Ted Cavanaugh's involvement. Can you dig into his background?"

"Absolutely."

"Just holler at me if you find anything good."

"Are you looking for something specific?"

Bennett sighed. "Yes and no. In the short time I've gotten to know Naomi, I cannot reconcile how she'd be involved with a deadbeat druggie. That tells me either Ted was a phenomenal actor, or a significant event or situation changed him. Money is a huge motivator for crimes, but it's not enough for this case."

"I'll drill down to his kindergarten enrollment years," Isla quipped.

"You're the best."

A fun ring tone chimed, and Isla glanced down. "Oh, that's my phone. It's the agency!"

Without exiting the call, Bennett listened as Isla answered. Her broad smile faded, replaced by down-turned lips and creased eyebrows. "What?" she said, panic suddenly in her voice. "But that's not true! None of it!" She listened more and seemed to calm down a bit. "Oh, I see."

Bennett leaned closer, feeling guilty for eavesdropping but concerned about his teammate's obvious distress.

"I understand. Yes, of course. Thank you." Isla set the phone down and looked at him. "My application to foster the infant—or any child— is postponed indefinitely." She swallowed hard and her lip quivered.

"What? Why?" Bennett asked, then mentally berated himself for interrupting her.

"Apparently, the agency received an anonymous report from a caller who claims I have drug and alcohol addiction issues. The person alleged witnessing me do both, starting in the morning and going throughout the day!" Isla's voice rose, anger replacing the sadness. "They're giving me a chance to rebut the accusations, but it'll take time."

"That's—" Bennett ground his teeth to keep from saying anything his mother wouldn't approve of. "Come on! That's so wrong! You work in law enforcement."

"Yeah, but what can I do? It's my word against this horrible accuser."

"Offer a drug test. Tell them the team will vouch for you."

Isla nodded. She leaned forward, and he saw the pain in her eyes. "Bennett, I've never touched alcohol or done any drugs. What is going on? And why didn't this totally fabricated report come up in my background checks during the certification process? Why now?"

"Exactly." Bennett's cop brain sped into action. "Why would someone want to stop you from fostering or adopting?"

"If I could answer that, I would. Who hates me that much?"

"No enemies come to mind?" Bennett probed.

"No, but don't you say everyone has enemies?" Isla gave a bitter snort. "Even if they're unaware?"

He winced at the repetition of his cold but accurate belief. "Isla, think hard. Is there anyone who found out about your foster-to-adoption journey who wasn't on your list of references? Someone who would take that as an affront?"

Isla considered his question and shook her head. "No."

Who would be so cruel as to interfere with Isla's benevolent dream? "Anyone who's been around you for more than a day knows how important this is for you."

She lifted her chin. "Well, whoever this person is, they're not getting away with it. I'll investigate it myself."

"That's the right attitude. Holler at me if there's anything I can do. I'll be thinking about ways to help too," Bennett assured.

"Thanks." Isla yawned. "I will."

"Get some rest."

"You too. Good night."

They disconnected, and Bennett closed his laptop. For every victory their team gained, there was another defeat. Would it ever end?

Chapter Twelve

Naomi joined Bennett on the morning walk with Spike. "That sunrise is captivating."

"Agreed." Bennett shot her a smile, and she fought her knees to keep from weakening.

They hadn't solved Ted's murder or discovered anything new since the day before, but she felt optimistic.

"Lost in thought?" Bennett asked.

"A little. Is Selena coming over today?"

"Yes, she and Kyle will be here around lunchtime to go through evidence and work the case."

"Oh, good. I enjoyed talking with her last night. Sorry again for crashing early. The day's events caught up with me."

"Don't apologize. You're supposed to rest," he reminded her gently. "I'm glad you got some sleep."

"I did. Like a rock. Guess I'd better soak up

as much of that as I can before little man makes his appearance."

"I can't offer any personal experience, but from the stories I've heard, yeah, you're going to want to bank energy for later."

They waited as Spike paused to sniff a row of flowers. Naomi's gaze roved the area where many houses had neatly manicured lawns awakening to spring. A woman dressed in leggings and a short-sleeved shirt jogged on the opposite side of the street. Despite Naomi's wave, the woman, who wore mirrored sunglasses and had EarPods inserted, was too focused on exercising to return the gesture.

Naomi glanced down, determined to add in exercise in her own life as soon as possible.

If only she'd be sharing the joys of motherhood with Bennett. *Ugh*. Why wouldn't those thoughts leave her alone?

He turned to face her. "Will you have any help with the baby?"

The man had an uncanny way of tackling contemplations before she spoke them. Naomi shook her head. "No, but I'll be fine. Once I return to work, it'll be nice to have little man ride along with me. I'll enjoy his company when I'm driving the tour bus. I mean after I get a new one. Thankfully, the insurance should cover the cost of the replacement, right?"

"I hope so."

Spike continued forward, and they resumed the stroll.

"You're going to take the baby with you on your tours? Won't that be hard?"

She shrugged. "It'll be challenging until we get a routine down, and I won't be able to do it every day. I have a daycare lined up, but the thought of being away from him tears at my heart." Naomi didn't add she couldn't afford full-time daycare. That wasn't Bennett's concern, and she'd troubled him enough with her personal problems. "I'll have to get used to being a working parent."

"Did your mom work outside the home when you were growing up?"

"Yes, part time. Somehow, she was always there for us, though. I don't know how she did it." Naomi recalled talking to her mother after school. Most teenagers wouldn't have spent their time in parental chats, but Naomi had enjoyed it. "She was my best friend. I miss her every single day."

"My mom is great, but I don't see or talk

to her as much as I should." Bennett groaned. "Now I feel guilty."

Naomi chuckled.

"Tell me about your family."

"We were close, probably because there were only four of us. My parents were supportive if Evan and I wanted to try new things. Especially when I started rodeo performance stuff."

"Do you miss riding?"

"All the time. It was freeing." A soft breeze fluttered her hair, and she tucked strands behind her ear. "If only horse care and upkeep weren't so expensive."

"Did your brother also ride?"

"No, not really. We've always moved in our own circles."

"Totally get it."

"After my parents' deaths, I was lost."

"The accident happened five years ago?" Bennett asked.

"Yes. Ted was a lifeline for me. We weren't married yet, just dating, but he was supportive and kind."

"The picture you paint of Ted differs from the one in my mind."

"I'm sure. I don't know how he got involved

in the mess he did, but I'm convinced he wasn't always like that."

"Naomi, I agree with you."

She stopped and faced him. "You do?"

"We're digging into Ted's life to explain the strange clues."

"Ted didn't have any living family and never talked about his past. He was touchy about it, and I only know his grandmother raised him."

"Where did he grow up and attend school?"

"He said he was from Denver and attended Northridge High School."

Bennett frowned. They started walking again. The older neighborhood's bungalows had established lawns. Birds trilled from the trees that towered overhead.

"Do you think he was lying?"

"I didn't say that. But I'm going to check it out. Did Ted have family in the area?"

"No," she replied, sadness sweeping over her. "His parents died when he was young. His grandmother—also deceased now—raised him."

Spike traversed the sidewalk, tail high and a bounce to his canine step.

"I'm sad little man won't have any living grandparents," she admitted.

"There's not much in the case file about your parents' deaths. But we don't have to talk about that if you don't want to."

"No, it's okay." Naomi sighed. "They were driving home on a winter night. They never should've been out at that time in the first place, but my dad always aided whoever was in need. When his buddy's water heater went out, my parents offered to help install a new one. The blizzard arrived earlier than predicted. The water heater installation didn't go easily— basically, the perfect storm. They hit black ice and dad lost control, rolling the car. They were both killed instantly." Her throat tightened.

"I'm so sorry." Bennett's tone held compassion, which only made the moment worse.

They walked on for several minutes before Naomi continued, "My mom oozed kindness. She took casseroles and pies to neighbors in need or just because. She would've been a wonderful grandmother. My dad was quiet, but strong and loving. I pictured him bouncing my son on his knee while regaling him with his exaggerated fishing adventure stories. I'm sad they're not here to celebrate this milestone with me."

"It's only you and Evan now?"

"Yeah."

"Will Uncle Evan be a big part of your child's life?" Bennett asked.

"He's got his job recruitment firm in Elk Valley—which you probably already know. He's super busy with that."

"Will you visit him?"

"Doubtful, until the baby is older." She crossed her arms over her chest, tugging her cardigan closed. "I have no desire to return to Elk Valley."

"Even for the reunion?" Bennett asked.

Naomi considered the question. "I'd toyed with the idea when I first got the invitation."

"What changed?"

"Honestly, going to Peter's ranch solidified my reasons. It's all reminders of that part of my life." Naomi bit her lip, contemplating. "Talking it out helps. I'm curious to see how everyone has changed. And to find out what they're doing now, but being in Elk Valley, especially after losing my folks, is…hard."

"I understand that."

Spike stopped again to investigate an unfamiliar smell.

"Well, hopefully your brother will visit you."

"Evan comes when he can, usually a couple of times a year."

"Why didn't he leave Elk Valley?"

"He's a creature of habit." Naomi chortled. "Evan is rooted and hates change."

They rounded the block and headed back toward the condo with Spike in the lead.

"Spike has me missing the joys of owning a pet," Naomi admitted. "Living alone, I might reconsider a canine protector. Not that I could handle caring for anyone else right now."

"Maybe when your son is older," Bennett replied.

Spike paused again, and they stopped, waiting for him to finish his exploration.

"After watching Evan's grief over losing his dog, Kiko, I'm unsure my heart could endure it." At Bennett's quirked brow, Naomi explained. "She was his female chocolate Lab. He did everything—to the extreme—to help her through her illness. Her death devastated him. The man is a dog lover to the max." Naomi whispered, "Don't tell him I told you that. He'd kill me for divulging his softer side."

Spike advanced, allowing them to continue walking.

Bennett chuckled. "Your secret is safe with me."

"I knew I could count on you." She winked and their hands brushed. Naomi scooted away. "Spike's made me realize I have a canine shaped hole in my heart."

Bennett grinned. "I have a feeling you're going to be very busy soon."

"Yes. It won't be the traditional family I had hoped for, but it'll be good." Naomi thought about the baby's arrival. Recalling the destruction of her possessions, especially the nursery, caused a wave of sadness to course through her. "When will law enforcement release my apartment?"

"I'll follow up with the department today." Bennett hesitated.

"What aren't you saying?"

"They should've released the scene, but it's not safe for you to go there right now."

Naomi caressed her belly. "I'm sort of on a fixed timeline here."

"I'm working on it, I promise."

They paused outside Bennett's condo building door as a couple exited, holding hands. Naomi exchanged a smile with the woman as they walked by.

Naomi's heart squeezed, reminded that she was alone. "Do you want a family of your own someday?" The question escaped her lips before she stopped it, and she longed to rewind the moment. The other part of her recalled all that Selena had told her. What if Selena was wrong? Had Bennett's heartbreak over Delaney destroyed his dreams?

They reached the elevator as the doors opened. A second couple entered with them, giving Bennett the opportunity to delay answering her as they rode to his floor in silence.

They entered the condo, and Bennett released Spike from his leash, hanging it by the door.

"I can't answer your earlier question without stating the obvious," Bennett began. "Selena told you about Delaney."

"Whew, I'm glad you brought up the emotional elephant in the room. I wasn't sure how to." Naomi sipped the water. "Yes, she felt bad, though. She assumed you'd told me."

"It's all right." Bennett took a swig from the bottle, then replaced the cap.

"She didn't give me any details. Only that Delaney was involved with drugs, and you ended up arresting her."

"I'd spent months building this case against a group of drug runners moving product in and out of Colorado." Bennett sighed and kicked his feet up on the coffee table. "I'd worked long hours, which means lack of sleep and unavailability to Delaney, both emotionally and physically. She seemed understanding and I assumed she accepted the sacrifice we'd both have to pay for my job." He snorted. "Imagine when I learned her 'understanding'—" Bennett made air quotes with his fingers "—was solely because she was working me for information to elude capture."

"How so?" Naomi didn't hide her confusion. "If you didn't see each other often, how was Delaney cognizant of where you were or what you were doing?"

"Whenever we got the opportunity to talk, she'd ask about case updates. Of course, I was thrilled she was interested."

"Isn't that a violation?"

"No, I didn't give her any classified details. Cops talk to their significant others. It's healthy to vent to someone safe," Bennett explained. "My captain had always taught us to include our spouses."

"I guess that makes sense." Naomi crossed her ankles, shifting on the sofa. "She was collecting information." Betraying Bennett's confidence and trust. No wonder he was bitter.

"Yes."

"What happened at the end?"

"I worked a straight seventy-two-hour shift, so I hadn't spoken to her during that time. One of our investigators got a lead, and we were closing in. Imagine my surprise when we busted inside for the takedown, and I found Delaney there with hundreds of pounds of cocaine."

Naomi leaned forward. "How awful." She understood the pain of betrayal now like never before, and an unspoken compassion passed between her and Bennett. "I'm sad she did that to you."

"Yeah, you totally get it, huh?" Bennett's tone was soft. "I'm sorry for both of us."

"Based on what Selena told me yesterday, I'm sorry for all of us," Naomi added. "There are lots of happy marriages and families as proof that's not the norm."

"And there are as many torn apart by divorce," Bennett contended.

Naomi looked down. "Selena said our past experience helps us to make wiser choices for the future."

"As true as that might be, I cannot see myself ever going down that relationship road again." Bennett frowned. "I gave up a lot. Sacrificed too much. Had the chance to do more in my career, which I passed on because I wanted to be there for my wife and kids." He snorted. "Won't make that mistake again. I don't trust people, period."

"That's not true," Naomi said, lifting her chin. "You trust Selena and Spike." At the mention of his name, the beagle hopped onto the couch and lay beside her.

Bennett frowned but didn't refute her argument. "Spike's incapable of deception."

"Okay, fair enough, but what about your team and your coworkers at the Denver PD?"

"They've proven themselves."

"Isn't that accurate of most relationships? We learn more about one another as we spend time together. Considering you were going to arrest me for being a serial killer when we first met, look how far we've come," she teased.

That got a smile out of him. "True that."

"Which proves that not everyone is unworthy of your trust. And you're saying you can't imagine that happening if you fell in love?"

"I won't put myself into a position to find out." Bennett's hardened tone and narrowed eyes stung Naomi. "Romance is out for me. I'd better get to work." Bennett rose and walked to his bedroom, closing the door softly behind him.

Naomi fidgeted with a string on her leggings. What possible rebuttal could she offer?

Selena had spoken truthfully.

Bennett wasn't a family man.

If only her heart accepted that reality.

Bennett immersed himself in the investigation, scouring the lists of recent murders in the surrounding states. There had to be a lead buried that they hadn't yet discovered. Working on the RMK and Ted's case simultaneously provided him a break from the uncomfortable and probing conversation with Naomi. She'd spent the morning busying herself rearranging tours with her contact, Addy, allowing him time alone to overthink.

He'd enjoyed their talk until they got stuck on discussing families and marriage. All that did was remind him of the things he'd never have.

Naomi was correct. Bennett trusted his teammates and coworkers, but after Delaney, he'd never offer that to another woman. He owed Delaney some gratitude. She'd awakened him to his lack of cop sense and how easily he'd set aside his skeptical nature for the sake of love. The risk had nearly cost his career and had taken a sizeable chunk of his self-esteem. A cost he wouldn't pay again.

The hurt and deflation of Naomi's enthusiasm had tugged at his heart while simultaneously activating his callous walls of self-protection. She hadn't pressed him, which made Bennett want to divulge his longing to trust her. At least he'd opened the door for that, until he'd chickened out before he spoke the words. Because as beautiful, sweet and fun as Naomi was to be around, she had the very real potential to break his heart.

A constant emotional tug of war had battled within him until he spotted the spark of hope in Naomi's eyes when they talked about relationships. He would not lead her on. That was far crueler. His harsh but firm replies squashed any erroneous ideas she might have about him. Hurting her wasn't his goal, but the alternative was telling her the truth.

He'd fallen hard for Naomi.

She'd endured hardship and betrayal, and Bennett refused to add to her pain by offering her hope. As excruciating as speaking the words were, it was for his own benefit as much as hers. His effort at stonewalling his heart required him to replay Delaney's treachery on an endless reel.

Naomi glanced up from where she sat talking to Spike, who lavished affection on her.

She was beautiful inside and out, and being around her would be his undoing.

He had to take down Roderick Jones and find the RMK so their time together would end. The reality of parting ways with Naomi saddened Bennett. Being without her sounded like a miserable life.

A text from Chase dragged Bennett from his ruminations. Video meeting now.

"Naomi, I have to take this conference call with my team."

She nodded mutely. With the hurt still evident on her face, everything within him wanted to comfort her, to tell her he was falling for her. Instead, he excused himself and went to his bedroom, closing the door behind him.

He logged in to the meeting. As his team members popped onto the screen, he replayed Naomi's comment about trusting them. To be fair, the trust occurred a little at a time. It wasn't instantaneous. When Chase had first recruited Bennett, he'd kept a distance until he'd verified their credibility. Was it possible to have that same emotion toward Naomi?

"Thanks for showing up on such short notice," Chase said, opening the meeting and commanding Bennett's attention. "Let's do a status check. Starting with Bennett."

"Selena already updated you all on the incident in the mountains. I doubt we'll ever find who attacked me, and all we have is the picture of Ted's note to go on."

"Yes, but we've got a solid connection to Roderick Jones," Selena added.

"He'll rear his ugly mug soon enough," Kyle replied. "He's behind the attacks on Naomi."

"I've requested DPD to keep the discovery on the down-low as much as possible, but Jones has deadbeats everywhere," Bennett explained. "By now, he's probably aware we confiscated the drugs from her van."

"But we believe there are more drugs?" Ashley asked.

"There must be. The money was significant, but it's not enough to get Jones's attention. There's something more he wants, and for whatever reason, he believes Naomi has it. That keeps her in danger," Bennett replied. "We need

Jones to crawl out from under his rock, which his determination to get the stash provides."

"As a precaution, Kyle and I are assisting with Naomi's security detail," Selena said.

"Good work," Chase commented. "However, I'm stating the obvious here. That cannot continue indefinitely. If we don't get a lead on Jones soon, we'll have to surrender Naomi to another jurisdiction and focus on the Rocky Mountain Killer."

The order was a kick to the gut for Bennett. He couldn't pass Naomi off to just anyone. Determination fueled him to bring down Jones, and fast.

Chase continued, "We have no news on Cowgirl. The motive remains a mystery, although there are plenty of theories simmering down to a jerk who steals people's dogs." He sighed. "At this time, we do not believe her dognapping or missing status is a personal vendetta against our team."

"Could be a criminal backyard breeder," Bennett said, a sick feeling in his stomach at the thought.

"Let's hope not," Hannah said.

"Where are we with the RMK investigation?" Chase asked.

"We're still scouring the lists Isla provided, but thus far, we have nothing on any of the victims' enemies," Ashley reported. "Not to mention, with all the fights they were involved with and instigated, multiple incidents of cheating on their girlfriends, etcetera, they accumulated a lengthy list of haters."

"Kyle and I are headed back to Bennett's to do the same," Selena added. "We're also comparing the lab results from both the Montana and Colorado crime scenes."

"Currently, it's not much," Kyle said. "We also have no leads on the shooters from Bennett and Naomi's most recent attack. We found the truck—stolen of course—and the perps ditched it on a rural highway."

"We're spinning our wheels, people," Chase grumbled. "What're we missing?"

"The RMK is from Elk Valley or has a personal connection there," Isla said.

"The RMK was involved with or has some attachment to the Young Ranchers Club, which means, more than likely, they were from Elk Valley, too, and attended Elk Valley High School," Bennett added.

"Let's scour the yearbook and YRC enrollments," Rocco offered. Like Ashley, the cop had attended high school in Elk Valley at the time of the murders…it was a good idea.

Meadow said, "Bennett, maybe Naomi will have some input to help us?"

"I'll ask her."

"Excellent," Chase commended.

"I'll upload the electronic files to the shared folder," Isla advised, referencing the online system that housed the team's working documents.

"Update the team with all potential leads," Chase said.

"Naomi asked about accessing her apartment," Bennett explained. "Denver PD released the scene, but I contend she's not safe there until we apprehend Jones."

"Agreed. Selena and Kyle, please continue assisting in Naomi's security detail with Bennett," Chase ordered.

"Roger that," they replied.

Had he imagined the knowing look in Selena's gaze?

They disconnected, and Bennett returned to the living room to talk with Naomi.

His phone chimed with a text message from Isla, advising the files were ready. Bennett lifted his laptop and pulled up the documents. "Hey, Naomi. I need your help looking through the yearbook and YRC annuals for connections between the murder victims beyond what we already know."

"Sure."

He moved to sit beside her, not missing how she quickly scooted to the right and placed a pillow on her lap to hold. Her body language spoke clearly. Naomi had distanced herself from him.

And rightly so. He leaned back, sharing the laptop screen. "Let's start with the Young Ranchers Club."

He scrolled the pictures.

"It's hard to say," Naomi said. "We weren't a vast community, which means interacting with the same people every year. In a way, everyone is connected."

"That's what I was worried about." Bennett sighed.

Chapter Thirteen

Bennett's obnoxious ring tone jolted him awake. He glanced at the clock on his nightstand where the LED light flashed 05:30 a.m. Isla's contact information appeared on the screen, gaining his full attention. He swiped to answer, "Isla, what do you have for me?"

"Good morning to you, too," she jested. "I ran the concealed carry permit information, and discovered Ted Cavanaugh changed his name about ten years ago."

Why hadn't Eduardo picked up on that? No time for placing blame. "Any idea why?"

"Hang on, it gets better. Ted Cavanaugh, originally Theodore Pritchard, was born in North Platte, Nebraska. Orphaned at two years old and raised by his grandmother, Twila May Pritchard, née Cavanaugh, in Benser, Nebraska. She passed away right before Ted's nineteenth birthday."

"Naomi nailed it." Bennett sagged against the headboard. "He took her name out of respect."

"Hmm, but get this. Prior to the name change, police questioned him in eighteen-year-old Otto Lewis's missing person case."

Bennett sat up. "Why?"

"Apparently, Otto, Ted and Glen Kappel were friends. The local sheriff noted Otto and Ted were troublemakers, but weren't involved in criminal activities. By comparison, Glen had multiple arrests with a rap sheet ranging from theft to assault. He bounced from juvenile hall to jail numerous times. He was also questioned about Otto's disappearance."

"Where's Glen now?" Bennett asked.

"Hard to say. He doesn't have a bank account, credit cards or property. Tracking him hasn't proven easy."

"Were any of Glen's crimes related to narcotics?"

"His last arrest was for possession of meth in Big Springs, Nebraska, six years ago," Isla said. "He served two years, then was released on parole."

"Interesting."

"Was Otto found?"

"Nope. Investigation went cold."

"Without a body, they probably struggled to prove Otto was dead," Bennett thought aloud. "I wonder if the sheriff remembers anything about the case."

"It wouldn't hurt to ask. His name is Zechariah Motega. He retired five years ago."

"Got a LKA for me?" Bennett referenced the acronym for the last known address.

"Yes, Motega's a resident of the Pine Meadows Memory Assistance Retirement Home."

Bennett considered the information, then asked the inevitable question. "Alzheimer's?"

"Yes." Sadness hung in Isla's reply.

"Okay. What do we know about Otto?"

"His parents were less than desirable. They offered a weak justification for their inability to specify the date Otto had gone missing. All they claimed was he'd disappeared in early October." Isla grunted. "And I'm struggling to get approved as a foster parent."

"Gotta love the irony." Bennett blew out a long breath. "Ted Cavanaugh died in October, too."

"Yeah, I didn't consider that a coincidence, either," Isla said. "There was no evidence to indicate Theodore, aka Ted, or Glen were involved in Otto's disappearance other than the trio were friends."

"Except it's interesting Ted changed his name shortly thereafter and moved to Denver," Bennett replied. "Not to mention, he lied to Naomi, claiming he grew up in Colorado."

"Definitely suspicious."

"Outstanding work." Bennett leaned forward, wheels turning. "What about LKAs for Glen, Otto and Twila May?"

"Already sent it to your phone. Along with pictures of them."

Even as she said the words, Bennett's cell phone pinged with a PDF file. "You're the best."

"Tell me something I don't know." Isla chuckled.

"Any word on the investigation of your foster approval? Or ideas who's making false accusations against you?"

"Not yet." Isla sighed. "I'm hoping to talk to Chase about it this afternoon."

"Holler if I can help."

"Will do."

They disconnected, and Bennett googled Otto's case, locating an old news story on the web. Other than the suspicious nature of his disappearance, there was no proof of foul play. His parents assumed he ran away. Both Glen and Ted claimed they had last spoken to him the day before they went fishing at Lake McConaughy in Ogallala, Nebraska.

Bennett threw off his covers, eager to talk to Naomi. He walked to the living room, debating whether to wake her. To his surprise, she sat on the couch watching an old sitcom with the volume turned down. "I'm sorry. Was I too loud?"

"Not at all." He dropped onto the recliner. "I just got off the phone with Isla and have something I wanted to run past you."

"By the tone of your voice, it doesn't sound like good news." Naomi shut off the TV and faced him.

"Why are you up this early?"

"Bathroom break and I couldn't fall back asleep." She tilted her head. "What's up?"

"Just to clarify, Ted told you he'd grown up in Colorado?"

"Yes, in Denver. Why?"

"Apparently, that's untrue."

"Look at my shocked and amazed face," she deadpanned.

"He grew up in a small town near North Platte, Nebraska, called Benser, where he lived with his grandmother, Twila May Cavanaugh. Did he talk about his parents?"

"No, only that they died when he was young. He spoke of wanting to be a better father to our baby, since he'd never had one. Why are you asking all of this?"

"Were you aware Ted's birth name is Theodore Pritchard?"

Naomi blinked. "He lied to me about his name, too?"

"Technically, no." Spike strolled over to Bennett and hopped on his lap. "He legally changed his name to Ted Cavanaugh, taking Twila's maiden name."

"How negligent of me not to ask, 'Do you have any other identities,' when we were dating," she mumbled sarcastically.

"You're starting to sound like me," Bennett teased.

"I'm starting to appreciate why you feel the way you do."

Bennett grinned, though her words gave him a twinge of sadness. His pessimism had brought down the optimistic Naomi Carr-Cavanaugh.

"On second thought, perhaps after Twila's death, he changed his name to honor her?" she said.

There it was. Naomi thought the best of others. Even her deceitful husband.

"Possibly." Bennett prayed for wisdom. How much should he share with her?

"Is there more?" At his hesitation, she added, "After all we've been through, just tell me whatever it is you're trying hard to say nicely or not at all."

Bennett shared the information about Otto Lewis's disappearance, Glen Kappel and Ted's police questioning, and Glen's subsequent arrests for petty crimes. "Did Ted ever mention either man to you?"

"No. I've never heard of them." Naomi exhaled.

Bennett handed her his cell phone, displaying the pictures of the three men. She studied them, lingering on Ted's picture. Did she miss him? As if in response, she swiped back at Glen's mugshot taken from his last arrest. "Now that you mention it, there's something familiar about him."

"Did he come to your house?" Bennett leaned closer. "Hang out with Ted?"

"No." Naomi reviewed the phone. "I'll keep pondering, though. Were Glen and Ted suspected of Otto's disappearance?"

"Possibly. Otto's body was never found. I'd like to take a road trip to Nebraska and do a little checking for myself. Hoping to talk to the sheriff who handled the case. I'll ask Selena and Kyle to come here—"

"No way!" Naomi jumped up. "I'm tired of sitting on the sidelines. I'm going with you."

"Your doctor won't approve."

"Then don't tell her." She offered him a wan smile.

"Naomi." A warning hung in his voice. "This isn't a good idea."

"Bennett, I want to understand why the man I loved lied to me. If visiting his hometown will explain that, I'm tagging along. How much more stress is involved in riding in a car as opposed to waiting here?"

Bennett sighed. "I won't get approval to take you with me."

"Then ask for forgiveness when we return." She winked. "When do we leave?"

He got to his feet. "Twenty minutes. I'll shower quick first, and you must eat a healthy breakfast. It's a five-hour commute, which puts us at the state border around eleven o'clock."

Against the voice in his head warning against taking Naomi, Bennett gathered supplies for a road trip. Chase had said without leads on Roderick Jones, they'd assign Naomi's detail to someone else. Bennett reasoned he had no time to waste.

He sent a text to Selena and Kyle. Following up on a possible lead. Will be in touch.

Selena responded immediately. Need us to stay with Naomi?

He replied, Not yet. Then he prayed he wasn't making the biggest mistake of his career by taking her with him.

What skeletons did Ted Cavanaugh have hidden in Nebraska?

"Is it strange that I'm grateful those thugs attacked me at Peter's ranch?" The drive to Nebraska offered Naomi plenty of time to think.

Bennett flicked a glance her way. "Dare I ask why?"

"How else would I have discovered these things about Ted? Maybe it's part of helping me to let go. Not just of the dream of what I thought we had and lost, but to allow me a fresh start. I could've died without knowing why. Although ignorance is bliss." A truer statement could not be made. "I'm compelled to understand why Ted kept his background a secret."

"Agreed. And is the person after you actually Ted's enemy?"

"As in, something triggered that individual to want to kill me?"

"Yes." Bennett remained quiet for several minutes, then said, "You continually amaze me. What other person views the assaults you've encountered as God working in your life?"

"God is always active in our lives. Recognizing it is the key."

"You're the kind of person I want to be when I grow up," he quipped.

She giggled and swatted playfully at him. "Whatever."

"Now that we are armed with this information, which, for the record, could turn out to be absolutely nothing at all—"

"Or essential to the case," she interrupted.

Bennett chuckled. "I wonder what secrets Ted's enemy has on him."

"Yeah, and why now?"

"I'm hoping that talking to Sheriff Motega will answer that."

"If he's an advanced Alzheimer's patient, do you think he'll remember anything?" Naomi asked.

"Good question. He doesn't have living relatives, and the electronic case file Isla sent me was basically useless."

"I guess it takes the term *long shot* to a whole new level," Naomi said. "Any word on when you'll get your pickup back?"

"Not yet. I kind of like this sedan. Cheaper on gas," he kidded.

They'd driven through the Sand Hills, where rolling land spanned acres in all directions. "This is actually pretty."

"It's a huge contrast to Denver."

"Hmm. Maybe that's why Ted chose to move there."

The GPS automated voice advised Bennett to take a right from the highway into North Platte. He continued to the Pine Meadows Memory Assistance Retirement Home. A duck pond and blooming trees enhanced the serenity of the single-level facility.

He parked, and they exited the vehicle. Bennett leashed Spike with his official harness, which had the MCK9 logo, and they made their way to the front doors.

"Are they going to give us a hard time since we're not family?" Naomi asked.

"Isla called ahead and got us clearance with the director."

Bennett approached the young woman behind the reception desk and offered their names. She confirmed they were approved. After buzzing them through the doors, a nurse led them to a sunroom. One entire wall comprised of glass contained the biggest aviary cage Naomi had ever seen. Birds of every color, shape and size fluttered around inside.

A husky man with snow-white hair sat at a table fixated on the scene.

"Mr. Motega, you have guests," the nurse said as they strolled toward him.

Motega turned, spotting Spike. A wide smile spread across his weathered face. "Poochy!" He reached out a hand, and Spike glanced at Bennett as though seeking permission.

"Be nice," Bennett said, kneeling beside the beagle.

Spike sniffed the older man's outstretched hand, then offered a lick of approval.

"You remember me, Poochy!" Sheriff Motega exclaimed.

Bennett and Naomi exchange worried glances. This might not pan out after all.

Naomi had enjoyed her time working with hospice patients, and her training returned.

"Hello, Sheriff Motega," she said, intentionally using his title.

He glanced up, and awareness swept over his expression. "Hello, young lady. Have we met?" He patted his leg.

Bennett gave Spike a nod, and he hopped into Motega's lap, earning him a soft stroke of the head.

"No, sir. My name is Naomi—" she began.

"Like the woman in the Bible?" he asked, intrigued.

"Yes, sir."

"That's how my mother named me, too." He smiled.

"Sheriff, could Naomi and I talk with you about an old case of yours?" Bennett asked cautiously.

"Who're you?" Motega surveyed Bennett warily.

"Detective Bennett Ford, sir."

"Ah, a fellow lawman. All righty, have a seat." He gestured toward the chairs across from him.

Bennett quickly dragged the seats closer, then assisted Naomi into one before sitting beside her.

Naomi took the lead. "Sheriff, we are looking into the Otto Lewis case."

Motega's blank expression worried her.

After several seconds, he looked past them toward the birds, still absently petting Spike, who sat patiently, receiving the kind affection.

"Good boy, Spike," Bennett whispered.

"Birds should fly free. Not live in cages," Motega said. "Otto must have wanted to be free."

Naomi and Bennett shared a look. Neither was willing to interrupt the sheriff's moment of clarity.

"Never found him," he concluded.

"Sir, your notes mentioned little regarding your questioning of Otto's friends, Theodore Pritchard and Glen Kappel."

Motega's gaze slowly traversed to Naomi. "You a first-time mama?"

"Yes, sir." She placed her hands on her belly. "I can't wait to meet my baby boy."

"Boys." Motega snorted. "They keep secrets."

"Did Glen and Theodore keep secrets?" Bennett pressed.

Motega shook his head. "Hoodlums." His gaze reverted to the aviary, and he mumbled, "Poochy, critters don't wanna be caged. Like me."

Naomi's heartstrings tugged at the man's quiet confession. She looked around the room.

Though pleasant and well maintained, the man before her no doubt missed his independence. Here, they monitored him constantly for safety reasons.

"Sir, can you tell us anything about Otto, Glen or Theodore?" Bennett pressed.

Naomi shook her head. Pushing Motega wouldn't help. Patience was the key.

"What's that funny vest you're wearing, Poochy?" Motega ignored Bennett.

"It's his uniform," Naomi explained. "He finds narcotics."

Motega looked up at her, wonderment in his eyes. "He learned to do that?" He smiled at the beagle. "And all that time, I thought you could only fetch slippers." He chuckled.

Bennett's expression fell.

Naomi wanted to assure him not to give up, but not at the risk of interrupting the moment. "Yes," she continued. "He helps Detective Ford."

Motega nodded, glancing at Bennett. "The factory."

"Beg your pardon," Bennett asked.

"They closed the old dairy factory outside of town." Motega shook his head. "Shoulda tore it down instead. Like everything in Benser, they abandoned it."

The nurse approached. "I'm sorry, but Mr. Motega needs to rest now."

Bennett sighed. "We understand."

"Thank you, sir." Naomi placed her hand over Motega's. "I enjoyed talking with you."

"Well, hello there." He met her gaze. "What's your name?"

The nurse offered her a supportive nod.

"My name is Naomi, Sheriff."

"Like in the Bible." He smiled.

"Yes, sir."

Bennett rose. "Come on, Spike, time to go."

The dog offered Motega another minute before hopping down.

"Thank you," Bennett addressed both the nurse and the sheriff.

Naomi led the way out of the facility.

"Well, that was a waste," Bennett groused.

"Are you kidding?" Naomi responded, sliding into the passenger seat. "He told us where to look."

Bennett loaded Spike and slid behind the wheel. "The factory?"

"Yes."

"He was confused, though. Rambling."

"At times, but the factory connected to a memory."

Bennett scanned his phone for any abandoned buildings that might fit the criteria. "There's one on the other side of Benser. I'd like to check out Twila May's house, too."

"Sounds good to me."

He started the engine. "Are you doing all right?"

"Yes. I forgot how much I enjoyed talking with patients. Maybe I'll get my nursing degree?"

"Really?"

"It's not as if I have a tour company anymore." She grunted.

"You do. It's just on a temporary hiatus."

"Right."

Bennett drove out of North Platte and headed northeast. Again, they traversed the Sand Hills until, out of nowhere, a smattering of brick buildings appeared in the distance. A rundown sign covered by vines and weeds, neglected and forgotten, advertised Welcome to Benser. A few small storefronts lined the main thoroughfare, and a gas station sat on the edge of town.

"Guess Benser isn't the local hot spot," Bennett quipped.

Following the GPS directions, they traveled to the address Isla had provided as Twila May's last known residence.

"Ted didn't talk a lot about growing up, but when he talked about his grandmother, he lit up," Naomi reminisced. She prayed his adoration for her was the sole reason for his name change.

A long, winding road led to the deserted property where weeds and trees swarmed the tiny house in overgrowth.

"Not sure what I thought we might find here," Bennett said, leaning forward to look out the window, "but this wasn't it."

"Didn't Isla already tell you it was abandoned?"

"Yes, but I hoped it wasn't in this bad of shape."

"Why not just tear it down?" Naomi asked. "It would be kinder than leaving the structure to slowly cave in on itself."

They pulled up to the broken chain-link fence gate and stopped. "There's no way you're going inside that dilapidated house."

"No argument here."

"Let's check out the factory."

Spike yawned, emitting a squeak as he stretched out on the seat beside her.

They drove ten miles east of Benser. The massive brick-and-iron structure stood amid the immense overgrowth of weeds and foliage. Bennett parked as close as possible to the building.

The factory had two floors, and multiple windows were missing or broken out. A tall steel cylinder protruded into the sky from one side and an old pipe lay in the parking lot—strange and out of place, yet simultaneously fitting with the scene.

Naomi scanned the area. "Do you hear horror music playing in the background?" she jested.

"A little bit," Bennett teased, shifting into Park. He withdrew his gun, checking the magazine. "You wait here. It's not safe."

"Are you kidding? That's right out of a slasher movie. You leave, and I'm sitting here alone when the killer finds me." Naomi shook her head. "No way. I'm going with you."

Bennett chuckled. "All righty then."

They exited the sedan, and Bennett passed Naomi a large flashlight. They slowly approached the structure, walking up the long cement loading dock. No doors restricted their access. Naomi flicked on the light and swept the beam through the room. Graffiti covered every wall, and a combination of atrocious smells assailed her senses. Bottles, cans and trash littered the floor of the main level.

"I can picture this as a teen hangout," Naomi said.

"Yeah, unfortunately, it provides ample space for nefarious acts." He kept Spike tucked under one arm as their feet crunched on broken glass. "Maybe that's what triggered Motega's memory of it. You talked about Spike searching for narcotics. This dump could've been used for drug deals."

"I hadn't thought of that. Otherwise, what did this place have to do with Motega's investigation?"

"Ted and Glen both claimed to be fishing when Otto went missing," Bennett said.

They moved cautiously through the room to the stairs at the far side.

"Dare we check out the upper level?"

"Stay close to me in case the floorboards aren't strong enough."

Naomi swept the beam overhead, illuminating the ceiling still intact.

Bennett placed Spike on the ground and activated a flashlight connected to his gun. Together, they slowly ascended the steel staircase to the second floor, then inched to the center of the room. They stopped, surveying the space where old dust-and-cobweb covered machines and furniture filled the space.

Naomi stepped forward and felt the board shift slightly beneath her feet. She quickly retreated. "That's unsafe."

Bennett looked down and gently helped her to move closer to the wall.

"What was this place?"

"Some kind of clothing or material factory," Bennett said.

Naomi rubbed her arms to ward off the chill that had nothing to do with the temperature.

"I told you they'd show up."

Naomi and Bennett spun to see two figures looming in the shadows behind them. The man's voice was familiar. As the duo—male and female—closed the distance, both wielding guns, she recognized the intruder who had threatened her at the hospital. The woman was also familiar, but Naomi couldn't place her. She opened her mouth to speak, but no sound came out. She had to warn Bennett. *God help us.*

"Put down the gun, cop."

Spike barked and growled, taking his guarding stance in front of Bennett and Naomi.

"Let me kill the dog," the woman said, staying in the shadows.

"Shut up, Hetti!" the man barked.

Awareness flitted over Bennett's face. "Hazel."

Naomi recalled his strange question about Hazel Houston.

"That's my alter ego when riding your tour bus, darlin'. I'm Hetti Miller." The woman chuckled, stepping closer into the light.

"I saw you." The same person Naomi had spotted on several occasions around Bennett's condo.

"Duh. I watched you." She aimed her gun at Spike, still growling.

"Spike." Bennett silenced the beagle, who remained on guard.

"Put down the gun," the man repeated.

"Can't do that." Bennett replied, slowly moving toward Naomi. "Get behind me," he whispered.

Naomi started to move, and the woman fired, striking the floor in front of her.

"Don't you dare," the woman ordered.

Naomi gasped and froze.

"Hello, Glen," Bennett said, tone steely.

"Do what you're told, or we'll shoot all of you." The man stepped closer, where sunlight streamed through the broken windows, illuminating his face and the familiar scar over his left eyebrow.

Realization slammed into her. The mugshot Bennett had shown her of Glen was a younger and thinner version. "That's why he looked familiar to me! He's the guy who threatened me at the hospital," Naomi gasped, finally finding her voice.

"I'm touched you remember me." Glen cackled. "Would've saved a lot of trouble if that stupid nurse hadn't interrupted us."

"Was Nolice working with you?" Bennett asked.

Glen tilted his head, clearly confused. "Who?"

"Stop wasting time!" the woman fired again, nearly hitting Spike. "Drop the gun!"

"Enough!" Bennett's jaw tightened as he lowered his gun to the ground.

"Kick it away from you!" Glen ordered.

Bennett complied. "Why did you kill Ted, Glen?"

"It was an accident," Hetti replied in defense.

"No. Ted did it to himself. He told you everything. Didn't he, Naomi?" Glen addressed Naomi, slurring his words.

Great. He was intoxicated. And armed. Not a good combination.

Naomi took a half step to the right, feeling the weight of the board shift under her. She hesitated. The same place she'd warned Bennett about. Death by gunshot wounds or falling through the floor? Neither sounded appealing.

"Until this morning, I'd never heard of you, Glen," Naomi said.

"As if I'd buy that," Glen growled. He fired into the rafters, and a cloud of dust rained down on them. "Gimme my drugs!"

"Boards are weak," Naomi whispered.

Bennett gave her an almost imperceptible nod. "You mean Roderick Jones's drugs."

Glen glowered at them. "Where are they?"

"Tell him!" Hetti hollered. "Roderick will kill Glen! Don't you understand?"

"Shut up, Hetti!" Glen barked.

"Ted lied to me," Naomi said.

"No. He told you," Glen insisted. "Now, I'll ask once more. Where are the drugs?"

"They're in police custody," Bennett responded.

"Some, but not the big stash," Glen argued.

"Give me them, and I'll let you go. I've protected you, Naomi. You owe me."

She blinked, confused.

"Do it!" Hetti screeched.

Glen glared at her. "I'll shoot you myself if you don't keep quiet!"

Hetti cowered.

"I… I don't know," Naomi stammered. Visions of the assault at Peter's ranch fluttering around her in the repeated scene.

"Why else are you here?" Glen challenged. "You just happened to show up at this decrepit factory? Of all the places in the world? Ted told you about everything! Including Otto!"

"Where is Otto?" Bennett said.

"Ted was such a wimp. Whining about confession and judgment before his kid was born. It's too late. You can't fix everything with the truth!" Glen threw back his head and hollered. "That was our secret! I covered Ted. He's the reason Otto died! But I helped Ted. He never would've survived prison. So, you owe me now, too, Naomi. For your husband's betrayal."

She'd use the illusion of them sharing a common enemy. "He betrayed us both," Naomi said.

A cackling ringtone filled the cavernous

space. Glen withdrew his phone with one hand, keeping his gun trained on them, and answered, "Yeah. I'm getting it. Yes. I'll have it today." He slid the device into his pocket and swallowed hard enough that Naomi could see his Adam's apple bob. "Time is running out for us. If you want to live, speak."

"It's over, Naomi," Bennett said. "I'll take you where Ted hid your stash. Look, Spike is a narcotics dog." He gestured to the beagle. "He can help."

Naomi blinked. What was Bennett doing?

He lifted his hands in surrender. "C'mon. I'll go with you."

"No way," Glen argued. "Just tell me."

"Thing is, we're not positive. It's somewhere on Twila's land."

Glen seemed to consider the news. "Then I don't need you." He aimed the gun.

"Except you'll be digging for days looking, right?" Bennett said. "But with him, we'll find it fast."

"Then gimme your dog."

"Can't, dude." Bennett shook his head. "He'll only obey me. Just one condition. Let Naomi go."

"Okay, you and the mutt come with me."

Glen paused. "Hetti, you keep Naomi here." He waved Bennett closer with the gun. "She's insurance. If the cop's lying, kill her."

"You got it, honey," Hetti replied.

Bennett stepped in front of Naomi, surreptitiously passing her Spike's leash. He held up his hands. "I'm unarmed. See?"

Naomi kept the leash low, out of sight.

Bennett now shielded her with his body.

Spike stood at her feet, whining.

He took two more stalking steps, closing the distance between himself and Glen. "We'll get the drugs and come right back," Bennett cooed.

Then, like a flash, Bennett's arm swung out and swatted the gun from Glen's unsuspecting hand. The pistol toppled to the floor.

Hetti screamed.

Glen lunged for Bennett, tackling him. They rolled in a flurry of fists and kicks.

Naomi tugged Spike closer to her and moved against the wall.

Hetti lifted her weapon, meeting Naomi's eyes. "If Roderick doesn't get those drugs back, you will die tonight."

Bennett and Glen wrestled, rolling too close to the weakened floorboards.

Then a loud crack as the wood gave way.

Hetti and Naomi screamed.

Chapter Fourteen

Bennett rolled away from the gaping hole in the floorboard and peered down to where Glen's lifeless body lay below.

Hetti screamed and rushed to the hole, falling to her knees.

Naomi stood frozen, Spike at her side.

Bennett wasted no time. He jumped to his feet and jerked the pistol from the weeping woman. "Hetti Miller, you're under arrest." He helped her to kneel, kept her hands behind her back and snapped on flexicuffs. "Stay here."

"Glen!" she cried. "Get help!"

"I'll call for an ambulance," Bennett assured her. "Naomi, take away her gun and keep an eye on her while I check on Glen."

The fight withered from Hetti. Her head hung as she cried and repeated, "Roderick is going to kill us. We must find the drugs."

Naomi held the woman at gunpoint, still looking unsure about it.

"I'll be right back. Spike, stay. Guard."

The beagle took his stance in front of Naomi.

Bennett rushed to the main level, calling for backup as he approached Glen's body. He checked his neck, confirming there was no pulse. Then hurried up to the second floor, where Hetti still rambled and bawled.

Naomi passed Hetti's gun to Bennett, and he helped her to sit against the wall. Bennett called Chase and offered a speedy synopsis, promising he'd update the team with a full report ASAP.

His commander was clearly unhappy, but agreed they'd discuss it later.

Naomi huddled close to Bennett as Spike sniffed the area.

"Spike, stay over here," Bennett ordered, tugging the leash to prevent the beagle from falling through the rotted floor.

"Hetti, this is your opportunity to confess."

The woman sniffled and looked up, mascara streaming in long black rivers down her face. "Ted hid the drugs. Glen knew Ted told you." She jerked a chin toward Naomi.

"He didn't," Naomi assured her.

Hetti blinked as though seeing her for the

first time. "But you said—" she addressed Bennett "—you'd take Glen."

He shook his head.

"You protected her." Hetti's gaze bounced between Bennett and Naomi.

"Yes." Bennett folded his arms. "What happened to Otto? What did Glen mean when he said Ted killed Otto?"

"If I tell you—" Hetti lifted her chin "—I want immunity."

"I can't make that agreement, but I'll tell the prosecutor how you complied."

She sighed with resignation. "It was a game. Ted, Otto and Glen were all drinking and hanging out here. Ted dared Otto to walk the rafters." Hetti jerked a chin toward the ceiling.

Long steel beams ran the full length of the building, spaced about two feet apart.

"Otto fell and broke his neck," Hetti said softly. "Just like Glen." She gazed at the hole in the floor.

"Where did they put Otto's body?" Bennett asked.

"They buried him on Ted's grandmother's property."

Spike sniffed where the dust from the rafters

littered the floor. Bennett recognized the dog's attentiveness. "Spike. Find the cookies!"

The beagle's white-tipped tail wagged, and he continued circling the area. He barked twice. Paused. Barked twice again. Bennett illuminated his flashlight and swept the beam overhead, spotting the package sticking out from the side of the rafter.

Naomi looked up. "Is that...?"

"Yep, there's Jones's drug stash. When Hetti shot at the ceiling, she must've hit the bag."

Hetti blinked. "It was here all along?"

The sound of sirens filled the atmosphere.

Nine hours later, Bennett sat in his bedroom, laptop perched on his thighs, updating the team.

"You can't make this stuff up," Selena said.

"Tell me about it. Hetti talked freely, though doubtful they'll offer any leniency in her sentence. She was fully cognizant of her actions."

"I'm astounded she stalked Naomi, riding along on her tours," Meadow replied.

"She and Glen assumed she'd find the drugs if she stuck with Naomi long enough," Bennett said. His cell phone rang. "It's the Nebraska State Patrol."

He answered while his teammates watched from the other side of the screen.

"Detective Bennett, cadaver dogs located human remains at Twila May Cavanaugh's property," the NSP trooper advised. "We'll get DNA confirmation but looks like it's Otto Lewis."

"Thank you." Bennett disconnected. "They found Otto."

A quiet silence hung over the group.

"At least his family will get closure," Rocco said.

"If Ted and Glen had gone to the police and told them Otto's death was an accident, it would've changed everything," Bennett said. "Instead, Glen talked Ted into hiding the body, using fear to make him complacent."

"And giving Glen something to lord over Ted, to control him later on," Kyle replied.

"Hetti said Glen got in deep with Jones while incarcerated," Bennett said. "He'd kept tabs on Ted over the years, ensuring their secret about Otto remained a secret."

"Then when Ted went to Glen looking for a way to make fast money, Glen connected him with Jones," Selena surmised. "Hetti confirmed Ted hid Jones's stash, then buried the box before telling Glen he planned to confess everything to the cops." Bennett shook his head. "They fought at Beaver Brook Trail, and he shoved Ted off the cliff."

"He'd witnessed how twisted Glen was," Meadow chimed in.

"Definitely," Bennett replied.

"Naomi recognized Glen at the factory, but not from the pictures?" Rocco asked.

"Yeah. It wasn't a current photo. He'd aged and gained weight. He also didn't have the scar she'd focused on until his battle with Ted, so it wasn't in his mug shot," Bennett explained.

"Ted had fought for his life," Kyle surmised.

"Yes," Bennett said.

Ashley chimed in. "Glen was the one who attacked you and stole the box at Beaver Brook Trail?"

"Hetti said when he found it was empty, he was furious." Bennett wiped a hand over his head. "Jones pressured Glen. Even called him at the factory. Glen and Hetti followed us to Nebraska, assuming we went to retrieve the drugs. He planned to kill us as soon as he got them."

"Still no word on Roderick Jones's whereabouts," Chase grunted. "We've got APBs and

BOLOs out." He referenced the "all points bulletin" and "be on the lookout" law enforcement notifications.

"He'll pop up somewhere," Hannah assured the team.

"The scripture Ted scrawled on the letter to Naomi was his confession. He wanted to make things right, but Glen got to him before he could," Bennett said. "Without Naomi's help talking to Sheriff Motega, I'd have never considered the factory." Bennett hoped Chase would lessen the disciplinary action he no doubt had planned for Bennett for taking Naomi into the situation.

"Yes, Naomi's been invaluable," Chase replied. "We'll discuss it further privately."

Selena offered a sympathetic glance.

Bennett should expect administrative leave. He sighed.

"We still have no updates on Cowgirl," Ashley said.

"Keep praying, people. On that note, please add Isla to your prayers," Chase replied. He'd updated the group on the foster approval situation earlier in the day.

"Thank you," Isla said.

"All right, team, get some rest." Chase prepared to end the meeting.

"Before we disconnect, Bennett, Kyle and I will wrap up here at the Windham Ranch and head your way," Selena added. "We'll swing through and grab takeout from that great little Mexican restaurant off Hampden Avenue."

"Outstanding," Bennett agreed. "I love that place."

"Not fair," Ashley whined with a teasing grin.

"It's the perks of living in Denver," Bennett shrugged. "Thanks, guys."

The group disconnected, and he closed his laptop, concern returning for poor Cowgirl. *Lord, please help us find her.* He struggled to accept that a loving and kind person would steal the dog but then treat her well. Bennett prayed it was true, because the alternatives made his stomach roil.

He exited his bedroom and padded to the living room. Naomi sat up at his approach, apprehension etched in her expression. "Everything okay?"

Bennett shrugged, dropping on the recliner. His cell phone rang before he answered Naomi. "Hey, Selena."

"Does Naomi have any aversions or cravings?"

"Selena and Kyle are picking up Mexican food for dinner," Bennett relayed to her. "Do you have any requests?"

A wide grin spread across Naomi's face. "Yes, please! A green chili smothered beef and bean burrito."

Bennett repeated the order.

"A girl after my own heart," Selena chuckled.

"Yeah, add two of those for me, too," he said.

"Got it. See you soon."

They disconnected, and Bennett slid his phone into his shirt pocket.

"There must be something to the power of suggestion," Naomi said. "I wasn't even hungry, and now I'm craving that burrito big-time."

"What a day." Bennett flopped into his recliner.

"I like law enforcement work," she teased.

"I'll notify the team you're interested," Bennett chuckled.

A chime from the bedroom got their attention.

"That's my cell phone."

"I'll get it." Bennett hurried to the spare room, retrieving the device and passing it to her.

She swiped at the screen. Her forehead creased and her brows lifted.

"What's up?"

She held it up for him to read the text message.

Naomi, go to the ER ASAP. Have results from bloodwork and found something. Meet you there.
Dr. P.

"Your doctor texts instead of calling you?" Bennett asked.

"Yes, she often communicates that way with me, especially if she's multitasking with deliveries at the hospital."

"Oh. I suppose that makes sense."

"What do you think it means?" Her lip quivered. "Bennett, is there a complication with the baby?" Her hands covered her belly protectively.

"Let's stay positive. Might be a simple low blood sugar issue." Though apprehension consumed his heart. Bennett checked the clock display on his cell phone. "The doctor's office is closed now. She wants to make sure we don't wait until morning." Even as he spoke the words, he realized how it sounded. What was urgent enough that it required her to go to the ER? "Let's not waste time second-guessing."

He steadied his voice and inflection to keep her calm.

"You're right."

Bennett helped her to her feet, and she hurried to the spare bedroom to put on her shoes.

He glanced at Spike. He'd be fine alone for a little while, but if it took hours, Bennett didn't want to leave him unattended. He'd text Selena and Kyle on the way.

Bennett snapped on Spike's leash as Naomi returned to the living room. He gave her a sideways hug. "Don't let your imagination take you to dark places. It'll be all right." He prayed that was true. "Would you like me to bring the car to you?"

"No. I'd rather walk."

He started to argue with her but didn't want to add to her worries and stress, fearing that would be worse.

They hurried from the condo and down the elevator to the basement level. Bennett's rental car sat in his assigned spot at the far end of the garage. As usual, automobiles filled the other spaces.

As they neared the vehicle, Spike barked twice, paused and barked again.

Bennett hesitated, placing a hand on Naomi's

arm to halt her. A large pillar stood between them and the vehicle.

He withdrew his gun, cautiously inching toward the cement structure, while motioning with his other hand for Naomi to follow him.

Bennett peered around the post.

A bullet pinged the cement beside his head.

"Naomi, down!" Bennett ducked and turned to look behind him.

He'd made a huge mistake.

Naomi didn't dare move or breathe. The man's arm snaked around her neck, constricting tighter, and nearly eliminated her oxygen supply. Her eyes pleaded with Bennett.

His dire expression added to her fears.

"Roderick Jones." Bennett practically growled the name.

Awareness pummeled Naomi. She hadn't seen her attacker before he'd taken her hostage.

Unable to speak, she focused on guarding her throat. Her hand clamped onto Jones's arm, creating a small gap to keep him from strangling her.

He tugged her backward, and she stumbled off-balance, dropping her hands to steady herself.

Familiar muscle pain tightened across her back and belly.

Please God, not again. Not now. The contractions had been sporadic all day, but they weren't coming at regular intervals. She'd timed them to be sure. Plus, they'd felt similar to the Braxton-Hicks ones she'd experienced before.

Naomi processed the implications. If she was in labor, the stress of Jones holding her hostage was adding to their intensity. The nurse had instructed her to take deep cleansing breaths to calm herself, but Jones's hold restricted Naomi's attempts to comply.

Spike continued barking and snapping from his leash, but Bennett kept him nearby.

A sardonic guffaw too close to her ear preempted the man's response. "Shut that dog up, or I'll silence him for good." He positioned the gun, ensuring the barrel sat directly in front of Naomi's face.

"No!" she cried, arms outstretched as though she could protect Spike.

Bennett quieted the beagle with a single tug on his leash.

Spike dropped to sit beside him. He laser-focused on Jones, emitting a low growl.

"She doesn't have what you're looking for."

"Of course not, because my drugs belong to the stinking Nebraska State Patrol." Jones jerked her harder, causing Naomi to flail her arms for balance and forcing her to lean back against the man's chest.

She cringed at touching him. "Then what do you want?" Naomi choked, stalling for time and trying to breathe. Somehow, she didn't think Jones would put a pause on holding her hostage so she could give birth. If he got her alone in a vehicle, she was dead for certain.

"You're kidding, right?" Jones snorted, speaking too loudly for their proximity. "You owe me. And you're going to pay."

"You used a texting app and sent her the message, making it appear as though her doctor sent it," Bennett said, clearly stalling as he moved in a stalking motion. He was searching for a way to shoot Jones without hitting her.

Naomi pieced together the details. Her number was plastered all over the side of her tour bus. Easy access for Jones.

"See? Too bad you didn't use that brilliant deduction skill before all of this." Jones laughed again. "That's how you cops are, right? Too little and too late, always behind in the chase. But I'll admit you got me this time. You found my drugs before that loser Glen did." He jerked harder on Naomi.

Stars danced before her eyes as the lack of oxygen started impeding her ability to function. Pain erupted through her back and belly. The contractions were coming on stronger.

"Since I lost all that important revenue, I'll make sure Naomi here pays sufficiently." His hot breath against her ear made her want to vomit.

Bennett worked his jaw, still holding his weapon steadily.

"Drop the gun, cop. Then get in your car with your dumb dog and wait until I give you further instructions." Jones's voice went up several decibels, rattling Naomi's brain. "Gimme a reason to kill her in front of you."

"You'll never get away with this. She's nine months pregnant. If she knew anything, she'd tell you to protect her baby."

Naomi swallowed hard against Jones's tight grip around her throat. *Lord, please somehow save my son.*

"Naomi's been in on the whole thing from the beginning." Jones's sardonic laugh was like nails on a chalkboard. "She had you buffaloed, right? All innocent-acting."

A flash of what Naomi guessed was fury passed over Bennett's face. After all he'd endured, would he believe Jones? Her heart hurt at the thought. No, she loved Bennett. She'd never hurt him.

Lord, help me. How do I prove to Bennett that Jones is lying? She met Bennett's eyes, hoping with all her being that if she died today, he'd recognize Jones wasn't telling the truth. She'd never told Bennett that she'd fallen in love with him. But she couldn't bear for him to think she'd betrayed him.

As though understanding passed between them, Bennett's expression softened. "No. You're a liar. Naomi was never involved with Ted's crimes. She has nothing to offer you, so let her go."

Naomi squeezed her eyes shut. If this ended badly, at least he knew she hadn't lied to him.

"That's the difference between us. Revenge is sufficient for me." Jones tightened his hold until Naomi could barely breathe. "Put down the gun, cop. Now!" He fired a shot beside Spike. The beagle never wavered from his glowering stance.

Bennett's murderous stare didn't shift from Jones as he slowly placed the weapon on the ground. But as he glanced up, Naomi noticed a slight flicker in his eyes. She watched him for any signs or instructions. Did he have a plan?

Screeching tires had Jones jerking Naomi to the side.

She spotted Selena's familiar SUV as it barreled toward them.

Jones relaxed his hold slightly on Naomi's throat.

She took the opportunity and threw her elbow back, catching him under the ribs. He gasped.

Spike bounded toward them, barking and snarling just as Selena skidded to a halt in front of them.

Jones shoved Naomi to the side. She crashed into the door of a minivan parked to the left and caught herself before falling.

He lunged over Selena's hood, attempting to escape, and ran in the opposite direction.

Naomi ducked and scurried to hide behind the minivan.

A blur passed her. Bennett. He dove for his weapon and raised it. A single blast echoed in the cavernous garage.

Naomi peered around the quarter panel to

see Jones stumbling, the back of his shirt already absorbing a crimson stain.

Bennett's bullet found its mark.

Jones spun and aimed. Barking erupted as Scout and Spike bolted straight for him. The man lowered the weapon, then turned to run. The dogs easily caught up with Jones, tackling him face down to the ground in a tag-team attack.

Jones hollered, swatting at the unrelenting K-9s. Scout clamped his jaws on Jones's gun-wielding hand. The man screamed, dropping the weapon.

"Stop moving, or the dogs will not let go!" Kyle shouted.

"Stop moving!" Selena repeated.

Jones relented and lay prostrate on the garage floor.

"Scout, Spike, release!" Selena said.

The Belgian Malinois immediately released hold of Jones's arm and slowly backed away. Spike gave one more warning growl, tugging on Jones's pants before releasing the fabric. He panted, satisfied beside his K-9 partner.

Kyle rushed forward and snapped cuffs onto Jones's wrists while Selena collected his gun.

Bennett closed in on them, keeping the drug dealer at gunpoint.

Jones cursed. "I'm injured. Call an ambulance, I'm going to die!"

"Nah, you'll just hurt for a while," Kyle replied, checking over the wound.

"Prison provides plenty of healing time," Selena added.

Kyle hoisted Jones to his feet while the man spewed curses.

"This isn't over!" Jones threatened.

"Oh, but it is," Bennett said. "Remember, we have you and your drugs, and based on the amount, your supplier will be very upset."

Jones glared, then returned to hollering a few more choice words as Kyle placed him in the back seat of the SUV.

While Kyle and Selena dealt with Jones, Bennett spun and ran to Naomi, pulling her into his arms. "Are you okay?"

"Yes," she croaked against her sore throat. She clung to him, unable to let go. Spike hopped up, planting his paws against her thigh. She glanced down and smiled. "Thank you, Spike."

"I've got you. You're safe," Bennett whispered.

"You believed me."

"I might not have the best track record with trusting people, but my heart said you weren't involved with Ted's crimes." In Bennett's embrace, Naomi clung for life, allowing him to bear the weight of her relief, her fears and all that she'd endured since the start of Jones's terror. "I've got you." He pressed a kiss against her temple and Naomi closed her eyes, accepting his comforting hold.

"Are you okay to walk?" Bennett asked.

Naomi realized the contractions had slowed sometime during the chaos, proving they were Braxton-Hicks. She nodded.

Bennett placed a hand on the small of her back, supporting her arm as they walked toward Selena's SUV. Spike trotted happily beside them. "How'd you know where to find us?" Naomi asked, rubbing her throat.

"We had the windows rolled down. When we pulled into the garage, Jones's voice carried to us. Then we heard Spike barking, and it was apparent something was wrong," Selena explained.

If not for Bennett's powerful hold on her, Naomi was certain she'd crumble. Her body felt weak and achy all at once.

"Naomi?" Bennett asked, looking into her eyes.

"My." A cramp gripped her harder than anything she'd experienced before, tightening around her back and stomach like a giant hand. "Oh." She gasped, clinging to Bennett. A puddle beneath her indicated what she already knew. "My water just broke."

"What?"

"She's in labor!" Selena cried.

Wordlessly, Kyle took Bennett's keys and ran to the rental car. He returned within record time and jumped out, allowing Bennett to slide behind the wheel. Kyle helped Naomi into the front seat and snapped on her seat belt.

"We'll call the hospital and notify them you're on the way," Selena advised.

"Thank...you." Naomi gasped.

Kyle hoisted Spike into his arms, and Bennett drove from the garage.

"Breathe, breathe," Bennett said, concentrating on the windshield, his tone steady and calm.

"I guess that was the stress Dr. Pankratz warned us about," she joked, then sucked in a breath to get through the approaching pain wave.

Bennett pulled onto the street. "Yeah. Remind me to charge Jones with that, too," he retorted sarcastically. "Okay, tell me when the next one starts, and I'll time it."

Naomi tried to laugh, but another contraction took hold. "Now," she gasped, breathing through it. When it ended, she exhaled.

"Doing all right?"

"Yes," she said.

"The contractions came on suddenly?" he asked.

"Sorta. I've had them sporadically most of the day, but I didn't think much of it since they were in my back."

"Why didn't you tell me?"

She winced.

The drive to the hospital seemed to last for hours, though the dashboard clock testified to a twenty-minute commute. Bennett did a great job of remaining calm, and his presence helped Naomi.

When they reached the emergency entrance, Bennett parked the car under the ambulance awning, then rushed to help Naomi from the passenger seat. A nurse hurried toward them with a wheelchair, guiding Naomi into the building.

"Her contractions are steady at five minutes apart." Bennett provided a recap.

"Stay with me, please," Naomi pleaded, suddenly afraid to be alone.

"I will. I'm here."

"Park your car and meet us in L and D," the nurse ordered.

He nodded and scurried outside while the nurse guided Naomi's wheelchair to the Labor and Delivery Unit. There, the nursing team helped Naomi change into a birthing gown, then settled her into the bed. The contractions remained constant.

Bennett returned shortly thereafter, though Naomi lost track of time in the chaos.

"Please hand me my cell? I want to tell Evan."

"Sure."

He dug her phone out of her purse and passed it to Naomi. She unlocked the screen and opened the running thread of text messages with Evan.

You're about to become an uncle. Come to Rose Faith Hospital ASAP!

He responded within a few seconds. Congrats, can't wait to meet my little nephew. Be there in the morning. He'd even added a heart emoji.

Unable to contain her joy, Naomi's eyes welled with tears for her brother's support. No matter how many years, tragedies and miles separated them, Evan was still her big brother. Always there for her.

She glanced to her right where Bennett sat. She passed him her phone, and he held her hand as she breathed through another contraction. "This is the real deal."

Chapter Fifteen

Bennett sat in the waiting room, staring at the massive TV screen on the wall.

"Has Naomi delivered?"

He glanced up at the familiar voice. Addy Everett entered, clutching a stuffed bear. "How did you know she was here?" Something about the woman rubbed him wrong.

"She texted me."

Bennett quirked a brow, still guarded.

"I can show you if you don't believe me." Addy held out her phone. "I agreed to take her tours until she returns to work." She lifted one hand in surrender.

He hesitated, contemplating if Naomi's assessment of the woman was accurate.

"We didn't start off on a good foot or shoe—however that saying goes." Addy closed the distance between them, then sat in the chair opposite Bennett. "Naomi is a wonderful person. I'm glad she has someone looking out for her finally. She deserves to be happy."

Bennett blinked. "I think so, too." He relaxed a little. "The doctor is with her now."

"I have a tour in the morning, so I wanted to bring by a new agreement." She handed Bennett an envelope. "This is the list of tours I'm handling for her temporarily. We agreed on a split profit, but I changed it."

Bennett opened his mouth to defend Naomi.

"She'll get the entire profit. They were her customers to start." Addy tossed him the toy. "I can't stay, but will you tell her?"

"Yes." Bennett balked, slightly taken aback. Had he totally misread Addy?

"See ya." She stood and walked away without another word.

A strange person, but not unkind.

He dropped onto a chair, leg bouncing with the stuffed animal tucked under his arm.

The nurse handling Naomi's delivery approached.

He opened his mouth to ask about Naomi's status, but she stopped him with her lifted palm. "She's progressing, but the doctor's not quite finished with the exam."

He exhaled.

"I see tons of fathers-to-be, but I have to say, you're making me nervous," she laughed. "Go walk off some of that antsy energy."

"You think there's time?" Bennett halted in place. "A short one?"

"Babies arrive when they're good and ready and not a second before."

"Right." Having never been in this position before, he was unsure where he was supposed to be during that time. Naomi hadn't asked for him to witness or assist in the delivery, and he didn't press. But he also hesitated to leave her, even for a second. The threat of Jones hurting her was finally over. So what was his compulsion?

"Get out of here. Grab a coffee. A candy bar. Something," she said, shooing him with one hand and a wink.

Had Naomi changed her mind? Maybe she didn't want him in the room while she delivered? The look on the nurse's face remained stoic. He took the hint and didn't press.

"Okay." Bennett strolled toward the stairs, opting to take those instead of the elevator while his mind roamed wildly.

He cared for Naomi, and he wanted to tell her. What right did he have to do that? What could he offer a wonderful woman like Naomi Carr-Cavanaugh? He was broken and scarred. She deserved the best. Better than him.

Was that a cop-out? Probably. The truth was, Bennett feared getting hurt again.

Seeing Naomi vulnerable with Jones triggered him to save her and express his love. He'd never felt this way. Not even for Delaney.

This was the real thing.

And it terrified him.

Naomi had endured indescribable pain and obstacles, yet her faith remained strong. She didn't place what Ted had done on anyone other than him. How had she worded it? He owned his mistakes. They belonged to him, not those who came after him. The words struck him afresh as they had the first time. He was trying to make Delaney pay by putting himself in a prison of solidarity and shutting out everyone else in his future. She wasn't paying for hurting him; he was. The ridiculousness of it smacked Bennett.

His feet seemed to move on their own as his brain traversed the complicated relationship road. Before he realized it, he'd made his way outside to get some air. The moon was bright in the cloudless sky.

As he stood staring up, he accepted the truth. He wanted Naomi in his life and longed for a future with her and her sweet baby. Though he feared the risks, the idea of joyful holidays, and first everything like birthday parties and Christmases offered a newfound joy to his heart he'd never experienced.

He spun on his heel, then paused.

Though timing was essential.

She was busy now and needed to rest. But as soon as he could, he'd tell her. He wouldn't waste a single second. He would confess he'd fallen in love with her and wanted a future with her.

Bennett dropped onto a bench outside the hospital and texted Selena and Kyle for a status check.

Within a few minutes, their reply bounced through.

Dogs secure at Denver PD. J in jail. En route, ETA thirty.

Another message pinged through his cell phone with a task force text from Meadow.

UPDATE ON COWGIRL. I'm in Elk Valley at HQ. I spotted Cowgirl darting around in a restaurant alley for food earlier! I used food to lure and coax her, and although I got close, Cowgirl fled across the street, into the park and then into the woods. Still searching. Keep praying!

The group quickly responded with promises to continue praying for Cowgirl and a quick rescue return.

Bennett bowed his head to pray for Naomi and a safe delivery, for Cowgirl's safe rescue and for the courage to tell Naomi that he'd fallen for her. And for the first time, Bennett offered his hopes, dreams and future to God, trusting His plan. A peace he'd not experienced since before his days with Delaney swept over him.

Satisfied, he stood and strolled back to Naomi's room.

The door was ajar, so he rapped softly, then startled as a nurse peered out. "Perfect timing."

Bennett quirked a brow, unsure what she meant until he entered and found Naomi holding a tiny, blanketed bundle.

He gaped. "Was I gone that long?"

Naomi chuckled softly. "Nope, little man was just ready to make his appearance."

"Don't let her fool you," the nurse said. "She

was a rock star. Made delivery look easy." She winked and exited.

"I don't know about that," Naomi whispered, brushing her lips over the infant's head. "Come and meet August Lee. I named him after my dad, but I think we'll call him Augie for short." She yawned, then glanced down at the baby, her long eyelashes shadowing her cheek. Even in her exhaustion, she'd never looked more lovely.

Bennett quickly moved to her side and studied the perfect baby with his soft skin and bright eyes, mesmerized by Naomi. Bennett smiled. "He's beautiful."

"Would you like to hold him?"

The offer to hold the most precious part of Naomi's heart overwhelmed Bennett. The ultimate level of trust. Emotion swelled within him. "Yes. Please."

Bennett gently took Augie from Naomi's arms, cradling the infant close to his chest. The baby's tiny hand emerged from the blanket, gripping Bennett's finger. Like a wave, protectiveness and the overwhelming urge to care for this little person overtook Bennett. Tears filled his eyes, but he dared not wipe them away for fear of not properly cradling the baby. "He's perfect," he croaked through his tight throat.

"Yes." Naomi's reply was soft and tender. She nestled down under the covers.

"Rest." Bennett slid into a chair beside her bed, still holding the tiny infant. "I'll be here when you wake." *And every single day hereafter. If you'll let me.*

Naomi nodded. "Just two minutes."

Bennett tore his gaze from Augie long enough to see her drifting off to sleep. Within a few seconds, her soft breathing suggested she'd fallen asleep. He whispered to the baby, "You have the most beautiful mommy."

Augie never released his hold on Bennett's finger, and his stare fixed on him as though asking his intentions. In that moment, Bennett promised his commitment to Naomi and Augie. Even if she rejected him romantically, he'd be there for them and help any way possible. If Naomi allowed him. Because the idea of being away from either of them was unbearable.

The night passed quickly. Naomi had gotten short bouts of sleep between Augie's grunts. It might take a while for them both to get their schedules lined up. Morning sunlight streamed through the blinds, and gratitude filled her heart. In juxtaposition, the new day reminded her that today she'd part ways with Bennett. She glanced around the room.

True to his word, Bennett hadn't left her side, except a few minutes ago, upon her request for a blueberry scone.

Their time was ending, and she needed to accept that. She'd contemplated telling him a hundred different ways that she'd fallen in love with him. But he'd chalk it up to the emotions arising from Jones's attack and Augie's delivery. As Selena had said, he'd see it as emotional attachment during trauma. She'd treasure their moments—even if it was filled with life-threatening events—and hope they maintained a friendship.

Naomi thanked God for the time they'd had, and she prayed Bennett would find love again—with or without her.

Augie sighed, regaining her attention. He slept, soft breaths emitting from his perfect rosebud mouth.

Naomi brushed her lips over his head, inhaling his sweet scent that filled her heart with the purest contentment. She glanced at her cell phone on the bed table. Still nothing from Evan. She'd sent a picture of Augie along with his birth information. But knowing her brother, he got busy at work and couldn't leave as planned. He'd show up. She considered sending a follow-up message, but didn't want to annoy him. Evan was a faithful brother. He'd never let her down.

The door opened, and Bennett entered, carrying a paper sack. "You wouldn't believe the line for that coffee cart downstairs."

"Thank you for enduring it," Naomi said, pushing herself to a sitting position.

Bennett set the scone on the bed table and added a few napkins. "How about if I hold Augie while you eat."

"You talked me into it." She gently passed her son to Bennett, wrapped tightly like a burrito in his blanket.

"Sleeping good?"

"Now—" she snorted "—if he could figure that out between two and four a.m., that would be great."

Bennett lowered himself into the chair beside her bed. "Any word from Evan?"

"No, but he'll be here," she assured him and herself. Naomi extracted the scone from the paper covering and broke off a section. It melted in her mouth. "Best. Scone. Ever."

Bennett chuckled. "I aim to please." His

brown eyes captured hers. There was a new tenderness she'd not seen before.

"Why are you looking at me like that?" Warmth radiated up Naomi's neck. She munched on her breakfast, stalling for time.

Augie stirred and Bennett glanced down, then jerked to look at Naomi. "Is something wrong?" His eyebrows peaked. "Should I get the doctor?"

Naomi chuckled. "He's fine," she assured between bites of the scone. "He's just dreaming."

Bennett exhaled. "Whew. Okay." His shoulders visibly relaxed.

She relished the sight of Augie cradled against Bennett's muscled chest, outlined beneath the light T-shirt he wore. "I need help, little man," he whispered to the baby.

Naomi tilted her head, hanging on his every word.

"See, I wanna talk to your mommy, but I could use some advice on the best way to do that." Bennett lifted Augie closer to his ear as though listening.

A grin tugged at Naomi's lips at the silliness.

"Roger that. Okay. Thanks."

Augie grunted, then emitted a tiny mewing, his face screwed up in protest.

"I guess he's missing you already," Bennett chuckled.

Naomi took one more bite of the scone, then set it on the bed tray. "The feeling is mutual."

Bennett gently passed the infant to Naomi.

"What's up, Augie?" At the sound of her voice, Augie calmed, his wide eyes watching her. She nestled him, memorizing every detail of her son. "And what great wisdom did Augie offer you?"

He leaned closer, putting his hands flat on his thighs. "Naomi, I have to tell you something."

She swallowed hard, bracing her heart for his goodbye speech, and plastered on a smile. "It's all right, Bennett. You don't have to say anything. I've enjoyed our time together and would be grateful if we stayed friends. If you want to."

"I've fallen in love with you."

Had she heard him correctly?

He'd paused, eyes fixed on hers. Anticipation in his expression.

"You what?"

"Not the reaction I was going for, but it's not a rejection, right?" He smiled and her heart melted straight to the floor.

"With me?" *Brilliant, Naomi.* Why had she said that? "But you said…"

"Let's just say I had an epiphany yesterday about trust and faith. I've put them both in the wrong things and people. God alone deserves them." His brown eyes bore into hers.

"I'd agree with that."

"I recognize it's poor timing. You have your hands full. But I couldn't wait another second." He glanced down. "I needed to tell you I've fallen in love with you. And the funny thing is, I want to trust again. To love again. Seeing you and Augie makes me want to be a part of this something wonderful you two have going on."

Naomi studied Augie. Was Bennett certain what he was getting into? She couldn't afford to make a mistake by casually dating. "We come as a packaged deal. A ready-made family." She offered him the out he needed.

"Yep, like getting the best of both worlds. I've wasted too much time running away from love and a future with kids and a wife. I never realized I wanted that until you came into my life."

She blinked. "Bennett, I'm a little foggy here between lack of sleep and people trying to kill me. Just to make sure I'm understanding you correctly… What're you saying?"

"Naomi, I want to marry you, be a father to

Augie, and have a future with you both. The whole family deal."

"A few days ago, you were determined to arrest me as a serial killer." Her tone was teasing, and she was grateful Bennett didn't appear offended.

"Well, that's what brought us together in proximity. But your incredible faith and compassion and beauty and humor—those are the things that stole my heart, Naomi."

"You won't arrest me for robbery?"

Bennett laughed. "Nope, but I'd take fifty to life with you."

"Then I'll admit to being guilty as charged." Naomi's heart swelled until she thought it would burst. "Bennett, I am so glad to hear you say that. I'm madly in love with you."

"Sorry it took me so long to get here."

"You were worth the wait."

He leaned closer. "Does that mean you'll allow me to court you—for a short time—and marry you super soon?"

"Yes."

Bennett got to his feet, standing beside her. "I'd like to kiss you now."

"Don't let me hold you back. Besides, my

arms are full." She gestured toward Augie, contentedly snoozing.

"A captive audience. I love it."

Naomi lifted her chin, and Bennett pressed his lips against hers. Once they connected, the hunger grew stronger, bringing to life all the hopes and dreams for their future.

"Ahem." A woman's voice interrupted with the sound of her clearing her throat.

Regretfully, Naomi and Bennett parted but kept their heads close together as they both turned to see Selena standing in the door holding a giant stuffed giraffe. "Didn't mean to interrupt."

"No. It's okay. We've got a lifetime to figure it out," Bennett said with a wink. "Come on in. I need to grab a bottle of water. Be right back." He excused himself from the room, and Naomi immediately missed him.

"Didn't expect to see that," Selena said, approaching with the stuffed animal.

An awkward silence hovered between them. Would Selena disapprove?

"It's about time."

Wait. What? Naomi's neck jerked upright, and her gaze landed on Selena.

"The attraction was pitifully obvious." She

gently placed the giraffe at the foot of Naomi's bed, then dropped onto the chair beside her. "When's the wedding?"

"Soon, by the way Bennett spoke."

"I'm dumbfounded."

Her heart deflated at the presumed disapproval.

A genuine smile covered Selena's face. "Oh, Naomi. No, it's great!"

"Really?" Naomi exhaled relief.

"Absolutely. Bennett's a sound judge of character, and you're as real as they come. It's a wonderful thing." Selena inched closer. "Is there any possibility that I could hold your precious baby?"

She turned and spotted the sink in the corner of the room. Selena quickly hurried to it, not waiting for Naomi's response. She washed her hands and returned. "Okay, let me try that again. Now, could I possibly hold your beautiful baby?"

"Absolutely." Naomi adjusted Augie and passed him to Selena. "Meet August Lee."

A soft gasp escaped her lips as she glanced down at Naomi's son. "Oh, he's perfect."

"I agree, but I'm horribly biased."

"Makes me optimistic that I'll find love again."

"I thought you'd given up on romance."

"I had, but remember that ex I told you about?" Selena leaned to the side, exposing a vulnerability in her green irises.

"Yeah," Naomi urged conspiratorially.

"Turns out they just granted him a court hearing for new evidence they found that might prove he's not guilty."

"Wow, that's huge. What do you think of it all?"

Selena shrugged. "I don't know."

"But…"

"True confessions?" She glanced up, meeting Naomi's eyes. "Am I dreaming to hope it's true?"

"Never. I like inconceivable situations that become possible." Naomi smiled. "Bennett and I are proof it happens. I'll have to explain to Augie that we fell in love while Bennett was preparing to charge and arrest me as the Rocky Mountain Killer."

"From serial killer to bride." Selena laughed. "Sounds like a reality TV show."

"I should probably wait until Augie is thirty-five to share that."

The women fell into a burst of giggles.

Bennett returned, and Selena faced him, still cradling Augie. "Congratulations!" Her cell phone rang, and she frowned. "Ah, I don't want to give him up."

"You aren't limited to one holding," Naomi promised.

"Okay." Selena reluctantly passed Augie to Bennett. "I'll be right back. It's Chase. Can I tell the team the good news?"

"Yes!" Bennett moved closer to Naomi.

Selena hurried from the room, leaving them alone.

"I love you, Naomi."

"I love you, Bennett."

"Are you going to keep Carr-Cavanagh as your name?"

"That might be a little much with Ford, too." She tilted her head. "Actually, it's the prime opportunity for a fresh start. Naomi Ford."

He kissed her forehead. "I like the sound of that."

"Me too." And in that moment, Naomi realized everything she'd ever wanted was real, present and in her life. "Lord, thank you. You really go above and beyond with blessings."

"Amen," Bennett said, capturing her lips again in a kiss.

★ ★ ★ ★ ★

Don't miss the stories in this mini series!

MOUNTAIN COUNTRY K-9 UNIT

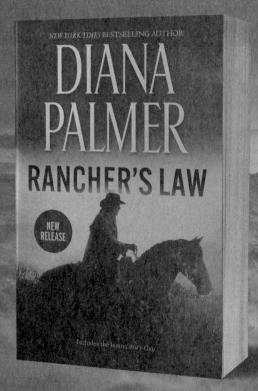

NEW RELEASES

**Four sisters. One surprise will.
One year to wed.**

Don't miss these two volumes of
Wed In The Outback!

When Holt Waverly leaves his flourishing outback estate
to his four daughters, it comes to pass that without an
eldest son to inherit, the farm will be entailed to someone
else…unless all his daughters are married within the year!

May 2024

July 2024